Thumb

by
John Guy Collick

The first volume of The Book of the Colossus

Published by John Guy Collick

ISBN: 978 0 957643918

for Naomi and Owen

At the end of time all directions are given in relation to the
body of God. His head lies to the north, and his feet point
south.

CHAPTER ONE

A FLAT SINGULARITY carried the unfinished body of
God through an empty universe. The colossus lay on his
back, a being so vast he might easily have put his arms
around a world, if any still existed. His left hand rested
palm upwards. In the shadow of the Thumb a brass and
wooden flying machine sped southwards. Max Ocel sat
in the forward cabin of the *Bricolage*. If he glanced
through the porthole to his right he could see the
Knuckle, thousands of miles away, like a wall cutting
the sky in half.

A map rested on the table in front of Max. He knew
they flew somewhere between the fortress of Abductor
to the north and the second joint of the Thumb, heading
home to the city of Metacarpi. The chart covered almost
fifty thousand square miles of nothing. Whistling to
himself he pored over his notes, marking the wormholes
they'd explored this trip. *Dead, dead, sealed, live, dead, live,
dead.* Not good. The descendants of the people who built
the Thumb relied on these portals for supplies and luxuries to wile away the boredom as they waited for
everyone else to finish their part of the Great Task. Max
was a Time Scavenger, searching the wormholes for anything of value. *It's getting harder,* he thought. Each time
he found fewer open shafts into the past. Only this
morning he'd stood on a landing and stared down an-

other infinite well lost to them forever. The stairs ended in a rusted tangle at his feet. Below lay doorways to thousands of worlds full of treasure and wonders. Just half a dozen could make him rich, but they might as well have been in another universe.

At this rate the city'll be out of food in decades, he mused. *It's no good hiding behind the walls with our heads up our backsides, we'll have to open the old trade routes to Abductor and Tip, otherwise we'll all starve. Time to tell the news to Father.* When had he last seen the ruler of Metacarpi? Five years ago? He remembered the sour old bastard standing silhouetted against the windows of the tower they called the Carceral Archipelago, all rage and austerity. He shuddered. The thought of meeting Herman Ocel gave him a pain behind his eyes.

Max flew over long-dead worlds ground into dirt and spread over the singularity to make a land for all the kingdoms and empires around the body of God. One day, so the story went, he'd come to life and save humanity. The God Door waited out there in the void, leading to another universe filled with stars and planets. Max didn't care. He wouldn't live to see the new cosmos. That lay aeons in the future. He'd be long gone by then, just more dust under another scavenger's flying machine.

Max wore baggy khakis, a linen shirt and a waistcoat made from lizard skin. The scales still lived and moved across his chest and back, making the garment shimmer. He ran shaky hands over his head. At thirty he found it harder to bear the energies locked inside the wormholes. They dried him out, consumed him, leaching the colour from his cropped hair.

Dynamos crackling, the vessel flitted across the Wasteland. Everywhere lay scraps of scaffolding, frames as big as mountains and machines rusted into meaningless shapes. Each time they passed over metal the *Bricol-age* discharged arcs of electricity and the inside of the cabin flashed blue-white. Max tasted ozone on his tongue and saw the hair on his arms stand up.

He heard music. Puzzled, he looked up. Abby Fabrice sat cross-legged on the forward deck, picking at a lute she'd found on their last successful forage. Despite his tiredness he couldn't help but smile at the expression on her face and the melody she was slaughtering. It sounded truly hideous. He wasn't ready to forgive her though. He thought her a pain in the arse, reckless and insolent. That stolen lute had led to a running firefight with a squad of lizard men in a storm-lashed forest on an ancient planet, followed by a screaming row lasting the entire five-mile climb up the wormhole stairs. In the end she'd tearfully pledged to be more obedient to her captain's orders, if he let her keep the lute. Max knew the promise wouldn't last. Stray electricity from the engine arced behind her. A spark caught the strings and she snatched her fingers away with a yelp of pain. *Serves her right*, thought Max, turning back to his map. He smoothed its folds, lay his head on the table and closed his eyes.

He woke to the sound of Abby banging on the window. She waved for him to come outside. She'd swapped the lute for a telescope and he saw excitement in her face. Never a good sign. He stepped onto the deck, shielding his eyes against the light. The wind tasted bitter and the ground beneath the flyer shimmered as it sped past. Abby handed him the spyglass and pointed. Dreading what he might see, Max tried to focus but the *Bricolage* moved too fast and the ship rocked under his feet. He staggered.

"Come on, you're not that ancient," said Abby, standing in front of him so he could rest the telescope on her head. Looking again he saw a house canted at an angle on top of a ridge. *That's impossible.* Abby gave him a mad grin over her shoulder. He could see in her eyes that he hadn't imagined it. Even so, he had to say it.

"That shouldn't be there."

No-one lived this far away from the city. Who'd erect a building in the middle of this Wasteland, amid the junk left by the creators of the Thumb? He tried to make out the details. It didn't even look like a real dwelling. It reminded him of a child's drawing. He counted a single door and four windows, all different sizes.

"I know," said Abby, "isn't it exciting?"

Max rolled his eyes. That was her first response to anything that looked like it might kill them. His skin crawled with fear. They should open the dynamos till they roared with blue fire and put a hundred miles between them and that house.

"Over there, in the shadow of the slope," said Abby.

Max saw a flyer crumpled at the bottom of the hill. Two black fins stretched from a tear-drop fuselage, one looked broken. *It hit the ground at an angle and slid across the floor into that clump of rocks, going at speed judging by those gouges in the dirt.* Where in God's name did it come from? He looked around at the shabby wood and brass of the Bricolage. *Not one of ours then.* He noticed the hunger in Abby's green eyes.

"There's nothing like that ship for thousands of miles," he heard the longing in her voice. "I reckon it could fly above the atmosphere, even to the Palm itself."

He couldn't reason with her when she spoke like this, but he tried.

"OK. Before we go charging in, like we did in the lizard men's temple," he said, "why's it crashed? Why's it crashed there? And what about that house?"

Abby gave him a lopsided grin of disbelief.

"Max, we scratch a living from the few remaining wormholes because they're all we can reach with steam and electricity," she said, "and they're closing one by one, you know that."

He looked at the wreck once more while Abby's voice murmured beside him.

"With a ship like that we could open up the old trade routes again, make proper contact with the other cities, not just Abductor but Tip as well, perhaps as far as Wrist or beyond."

Max trained the telescope on the house. Now that he looked at it more carefully it appeared oddly familiar. He knew for a fact Metacarpi had no buildings like it, but it still nudged at something deep in his mind. Fear gave way to curiosity. He cursed Abby, how did she manage it every time? He knew from experience that if something didn't make sense it was probably out to get you. Anyone with half a brain would run away, but a nagging feeling of déjà vu and that bloody woman's voice in his ear made a lethal combination.

"Just a quick look, please?" begged Abby. "We'll keep down in the shadows, first sign of any trouble and we'll leave."

"This is completely mad," he said wearily.

Abby laughed in triumph and slapped him on the shoulder

"Come on you coward," she said, "we'll survive, we always do."

She ducked back inside the cabin. Max looked at the building again. *Where, oh where have I seen you before? In a photo, in a painting, in my dreams?*

The dynamos span up and the ship turned towards the ridge. Olaf came on deck. The engineer stared moodily ahead, a slab of a man with the eyes of a sad wolf and a pigtail down to his waist. They'd signed him on for this trip after their last mechanic fried himself with a faulty accumulator, but his grumbling was already getting on Max's nerves.

"More fighting?" asked Olaf. Max shook his head and gave him the spyglass.

"Recognise that ship?"

Olaf whistled.

"Nope, it's an evil looking machine though," he said, "and I don't like the look of that house either. Is that lunatic making us take a look?"

Max bristled. As irritating as Abby could be, she remained his closest friend and she'd saved his life more than once.

"Just take us in," he said. Olaf spat over the rail and went back to the engine room.

The *Bricolage* slowed to a stop. From the bottom of the ridge the house carved a cliff-sized chunk of darkness out of the sky, the windows dead shadows on its facade. No lights shone. It still looked familiar, like the fragment of a barely remembered song tugging at Max's memory.

We're five thousand miles north of the city. There's nothing here but debris left over from the Great Task, and a few undiscovered wormholes, most of which are useless. No-one could live in this place, and yet here's a house I half recognise. Mysterious sights filled the land around him, the legacy of a million years of construction as the cities of Tip, Abductor and Metacarpi brought machinery and materials out of deep time to create the Thumb. In his travels Max found buildings, machines, even the remains of creatures of such terrifying proportions that they haunted his dreams. Yet that simple dwelling on top of the crest, with its lopsided walls and picture-book windows, disturbed him far more than the strangest relics he'd found abandoned in the Wasteland.

"Come on." said Abby, jolting him out of his thoughts. They climbed over the side of the flyer and lowered themselves to the ground. The slope reared up above them in an arc. A quarter of a mile away the house leaned over the edge of the crest. To Max it looked ready to topple any minute. He tried to ignore it as they made their way towards the wreck. He stepped warily across the slippery ground. It looked like melted plastic.

Abby walked a few yards to his right, scanning the surroundings. She'd tied her red hair into an unkempt bun on top of her head, fixing it in place with two long pins. With her tight-waisted, high-collared jacket, culottes and boots her silhouette carved a jumble of triangles in the dusty light. Secretly he admired her stupid bravery. She made it look so effortless. He always had to fight the sick fear nibbling at the edges of his mind. Abby scampered into peril without another thought. She held a square machine pistol in both hands. To Max's relief she kept it pointing at the ground. He didn't want to provoke anything in the ship or the house.

Max reckoned the crashed flyer looked like a single man fighter or a reconnaissance vessel. He pointed at the red spiral painted on the side.

"Recognise that?" he asked.

Abby shook her head. She lifted a fragment of wing and handed it to Max.

"This engineering's way beyond ours," she said.

He held it, trying to guess at the metal. Some kind of alloy? In his hands it felt as light as paper. They walked round to the front, guns trained on the cockpit window.

To Max's surprise the cabin was empty. Through the cracked glass he could make out a couch, two steering handles and a control panel. With a chill he saw blood smeared on the dials and buttons. His hands started to tremble. They continued round to the far side of the ship, into the shadow of the slope. Max almost tripped over a hatch cover lying on the ground. *Stay alert dammit! God knows what's watching us from that house.* Beside it a tangle of bloody webbing spilled out of the interior. Abby stuck her head inside.

"They're not here," she said.

She looked at Max. He saw the worry in her eyes. He peered past her into the ship at the open locker under the couch, and the bloody hand print on the inside of the lid. Abby touched it and showed him wet fingertips.

"We must look for the pilot," she said. Her voice fell to a whisper and she nodded towards the house. Max seethed. *Oh you've seen it now, have you? You realise what you've got us into.* It was never simple, never easy. The parameters shifted all the time, and always in the wrong direction. Up to this point he'd itched to tell Abby to get back on the *Bricolage,* but now duty kicked in, prodding him up the slope with an insistent finger.

"So now we're on a rescue mission," he said pointedly. She nodded with that expression of desperate confidence and sheer terror she called her 'brave face'.

"For God's sake, Abby," he muttered. *One day you'll kill us all.*

She walked a few steps up the slope, her gaze on the ground.

"There's more blood," she said. Max followed her. Scattered drops led away from the craft and up through the shadows. Here and there he could just make out footprints along a path that barely made a crease in the surface. At least the pilot could still walk. Unfortunately, they'd walked up to the house.

"They probably just smacked their head on the controls when the ship went down. Maybe they're dazed, that's why they headed that way." Abby pointed up at the ridge. Max forced himself to look at the building. Where had he seen it before? It still tugged at his mind, quietly stoking his curiosity, yet at the same time it frightened him. He wanted to flee back to the ship, dragging Abby with him, but his feet carried him onwards up the slope. The closer he got, the stranger it looked. His gaze kept sliding off the walls. Details blurred or suddenly jumped out at him. Was some strange quality of the light messing with his eyes? He stopped and Abby banged into his back.

Enough is enough. Danger filled the air. It flowed over him, seeping under his clothes, soaking him in sweat. All his experience and instinct told him to turn around. He wasn't going to risk their lives for a dead or dying stranger. He'd order Abby back to the ship, carrying her if he had to. Olaf could help if she put up a fight.

He saw a woman appear in one of the upper windows. She glanced down at him for a second, before fading back into the darkness. She didn't look like a pilot, he could have sworn she wore a purple dress.

"She's up there," he said, his voice tight.

"She?" asked Abby.

"The pilot, I think. I saw her, at the window."

They couldn't leave now. He looked into Abby's face, gathering his courage. *Here we go again*, he thought. She nodded.

"OK, please don't do anything too stupid," he said.

"Of course," said Abby, her face a picture of sensible innocence.

They climbed the slope. Max led the way. The surface curved above his head like a wave. He kept his eyes on the ground, searching for more blood. He knew where to go, but he didn't want to look at the house. He could sense its presence above him. It filled him with dread. Invisible hands squeezed his chest, forcing the breath out of him and pressing his heart against his ribs. He glanced behind at Abby's drawn face. She looked tired and frightened. That made it worse. Nothing fazed Abby Fabrice, but he could see his own feelings of growing panic mirrored in her eyes. *God, it's affecting you too. That building radiates fear. Maybe it's some kind of defence mechanism.* With relief he saw the *Bricolage* lift into the sky and move towards the ridge. Thank God for Olaf. The morose bastard, anticipating their plans, tracked them with the ship. He raised the steam powered chain gun from the deck and pointed its barrels at the house. If worse came to worse he'd have them off the path and a hundred miles away in minutes. Max looked down at Abby to reassure her but before he could say anything the ground beneath his feet gave way and he fell down the hill.

He flipped over and over, arms flailing as he tried to stop himself. His head banged painfully against a rock and the sudden agony disoriented him. Yet amid the pain, disquiet tugged at his mind. *I'm falling upwards.* The ground hit him hard, driving the breath out of his chest. Silence descended. Instinct kicked in. He forced himself onto his hands and knees, searching for his gun. *Gone. Damn. I must have lost it in the fall.* He looked up. A dark shape loomed over him. Panic sent him scrabbling backwards on his bottom until he fetched up against a boulder.

This isn't possible. The house stood in front of him, but not on the ridge. He glanced around, heart still pounding, expecting something shadowy and full of claws to attack any second. He sat at the bottom of a circular amphitheatre. Jagged hills curved away on either side. Sheer slopes disappeared into a sky filled with mist. Where the hell was Abby? Nothing stirred amid the rocks. He crept round on all fours, feeling the cracked ground bite his knees. He forced himself to breath slowly, calming the gibbering idiot inside his mind.

Had he fallen over the other side of the ridge and found a second building in the valley beyond? No, they'd scarcely made it halfway up the slope. Maybe the ridge collapsed, but he saw no rubble. Winded, and desperately scared, he checked himself but found nothing but bruises. He needed Abby. He ought to stay quiet, who knew what hid among these boulders or waited for him in that house, but he shouted her name anyway. The rocks flung it back at him in an echo. He dared to close his eyes and listen, trying to pick out the crackling hum of the *Bricolage*. Nothing, just wind stirring the mist.

When he eventually calmed down and death no longer seemed imminent he walked slowly around the perimeter of the depression, staying among the boulders. The cliffs rose vertically from the crater floor and he couldn't see any footholds in their rust-coloured faces. After a while he stopped scanning the shadows around him and kept his eyes locked on that damned building. *It's for playing,* he thought. He stopped. *Where the hell did that come from?* The house made him think of childhood games. *Why?* He stopped and peered at it closely. He could see detail at the periphery of his vision, but straight on everything appeared fuzzy. *Is it real, or an illusion? Will it vanish if I touch it?* As soon as he had the thought he found himself standing at the front door, his hand reaching out. It swung open, inviting him to enter.

Max did what he always did when scared and desperate. He focussed on his fear, moulding it into anger, fighting the gut-wrenching helplessness that threatened to overwhelm him. Why the ship and this crazy house? He couldn't ignore the nagging sense of familiarity. *I've been here before, I've stood in front of this very door. It means something to me, but what in God's name is it? Only one way to find out.* He stepped through into the darkness.

CHAPTER TWO

THE LIGHT WENT out. Max flailed in panic. His feet dangled over nothing. Shapes formed in the blackness. Perspective lurched and he found himself floating in a void. He yelled out in fear. A jumble of windows, stairs, walls and doors spread out before him across infinite space. Slowly they drifted together, merging into architecture.

He stood alone in a corridor. It stretched into the distance, narrowing down to a point. His heart lurched. Terrified, he pressed himself against the wall, hands shaking as he reached for a gun he no longer had. *Keep control, keep kneading your fear into anger. Terror will turn you into a corpse, rage might keep you alive.*

He ran through the possibilities in his head. *Am I in a wormhole?* But they were vertical, extruded from the singularity to plunge downwards to infinity, brick shafts lined with spiral staircases leading back through time. *Is this in the past?* He looked at his hands. He'd been born and raised in a universe so leached of energy it made him a ghost. When he stepped through doors onto planets long dead it felt like walking into a fire. On some of the older worlds he swore he could see the vapour rising from his skin as his body ablated in the glare of ancient suns. Not here. *It's freezing, like a street in Metacarpi in the early hours of morning.*

Wooden doors punctuated the walls on both sides, all closed. He looked behind him and his stomach twisted. The corridor stretched into infinity. The air around him seethed and details dissolved into shadows after a few yards. Ahead the same scene repeated itself, the passage shrinking to a point. He looked more closely at the peeling wallpaper. Where it still clung to the bricks he saw columns of printed flowers suckled by bugs that looked half-insect, half-machine. The nagging sense of familiarity grew. The atmosphere of the place dug deep into his memories. *Are you trying to tell me something, or do you just want to kill me? Either get it over with or tell me what it is you're trying to say.* He tried the doors nearest to him. Locked.

He noticed a picture hanging askew on the wall. Max struggled to make out the image through the dirty glass. Four men and four women sat on either side of a table. The men wore black suits, the women, dresses. *Brothers and sisters*, thought Max. They all had the same white hair and large eyes. The women folded their hands on their laps, the men thrust arms into their jackets like petty generals. The face of one of the men jogged his memory. *I know you, but where did we meet and when?* As soon as the question formed itself in his mind he grew aware of a faint whispering further down the corridor.

As he passed door after door the murmuring grew louder, not one voice but many. He tried to locate the source, and to catch some meaning from the incessant words. He knew they talked to him, desperately pleading, but he'd no idea what they said. He came across a second picture. He thought it a copy of the first, but with a twist of inexplicable terror saw that all the men and women now faced him. In that moment he nearly ran shrieking down the corridor into the jaws of whatever waited in the darkness. With a massive effort he forced himself to look into the faces in the photograph. *Have I gone mad? Is this a hallucination? Perhaps I'm banging my head against the walls of a cell in the lower levels of the Carceral Archipelago while Father tells everyone he's not particularly surprised.* No, he was awake - exhausted and scared yes - but fully aware. The floor under his feet, the damp air on his face, the incessant voices in his ear, they all existed. But why? Why the corridor, the strange pictures and the voices? *This house is full of messages, all for me and I don't understand them.*

"What do you want from me?" he called out.

The voices rose into a cacophony of sound. Max leaned against the wall, his hands to his ears. The whispering stopped. Silence hit him like a blow. He staggered, just as a woman stepped into the corridor ahead. This looked like something he could understand, even fight. He crouched, ready to defend himself.

She looked about fifty. She'd tied her hair up into a bun, held in place with a silver comb. Rings sparkled on her fingers. He recognised the face he'd seen at the window, but Max knew at once she wasn't the missing pilot. She looked more like one of the bourgeois mistresses that lived in the houses in the northern quarter of Metacarpi. She wore a tight-sleeved purple dress, high at the neck; the clothes of a hostess greeting someone to a dinner party. She folded her hands together and smiled. Despite his fear her face entranced him. Unusually chiselled for a woman, it somehow comforted him, suggested safety and warmth. He took a step backwards. *You know what this is, don't be fooled, this is the monster that built the house and lured you in. It doesn't really look like this.*

"Who are you?" he asked.

"Max, don't you know?"

So she could speak. That brought some relief. If he could talk to her he might yet leave this place alive. The fact that she appeared like an ordinary woman to him suggested she wasn't planning on killing and eating him straight away.

"You're a creature from the Wasteland. You built this place, and now you appear in this shape. Why? What do you want from me?"

She looked at him as if he was the biggest idiot in the universe. To his complete bafflement his face turned red with shame and he felt an inch tall.

"Maximilian Ocel. Do you really not recognise your own mother?"

Despite his knee-buckling fear Max couldn't help but laugh. Was that the best the creature could come up with?

"My mother died when I was two years old," he said. "You'll have to try harder than that." If it'd just played its best card, it had a poor opinion of him.

He paused, noticing something familiar in that long face. Could he see softer echoes of his own features? He couldn't remember what his mother looked like in the flesh, though, as a young boy, he'd seen a painting of her every day. He recalled sitting at breakfast with his father on the top level of the Carceral Archipelago. The portrait hung on the wall above Herman Ocel, who always sat with his back to it as if he couldn't bear to look at his dead wife. For Max it became the only human thing in the room. During the meal he watched the man opposite slowly assume the face of the Lord of Metacarpi. The frown deepened, the jaw muscles tightened and the beard grew sharper. Each morning the process started earlier. Once Hermann Ocel had looked occasionally at his son across the table with the hint of a sad smile. Now the mask went on as soon as he sat down, his father growing as implacable and austere as the stone walls around them. Max felt desperately lost, so he gazed into the shadows beyond at the picture of his mother. He remembered the oval face, the sharp nose and those eyes. Come to think of it, this woman did look more like his mother as each moment passed, as if the recollections brought her into sharper focus.

"You see, you do remember me, deep down," said a voice soft, reasonable, kind and utterly terrifying.

"Is that where you come from? Whatever you are, you've plucked this woman from my mind, this whole house, haven't you?" He looked carefully at her face. She smiled and in that second her eyes unlocked a door in his head. A thousand recollections roared back, filling him with long forgotten sights, sounds and feelings. The woman smiled and clapped her hands as if congratulating a clever child. He went down on one knee, knowing that if this creature attacked him now he couldn't defend himself.

"What do you want?" he heard himself whimper.

An elegant finger lifted his chin. He looked into a face he hadn't seen since he could barely walk - vast, kind and filled with love. A distant part of him longed to be picked up and held. He pushed himself back and staggered to his feet. Memories flickered through his mind in an incessant stream like a magic lantern show. A warm room, a fire, the smell of cake and rich wine, soft sheets, lamplight on polished wood. A lullaby. A game with wooden animals.

"Get out of my head," he said. "Stop it."

"That's it Max, that's it, that's the place," cooed the woman. "Look."

She opened the door behind her.

Get a grip, fight it. His nails dug into his palms. The creature was playing with his memories, parading his childhood before him for its own cruel amusement. He hated it, and from that anger came defiance. He looked through the door and gasped.

It was more an impression of a room, than a room itself. He sensed a low ceiling and wooden panelled walls. Lamps cast reflections across the furniture, a thick carpet stretched to a fire where flames danced upwards from spitting coals. He smelled cake, milk and the faint aroma of cigars and wine. He knew this place. The vague sense of familiarity that had plagued him when he first saw the house had vanished, replaced by certainty. He'd been in this room before, but when? Without thinking he stepped through the doorway. He stood next to a table but the top of his head barely reached it and when he looked up he saw lamplight twinkle through a decanter as large as a man. *Why is everything so big*?

"Max, we used to play here, remember?" his mother's voice floated in the air. Was she asking a question or stating a fact? He turned and found himself looking at a wall of purple silk. She towered over him. He felt his fingers enclosed in a hand twice the size of his own.

"I recognise this place," answered Max.

"Do you remember where it is?" she asked again.

Not in the Carceral Archipelago, he knew that. Stone and iron, steel and cold tiles covered the walls and floors of that tower. This was like the rooms he'd dreamed of when younger; places warm, secure and filled with laughter. But he couldn't dismiss this as the echo of a childhood fantasy. He knew he'd walked here before, and felt carpet under his toes. He tried to focus on the details around him, but everything looked blurred, like images projected on smoke. To the left of the fire, in the corner, he thought he saw a doorway opening onto a passageway. He couldn't see down the corridor, but something about that entrance frightened him.

He used to come that way, said a voice in his mind. Was that his mother speaking, or himself? *You were frightened of him at first, but later you played together.*

"Who used to come that way, Max?" He heard tension in her voice, echoing his own rising dread. A man stood in the passageway, just inside the entrance. A shadow among the shadows, but this one had white hair. He tried to pull away from his mother's grip.

"Where is this Max, where is it?" A babble of voices replaced hers, insistent, rising in pitch, blotting out all reason, asking the same question again and again. *Where is it, where is it? I don't know, I can't remember.*

A searing pain exploded in his shoulder. Max yelled. The floor lurched and he fell. He looked wildly around and saw that he no longer stood in the room of shadows. Instead he knelt on a dirt floor encompassed by bare walls. Daylight crept through gaps at the bottom where they rested on the uneven ground. More spilled through four windows and a door to his left. A woman sat in the corner, her head slumped on her chest. She wore a leather flying suit with a red sigil on the left breast. Max could just make out a pale face fringed by black hair and smeared with blood. From outside came a thudding sound, as of giant footsteps. With each crash of sound the room shook and threads of dust trickled down through the air. Hands jerked him to his feet and slapped him across the face.

"Max, get up! We have to leave, now!"

"Mother." He glanced wildly round. Now the creature looked like Abby. She held a hairpin in her fist. His right shoulder hurt like hell.

She slapped him hard. *She insists on wearing all those bloody rings,* he thought.

"It's in your head. It's a trap. Wake up you stupid bastard or I'll stick you again, God help me."

He pushed her back against the wall, his fingers around her throat. Another image plucked from his mind, another illusion in this insane trap. He summoned up the last of his strength and sanity to fight back, furious that the creature still plundered his mind for bait, feeding him with false images of the people close to him.

"For God's sake Max, get a grip," yelled Abby, as much in frustration as fear.

She twisted out of his hands and threw him across the room. He banged his head against the far wall and the building shuddered. Abby took a few paces back, the bloodied pin at the ready. Behind her the injured woman lay unmoving in the shadows.

"Max?" asked Abby uncertainly.

Swaying like a drunk, Max held up his hand to quieten her.

"You ran into the house, and when I came after you I found you just standing there in some kind of trance. I've been screaming at you for the last half hour."

"Shut up," Max said. "Shut up and listen."

He closed his eyes, despite the vertigo, and tried to concentrate. Outside something walked towards them with titanic steps. With each footfall the walls shook. He pointed at the woman behind Abby.

"She's real?" he asked.

Abby nodded.

"Sure?"

Abby nudged the woman's leg with her toe.

"I think so."

Max leaned down and lifted up the woman's hair. A ragged gash marked her forehead and bruises covered the left side of her face. He felt her pulse. She was alive. He picked her up and slung her over his shoulder, surprised at how light she seemed. Abby kicked the door open and they stumbled out of the house.

"Max!" his mother called.

Despite himself he stopped and looked back. Instead of shabby walls and a dirt floor he saw the warm room again, more precise now, as though the images in his head had finally come into focus. A fire roared in an iron grate. He saw a bookshelf filled with wonderful stories and next to it the end of a child's bed. *Is that mine?* Two glasses stood next to the half-filled decanter on the table. He saw points of light distorted by the crystal, biscuit crumbs scattered over the polished wood. Details leaped out at him in rapid succession, as if he stitched together a tapestry from fragments of long forgotten memories. His mother stood in the centre of the room, her arms stretched out, beseeching him to return. Beyond her he could just make out the passageway and the outline of the man hovering in the shadows.

"Please Max, tell me where this is," cried his mother. *Get out of my head.* He stumbled away, trying to shake his mind free of the images. The room blinked out and the door slammed shut. With horror Max realised a wall of mist filled the sky beyond the house. Threads drifted over the ridge towards him. He turned and ran down the slope. Behind him the footfalls came so loud that with each step the ground shifted. He stumbled and fell to one knee, almost pitching the woman down the slope. He heard his name again, but this time it rolled over the landscape like thunder. Ahead of him Abby slammed her hands to her ears. She turned back towards Max, blood pouring from her nose, before looking up into the sky with an expression of fear that appalled him. *Nothing fazes Abby,* he thought, *nothing ever fazes Abby. What in the name of God is behind me?* Crying in terror Abby fled down the slope. Ahead of him a gun chattered and bullets sped over his head back into the mist. He saw Olaf, far below, sitting in the saddle of the chain gun, shooting into the fog. He staggered on, his boots slipping on the incline. By the time he reached the bottom the voice incessantly shouting his name was nothing more than a whine, the drone of an insect in his mind. Abby stumbled on in front, weeping hysterically and wiping the blood from her face with trembling hands. Max grabbed her by the scruff of her neck and managed to manhandle her and the unconscious woman into the shadow of the ship. Olaf leaned over the rail and dragged them onto the deck like a man fishing three kittens out of a pond. Abby yelled commands at the engineer and they ran into the cabin.

Max looked up at the ridge. The fog filled the sky. In its midst the silhouette of a man, vaster than a mountain, looked down at the *Bricolage*. *He's as big as the Carceral Archipelago.* He couldn't see any features, he didn't want to. He couldn't speak or move, terror paralysed him. The shadow bent forwards, reaching down to the house. The building teetered forwards like a toy made of card. That hand, how big was that hand? The dynamos span up, blue fire sparked across his field of vision. *He's in no hurry*, thought Max, *we can't escape, he'll just extend his finger and grind us into the dirt like a boy crushing an ant.*

He closed his eyes, waiting for the end. He heard the sound of splintering wood and shattered glass. Surprised to be still alive he looked up in time to see the house tumbling down the slope. Four walls and a roof collapsed inwards like cheap scenery and slid down the jagged ground, breaking apart as they gathered speed. Above them, the giant clutched the ridge. Max saw grey fingers tipped with black nails, cracked and splintered where they gouged furrows in the rock. The engine kicked into life and the ship turned. It accelerated away, rocking from side to side, making it hard for Max to see properly. *If it chases us*, he thought, *we're finished.* But the giant stayed perfectly still, with only his monstrous hand emerging from the mist. As the distance increased, Max gathered enough courage to stand. The injured pilot lay on the deck, her head lolling back and forth. Keeping one eye on the receding titan he gathered her up in his arms. As the ship sped away from the mist and the immense shadow, Max began to hope. Perhaps they'd escaped. Perhaps despite all the hallucinations and terrors plucked from his mind, he'd defeated the giant.

CHAPTER THREE

MAX CARRIED THE pilot into one of the cabins. His hands shook and he fought the urge to be sick. *Shock, it's the shock. You're still alive. You survived again.* It hadn't beaten him, though it tried to turn his mind inside out. He didn't know whether to laugh or collapse in a sobbing heap. Instead he forced himself to get a bowl of water and bandages. The woman lay in the bunk, as still as death. Her long face made him think of the sculptures in alien temples he and Abby plundered during wormhole trips. Long black hair framed sharp features and upward-tilted eyes. The skin turned almost translucent in sleep, as if carved from frosted glass. He tried to guess her age but found it impossible. Injury lay an inhuman patina over her features. He touched her forehead. It felt hot.

Ten minutes later a dressing covered the cut on her forehead and a bowl of bloody water sat on the shelf by the window. Max hadn't found any other injuries. He pulled the blanket up to her chin. She opened her eyes. He almost screamed. *I'm still a mental wreck, the slightest thing sets me off.* Despite the shock, he noticed she had astonishing pupils, a deep violet flecked with silver, like scraps of mica.

"You're safe," he tried to sound reassuring but his voice trembled.

She didn't look at him. Her unfocussed gaze flickered round the room.

"The Dogs set up barricades on the third deck," she whispered. "He's locked himself in the Iron Core. I don't think he's injured, at least not badly, but I'm the only one who can open it. Please don't let them send me away. They're disloyal bastards. Aren't I his daughter?"

Her eyes rolled up and her head fell back onto the pillow.

The monster got inside your mind as well, thought Max, *showed you memories you didn't want*. He remembered the fire-lit room and his mother. Panic grabbed him and he found it difficult to think. The *Bricolage* rocked from side to side. Had Olaf forgotten how to steer the damn thing? He could smell burning. What the hell was the engineer playing at?

Olaf sat on the navigator's stool in the forward engine room. He stared into the mirrors at the landscape speeding beneath the ship, his eyes wide with fear. Max noticed he'd turned off the rear viewer. The dynamos shrieked, static sparking across the machinery. *He's going to destroy the engines*. He shouted in Olaf's ear. The man ignored him. Max shook him but the engineer shrugged his hand away. In the end Max prised his fingers from the accelerator wheel. He ducked just in time and Olaf's fist smacked into the side of a fuse box, leaving a dent.

"For God's sake Olaf," shouted Max. All his fear and rage boiled up. If he'd had his gun with him he'd have shot the lumbering bastard and tipped him over the side. Olaf's face crumpled and he began to sob. Max stared, appalled. He felt ashamed, remembering how the engineer had tried to defend them against the titan.

"It hasn't followed us," he said, putting a hand on the Olaf's shoulder.

"It's too big, too huge, it'll hunt us down, no-one can escape," whispered the engineer. He looked dangerously close to the edge.

"It crawled out of a wormhole," Max said, desperate to reassure the man. "It got into my head and tried to trap us with my memories. It won't live for long, nothing from the past ever does. They perish in days, if not hours."

He hoped he was right. In the threadbare reality at the end of the universe, monsters from the past never survived. Aeons ago the builders of the Thumb had brought creatures and machines out of the past to help in the Great Task. They all perished, eyes fading, energy leaching away. Max still found giant skeletons in the Wasteland, but nothing like the mountainous shape that loomed in the mist beyond the house. Max knew of tales of horrors from deep time finding their own way into wormholes and crawling up the shafts. When that happened his father sent ships to drop bombs into the pit before sealing it forever. He shuddered. Someone else could do the job, he didn't want to see the giant ever again. Even so he couldn't shake the feeling he'd met something more than just an escaped demon from the past.

Olaf dried his face with his sleeve and nodded, but Max could tell by his eyes that dread still lurked in the engineer's mind. *We're at least five days out from Meta-carpi*, he thought. If Olaf cracked he'd no idea how they'd get home. The *Bricolage* needed a crew of three. He didn't like leaving the man alone in the engine room, but he wanted to find his partner. Abby Fabrice had fought stomach-churning horrors in the darkest places with a mile-wide grin on her face. He remembered her look of fear when she saw the giant in the mist above the house. He'd never seen her so scared. He went searching for her, dreading the state she'd be in.

Abby sat in the chart room drinking her way through a bottle of red spirit they'd stolen in the slums of a planet-wide city. Her gaunt stare shocked Max, but when he looked into her eyes he saw she was still with him.

"You're as white as a sheet," she slurred.

Something wasn't right. His friend shouldn't be like this. They'd faced horrors enough in the past, why had the giant scared them so badly? He knew it could reach into their minds. It must have made them fear it, paralysing them with terror like a spider injecting venom into its prey. He shuddered at the thought.

"It was as big as a mountain," said Abby, pouring another shot. Her hands shook. "I felt helpless, almost mad. I couldn't think, all I wanted to do was run."

He remembered the shadow rearing above them, vast and remorseless.

"It messed with our thoughts, showed me visions, terrified you and Olaf with some kind of psychic attack." He paused, realising what he'd said. The creature sent his companions delirious with fear, but not him. True, he'd been terrified, but his hallucination had also been filled with images of comfort and warmth, more like a dream than a nightmare. Why?

"So what happened in that house?"

He took a swig and passed it back. God it tasted foul - like alcoholic engine oil - but it roared through his system in seconds, numbing his ragged nerves. He told Abby what he'd seen in the corridor, about his mother and the room.

"She died when I was two, I only recognised her from a painting in the Carceral Archipelago," he said. In the fug of the alcohol he saw her features again. God she'd been beautiful. Even a man like his father might fall in love with her. No, impossible. Herman Ocel a lovesick suitor? Too bizarre.

"Everything about it felt familiar, the house, her, the room."

He took another drink and searched his earliest conscious memories; the tower, stone and iron, four chains stretching down into mist. How long ago? He'd be four or five. The creature had unlocked thoughts far older, memories he didn't even know he had. Why? That room looked so comforting, full of calm warmth and security. Only the shadowy figure in the passageway scared him. He remembered the white hair, a pale face and large eyes, like the people in the photograph. *What does it mean? Was it really just a trap?*

"Is it a room in the Carceral Archipelago?" asked Abby.

Of course not. He felt the bitterness well up.

"No," he managed to say. He shouldn't have drunk that spirit. He blinked, angry at the emotion that caught him unawares. Abby reached out to touch him and he instinctively flinched back. He saw the hurt in her eyes.

She jerked her head towards the cabin door behind her.

"How is she?" she asked.

"Unconscious, it got inside her head too."

What had she said? *The Dogs are barricaded on the third deck?* It sounded like the memory of a battle.

"Any idea where she's from?" asked Abby.

He hadn't a clue. He reached for the bottle and nearly knocked it over. Abby put her hand on his shoulder. This time he didn't pull away.

"You need rest," she said.

"I need air," he muttered. "Keep an eye on Olaf, he's close to cracking."

He blundered out of the room.

Max walked out onto the deck of the *Bricolage*. Through the haze of his exhaustion he stared at a plain littered with a patchwork of chasms. Here and there immense cubes or pyramids of ebony thrust out of the ground. *What are we doing here? Look at this place, how many more million years are we going to have to grub our lives out on this glorified carpenter's bench?*

He rested his hands on the rail of the airship and looked up at God's left thumb, thousands of miles to the west. He knew beyond it lay the Hand, palm-up on the floor of the universe, but the mass of the Thumb hid everything else, a curved wall filling half the sky with its shadow. All detail merged into a patchwork jumble. Straight ahead lay the folds of the Knuckle, too close for him to get a true sense of its shape. He tried to see the beginnings of the Cuticle three thousand miles to the south, but everything faded into the haze and exhaustion made it hard to concentrate. *When are you finally going to wake up and carry your children into the new universe, you lazy bastard?* It wasn't much of a prayer and besides, the unfinished god still slept, oblivious to his creators.

He saw dots of light peppering the skin. They shone in the purple twilight; some steady, some moving, some dying while new ones sprang to life. Max craned his head back. The air stopped less than a hundred miles above his head, beyond that the Thumb rose over five thousand miles into space.

He could stare at it forever. As a child, trapped in the iron and stone cylinder of the Carceral Archipelago, he'd often looked from his bedroom window across the city towards the Thumb. He longed to journey to it. He imagined himself threading his way across the Palm, high above the atmosphere, or walking through the wooden and steel pores of the sleeping titan. He knew

Abby felt the same way. The Thumb called to both of them. She had the advantage of an older sister to fill her head full of stories about the kingdoms scattered over and around the dreaming colossus. Names filled his mind; the Steel Queen ruling her city encased in a hollow ball as it floated along a river of mercury, the Ocean of Forgotten Guns, the Philosophers navigating their trains across the airless wastes of God's face and chest. Stories for children, filled with strange wonders and impossible bravery. He thought of the ghost of his mother in the giant's house. Had she told him stories from those books in the mysterious room? Whatever tales she recounted to him ended when she died. He couldn't remember a single one.

At the thought of his encounter in the creature's house fear rose up in him like a sickness. He pushed it back. *You're such a coward, Max, fight it.* He tentatively eased himself back into the new memories. In his mind he saw the blurred interior of the room and the shadowy figure standing in the passageway. *Where is this place?* That's what the creature asked. He didn't know. A house in the city perhaps? Certainly not the Carceral Archipelago. He'd lived his life in that stone tower. It was his whole world. No, not his. It belonged to his father, and he understood the old bastard well enough to know he'd never dwell elsewhere. Would he tell his father about the house and the monster impersonating his dead mother? He quailed at the thought. They hadn't exchanged a word for over half a decade. Even when they had spoken, Herman Ocel never mentioned his wife once in thirty years. What made him think the Lord of the Carceral Archipelago would discuss it now with his estranged and despised son? He lowered himself down onto the deck, leaned against the bulkhead and looked up at the Thumb, letting its massive presence fill his mind. He fell asleep.

"A thumb is an easy thing to build, far simpler than a heart the size of a world, or the mind of a god. A thumb is made of skin and flesh with three bones in the core, stretching from the fat palm muscle we call the Abductor Pollicis Brevis down to the edge of the Nail. Simple mechanics, nothing more. A million years ago we began the Great Task, to build a god that would carry us from this dying universe to the new cosmos. But we had nowhere left to make such a deity. All the planets turned to rubble long ago, torn asunder in the death throes of the galaxies. Even if one still existed it wouldn't be big enough. Our god is over half a million miles long from toe to crown. What human realm could support such a titan? By this time we lived in our metal spheres floating in the void, tiny man-made worlds sheltering the remnants of humanity.

"But we had friends. The Black Roses, children of another, far stranger god. They knew the science we'd forgotten. Taking pity on us, they unrolled a flat singularity and covered it with the remnants of long-dead worlds. It became our workbench and our home; five light years square, a floor for the universe upon which we build a new god. But what materials could we use to create him? There's nothing here. The universe is empty.

"The Black Roses drilled holes back through time and space, shafts of darkness studded with billions of doors, each one leading to an ancient world. Everything we needed to make our saviour lay in the past. Wood, metal, jewels, rare stones and furs, wondrous tools as big as cities or smaller than a human cell. We became the last craftsmen, engaged in the most glorious work ever attempted, the Great Task, the building of a new god."

Despite the man's best efforts, his teacher's voice sounded as grey as the light that barely penetrated the classroom. Outside sheets of rain hammered against the window. Cloud swathed the city two miles below. Max sat with his face on his fist, his cheek pushed up so far it felt as though his ear rested on top of his head. He'd heard this story so many times before and he knew what came next.

"Three kingdoms dedicated themselves to building the left thumb of God, a titanic feat of engineering for that single digit is how big?"

"Twenty seven thousand miles long and six thousand miles wide," intoned Max. How many times did he have to repeat it?

"To the north, the people of Abductor fused the Thumb to the Palm, moulding vast forces and materials in their immense fortresses. Here," the teacher gestured out of the window, "Metacarpi built the Knuckle, all the way down to the start of the Cuticle. Finally the people of Tip made the Thumbnail and the Pad. They're all mad in Tip, mad and arrogant. They've got it into their heads they'll be the first into the new cosmos, when God reaches forward with his fingers to touch the boundary between universes. The idiots don't realise that God is right-handed, and that the other thumb will lead the way." The teacher waved his right hand at Max and chuckled to himself. *He's well over a hundred years old, where do they find these idiots? You're supposed to be training me to be the next Lord of the Carceral Archipelago.* Max suspected his father wasn't taking his education seriously. This teacher dribbled when he got excited, wore odd socks and smelled faintly of piss. Max wanted to ask how he knew God was right-handed, but the tutor was a fool and Max too old to bother making it obvious.

"Abductor, on the other hand, is a kingdom built from fear, a patchwork of castles bristling with armaments that no-one remembers how to use. The men of Abductor convinced themselves that somewhere in the empty universe other godless beings still lurked. Desperate to escape the dead cosmos, but with no god themselves, these creatures of darkness wait to steal ours or destroy him out of hatred and spite. The fools of Abductor think they will defend the sleeping deity with weapons stolen from the past. Mad and arrogant again, full of their own self-importance, completely deluded.

"Now in the beginning . . . when the three cities created the Thumb the kingdoms worked together, labouring night and day without cease for thousands of years. But a thumb is an easy thing to build, and they finished it long before the other parts of God. Foolish and impatient, the people thought that because they'd played their little part the deity would spring awake and carry them to the God Door straight away. They waited, and they waited. The wormholes no longer supplied honest labour with the materials for the body of God. Now they vomited forth luxuries; spices, drugs, liquors, foul passions and dangerous ideas. Boredom and decadence gave way to cruelty and ambition.

"Abductor fell upon Metacarpi, Metacarpi warred with Tip for thousands of years, and each war diminished us. Empires became nations, nations became kingdoms and in the end kingdoms became cities, inward looking and inbred. We turned upon ourselves and lost contact with the fortresses of Abductor and the fools of Tip. To the north they still point ancient weapons at the empty sky, thinking that monsters and aliens wait to take our God from us. God himself only knows what they do in Tip. Dance themselves into madness each night, I expect, bedecked in ragged silks and intoxicated on chemicals plucked from the cores of long-dead suns."

The teacher impersonated them with his own little dance, high stepping and ludicrous in front of the rain-lashed windows. He stopped and massaged his chest. Max's interest perked up. *The old fart's going to drop dead at last.* The tutor disappointed him.

"Write an essay on why no-one will ever attack Metacarpi again," he wheezed. "Describe how the mighty tower of the Carceral Archipelago is a moral axis of strength and resolve into whose shadow no fool dares step. Five hundred words, on my desk by tomorrow morning."

Max woke in his bunk, his body a mass of pain. Blood crusted a puncture wound just below his collar-bone. He remembered. *That harridan stabbed me with one of her hair pins.* He sat up, groaning with the effort. *At least it wasn't the poisoned one.* Outside the porthole a pale landscape slid past, littered with rusting canisters as big as the ship.

He found Abby Fabrice on the forward deck.

"Are you OK?" she asked.

He grunted, aware of her green eyes scrutinising his face.

"I haven't gone mad yet," he said. He worked his arm as he massaged his shoulder.

"Sorry," she said, nodding at the dried blood on his shirt. He noticed her haunted look. Dark circles ringed her eyes, remnants of an uneasy sleep.

"Bad dreams?"

She shook her head.

"Just crap left over from that monster's psychic attack; old stuff, history," she looked away. Max knew better than to probe further. He wondered how long they'd suffer the after-effects of the assault, they'd never met anything that messed so badly with their minds before.

He looked behind, trying to work out their position. A mountain of rusted nails slid past, each a hundred yards long. The ground briefly changed to a patchwork of iron plates. Sparks arced out of the dynamos and played across the metal. The landscape disappeared into haze on all sides. He looked for any giants striding towards them. Nothing. Red land below, purple sky above and the eternal wall of the Thumb to the west. The creature was probably dead by now. A thing that size from a wormhole wouldn't last long at the end of time. In his imagination he saw a vast body stretched across the floor of a dusty valley, light fading from its eyes, a broken house cradled in its hand. He shuddered. *This is going to haunt me for years.* He turned back to Abby and realised she felt the same way.

"Olaf?" he asked.

"Still with us, barely," said Abby. "He's jumping ship the minute we get back. Never wants to see us again. I doubt he'll step in another flyer."

"He didn't last long." Bravery wasn't essential in an engineer. They usually stayed with the ship while the Time Scavengers went into the wormholes. Olaf had joined the *Bricolage* a few weeks before, probably thinking he'd have an easy life taxiing the pair of them across the Wasteland, snoozing on deck while they clambered up and down through time and space. Poor bastard.

"That woman's sick, she needs attention," said Abby.

He did a quick calculation in his head.

"We're five days out from Metacarpi."

"She needs help sooner. Odilon's a day from here," said Abby.

"That loony? What makes you think he'll be any use?" He sensed Abby's sudden irritation and mentally kicked himself.

"Give me a better suggestion then, Captain," she said acidly before stalking back inside.

Max brooded. A ring of towers once marked the northern perimeter of the old kingdom of Metacarpi. Only one remained, a spire of crystal and metal rising over a sheer cliff, home to Odilon the Watcher, a recluse who spent his days trying to piece together the knowledge of the first builders. In Metacarpi he carried the reputation of a hermit, but he also patronised Rebecca Fabrice's theatre, and Abby adored the man for his kindness towards her family. He made Max uncomfortable. Odilon also advised the Lord of the Carceral Archipelago. Max knew him as the eccentric who came by night to the stone tower to whisper advice in the shadows with his father. As a child he'd been terrified of the recluse, with his bald head, eyes of amber and the robes that hissed over the floor as he walked beside Herman Ocel. *You always had time for Odilon the Watcher*, thought Max. He remembered the philosopher bending down to pat his head, compassion in his penny-coloured eyes. *And Odilon always had time for me.* But when the hermit came to the tower he and his father disappeared for days, sometimes weeks, leaving Max even more alone. He always feared his father wouldn't return from these adventures, a childhood anxiety he'd found difficult to shake off. In later life he realised the recluse was nothing more than an eccentric philosopher whose advice oscillated between the cryptic and the surreal. In his mind's eye he saw the two old men, his iron-faced father and the dreamer. They probably went and got debauched in the jazz bars and whore houses down by the Brick River. He thought of his mother, and somehow the recollection made him ashamed of his cynicism. He went in search of the injured pilot.

She lay in her bunk, eyes closed. Her ragged breathing worried Max. Her forehead burned. When he wiped the sweat from her skin he found himself staring in fascination at her face. Her porcelain features made him think of airless wastes of steel and light. He had to agree with Abby. She didn't look well enough to make the journey to the city. As much as he wanted to get back to Metacarpi, he couldn't think of any option but to take her to Odilon's tower.

"Your mouth's open." Abby leaned against the doorway, her arms folded and her eyebrow arched.

"Has she said anything?" asked Max, ignoring the jibe. At least Abby sounded like her old self. She shook her head. He picked up the woman's jacket, tracing his thumb over the red spiral, trying to make sense of the symbol.

"Where do you think she's from?" he asked.

"Her ship's a short range scout. A few thousand miles, Abductor?"

No, not Abductor. Their technology's no more advanced than ours. They flew ships shaped like iron crucibles that belched oily smoke and sounded like coffee grinders. No, something else was approaching the Thumb, another, more sinister power. It came with sleek machinery and disturbing beauty.

CHAPTER FOUR

MAX CAUGHT HIS first glimpse of the Watcher's tower as the light faded from the sky. In the absence of any stars, energies embedded in the atmosphere by the Black Roses waxed and waned as the hours drifted by, giving the semblance of night and day. It grew cold so he wrapped himself in a fur coat he'd taken from a dead soldier on an ice plain beneath triple suns. He held a mug of coffee to keep his fingers warm and watched the threaded silhouette grow larger with mixed emotions. Odilon's home proved to him how low the city of Metacarpi had fallen. He thought of its stone streets, grimy windows and the crumbling tenements south of the Brick River. In his mind, streams of grey-faced people stumbled back and forth beneath the lamps, grim, tired and resigned to centuries of waiting.

That spire belonged to an earlier age, built with a science long forgotten. He looked at the lines of steel and copper, woven between sheets of crystal. To Max it merely underscored the emptiness of the land around it. Once factories bigger than a city had filled this realm, surrounded by warehouses, cranes, flying platforms, docks, foundries, refineries, copies of every single type of workshop mankind had ever known, from simple coppersmiths to laboratories where alchemists stitched together the last remaining shreds of existence with the quantum threads that bound the universe. Millions upon millions of craftsmen, artists and technicians brought materials out of the wormhole shafts and welded, riveted, glued, bonded and sewed them together to make the Thumb. Arts and science flourished, philosophy and culture created hitherto undreamed-of wonders.

Max remembered the pictures in his school books. Men and women, slender and noble, stood on mountains and scaffolds and pointed in admiration at the Great Task. Beneath them millions of labourers, machines and fanciful creatures from the artist's imagination hauled pieces of the new god across the Wasteland towards the Thumb. Hundreds of spires communicated through chains of mirrors, speaking to each other in light, co-ordinating this one part of the greatest single piece of work man had ever attempted, the building of a god. After they'd finished the Thumb, they continued to broadcast in preparation for the awakening that never came, praising the people for their efforts and begging them to wait in patience. Wars came, and the spires turned into fortresses. As a child Max always found this the most exciting part of the otherwise tedious history lessons. In his imagination he saw vast aerial battles fought between the towers, the squat crucibles of Abductor exploding in flame and smoke as the tower's fire lances swept among them, Metacarpi's fighters picking off the survivors in a hail of missiles. Yet despite his city's inevitable victories only a single tower remained, while in the valley heaps of scrap and fragments of machines stood as decaying monuments to lost centuries of struggle.

Abby joined him on deck.

"Decent food and a hot bath," she said. "I smell like a pig."

"Don't tell him I saw my dead mother in the house," said Max. Abby looked at him in surprise.

"It's OK, Max, it sent us all crazy. There's no shame in that."

She didn't understand how much the encounter in the house still preyed on his mind. Abby bounced back from fear too easily. Max struggled to explain, but gave up.

"Just don't say anything. I don't want him to know, not yet," he replied.

He didn't trust Odilon. If he told him the monster had given life to a memory from his childhood he knew the Watcher would pass it on to his father. How would the old man react to the news that his son had come babbling out of the Wasteland talking about ghosts and giants, making up ridiculous stories about the woman he'd lost? *He'd lock me up in one of the rotating cells at the bottom of the Carceral Archipelago, the ones reserved for traitors and maniacs. I'll tell him when I'm ready, if ever.* He noticed Abby studying his face, trying to read his thoughts.

"We'll tell Odilon about the giant," he continued. "He might know where it came from. But don't mention the visions."

"OK," said Abby. He nodded in gratitude, at least he could trust mad Abby Fabrice.

The tower stood on a six-mile high plateau that angled out over the landscape like the edge of a book. In the valley below scribbles of light scored the surface, interspersed with the gleam of copper and corroded bronze. As the *Bricolage* coasted over the surface Max saw strands of metal hundreds of feet in diameter snaking in and out of the ground. A road made of white stone crept down the cliff face and disappeared north. The ship followed the broken highway into the shadow of the slope before rising up to the fortress. Odilon waited for them at the base of his tower. He held up a lantern to guide their way as night fell. Beyond his silhouette the bruised sky shifted to black. Guidance lights winked at the entrance to a hangar. Olaf steered the *Bricolage* inside, bringing it to rest in the corner of the vault. Max wondered what vessels once rested here; the dreadnoughts of his childhood dreams, all polished wood, brass and steel with bright silk pennants? In the empty cavern his own ship looked like a speck of dirt blown in from the night. Olaf shut off the engines and arcs of electricity discharged into the floor.

The doors rolled closed as Odilon walked towards them. To Max he hadn't changed since they'd first met in the stone corridors of the Carceral Archipelago. He wore the same soft blue robes. They slithered over the concrete behind him. Lamplight glistened on his bald head. Eyes the colour of pennies watched them as they disembarked. Abby walked up to the Watcher and hugged him. He towered over her. Max shuddered. How could she do that? He, on the other hand, felt like a four year old again, desperate not to be asked questions about lessons he'd already forgotten.

"Abby, my child," said Odilon, his voice rich. His features cracked into a friendly smile. Max thought he had a face like a rubber toy with someone's hand inside his head, squishing it to make him look very happy, very sad or filled with compassion. He possessed the uncanny knack of mirroring and amplifying every human emotion he encountered. If you were miserable he met your gaze with the profoundest expression of sympathy; if you laughed his features glowed in utter delight. When Max spoke to the Watcher he felt as if his entire unconscious mind pulled faces back at him. He found it unsettling, yet it seemed to put everyone else at their ease. He saw the tension drop from Abby's shoulders as the sage embraced her.

"We need your help. We found a stranger, she's injured," said Abby. The Watcher nodded.

"Of course, we'll do what we can to make her better."

He walked towards Max, who steeled himself, ready to be alarmed at whatever came next. Odilon stopped.

"Maximilian Ocel." He narrowed his gaze as if peering past the Time Scavenger's eyes into the depths of his brain. For a split second the soft smile froze. *Has he seen what I saw?* thought Max with a surge of panic. *Does he already know about my mother and the room with the white haired stranger?*

"What did you find out there?" Concerned interest filled Odilon's voice.

"A giant," grumbled Olaf.

The Watcher laughed but although his grin showed delighted surprise, his eyes said something else. Was it fear, anger? Max had never seen either in Odilon's face. He doubted he'd even recognise them in those gentle features. Even so, as expected, the other man rattled him. *So much for discretion, the mad bastard knows everything and we've only just got here.* Did the others notice the change in the Watcher's face? Abby looked on the old man with fond adoration and Olaf was as bovine and sullen as ever.

"A giant? How interesting. How large was this creature?" asked Odilon.

"As big as the Carceral Archipelago itself," said Max. He tried to keep his voice even but he realised it sounded like a challenge. *Explain that you smug, bald-headed clown.* Odilon's mouth fell open in a textbook picture of surprise.

"Two miles high? Really? Astonishing!" he said. "You must tell me all about it, but I expect you're tired and I need to see this casualty of yours. Bring her into the tower, and after I've tended to her we can eat and talk."

They brought the pilot out of the ship. Olaf, anxious to redeem himself, insisted on carrying her. She looked like a sick child cradled in his arms. Odilon led the way as they climbed through the tower's interior. Max had never been inside the spire and he marvelled at the contrast between the delicate exterior and the metal-walled spaces within. They climbed stairs of ridged nickel. Max felt the texture through the soles of his boots. They walked along curving corridors made of interlocking shapes forged from alloys tinted in different shades of blue, from midnight to the dusty cobalt of Odilon's own robes. Doors opened on gantries running along the inside of curved sheets of crystal and glass. Max guessed these spaces had once housed machines, weapons and laboratories dedicated to the study of the forces needed to hold God together. Now only a few scraps of wire or metal littered the polished floors, undisturbed for millennia; yet despite the tower's great age Max didn't spot any dust or corrosion during their entire journey. Once they traversed a bridge spanning a vault filled with shining water. Beyond it a side corridor led into a library. Abby whistled and Max saw she wanted nothing more than to lose herself among the books, but Odilon's lamp receded along the corridor and they hurried to catch up. The spire filled Max with wonder, tinged with melancholy and a sense of irredeemable loss. *I'm creeping through the guts of a dead machine we no longer understand.*

They stopped at a ring of cubicles in the upper part of the tower. The engineer placed the woman on a bed. Odilon leant over her, his body forming an elegant curve. Max thought he looked like a snake. Abby must have read his mind because she elbowed him in the ribs. *I've got to stop it*, he thought to himself. *He's always kind and helpful, and she loves the old lunatic.* Even so he couldn't forget the glimpse of uncertainty in the Watcher's eyes when he'd spoken about the giant.

"Do you recognise that?" Abby pointed to the patch on the woman's jacket.

"That's the sigil of the Empire of the Ear," said Odilon.

"The Empire of the where?" asked Max incredulously.

He ran through his memories, trying to recall any such place. For the people of Metacarpi geography stopped at the Wrist, beyond that lurked only legends and rumours. He'd guessed other kingdoms and cities lay scattered across the body of God, where else did Abby's stories come from? But the Ear of God? That was over a quarter of a million miles away. It didn't make sense. The pilot's scout craft had a range of a few thousand miles at best. She couldn't have flown it from the Ear. Something else must be close behind. He swallowed. *Something bigger and more deadly.*

Max looked at the woman. Her narrow face and pale skin contrasted with their own rougher, weather-beaten features. She had an inhuman air about her, as if she spent her life in a sealed, antiseptic world deep in Trans-Atmospheric space. If Odilon was right and she came from the Ear, what in the name of God himself was she doing next to the Thumb?

The Watcher reached into the folds of his robe and took out a phial. He let a drop of yellow liquid fall on the woman's lips. Her breathing deepened.

"Odilon's magic," he explained. "She has a fever, but it will pass."

He turned to Max and, raising the lantern, peered into his eyes again. *What are you looking for?* thought Max, fighting the urge to look away.

"I'm fine," he said tightly. Odilon patted him on the shoulder and smiled.

"Eat, then sleep and we'll talk tomorrow about giants."

In the morning Odilon took them to a dome at the very top of the tower. Max hauled himself up a spiral staircase into an observation chamber. Dials and controls covered every inch of the walls. He gazed around in awe, wondering if Odilon actually understood what each one did. This spire contained thousands of years of arcane science. He doubted even someone as sage as the Watcher comprehended more than a fraction. He looked at Odilon busying himself with a set of levers at the far end of the room. *How old are you? Sixty, a hundred?* He'd never questioned it before but now he thought about it the Watcher didn't look any different to the man who'd visited his father all those years ago. He chalked it up as another example of his strangeness and turned his attention to the room.

In the centre stood an onyx table. Max swept his fingertips over a surface so cold it hurt. It reflected the faceted glass above his head and the sky beyond. Odilon reached underneath the slab and pulled out several maps, each the height of a man. Max and the others gathered round as he unfurled each roll in turn, bending into a boneless curve to study them with a magnifying glass that dangled on a chain around his neck.

"So, where did you see this giant?"

Max didn't want to talk about the house. He couldn't understand Odilon's persistence and Abby seemed to be egging him on. Surely the pilot downstairs held more significance than a creature stumbling out of a wormhole? He seethed as she unrolled another map. *That's the one I fell asleep on just before we found the house.* Abby gave him one of her looks. *OK, give them what they want and get it over with.* He joined her and they compared the two charts. He tried to remember the route of the *Bricolage*. He reckoned he'd slept for an hour before Abby woke him. He did the calculations in his head and gestured vaguely at the contours. Odilon nodded and walked to the side of the room. He reached up and pulled an inverted cone of steel and leather along a rail until it pointed down at the centre of the table. The apparatus terminated in a lens. Odilon threw a switch on the machine.

Max gasped. He saw a pyramid of glowing squares fall across the onyx slab like cards dealt across a table. As the images spread they shrank. At the tip of the triangle the last picture was half the size of his little finger nail.

"These are my eyes," said the Watcher, sounding like an excited boy. "Once thousands of thinking mirrors carried the voices of the builders from the Wrist to the uttermost Tip. Now there are barely a hundred left. Each light shows the view reflected in a single mirror. The chain is seventeen thousand miles long. The oldest mirror dates from half a million years ago. The size of each image is determined by the distance of the glass that feeds it."

They gathered round. The scenes entranced Max. He saw glimpses of crumpled ground, fragments, shattered wheels, frames, broken machinery and mountains of metal and wood. He leaned over the table and gawped in wonder at each patch of light, his unease forgotten.

He couldn't see anything that looked like a house or, God forbid, the giant. He finished at the smallest square. Something in the shape woke uncomfortable memories. Odilon positioned the lens of a second projector above it.

The magnified picture appeared on a screen behind them.

Max felt his legs go weak. He reached behind for the edge of the table, steadying himself against the sudden rush of fear. *Fight it, don't be a coward, turn it into anger. That's the ridge alright, where's the giant?* The grainy image made it hard to see details. *My God, is that a handprint?* Everything else had vanished; the house, the mist, even the broken ship at the foot of the slope.

"Well, well, well," said Odilon. He studied the image with his magnifying glass for what seemed like an eternity. Eventually he looked up at his guests.

"In the records of the beginning of the Thumb there are stories of giants," said Odilon. "Men found the beings on a long-forgotten world in the depths of a wormhole shaft and brought them here, though others believe that the alchemists who built this tower created the monsters themselves to work as slaves. But the giants were cruel, arrogant and violent. They possessed powers that couldn't be tamed. They rebelled against us. The ancient lords of Tip, Metacarpi and Abductor united to destroy them. They hunted the monsters down until none remained. That's what the records say. It looks as if they're wrong."

That didn't make sense to Max. He remembered the house, the long corridor and the ghost of his mother. There had to be more to this than just a deranged monster on the rampage. He toyed with the idea of telling Odilon about the visions but decided against it. All hell would break loose if his father found out.

"What made them cruel?" he asked.

"Their nature," answered Odilon.

"So you're saying that one of these giants from, what, nearly a million years ago, is out there still?"

asked Abby. Max could see she struggled with the explanation.

"I doubt it. I think this one escaped from a wormhole shaft. It may be a descendant of the original brood, in which case it proves they came from an ancient world. It's a simple task of finding the shaft and closing it," said Odilon.

"And killing the one that's escaped," muttered Olaf. He pulled a clay pipe out of his pocket with trembling fingers and lit it.

"No need. It'll perish soon of its own accord," said Odilon. "A giant from the past won't last more than a couple of days."

"It got inside my mind," said the engineer. Max froze. He swapped a panicked glance with Abby. Odilon looked curiously at Olaf.

"It made us all scared." The man nodded towards Abby. "She was screaming like a child."

Odilon turned to Abby.

"We think it generated some kind of psychic field to trap us," she said.

"What did you see?" asked Odilon. He looked like a sculpture made from blue steel. Abby shrugged.

"Blood, dead faces." She shook her head, clearly not wanting to continue. The silence that followed seemed to fill the universe. At last the Watcher smiled and took her hand, as if comforting a child.

"The ancient giants were terrible creatures," he said.

This isn't right, thought Max. *It's too simple an explanation, too easy.* Abby caught his eye as the sage turned away. He took her cue and changed the subject.

"What about the woman downstairs?" he asked.

"While you slept I worked out her route," said Odilon. He pulled his very serious face and Max's throat tightened.

"Turn mirrors fifteen, thirty-five and eighty nine," called Odilon. Springs and relays clicked behind the wall of brass dials.

"The craft you found travelled two thousand miles from the direction of Abductor Pollicis Brevis," he continued, turning back to the projection screen. Max heard a sharp intake of breath from Abby. Dread swept through him as he looked at the image. Two ovals hovered over a range of hills. For a second he failed to understand what he saw and turned to the others for an explanation. Olaf and Abby stood side by side, their mouths open. They looked like a pair of tragic masks.

"Oh my God," hissed Olaf. Max turned back to the wall and comprehension dawned.

The dreadnoughts floated in the purple sky, immense lozenges of steel and brass fringed with glass canopies, fins and weapon blisters. Orange lights flickered along their outlines. Max noticed dots moving back and forth against the colder radiance of cabin interiors. *God, that's the crew.* Each of the ships bore a red sigil in the centre of the prow. *They'll destroy us. They'll wipe us out of existence. This is what the ant sees before the boot descends.*

Max walked up to the image on unsteady legs. Abby joined him, her gaze flickering back and forth over the ships.

"What are they?" Max asked. The size of the machines astounded him. God only knew what powered them, what energies lay encased beneath their black hulls.

"Battleships. Big, god-awful, mighty, death-dealing, shit-kicking battleships," said Olaf.

"Look at those turrets," whispered Abby, her face a picture of horrified fascination. "One of those could destroy the entire city."

Max peered at a gun on one of the upper batteries. *I could fly the* Bricolage *down that barrel without even scraping the sides.*

"The ships belong to the Empire of the Ear. The pilot is a forward scout. She flew too far in her vessel, it ran out of energy and crashed. You saved her before your giant could kill her," said Odilon.

My giant? For some reason Max thought of his mother. He noticed Odilon watching him with copper eyes. Max still couldn't shake the feeling the sage knew about his visions in the house.

"What do they want?" Abby asked. "Is this an invasion?"

"We've nothing worth conquering," said Max. *This is ridiculous. Who'd send two battleships like that to an undefended city in the middle of nowhere?* Their own fleet consisted of half a dozen battered frigates with a couple of cannon each, and a handful of transport vessels. They had comedy value but nothing more.

"How long do we have?" he asked.

"With those engines? Six weeks, maybe two months," said Olaf.

"Now what?" asked Abby.

I've got to tell my father. I've got to face the old bastard and tell him . . . what? Of his approaching destruction? The thought of running away to the Thumb suddenly seemed very appealing.

"Is there anything in the Carceral Archipelago that can help us?" asked Olaf.

"Such as?" snapped Max, unnerved by the sight of the dreadnoughts.

"I don't know," said Olaf plaintively. "A secret weapon, from ancient times."

"Not that I know of," said Max. *You should know. You're supposed to be heir of the Carceral Archipelago, but if*

Father has mighty defences secreted away he never told his son.

Odilon gave a polite cough, Max looked at him in surprise.

"The Lord of the Carceral Archipelago is ever resourceful," he said. "You should tell him about this as soon as possible."

What did Odilon know that he didn't? Did Herman Ocel have something powerful enough to meet a foe like that? Max looked at the dreadnoughts. He doubted it. He found Odilon's platitudes maddeningly unhelpful.

"He won't believe me, unless you can get a photograph," said Max, studying the ships. Black and silver armour plating covered the hulls.

"The light from the final mirror is weak, it takes hours to capture the images," said Odilon.

"Then start the process now," said Max, his patience wearing thin. "Get anything you can."

Under Odilon's direction, Olaf and Abby slotted a glass plate into the projection mechanism.

"The ships are moving. We'll get a blurred ghost at best," explained the Watcher. His languid manner angered Max. Despite himself he started to lose his temper.

"The Carceral Archipelago won't be the only tower to fall if they get here!" he snapped. "Your precious spire is as much a target, Odilon. Don't think your patronising indifference will save you when those battleships float down the valley. Any picture will do, just get me something to show my father."

"Max!" said Abby, aghast. The sage fixed Max with steady gaze, his expression unreadable. Max struggled to contain his anger. He'd overstepped a mark and knew it. Odilon's features broke into a self-deprecating smile.

"Of course, I'll do my best," he said.

The image vanished. Despite himself Max rounded on the Watcher. For a second he thought he'd deliberately switched the projector off.

"What happened? Bring it back!"

"I can't. The mirror's broken," Odilon said, staring straight back at him. "They're so old, the eyes of the tower, they're dying one by one."

"What about the other mirrors?" asked Abby in a frightened voice.

"Too far away," he answered.

Max placed his fingertips on the edge of the onyx table, closed his eyes and forced himself to calm down. *I've been running on empty for too long. It's too much. First the giant, my dead mother and now this.* He felt as if the universe had him beneath its own vast thumb, grinding him into the dirt.

"My father won't listen to me," he said, "he never listens. He only believes what he sees with his own eyes."

"Max," said Odilon, "I'll visit your father and tell him what we've learned. He'll believe me."

Max winced at the implication of the Watcher's words. *He'll listen to you because he won't believe his own son.* He sighed. It was what it was. No use raking through the dead coals of their relationship yet again. The only thing that mattered now was warning the Lord of the Carceral Archipelago of the coming threat.

"There's one person who can tell us why those ships are heading this way," he said. "Odilon, please will you wake her up?"

CHAPTER FIVE

THE PILOT SAT propped against a stack of pillows. Max saw her astonishing purple eyes change hue as she turned her head towards him. She looked frail, but he couldn't tell whether it was the fever, or she always looked like a delicate statue.

"What happened to me?" she asked in a soft voice. She spoke with a strange accent, it sounded like she sang the words.

"Your flyer crashed. We rescued you," said Abby. "You've been out for over a day."

The woman closed her eyes.

"I was in a house on a hill."

Max and Abby exchanged glances and he shook his head. *Forget the giant, we need to learn about those god-aw-ful battleships, we can talk about monsters later.*

"Are you from the Empire of the Ear?" asked Max. She nodded.

"There are two dreadnoughts to the north of here, heading this way. Why?" said Abby.

Tears welled up in the woman's eyes and she clutched at the sheets.

"They betrayed him. The filthy traitors. Hathus, all of them. They attacked the Dogs while they slept. The survivors barricaded themselves in the accumulator rooms. I fled. He made me go. I wanted to fight beside him but the Dogs forced me into a flyer. He is the noblest warrior, the mightiest general, a god among men, and his best officers turned against him. Even Captain Andagis betrayed him. He's locked himself in the Iron Core, They can't get at him. But he can't get out. He'll die in there."

Her face crumpled and she began to sob. Max felt at a loss, she looked so helpless.

"Who was betrayed?" asked Abby.

"My father, Alaric," murmured the woman, tears running down her cheeks.

"General Alaric an Vircana?" asked Odilon. *Who?* thought Max. The Watcher stared at the woman with an intense interest that did nothing to reassure him. Judging by the old man's expression everything had just got significantly worse. Abby shrugged at Max. She didn't have a clue either.

"We're friends, you're in no danger here," said Odilon. Max wasn't sure how comforting she'd find his words. *We're an alarming looking lot, especially Odilon.* The Watcher took the woman's hand in his. To Max's surprise she stopped crying.

"I'm Ruth an Vircana. My father is Admiral of the Seventh Fleet of the Empire of the Ear, Condottieri to the Emperor Demetrius and Commander of the Dogs." Tears leaked down her face. "The faithful Dogs."

Emperors and armies, unfamiliar names; none of it meant anything to Max.

"Why are you here?" he asked.

"We came on a mission from the Emperor himself to the Thumb. I don't know why," the woman said.

An uneasy hauteur settled across her features. He recognised the expression, she'd put on a mask to hide herself from the world. He'd seen his father do the same countless times. *She's not as desperately helpless as she looks.*

"What does the Empire of the Ear want with the Thumb?" asked Odilon gently.

"The Emperor gave my father orders to open once we got beyond the Wrist. When the day came we breakfasted on his balcony in the bright, cold air. Everywhere looked empty, this landscape is so dead and empty." Her lips trembled.

Of course it is, thought Max. *It's the end result of thousands of years of self-destructive boredom. A thumb is an easy thing to build, we finished it too soon. An ear on the other hand, how many aeons does it take to give God the ability to listen?*

"He kissed me and told me the Emperor had chosen us to perform a task that would change the fortunes of every human left alive. He went into the study and opened his orders. When he returned his face was white and he wouldn't speak to me. The Emperor's letter robbed him of his voice."

"What frightened him?" interrupted Abby.

"Nothing frightens him, nothing frightens any of us," spat Ruth in sudden fury. "We are the Lords of the Long Lock, the Athanatoi of the AntiHelix. This wasn't fear!"

Max lay a hand on Abby's arm. At his touch she relaxed a little. He heard her mutter something like 'snotty little shit' under her breath.

"He summoned his captains, Andagis of the *Geryon* and Hathus of the *Beatrice*," continued Ruth. "After their meeting, Andagis went back to his ship. I returned to my rooms. Shortly afterwards fighting broke out. Dogs came to my room. I ordered them to lead me to my father, but they took me to the hangars instead. They put me into a scout ship and fixed the autopilot so I couldn't return. I flew for days, weeks, I don't know how long. My supplies ran out. In the end the ship's accumulators emptied and I crashed. I remember a house. That's all."

"Who's in charge of those dreadnoughts now?" asked Max.

"Hathus."

Max saw her pour all her hatred, loathing and misery into that name.

"Is he still heading for Metacarpi?" he asked.

"How should I know?" Her cold contempt gave way to an expression of desperation. *We've pushed her too hard*, thought Max. Ruth an Vircana looked at each of them in turn, then lay her head back on the pillows and closed her eyes. *We need to get her to the city, and let the Lord of the Carceral Archipelago know what's coming.* Colour drained from the woman's face and her breathing became ragged. Abby made to ask another question but Odilon laid a hand on her shoulder and shook his head. He ushered them out of the room and led them back to the observation dome.

Odilon unfurled a map on the table. Max saw the simple outline of a man lying on his back, arms by his side, palms upwards, fingers spread, surrounded by an intricate web of lines and symbols.

"We are here," Odilon gestured at the left thumb. Max looked at the body of God. Following convention the artist had left the face blank, but the hair spread out in a ring around the head like the petals of a flower. Max peered closely. Written along one curving line he read *Long Lock. She comes from the Hair*, he thought. As if he'd read his mind Odilon pointed at the map.

"Each strand is a hundred miles thick. You could fit all of Metacarpi on one single filament. Long Lock alone is home to over a billion souls. The Empire of the Ear is immense."

64

What could they possibly want with Thumb? wondered Max. *Are they planning on taking over the whole body of God?*

"I don't have any maps of the side of God's head," Odilon said, "but the Emperor of the Ear, Demetrius, lives in a fortress on the AntiHelix here." He pointed to the inner whorl of his own ear.

"That's beyond the atmosphere," said Abby. Max saw the excitement spread across her face.

Odilon nodded.

"It's over fifteen thousand miles above the air. Demetrius rules over nine kingdoms, including Long Lock, Buccinator, Upper and External Occipital, Lobe and Helix." The Watcher pointed in turn to the parts of his own face. Max found it hard to believe. Odilon spoke of realms actually on the body of God itself. He struggled to imagine whole civilisations clinging to the skin. How could people live in those airless wastes? His mind reeled, choked with wonder. *They have the knowledge we lost, the science we wasted in stupid wars with Abductor and Tip.* Odilon's voice filled the chamber around them.

"He keeps his petty kings and tyrants in check with a mercenary army known as the Dogs. The empire exists in a fragile balance of power. Demetrius sits in the centre of a constantly shifting matrix of jealousies, ambition and hatred. He is old, very old, and claims he talks to God."

"Talks to God?" asked Abby incredulously. Max looked at the Watcher, expecting to see his own disbelief echoed in the man's face. Odilon looked in deadly earnest.

"Once a month Demetrius visits a building deep in the ear; the Whispering House. In the uppermost room he sits alone and speaks to God. Apparatus stolen from deep time carry his words twenty-five thousand miles into the brain of the deity."

"What does he say?" asked Abby.

Odilon shrugged. "Perhaps he pleads on our behalf, who knows. His prayers are secret. In any case, beyond the Tympanic Membrane lies the Kingdom of the Machine Men. Only they can survive the forces used to knit the mind of God together. I doubt they pay attention to the musings of one old man, no matter how profound."

Odilon rolled up the map and stowed it under the table.

"They're an ancient people, with a civilisation far older than Metacarpi. They follow complex codes of loyalty that the long passage of time has made cruel, and they think we who live below the atmosphere are ignorant and decadent."

Abby snorted.

Odilon's face creased in thought. *There's something else*, realised Max.

"What is it?" he prompted.

Odilon walked to a crystal window, approaching his own faceted reflection.

"Three weeks ago Abductor fell silent."

Max and Abby swapped scared glances.

"What do you mean, 'fell silent'?" asked Max, dreading the answer.

"We never talk to them anyway," added Abby. "They just hide in their concrete bunkers waiting for the space monsters to turn up."

"I talk to them," said Odilon, "or rather, I did. Someone has to keep communication going between the cities." Was that contempt in the old man's voice? Max wondered what the Watcher really felt about his friends in Metacarpi. The room felt colder, the shadows longer. Behind him Olaf muttered a curse.

Max forced himself to approach the Watcher. Odilon stared out into the night. To their left faint lights speckled the wall of the Thumb.

"Odilon, what do you mean?" he asked again. He could guess the answer. In his mind he saw two dreadnoughts hovering over a sea of flame, burning citadels outlined in the blackness. A single turret carried enough firepower to flatten Metacarpi, that's what Abby had said.

"They destroyed Abductor," she whispered. Her hand flew to her mouth. "Why?"

"Alaric an Vircana is a brilliant General," continued Odilon, "and leader of the Emperor's own Dogs. He's ruthless, but he's not insane. He wouldn't order the destruction of an entire city. This Hathus is another matter. The name is not known to me."

"She might be lying," said Abby. "Can you get the truth out of her?"

Max wished Abby would think first before opening her mouth.

"If she's the daughter of a warlord in charge of dreadnoughts, forcing her to do anything is probably a bad idea," he said. He fought his rising anger. *We're all scared, none of us know what to do.* He wracked his brains. "Get her ready to travel tomorrow, we'll take her to my father. Odilon, I need you to talk to him as well, confirm what we've heard tonight."

"I'll follow you," said Odilon. "First I need to learn more about this Empire and its purpose."

Max looked into the other man's penny-coloured eyes. A thought hit him. *You know something, you know something and you're not telling us what it is.* For a split second he toyed with the idea of challenging the Watcher, but decided better of it. He didn't have time to pick fights with a lone eccentric in an abandoned tower. Let the old man keep his secrets. He realised whatever hold Odilon had over his childhood self had vanished in the shadow of those approaching battleships.

Max couldn't sleep. Images of dreadnoughts pouring fire onto the city of Metacarpi filled his mind. From what he'd seen, and Odilon's description of the Empire of the Ear, they faced an enemy against which they were utterly helpless. Ruth claimed she'd fled the ship at Wrist. That meant Captain Hathus, not her father, had ordered the destruction of Abductor. *What do we do when we face annihilation?* There'd always been rumours of mighty weapons hidden deep below the Carceral Archipelago or far beyond the Forbidden Sea. Max knew the tower held nothing in its vaults but ancient cells, torture chambers and dirt. His father, for all his implacable resolve, had nothing to match those battleships. Perhaps their only chance was flight - an exodus to Tip or even into the Thumb itself. Was that it? The end of Metacarpi? He imagined all the buildings empty of people, the streets silent, the wind blowing through the chains of the Carceral Archipelago.

He saw no answers, and eventually his thoughts drifted. With a shock he found himself thinking of the giant's house and the ghost of his dead mother. Once again he stood in the room next to a polished wood table, opposite a roaring fire. *Is this a hallucination or a genuine recollection?* He tried to pick out details to give the memory more solidity, but as soon as he focussed on the images they slipped away, or turned into tantalising fragments; light through a crystal decanter, a spitting coal, words on the spine of a book he couldn't read. He remembered holding a wooden animal, a painted cutout with a peg in the middle, part of a puzzle or a game. It was agonising, not knowing what any of it meant. He could see his mother, or the woman claiming to be her, but he didn't trust the recollection. The giant created the image from his childhood memories and the painting in the breakfast room at the top of the Carceral Archipelago; an ideal patchwork of stylised beauty and infant longing. He closed his eyes and tried to imagine walking through the room once more, but nothing grew clearer. A strange mix of emotions came with the memory; the feeling of calm love, warmth, cake and milk, the smell of perfume. But he also sensed uncertainty, a childish dread associated with the passageway in the corner, and the figure hovering just outside the range of the honey-coloured lamplight. *Is that you, Father*? The austere and unfeeling bastard would stand out like a sore thumb in such a place. But had he always been that way? Was there a time, long ago, when Herman Ocel had been kind, tender and in love? *Tender and in love? The only emotion I've seen on the old man's face is deep disappointment in his wayward son.*

Max wanted to escape his thoughts so he left his room and wandered through the corridors. He tried to lose himself among the featureless metal, glass and crystal. Everywhere the same lambent light cast blue shadows over the jigsaw walls. To Max the place felt inhuman, sterile. Strangely this brought a brief feeling of peace. This empty, dead machine was no place for ghosts, giants or sour fathers.

At the end of the corridor a small access hatch opened onto a metalwork balcony. Max stepped into the night. He found himself next to a huge gun. Intertwined barrels of plastic and copper flowed out of the wall like roots. They pointed west, towards the Thumb itself. Five thousand years of decay had turned the weapon into a ragged chaos of cracked plastic and verdigris. Max put his hand on its surface. He thought he detected vibrations beneath his palm. Machines like these might be a match for the ships from the Ear. He hunted for a firing mechanism - a button or a trigger - but found nothing. He knew he wasted his time.

He stared glumly at the incomprehensible cannon. Outside the city he travelled among the shreds of dead civilisations, echoes of greatness fallen into decay. He could understand why most people never left Metacarpi. Out here you couldn't escape the constant nagging undercurrent of terrified awe in the face of this immense past. The shadows of long-dead people braver, nobler and cleverer than anyone now alive filled the air. He looked at the landscape below, dark red where the lights fell across the ground. He felt like a bug crawling across the last page of a history book. *Any second now it'll slam shut and on the back cover there's nothing but fire and desolation. I need a drink.* He went back inside, hoping against hope that Odilon had a few bottles secreted away.

He ended up in the library. To his surprise he saw Abby sitting with her feet on a table, leafing through a book. Around her volumes rose up in mountains, spilling from overstuffed cases, mingling with the scrolls and papers that littered the floor. Books as big as a man stood propped open on their own frames. Abby looked up as he approached.

"How do you feel?" she asked.

Max sat down. He tried to pick an answer from his jumbled thoughts. In the end he just shrugged. A bottle sat on the table next to Abby. She pushed it towards him. He took a swig. The cold wine soothed him. He looked at Abby while she continued to turn the pages. Blue circles ringed her eyes. Freckles turned grey with tiredness dotted her skin. She looked like an old photograph.

"What's the book?" he asked.

"I'm looking for stories of giants," she answered wearily.

"And?"

She tossed the volume onto the table. She really did look exhausted. It worried Max. She always kept a spark of energy to goad him on when he'd lost his own. Relief came when she gave him a muted version of her mad grin.

"Not even fairy stories," she said. "Odilon must be right, it crawled out of a wormhole shaft. If that's the case it'll be dead by now."

Nothing from the past ever survived in the threadbare reality at the end of the universe. Max stared at his own hands. They looked solid enough. He rubbed them together, feeling the satisfying rasp of the callouses. He'd seen Abby topple men twice her size. *Are we really all so weak, so tenuous - mere ghosts at the end of time*? Abby gave him an arch look, she'd seen him do this before, get all philosophical. He changed the subject.

"How do you know Odilon?" he asked.

Abby stared into his eyes, he could see her gearing up to laugh at his suspicions.

"My granddad took it into his head to re-open the Theatre of Angels after your granddad got rid of that stupid law banning plays. He petitioned the Carceral Archipelago for, what? three years, and always got the same answer. He needed an official patron and half a million coins' security to stop him filling people's heads with dangerous ideas. A waste of time, they had someone lined up already. Then one day Odilon the Watcher turns up, says he'll be our patron, pays the money and the next day a licence appears from the Carceral Archipelago with an official seal dangling off the bottom. All he wants in return is his own box at the theatre, and once in a while a play of his own choosing, paid for by himself."

"Which plays?" asked Max.

"Just *The Gate of Light*, no others," answered Abby. Her mouth twitched. She had to be poking fun at him. He laughed out loud.

"That's a story for children."

The thought of Odilon entranced by giant puppets dancing across a stage was too absurd for words. He shook his head and took another drink. The powerful wine began to unstring his thoughts. Abby laughed too and it made him happy to see the worry leave her face.

"It's true. It's the only one he likes," she said, "usually once a month or so. Drives my sister crazy, but he's the patron."

And I had him pegged as the strange recluse in the mystic tower, learning things Man Was Not Meant To Know. A thought struck him.

"How old is he?" he asked.

"Don't know, he looks the same to me as he did when he first turned up at the theatre twenty-five years ago."

"He hasn't aged," mused Max. Abby rolled her eyes.

"Come on, he's a funny bugger with mysterious ways but I trust him implicitly. He's always helped my family, and probably yours too. Long life is not so bizarre in this universe. The Philosophers live in outer space for centuries."

Max shuddered at the thought of those spectres, their bodies leached of colour by years in the darkness; white hair, skin, eyes, clothes; pure and refined like the sciences they studied. He looked in relief at Abby's red hair and her tanned face. The wine brought the colours back. She stared around her, green eyes wide. She did that when drunk. Max grinned. *At least we're still human.*

She has mad courage and I have my cowardice which I turn into courage when I need to. We must be able to find some way to stop those ships.

"What are you looking at?" she said.

"Nothing," he replied, thrown by her stare.

Abby studied his face for a while. She looked about to say something. An odd tension filled the room. The moment passed. *Must be the wine,* thought Max. *God knows where Odilon found it.*

"I'm tired. Off to bed," she mumbled.

Abby stood up, staggering a little. She came round the table, put her arms round his neck and pressed her head against his, so hard it hurt. Her hair fell around him. He smelt perfume, sharp and weird, as expected.

"Glad you're ok," she said. She kissed him on the cheek and walked unsteadily out of the library. *She really is drunk. That's the second time she's given me a kiss in the five years I've known her.*

Silence descended. Max stared at his boots. He reached across and turned the book around. It offered nothing, not even pictures. He looked up at the crystal windows where they arched inwards to meet the roof. For a second he thought he saw a feathered shadow drift over the glass. He blinked and checked again. Nothing. He felt so tired. Sleep might come at last. He left the library and threaded his way back to bed.

CHAPTER SIX

HE DREAMED OF the room again. He held a wooden animal in his hands. The other pieces lay on the carpet in front of the fire. He felt firelight on the side of his face, smelled the hot cotton of his night shift. His mother passed back and forth behind him, gathering her pens and notebook, ready to ask the questions he never understood. "Do you see when Max laughs it means he is happy? Max is sad, but only for a few moments, look how love quickly cures tears."

Hesitant footsteps came from the passageway and his heart hammered in his chest. He looked anxiously for his mother. Her arm curled around him and her face appeared next to his. "Don't worry, little Max, he's as frightened of you as you are of him, but we'll soon be the best of friends."

The man hovered just inside the entrance, white hair across a pale forehead, large eyes peering fearfully into the room. "Look who's come to see you," his mother said.

But suddenly the firelight died and the air turned grey. Lamps sputtered. A cold wind from the darkest reaches of the void flowed over him. His mother grew angry, her words choked and harsh. "Max, how could you? This is our special room, our special place. Who have you brought here? What wickedness is this?" Her voice became bestial grunting filled with hate. All-consuming horror filled Max, the kind he only ever knew in dreams. He looked up and in the last flickering light of the fire saw a feathered shape on the ceiling.

The dream played over and over in Max's mind as he boarded the *Bricolage*. He didn't tell anyone, not even Abby. He wondered if he was cracking up after the encounter in the house and the shock of seeing the dreadnoughts in the mirrors. He'd always been haunted by his own fears. Uncertainty and cowardice plagued him whenever he confronted danger or the unknown. But he always found that kernel of courage in the end. At the last second he squeezed fear into a tiny diamond of bloody-minded stubbornness. It saw him through fights, chases, monstrous encounters and hopeless dead ends. That's how he got into the house in the first place, and how he'd escaped. But now he feared he'd reached his limit. Perhaps the giant's psychic attack had tipped some internal balance in his mind, and the battleships from the Empire of the Ear were just the icing on the cake. *What do I do? Am I losing it? Or is it just the thought of talking to the old bastard in the stone tower for the first time in five years?* What would he say to the Lord of the Carceral Archipelago? *Hello Father, I met your dead wife in a house built by a giant? Keep it simple, tell him about the battleships, hand over the daughter of this mighty general and get out of there. Pack your bags, load up the* Bricolage *and head for the Thumb.* It sounded so appealing. Duty was one thing when you rescued a beautiful woman from a monster, something else entirely when dreadnoughts more powerful than anything you'd ever dreamed of bore down on your city. His father wasn't stupid. *Let's face it. The only chance of survival is negotiation, even surrender. I only hope Captain Hathus will listen.* Looking at Ruth's icy face, even in sleep, made him seriously doubt he would.

Whatever drugs Odilon gave her had killed the fever, though she still struggled to stand up. In the end Olaf picked her out of her bed like a child and carried her down to the hangar, her head lolling against his chest as she drifted in and out of consciousness. She didn't speak, and when Abby approached her Odilon shook his head and told her to wait.

They left Odilon in his crystal tower and headed south. Flying home, Max traversed half a million years of history. Beneath him he saw the fossilised remnants of a nation shrinking into a single city like a puddle evaporating on concrete. On the dawn of the fourth day he watched from the prow of the *Bricolage* as they approached the outer boundary of Metacarpi, five hundred miles north of the metropolis itself. This marked the first ring of defences in the ancient wars against Abductor. Using the scrap left over from the Great Task, the lords of Metacarpi constructed fantastical redoubts. He saw them first as a low cloud in the distance, rising above a range of mountains. After a few hours it resolved itself into a wall four miles high. But 'wall' implied order and coherence. Here was no logic Max could see, and he wondered how it ever defended the city against anything. It looked like a child had upended a box of toy buildings and piled them on top of each other in a line. Straight ahead Max saw three arches cut into metal as black as night. To the right a twisted framework clad in armour plating leaned forwards over the Wasteland. Max felt a brief toe-curling moment of terror as half a dozen sheets, each as big as a house, broke from the upper section and fell three miles to the ground in a torrent of iron. Even at this distance he heard the impact, a dull concussion arriving a few seconds after the last fragment disappeared in an explosion of wreckage. On the other side of the arches a line of concrete cylinders peppered with gun ports stretched to the east. In the early morning, vapour hung around their tops. Long gouges from ancient weapons scarred the masonry. *If only we still had guns like that, we might stand a chance against those ships,* thought Max, *but we stole them from deep time and they shuddered to a stop. Now the wormholes are closing, the chances of us finding any new machines to defend ourselves are gone.*

Abby joined him on deck with two mugs of coffee. She kept giving him 'have you gone mad yet?' looks and it started to get on his nerves.

"Think we have a chance against those ships?" she asked.

"Don't know," said Max.

"What if the Carceral Archipelago really has got hidden weapons we can use?" said Abby.

Of course we don't. The biggest gun he'd seen was the triple barrelled cannon on the rear deck of his father's ship, the *Zephyr*. It could toss shells half a mile and that was it. *Might get us a laugh before the annihilation.* The *Bricolage* passed into the shadow of the wall. Max looked up at the underside of an arch four miles high. Dark holes pocked the surface revealing the tangled framework inside. *Some of those girders are thicker than this ship.*

The vessel emerged on the other side. They flew across a network of ditches littered with wrecked machines long decayed into rust. Beyond, the landscape turned into a mirror-smooth slope rising up to the south. Looking over the side Max saw the perfect image of their hull a quarter of a mile below, sliding over an inverted sky of blue and purple. The ancients made the surface frictionless to protect the city from land armies. *Bugger all use against dreadnoughts,* thought Max.

Abby elbowed him in the ribs and nodded southwards.

"We're home," she said. He steeled himself. It always appeared first, rising out of the mist. The tower known as the Carceral Archipelago lifted two miles into the sky. The rough stone cut a two-dimensional gash in the landscape. Four mighty chains anchored it to the shore of the Forbidden Sea. The first Lord of the Carceral Archipelago, in a fit of bizarre symbolism, christened them *Love*, *Hate*, *Sorrow* and *Joy*. He died raving in the lowest cells but the names stuck. One link, laid sideways, would easily encompass a city block. Everything else looked insubstantial in comparison, even the mirror ground below and the titanic arches receding far behind them. Max forced himself to face it. The simple, brutal reality of his old home hit him like a blow.

The *Bricolage* flew over the edge of the mirror and down towards the city. In the dawn light the buildings spread out beneath the ship. Flats, tenements, offices, government buildings, shops, cafes, theatres, slums and mansions rode the troughs and crests of the land like boats on a frozen sea. A recent snowfall turned to slush in the gutters.

Max understood how Metacarpi seduced so many. It was easy to lose yourself in the shadowed streets. He looked down on a world grown lazy, complacent and bourgeois. Every luxury stolen from the past lay spread out before him. Fantastic arts brought back to the end of time decorated the theatres, galleries, bedrooms, chambers and halls. Rare foods and spices, fabrics spun from threads thinner than an atom or the pelts of alien behemoths, filled the rooms. Every taste, every perversion, every delight and every sorrow played itself out behind shuttered windows and in the depths of the city's cellars.

Flying machines of brass and wood sped over the rooftops. Their captains chattered to each other on radios that turned their speech into the paper whispers of ghosts. He could smell the steam, soot and ozone. Along the boulevards trams carried workers past mansions and tenements, scattering sparks into the gutters. Atonal jazz and haunting opera filtered out of cellars. On all sides poets and artists descended into madness. Cigars, absinthe, dark wines and incense mingled at fantastic and desperate parties. *All this euphoria and luxury we wallow in makes us think we're the kings of the universe. It's just denial in the face of death. What'll we do when the last staircase in the last wormhole rots away?* He emptied the dregs of his coffee over the side. *It probably won't come to that, given what's heading our way.*

Beneath them a clerk in shirt sleeves leant on a windowsill and smoked his pipe in the morning air. Apprentices gathering by a pie stall on Salveter Bridge jeered at a half-naked woman slumped drunkenly on a balcony. Olaf steered the ship closer to the rooftops, a dangerous habit. *Probably trying to make us as small as possible, so you can't see me,* thought Max, looking over the houses towards the tower.

They left the rich districts to the north and flew across the Brick River. Olaf guided the ship between tenements and skyscrapers. Max noticed more empty buildings. Rows of blank and shattered windows rose up on either side, interspersed with the glow of guttering lamps and candles. Lines of washing sagged between blocks of apartments. On the street below, where daylight never reached, lanterns hanging from stalls and shop awnings picked out the silhouettes and tired faces of the people as they emerged from their homes. A few looked up at the *Bricolage*. They reminded Max of the man in his dream; anaemic and frightened. He shuddered. Did one of these buildings conceal the mysterious room? Had there been a time when the three of them lived as a normal family: Mother, Father and Max in a simple house? A stupid notion, each Lord of the Carceral Archipelago spent his entire life in the tower; father, grandfather, all the way back to the first. He remembered his mother's words, *someone's here to see you*. He realised he gripped the deck rail so hard his hands hurt. He plucked them away just as Olaf lifted the *Bricolage* above the skyscrapers and pointed her at the tower. He forced himself to look once more at the fortress and its four chains. *Welcome home.*

He went inside and knocked on the door of Ruth's cabin. She stood at the window, one hand on the edge of the bunk to steady herself. She looked deathly pale but he didn't know if it was the lingering illness or whether all people from the AntiHelix looked like exquisite ghosts. She turned and her purple gaze pinned him to the spot. He'd never felt attracted to aristocratic beauty - he'd no patience with the vacuous simpering of the city's debutantes - but this woman's other-worldly features drew him in. *Watch it Max, you know she's trouble.*

"That tower's called the Carceral Archipelago," he explained. "My father, Herman Ocel, is Lord there. He controls the city, including all our defences."

"Am I a prisoner?" she whispered.

"No, of course not," lied Max, "you'll be a guest, but they'll want to ask you about the battleships and what happened to your father."

"I need to get back to the *Beatrice*," she answered, turning back to the window. "I have to free my father, take back the fleet."

Max gawped at the back of her head. *You look like a poorly sixteen-year old girl, do you seriously imagine you're going to rescue your father from those ships? You don't think we're going to do it for you, do you?* God help them if she suggested the idea to Abby, she'd be off like a shot.

Mind you, Max noticed Ruth rubbed his friend up the wrong way. She might not give the pilot from the Empire of the Ear such a sympathetic hearing.

"We'll do all in our power to help you," he said, realising how lame he sounded. She turned to him, her eyes filled with tears.

"He'll be in the Iron Core. It's his personal refuge on the ship, sealed from the outside. But he'll only have enough food and water to last a few weeks. He might be injured. You must help me get back to him."

She took a step towards Max, desperation in her face, searching his eyes for some hope. Max fought a sudden urge to take her in his arms. Her beauty made her a powerful presence despite her fragility and he suspected she knew it. *God, do they train all their women to be like this? If so it works.*

"I'll see what I can do," he said, ducking out of the cabin before he did something he knew he'd regret. He bumped into Abby in the corridor. She gave him an odd look; part mocking, part disappointed. He couldn't meet her gaze. *That woman thinks we're ignorant bumpkins and I've just proved it.*

"The tower's hailing us," Abby said. "Come on, this is your world, you can do the pleasantries."

They drifted along the chain called *Sorrow*, following it as it rose in a diagonal towards the crown of the tower. A brief radio exchange cleared them for approach. The fortified edge of the roof slid past and they coasted over the oil-stained landing field atop the Carceral Archipelago. Olaf set the ship down next to the iron wall circling the summit. As Max climbed down the ladder an official and two guards strode up to him and saluted.

"Glad to see you back, sir," said the clerk. He wore the wool jacket and trousers of a bureaucrat, a heavy cloth threaded with steel intended to symbolise the efficient resolve of its wearers. The guards bore simple uniforms of dark grey, marked by flat silver buttons. He detected baffled curiosity in their gaze. How long since he'd stood here? Was it really five years? He thought it a miracle anyone remembered him. Olaf came on deck with Ruth holding his arm for support.

"This is our honoured guest, the Lady Ruth an Vircana of the Empire of the Ear," said Max, in as commanding a voice as he could muster. To his shock he heard his father's voice coming out of his mouth, and saw the men's backs stiffen in response. Their eyes told another story. *Empire of the what?* The clerk looked past Max and his mouth dropped open at the pilot's pale beauty.

"She's to be treated as our most valued and distinguished guest," said Max. "Place her in the state apartments on the top floor near my own rooms, and summon a doctor, she's ill."

"Yes sir, of course sir," barked the man. He gave an exaggerated bow to Ruth and gestured towards the tower entrance. Ruth shot Max a helpless look that took his breath away.

"Go with them. You'll be safe, I promise. I'm going to meet my father to discuss how we can help you." *Lying bastard*, he thought to himself. *You don't discuss things with Father, you quiver while he admonishes.* Ruth limped across the landing ground in the company of the three men, refusing the clerk's offer of his arm. He steeled himself. *Now to meet the Tyrant in the Tower.* He looked round for Abby. She leaned over the deck rail above him, staring after Ruth. The cold suspicion on her face troubled him.

"Goodbye Max," she said.

"You're not staying?" he asked in surprise.

He needed her there, she'd give him the courage to face his father.

"Here among the oppressors?" scoffed Abby, looking around with barely disguised contempt, "No, I'll be at the theatre with my sister." She looked down at Max.

"Take care, Max. Watch yourself, even here," she said. Before he could say anything she disappeared inside. A few seconds later the *Bricolage* lifted into the sky and dropped over the edge of the roof. Abby knew how to hurt him. He'd expected more than a curt goodbye. Now he faced the Carceral Archipelago and its Lord alone. So be it.

He walked across the landing field and descended a stairway into the top floors. He realised rumours of his return spread throughout the entire tower before he even touched the bottom step. For that reason he avoided the main passageways, using the secondary chain of secret corridors, ladders and lifts called the Shadows. He knew them from his boyhood, when he'd delighted in their labyrinthine complexity, hiding and spying on almost every part of the tower, concealed from view in false walls or tunnels that ran alongside the air vents between floors. His teachers forbade him from entering the covert maze, but he suspected his father told them to go easy on the punishments when they caught him. Watching silently from shadows was an essential skill for those who ruled the tower and the city. Now he hoped it'd buy him a few moments alone to summon his resolve before he met Herman Ocel.

If he thought he could sneak unseen through the Carceral Archipelago he fooled no-one but himself. Every time he crossed a main corridor he found his route flanked by men and women from every floor. Soldiers in tatty fur boots and short blue jackets, clerks in identical grey wool suits, wardens, cleaners, sweepers, post boys, quartermasters, pilots and soldiers all leaned out of offices, barracks, tunnels and spy holes to watch him pass. Some of the more athletic Level Runners, who sped urgent messages from floor to floor, hung down through air holes, their ankles grasped by their comrades above as they watched him walk by. Their heads hung from the ceiling like weird light bulbs. Max resisted the urge to thump a couple as he passed underneath. The complex chain of mirrors linking each room and corridor to the Gazers of the upper floors twisted and creaked as he went by. Their immaculately polished surfaces flickered with reflected light, a chain of stars twinkling in his wake. A low murmuring of remarks, sneers and comments flowed around him.

He walked a narrow gantry above a kitchen the size of football pitch, rode a service lift that shot upwards so rapidly it took his breath away, and traced a winding corridor that forced him to stoop. At last he came to a landing with doors on either side, opening onto offices filled with clerks in their ubiquitous grey and steel uniforms. In a room crowded with stacks of ledgers, a thin-faced woman pursed her lips at him and folded her hands over a book covered in brick dust. Her hair, waxed into a grey spike, rose from the centre of her head.

"So you've returned," she said pointedly.

She tapped red nails on the pages, causing the grit to dance.

"Hello Maria," he said, happy to see her despite the expression of rage clamped to her features. His father's private secretary looked out for him as a boy. Six-foot two inches of ball-shrivelling terror to everyone else, she smuggled him pastries from the kitchen and occasionally wiped away his tears with the hem of a steel-laced dress that left scratches on his cheeks.

"We're a loyal lot," she continued, "loyal to him. Fuck the city. The city can burn for all I care, the Carceral Archipelago will endure. It has a heart of iron and stone, like his."

"That's true," replied Max drily, before realising he'd said exactly the wrong thing. Maria's pantomime anger switched to genuine reproach.

"He's not what you think he is," she said quietly. "You're too cruel, Max."

Me? Cruel? He could have said so many things in reply - the years ignored, the cold expressions, the indifference. *I'm not the cruel one.* He held his tongue and stared defiantly at Maria while she glared back, rapping her blood coloured nails on the book in front of her. She sighed.

"He doesn't come out of his apartment much, not any more. I could run this place myself, but that's not the point. He spends too much time in his own company, in those dreary rooms. Don't be too harsh on him Max, don't judge him for what he was. We all change. You've changed," she added, looking him up and down, "you look more and more like him. He talks about you."

Really? I can just imagine what he says. He felt very tired, playing out the argument before he'd even met his father. Maria came round the desk. She towered over him, thin and spiky with a permanent frown. She enfolded him in a hug.

"Now bugger off and try and make your peace with him," she said, shooing him down the corridor.

CHAPTER SEVEN

HERMAN OCEL'S SUITE lay next to the staple anchoring the chain *Joy* to the top of the tower. The hidden passageways of the Shadows stopped short of his rooms. No-one watched the Lord of the Carceral Archipelago. Nevertheless a few servant corridors flowed past the apartment, like tree roots around a rock. One ran outside the tower itself, a metal walkway covered with nothing more than a tin roof. It led directly to Herman's office. As a child Max had crept along this balcony to peer in through the panes of the access door. Most of the time his father kept the curtain across the entrance to block out the cold, but once in a while he drew it back and Max could see his silhouette against the lamplight, bent over his desk as he worked his way through his daily stacks of paper.

Max chose this route. A passageway at the top of a spiral staircase led to a hatch. The wheel turned easily, though when he pushed the door open the hinges shrieked and rust and grit fell from the frame. Had no-one come this way for so long? Maria said his father spent too much on his own, shut off from the rest of the tower. The thought disturbed him. To Max his father and the fortress were one and the same. Why would he choose to withdraw from it?

He emerged by the side of the staple. Far above, the underside of the landing platform and parapet projected over his head. To his right he saw the first link of the chain, its metal so thick four men could stand abreast on its inner surface. Below him *Joy* curved down towards the city. Despite the mass of metal the chain barely sagged.

Max climbed a flight of stairs and walked along the covered gantry. A freezing wind poured up the tower and his coat billowed around him. He remembered running along this path, feeling the metal through his plimsolls, filled with the heady excitement of a boy at play. He smiled at the thought. If he tried hard enough he could still tease a few carefree memories out of these stones.

He found the door and stopped. For a second he became a child again, summoned to his father's presence, only too aware that defending himself to Herman Ocel was as futile as hammering with his fists on the Carceral Archipelago itself. *He's only a man, older and more tired than you. He never paid attention to you when you were young, why let him bother you now?* Anxiety turned to frustration at his own fear. He gathered his coat about him and tried the door. It opened. He stepped through into his father's office.

He stood in a circular room with a low wooden ceiling. For a second he thought the place empty. Then he saw his father at the window, in exactly the same position he'd stood five years ago when Max last spoke to him. Herman Ocel carved a silhouette out of the cityscape beyond. He wore a coat like Max's. It rippled around him like smoke. His precisely trimmed beard came to a point over a high collar. Max realised he was looking at the same face he'd started to see in the mirror. The recognition of himself in his father unnerved him. He'd no idea what to say. The Lord of the Carceral Archipelago didn't even bother to turn round.

"Who's the woman?" asked Herman in his low, warm voice.

I'm well thanks, and how are you, Father? thought Max.

"Ruth an Vircana, she's from the Empire of the Ear," he said.

The Lord of the Carceral Archipelago continued to look out of the window. Max hesitated, then joined him. His father's profile, all sharp nose and hollow cheeks, was unreadable. Max followed the old man's gaze towards the south west where the gash of the Brick River left the city and wound its way towards the Forbidden Sea.

"Two of the empire's dreadnoughts are heading this way, massive warships bigger than anything we have. Her father was in charge but the crew mutinied and she escaped. Someone called Captain Hathus controls the fleet now. We don't know who he is but he may have destroyed Abductor," Max explained.

Still his father said nothing, a maddening trick of old. He'd keep quiet and Max, terrified by the silence, would start babbling any old rubbish just to fill the air, digging a grave for himself as he did so. When he'd emptied his mind of all the drivel he could think of, his father would turn on him and with the precision of a surgeon extract his faults one by one, spreading them out before him in their full glory. Well, he wasn't going to play these stupid games anymore.

"Odilon is coming, he can verify what I've said," he continued. With a great effort he clamped his mouth shut. *Your turn.* He walked into the centre of the room. Through an open doorway he saw the table where they once ate breakfast together. The portrait of his mother hung on the wall above and without thinking he stepped towards it. His legs felt weak. He'd last seen that face in the giant's house; the same chiselled beauty, the lazy blue eyes beneath brows arched in amusement. She looked identical to the woman he'd met. Yet beneath the fear of that uncanny place, came a strange gladness. Those memories of his mother hidden deep inside must be accurate after all, in which case so must his recollection of that room. Where was it? Not here. He looked around and saw blocks of dusty furniture, functional and grey. He couldn't imagine his mother in this grim cell. With a shock he noticed his father staring at him from the other side of the table. Herman's gaze briefly switched to the portrait and back at Max. Was that alarm in those eyes? Sadness? Shock? He toyed with the idea of telling him everything, of the giant, the ghost of his mother, the stranger who hovered in the corridor beyond the fire. But the moment passed and Herman's face turned into a stony mask once more.

"Take me to this Ruth an Vircana," said the Lord of the Carceral Archipelago.

Max followed his father as he strode along the corridors towards the state apartments. *Some things don't change,* he thought, *here I am trotting along behind again like a beaten dog.* They picked up a handful of soldiers along the way, Herman's own personal guards, cold-faced men in lacquer caps and black uniforms.

Ruth wore a simple white dress. Max guessed Maria had found it one of the rooms filled with the belongings of the executed. The girl no longer showed the signs of the fever, though her face still shone with a lustre like translucent crystal. Grey furs lay heaped on the bed and floor. Coal roared white hot on the other side of a glass-fronted stove, luxury by the standards of the tower.

When Ruth stood to face her visitors Max saw her body faintly outlined in the firelight. He tried to ignore the stirring of desire, and the growing resentment of Father and his mirthless goons. Herman bowed.

"Lady an Vircana. I'm Herman Ocel, Lord of the Carceral Archipelago. Please forgive the inelegance of your surroundings. Have you eaten?"

Ruth gestured to a bowl filled with heavy stew and a lump of coarse bread. Max winced.

"My Lord," she said, her head bowed, her words hesitant like a child struggling over a memorised speech, "I beg you to help me rescue my father, the Condottiere Alaric. We are the rulers of Long Lock, and my father is commander of the fleet of the Emperor of the Ear. You will have undying friendship not only from my family and all our people, but from the Emperor himself."

Ruth formed a picture of desperate helplessness, beautiful and afraid. *You're good, very good,* thought Max. He'd be happy to pledge there and then to follow whatever insane scheme she proposed. *Won't work on the Tyrant of the Tower though, sorry.* He looked at his father's expression, unreadable as always.

"My Lady, Metacarpi is a minor city in the shadow of the Thumb," he said. "We simply have no resources to mount an expedition against two dreadnoughts. If these ships destroyed Abductor then what hope do we have in any kind of resistance? The idea we can rescue your father is a romantic one, but at this moment, impractical. Is there no help to be sent from the empire?"

Ruth dropped her head and Max heard a harsher note in her voice. *She's not used to pleading,* he thought.

"The distance is too great, it'll take half a year at least for more ships to arrive," she said.

"Do you know what the dreadnoughts intend for the city of Metacarpi?" asked Herman.

Ruth looked up, no more the wide-eyed child. Max saw an aristocrat struggling to contain cruel arrogance.

"Captain Hathus is now the commander of two of our Cerberus class battleships and over a thousand elite marines. They'll wipe this city from the universe without a thought. My Lord, you must get me back to the *Beatrice*, my father is the only one who can stop this." Her voice cracked with desperation.

"Your father singularly failed to do so the first time," observed Herman. Ruth shot him a look of loathing before staring down at the floor. Her fingers twined around each other.

"Please, I beg of you," she said eventually. She began to sob.

"I'll think carefully about what you've told me, and I'll do everything in my power to help," said Herman patiently. He gestured to the guards and together they left the room. Max followed but Ruth grabbed his arm, pulling herself against him as if seeking protection. He stared down into her purple eyes, momentarily breathless.

"Please make him help me, please take me back to the ships," she begged.

Max didn't know what to say. He nodded and left in pursuit of his father.

He found Herman conferring with a guard. The Lord of the Carceral Archipelago looked up as he approached.

"Odilon's arrived," he said. It sounded to Max like a dismissal.

"Do we have any weapons to defend ourselves?" he asked. Herman ordered the soldier to leave. They stood alone under hissing gaslight.

"There's nothing in the Carceral Archipelago," said his father.

"What can we do?" asked Max. Half of him wanted to plead to take Ruth back to the dreadnoughts, but the idea was insane, no matter how potent her skill at seduction.

"We?"

The question snapped him back to reality. He'd assumed that, in the emergency, his father expected him to take his place as the heir of the Carceral Archipelago. He looked into the other man's face and with a shock saw nothing but impatience to be rid of him.

"You can fly, can't you?" said Herman. "And navigate? Go and talk to Theodore. He's commander of the fleet now, we'll need every ship."

You bastard, thought Max.

"Is that it?" he said, keeping his voice steady with great effort.

"What else do you expect?" asked his father. He crossed his arms, a gesture Max remembered from childhood. "Was this to be a reconciliation, after, what? How long is it since you turned your back on your duty and left the Carceral Archipelago?"

Max couldn't believe his ears. *This isn't about us, you stupid old fool. There's an invasion fleet weeks away and you're still harping on filial loyalty?* Even so, bitterness welled up in his heart and he had to respond.

"Is that why you hate me? Because I ran away?" he asked.

"I don't hate you Max, I barely know you," answered his father. "We all run away. I did. My father did, and his father, and we all return. But unfortunately some of us don't come back until it's too late. Five years I've ruled this city by myself while you've hunted for wormholes. A Time Scavenger," he spat the title, "stealing knick knacks from the past to sell to the petit-bourgeoisie and their whores. I've no use for you."

The words bit deep.

"That's not the point," said Max, speaking as carefully as he could as he battled with his anger, "the city is under threat and I want to help you defend it."

"Yes, destruction bears down upon us but you have nothing to offer that'll make the slightest bit of difference," said the Lord of the Carceral Archipelago. He turned his back on Max and strode down the corridor.

Disgusted with his father and himself, Max walked back through the Shadows. Maria stood up when she saw the expression in his face.

"That bad?" she asked. Max nodded. Long moments passed as he struggled with his feelings, pacing up and down the room, forcing himself to breath deeply.

"Don't judge him too harshly," said Maria after a while. He opened his mouth ready to tell her exactly what he thought of the Tyrant in the Tower, then stopped as a sudden idea struck him. What did his father's secretary know?

"Do you remember my mother?" he asked.

Maria sat down at her desk and started to shuffle papers around.

"Why do you ask?" she said without looking up.

"I dreamed about her the other night," he said. "We played in a room with a roaring fire and wooden walls. I think it's a memory from my childhood, but there's nowhere like that in the Carceral Archipelago, is there?"

Maria shook her head.

"What was she like?" he asked, hoping Maria would remember.

Maria looked directly at him and he saw the tears in her eyes. Maria of all people. There wasn't a soul in the entire tower that didn't fear her.

"He adored Yvette, your mother. She, and you, were his entire life. The day she died a part of him died too. In his mind he's still with her, but can't understand where she's gone. I think he walks the Shadows at night, looking for her." She muttered a curse, wiped her eyes with her hand and went back to her reports.

"Did we ever live elsewhere, other than this tower? In the city perhaps?" Max asked. He desperately wanted to find the room. Not only did it speak to him of a childhood he thought he'd never had, one of comfort and love, but each recollection convinced him it held a message. Why else would he recall it after all these years? Why would a giant from a wormhole seize on that particular memory?

Maria thought for a while.

"You always lived here, although," she tailed off, nails rapping on the ledger as she searched her memory, "how old are you in this dream?"

A flicker of hope sprang up in Max.

"I can barely walk. One? Maybe two?"

"Your mother was a philosopher, a scientist studying the mind," answered Maria, her voice faraway. "Just before she died she started on a new project. It involved you somehow. She'd take you on long trips for a few weeks at a time. She said it was for her research."

Max seized on her words with elation.

"Where did we go? The city?"

Maria shook her head.

"No, she'd take a flyer. She'd never said where, but your father joined you sometimes. Each time she came back so happy, as if she'd discovered new wonders and wanted to tell the world, though she never spoke about her work. She and your father kept it secret. Not long after that she fell sick. Odilon did all he could but she died. It broke your father's heart."

Maria sighed and pressed her hands against her face. She looked very tired.

"If he's cold and filled with rage that's why, but he loves you," she said.

"He's an odd way of showing it," Max said without thinking. In his mind he stood in front of a fire, peering through the shadows at a man standing hesitantly in a corridor. Was it his father? Was the white-haired figure an early memory of the ogre upstairs?

"You're the only one he's got left," said Maria, anger rising in her voice. "You can't complain about being abandoned when you spend years flying the Wasteland, making it obvious you'd rather be anywhere else than here."

Maria's comment brought him out of his reverie. Her words held a truth that stung him.

"I'll be at the Theatre of Angels if anyone wants me," he said. He paused at the door. Maria had access to all the records of the tower.

"Could you find out where Mother used to take me?" he asked. His father's secretary shrugged.

"It was a long time ago," she said. She saw his face and relented. "I'll see what I can do."

"Find me the Charge Log for the ship," he said. If it existed he could at least work out how far his mother had travelled on her journeys.

"Don't rake up the past, Max, you've hurt him enough already," she answered, fixing him with her steel gaze. She went back to her ledgers. He knew better than to speak again.

Max could have hitched a lift from one of the ships on the roof, but he wanted time alone to think. He climbed down through the Shadows, creeping between walls and across chasms filled with scaffolding. He came to a door near the base of the tower, another secret from his childhood. It led to steps that spiralled round the outside of the wall, dropping down to the shore of the

Forbidden Sea. At the bottom he walked away from his home across a concrete beach, found a fuel drum on its side and sat down, staring across the water.

He'd faced his father after all those years, to what end? Part of him felt disappointed. He'd expected rage, shouting, anger and accusations from the Lord of the Carceral Archipelago. Instead he met indifference from a lonely old man facing destruction beyond his wildest imagination, and incapable of doing anything about it. *'I have no use for you' Father said. I'm worthless in his eyes, despite Maria's claim that the arrogant old bastard loves me.* He looked up at the tower, its top lost in the clouds.

He wanted to solve the mystery of his mother and the room. He'd never thought about her before his encounter in the giant's house, but now, with each scrap of information, he yearned to learn more. Once, long ago, he was happy and loved, and the woman who cared for him was beautiful, kind, and an explorer, like himself. What great secret did she work on before she died? His father knew, but he doubted he'd tell his son. *In his eyes I've no more right to know than the next stranger.*

She'd taken him away for days on end in a flyer. Where? West lay warehouses and the ruined building grounds. To the east lay nothing, light years of barren rock and dirt, untouched since the Black Roses created the vast workbench floating in an empty universe. Before him the Forbidden Sea stretched south into the distance. No one knew how large it was. As a child, on the rare occasions he'd been allowed out of the tower, he came here to play in the shallows. Often he walked out to sea. He'd wander for a mile before water covered his feet. Beneath it the ocean floor looked like the surface of a machine, scored with metal vents, lines and sealed pipes.

On a whim he walked into the ocean. He knew he broke the law, and the knowledge stirred a childish frisson of wickedness. The Forbidden Sea was strictly off-limits to pilots and useless to boats. He'd heard rumours that beyond its misted expanse lay a flaw in the singularity. The single step of an intruder, so they said, would make the entire landscape vanish like a bubble - leaving the body of God to disintegrate in the darkness, surrounded by billions of the dead. It sounded far fetched to Max, but his father's ships patrolled the fringes of the sea with orders to shoot anything that ventured away from the shore.

The expanse in front of him held no answers. He left the water and made his way along the edge away from the tower. Miles and miles of empty warehouses stretched in the direction of the Thumb. Nothing stirred in the landscape of blocks, angles, broken window frames and metal. After a few mental calculations he turned north. Eventually he'd find the terminus for one of the tram lines. He walked through puddles of stagnant water under a dead sky. To Max it was as if he journeyed through a world transformed into shadows and shapes leached of all meaning. Doors, walls, machines, wheels, cogs, chains, chimneys, generators, windows, glass, crystal, metal and wood became one vast, lithified chasm across which he scuttled like a tiny creature. *Of little use*.

Some buildings contained machines recognisable as lathes or generators, others were filled with objects whose purpose and meaning he could only guess at; a two-hundred foot long wing cast from a single block of steel, a glass-floored room the size of a park covered in desks set in rows, each with a single stool and a typewriter. In one warehouse he found stacks of paintings; thousands of poorly-executed landscapes and portraits in heaps several metres high. Every canvas showed the same dark background and every face frowned in anger or sorrow. At last he stepped out of a broken door and saw a tram rumbling quietly to itself at the end of the line. He dropped a coin in the conductor's hand and took his place on the wooden bench.

CHAPTER EIGHT

MAX ARRIVED AT the Theatre of Angels to find it in chaos. At the front of the house assistants ran back and forth pulling down posters for *The Protein Man* and replacing them with *The Gate of Light*. Beyond the lobby actors and stagehands argued with each other and manhandled props and baskets full of costumes along the corridors. Max found Abby outside the women's changing room, talking to two men. He paused when he saw their black caps and leather coats. One of them glanced up and nudged the other. Max recognised the contempt in their eyes. They exchanged a few more words with Abby and then faded back into the shadows.

"Anarchists?" said Max. Surely Abby wasn't that stupid.

"We need to warn the people, get them out of the city," said Abby. "Those guys move faster and are better organised than the morons in the tower. They reckon they can shift a thousand a day out to the warehouses through the old supply tunnels and sewers." She looked tired and unhappy.

"You could get arrested just for being in the same room," chided Max. Abby's recklessness came in handy in the Wasteland and on ancient worlds, but not here. He knew what the Carceral Archipelago did with dissidents. Her naivety became a serious liability in the shadow of the tower.

"I'm not afraid of your father," she said. Max ignored the gibe.

"What did he say?" she nodded in the direction of the Carceral Archipelago.

"We have no weapons, and we're not going to rescue Ruth's father," said Max.

"So what are we going to do?" she asked impatiently.

"Odilon's arrived, my father's talking to him," said Max. He could see the accusation in Abby's eyes. He should have done more, argued with the Lord of the Carceral Archipelago and demanded plans for the city's salvation, insisted he produce inconceivable weapons built with ancient science. Her expectations were absurd.

"He'll do nothing," said Abby contemptuously, "no weapons, no plans. He doesn't give a shit about the people, he's just the Tyrant in the Tower. That's why I talk to the Anarchists, they care about us."

Max felt his temper rise at her deliberate goading. What was the matter with her?

"And what will they do? Wave a few banners, stick on some street theatre and toss a couple of home made bombs? That'll work," he snapped.

"You can be such a shit sometimes, Max," said Abby. *What brought this on*? he thought, dumbfounded by her spite. They'd argued before, usually about plans gone wrong, wilfully flouted or not even formulated. This time he sensed a desperate disappointment in her words.

"If you mess around with revolutionaries you'll end up at the bottom of the tower, and I will not be able to help you," he said carefully.

"Don't tell me what to do, you're not captain here," Abby said with weary anger. A girl in floods of tears ran up to them, waving a script and babbling about the chance of a lifetime ruined. Abby tried to placate her. Max, fed up with her temper, left them to it and went in search of her sister, hoping to cadge one of the bedrooms in the theatre roof for the night.

Rebecca Fabrice sat on a desk in her office, a cigarette hanging from her mouth as she threaded a ribbon through a mask. She looked Max up and down.

"Maximilian Ocel, well well."

To Max, Rebecca appeared like a stretched out version of Abby, the illusion compounded by her wedge-shaped haircut. She resembled a nail in a black dress and he occasionally fantasised about finding a hammer big enough to drive her into the ground. In all their meetings she acted as if she were party to a joke only she understood, with him as the punchline. Abby's occasional cynicism manifested itself as a major torrent of sarcasm in her older sister, turned on full whenever their paths crossed. In truth a lifetime in the Carceral Archipelago had left Max with an admiration for plain-talking women who could look after themselves, especially in a firefight. Femininity bored him. After a few drinks he'd happily trade banter with Rebecca, each trying to outdo the other in scornful put-downs. Today he wasn't in the mood.

"How's the Tyrant in the Tower?" she asked. That old insult again, he'd heard it only ten minutes ago from Abby, but crossing swords with Rebecca merely encouraged her so he mumbled something vague and shrugged. He wasn't really interested in talking, he wanted to grab a drink and find a place to sleep.

"Can I stay here tonight, in one of the attic rooms?" he asked.

"Kicked you out did he? Poor Max." Rebecca's eyes never left his, they were green like Abby's. "Take the one at the end. We're using the others to store all these costumes we no longer need."

She put the mask on the desk beside her.

"Abby says you met a giant."

Max swore under his breath. Abby told her sister everything, but this merely added fuel to the fire. He could imagine what Rebecca would say on hearing he'd seen his dead mother in a house built by a monster. He waited for the blast of scorn, the laughter and a shake of the head telling him he'd lived up to his stupidity again. To his surprise she didn't sneer or crack a joke. She merely looked back at him through the cigarette smoke, judging his reaction.

"Odilon thinks it crawled out of a wormhole shaft, and it'll die in weeks, if not days," he said.

"Does he indeed?" She picked up another mask, the face of a young woman, slender and melancholy. It reminded Max of Ruth. He briefly thought of her body framed against the stove light of the Carceral Archipelago. He quickly pushed the image to the back of his mind.

"The Watcher's arrived, asking for his usual. Pain in the arse. *The Protein Man*'s due to open tonight, but oh no, now we have to change everything so he can watch his stupid puppet show yet again. You'd have thought he'd grown bored of it by now."

Odilon's here. That means he's spoken to my father. Max wondered what he'd said.

"Where is he?" he asked.

"In his box, waiting," said Rebecca. "Not to be disturbed under any circumstances," she added pointedly as Max turned to leave. He opened his mouth to argue.

Surely the emergency came before the Watcher's eccentricities.

"Those are the rules, talk to him afterwards," said Rebecca. "I've something to show you."

She jumped down from the desk and opened the backstage door. He hesitated when he saw the familiar glint in her eye.

"Come on Max, I'm not going to seduce you in the prop cupboard," she said. Half a dozen responses popped into his mind but Max wisely bit his tongue.

They threaded their way through the theatre cellars. Actors and hands argued and tussled with scenery, props and each other. Two men pulled a giant shadow puppet down from the distant rafters while a woman, still in make-up for her original role, struggled into a black body suit, swearing hideously as she hopped up and down on one foot. A few angry faces turned towards Rebecca but she ignored them all, deftly navigating the chaos while Max trotted to keep up.

Eventually they ended up in a unlit storeroom. For an awful second he wondered whether Rebecca actually intended seducing him. He'd no doubts that sex with her would be both bizarre and demeaning. To his relief a lamp flared and her face appeared at the far end of the room, bathed in the orange glow. The light danced across stained and faded walls.

"Giants," she said.

"What about them?" asked Max, still rattled by his own imagination.

"Four hundred years ago an eccentric actor manager called Peter Löwy founded this theatre."

"Never heard of him," Max said, and immediately regretted it. Rebecca let a few seconds' silence say it all before continuing.

"He developed an obsession with giants, so much so that he built this."

Rebecca picked up the lamp and walked to a curtain at the far end of the room. She pulled it to one side to reveal a door which she unlocked and opened. The lamplight showed stairs leading down into darkness.

"Where does it go?" asked Max.

"It ends up in the Brick River," said Rebecca. "Peter Löwy got it into his head he'd made friends with a giant, and he wanted to invite him to watch the plays. He planned it so the creature would come secretly to the city and enter the theatre by this passageway, unseen by the rest of the audience."

"That's insane, this corridor's tiny," said Max. He descended a few steps, Rebecca followed. In the lantern light tendrils of mist curled towards them from the darkness.

"Peter Löwy blew his brains out on stage one night. Maybe he realised he'd built this tunnel a bit too narrow for a giant," said Rebecca, the familiar tinge of sarcasm creeping into her voice. Max remembered the hand he'd seen emerging from the mist, fingers the size of the *Bricolage*.

"Why are you showing me this?" he asked.

"Peter Löwy was as cracked as they come, but when Abby told me you and she found a real giant in the wilderness it made me think."

"Of what?"

He turned to look at Rebecca. Her face hovered a few inches from his. He saw a familiar expression of mischievous curiosity cross her features in the half light. Those green eyes bored into his.

"I don't know, perhaps Peter Löwy wasn't mad after all. Perhaps he really did try to befriend a giant. Why would he do that, if they're just monsters from wormholes?" she said softly.

Behind them a gong sounded. Rebecca gave a moue of irritation.

"They need me, bunch of kids the lot of them. Come on, Maximilian Ocel, I don't want you wandering off and getting lost. Abigail would never forgive me, though God knows what she sees in you." She held the lantern up to light his way as he climbed out of the corridor on unsteady legs.

"One more thing," she said, "hurt my sister and I will personally rip your head off and stuff it up your arse."

Max bristled.

"I'd never lift a finger," he said stiffly. Rebecca rolled her eyes and shook her head.

"You're an idiot Maximilian Ocel, just like your father." She put her hand on the small of his back and pushed him forward.

"Run along, the play's about to start."

Max wanted to talk to Odilon, to find out what his father said and to ask him about his mother. Odilon had nursed her through her illness, tried everything to save her life, but to no avail. He might know where she'd taken Max on her research trips, and how to find the room of his memories. He doubted it still existed, but if he could stand beside that fire, within polished wooden walls once more, it'd open up a part of life he hadn't even known existed. It felt like the moment he paused in front of a newly discovered door in a wormhole shaft, one step away from the most astounding wonders or the grimmest horror.

He didn't want to wait in the bedroom upstairs while Odilon sat through the play, so he went to the lobby and bought himself a ticket. Max smiled to see families already walking up the street towards the theatre. Children loved *The Gate of Light* and news of a performance spread quickly. He noticed mothers entering the lobby with their little boys in hand. He looked for traces of himself in their eager faces, wondering if they were a mirror of what he would have been had his mother survived. The bell sounded. He went into the auditorium and took his seat on the balcony.

Odilon always sat in the same box. Max couldn't see him, the shadows were too deep. The lights faded and the curtain drew back upon a black void. The sound of a single flute drifted out of the orchestra pit. Despite himself Max jumped when the face of the narrator filled the gauze projection screen at the back of the stage. The eyes formed hollow pools of darkness, the gaunt features stern. It did look eerie, he conceded.

"Once upon a time, light filled the universe, spilling from burning fires called stars. They floated together in their billions, and these glowing clouds hung in velvet nothingness," intoned the voice, sombre and musical, following the strange rhythm of the words. *This is what God will sound like*, thought Max, *if he ever wakes up.*

"People journeyed between the fires in huge ships that moved faster than light itself. They built empires, fought their wars, loved and died, fragile patterns of life in an immeasurable void.

"The stars died. One by one they turned red and faded away into the blackness leaving their worlds cold and empty. The great ships rusted. Humanity gathered in the twilight and built metal spheres to enclose the remaining sparks like hands cupped around a candle flame.

"The last star perished. Hope guttered in the embers. It was the end."

The face vanished. Somewhere in the audience a child started crying. Her father comforted her. Max had forgotten the hold this story had over the people. Despite himself he felt drawn into the narrative. A soft wind from the end of time blew through him, chilling his heart.

In the bottom corner of the stage a group resolved itself around a fire made from lamps and tissue paper. Max recognised the familiar characters; the grandfather, the mother, the daughter and the comic servant, Salabanco, in his long tails and battered top hat. The grandfather complained that all the stars were dead and he had nothing to point his seeing machine at any more. Tomorrow he would have to sell his wonderful toys so they could buy fuel to give them light in these last days. When everyone else slept the girl sneaked into the old man's tower and turned his instruments on the distant void one last time. Lo and behold she saw a faint radiance, far beyond the husks of the most distant stars. An actor in a black leotard hung from the ceiling above Max and opened the window on a lantern. With a rustle every face turned upwards. The gasp of happiness and wonder from the children made Max laugh.

The girl woke her family and showed them the light. The next day the wise old grandfather went to visit the King of Men to tell him of the mystery and to beg permission to lead an expedition to find out whether it held any hope for humanity. But the King was mad and cruel. Desperate to cling to the power he still held over the people he cast the family into prison. In a scene that had the audience roaring with laughter, the girl and Salabanco fooled the palace guards, escaped and stole a spaceship. The brightly coloured vessel flew through the darkness over the spectators' heads amid fireworks and smoke while the King shouted and capered on the stage in his ragged yellow robes.

At the interval Max bought himself a glass of wine from the actor dressed as Salabanco and sipped it in the auditorium while the audience rustled and chattered around him. What in God's name did Odilon see in this play? He was a philosopher in a crystal tower, steeped in the most obscure and intricate knowledge. Clowns, fireworks and pantomime kings made strange entertainment for a sage who lived and breathed the rarefied wisdom of millennia.

The second act began with the spaceship arriving at the distant light, which proved to be a doorway to another universe, young and filled with stars. This scene contained the highlight of any performance; the Dance of the Gods. Huge shadow puppets of fantastic design pranced and leaped across a flickering red screen. Each alien god had its own unique solo, drawing gasps of amazement from the younger children. Max found himself perched on the edge of his chair as the Crystal God jerked her body back and forth, transparent cellophane in the puppet casting coloured shapes that moved with their own life across the theatre. Finally the God of the Black Roses appeared on the screen, a delicate mass of fluttering petals flowing in loops like water. Max had to admit it looked spectacular. Out of tinsel, gunpowder and smoke Rebecca's actors created an image that made the hairs on the back of his neck stand up and a shiver of excitement run through him. As the girl and Salabanco stepped from their ship, one of the Black Roses approached them, dressed in fantastic purple and black plumage.

"Where is man's God?" asked the Black Rose. The girl couldn't answer.

"This door is a doorway to another universe," continued the creature, "but mortal creatures cannot pass through the door, only gods. Therefore our deity has gathered us in its hands to carry us to the new cosmos where it will scatter us across worlds like seeds."

"We have no god," said Salabanco, pulling a grotesque face, "as far as I know, we never had a god."

"All creatures have gods", sighed the Black Rose, "go search for yours."

The girl and Salabanco returned home to tell the King of Men the message from the Black Roses. But the mad tyrant would hear nothing of it and cast them into the dungeon where her grandfather and mother languished. The old man was dying and as the scene unfolded to the sound of gentle violins even Max found his vision blurred. Quiet sobbing pervaded the auditorium. Max wiped his eyes on his sleeve and glanced around him. He suddenly saw the humanity in the people who filled the theatre, who could find delight and emotion in such a naive tale. Hathus's dreadnoughts would blot it all out in a second. A grinding hatred of the men and women who piloted those monstrous ships welled up in him. Abby spoke the truth, his father would do nothing. Perhaps he should throw his lot in with the Anarchists after all, help them get these people out of the city and to safety in the warehouses. There may even be wormhole doors near enough in time to give them shelter for a few weeks until the ships passed.

Next day guards led the girl, her mother and Salabanco to their deaths but as the executioner hefted his axe the air filled with Black Roses. They tumbled over the spectators in a breath-taking display of acrobatics, landing on the stage in a storm of ebony petals. The King fled screaming, chased by the boos and jeers of the audience.

"Man must create a new god to carry him to the next universe," declared the aliens, "and we will help him out of admiration for the courage of a little girl and her foolish servant."

The narrator's face appeared on the screen once more.

"The Black Roses took the dark fabric of the universe and rolled it out to make the floor upon which God now lies. They punched holes back into time so we could plunder the past for wood and metal, stone and glass, and so the Great Task began. Humanity started building God a million years ago, and we are still building. There are parts of Him that cannot be made by men of flesh and blood. Some places, the Face and the Chest, are far above the thin layer of air that the Black Roses poured out for us. Other parts, the Mind and the Heart, are fashioned by creatures designed for that purpose. Our children, the Machine Men, work in deep forbidden places. That, however, is another story. When the Great Task is finished God will wake, gather us in his arms, and carry humanity into the new universe. So be patient, children, be good and kind, and ever so patient."

The house erupted and Max found himself on his feet, clapping and whistling with the rest. He understood the hold the play had over the audience, how it lifted them from their grey inward-looking world and reminded them of why they were here. Perhaps that was the reason Odilon asked for it time and time and again. It wasn't for his benefit, but his gift to a weary and forgetful city.

After the last of the audience left. Max went in search of the Watcher. He found him in the cellars among the props, talking to the actor who'd played the herald of the Black Roses. Above them towered the mannequin of the Black Rose God, an elaborate machine of ropes and paper feathers interlinked with cables and gears. When Max approached, the actor - a narrow-faced man with large hands - bowed and drifted back to a knot of performers struggling to dismantle the spaceship. Odilon looked up at the puppet.

"Wonderful," he said, "truly wonderful." The Watcher's face split in a broad grin. Max saw tears in his eyes. Had the play moved him so much? Sometimes Odilon seemed almost a child, his face a constant pageant of simple emotions.

"Did you talk to my father?" he asked. Odilon dabbed his eyes with his robe, chuckling in embarrassment. His expression turned serious.

"Yes, we talked about the dreadnoughts and the city's options," he replied.

"Do we have anything to match those ships?" asked Max. He knew the answer. The Watcher confirmed it by shaking his head.

"Your father asked if I had any science to defend against the Empire of the Ear," said Odilon. "I have nothing. I gave him my advice, I said we should evacuate the city and surrender to the fleet. We've no option but to throw ourselves on their mercy, but your father is a stubborn man. My counsel sits uneasily with him."

Max doubted whether capitulation would save anything. According to Ruth a treacherous psychopath now commanded the battleships.

"Abby told the Anarchists, I hear. They'll start their own exodus," said Odilon.

"If my father finds out . . ." started Max. Odilon shook his head.

"Abby'll be fine, and once realism filters into the Carceral Archipelago she'll be a hero." He gave a comforting smile and patted Max on his shoulder.

"Odilon, you looked after my mother before she died." Odilon blinked, sighed and nodded, his face a mask of sorrow. He looked into Max's eyes, as if gauging his next words to match his listener's feelings.

"What happened?" continued Max.

"She developed a fever of the lungs. I tried everything in my power to cure her, I searched my library, every medicine I could lay my hands on in the short time I had. I even entered a wormhole and captured a machine doctor from an ancient world, but nothing worked. All I could do in the end was ease her final hours."

The Watcher's face crumpled and he looked away, blinking furiously. Max waited, touched by Odilon's emotion, even after all these years.

"She worked on a project studying the human mind. Not at the Carceral Archipelago but in another place," said Max. *Please remember, Odilon,* he begged in his head.

"Yes, something like that. It was so long ago," the Watcher said.

"She used to take me with her."

"Did she?" Frustration welled up in Max. He'd hoped Odilon would help him find out the location of the room and the identity of the man in the passageway, but the Watcher struggled to recall the simplest details. Odilon tapped the side of his head,

"I have too much in here, you know. You're talking about something thirty years ago, you can't imagine what has entered here since then." Odilon's penny-coloured eyes twinkled and he smiled. *He's treating me like a child again.*

"Please Odilon, it's important to me," he said, struggling to keep his voice even.

"Max!"

Abby ran across the cellar towards them. She looked furious.

"There's a bunch of your father's thugs upstairs with guns," she said, glaring accusingly at Max.

CHAPTER NINE

THREE GUARDS WITH shotguns and an officer from the Carceral Archipelago waited in the lobby. Rebecca stood in the corner with a couple of actors still in costume. They muttered to each other, staring defiantly at the soldiers. The officer, a short woman with spiky hair, snapped to attention when Max arrived.

"Sir, you are to accompany us to the Carceral Archipelago immediately, on your father's request," she said crisply.

"Why?" asked Max, anger rising. After calling him useless his father now sent guards to order him about. He was in no mood to co-operate. "He can ask me himself if he's that desperate."

"We have orders to bring you in," said the officer flatly. She looked at him and Max saw the plea in her eyes. She'd realised this could get ugly and desperately wanted him to co-operate. Rebecca folded her arms and enjoyed the show. Abby stood next to Max, watching the soldiers with open hostility, always a bad sign. He got ready to grab her, just in case.

"Take your men, go back to the tower, and tell my father that I'm not jumping at his command. I'll speak to him when I'm ready," *which will probably be never after our last chat.*

The officer sighed.

"Maximilian Ocel, I'm placing you under arrest. Don't try to resist, it'll be easier for all of us if you co-operate," she struggled to sound convincing. Rebecca let out a barking laugh of contempt. Max lost his temper.

"That miserable old shit sent you to arrest me? God's cock, who does he think he is?" he yelled.

"Leave my theatre," said Rebecca, pushing herself away from the wall. "This is the son of Herman Ocel, Lord of the Carceral Archipelago, and I think that carries more weight than a frizzy-haired tart in leather boots."

Colour drained from the officer's face. She turned on the spectators.

"I can close this place down in a second," she shouted, "you're all traitors and dissidents. Known Anarchists left this rat hole six hours ago. Under wartime regulations I could have you all shot here and now." The men behind her looked nervous, their gazes flicking back and forth as more staff trickled into the lobby. Her words brought Max up short. *Wartime?* His father moved fast. *If he's put the Carceral Archipelago on a war footing then at least he's doing something, no matter how futile.*

"Piss off," said Abby. "This theatre is licensed, only the Tyrant in the Tower can shut us down."

"Arrest him, and her too," said the officer, pointing at Abby.

She drew her revolver. *Oh shit,* thought Max. He wasn't fast enough. Abby lashed out with her foot. The gun span into the air. She swung at the officer, but Max deflected her arm with his own. He always forgot how strong she was and it hurt. All the soldiers drew their guns and pointed them at the crowd. One of them aimed a blow at Max with the butt of his shotgun. It glanced off his temple and knocked him sprawling. Abby tried another kick at the officer, who danced out of reach. A gun went off, fired into the ceiling, and a cloud of plaster fell onto the carpet. Abby slipped and fell on her back. The officer scooped up the fallen revolver and stood over her, aiming it at her face. Max realised she was a second away from pulling the trigger. He tried to throw himself across Abby's body. The actors shrieked and sobbed, pressing up against the wall of the lobby.

Odilon came into the room. Silence fell so suddenly that for a second Max thought the shotgun blast had rendered him deaf. The Watcher spoke.

"Put your gun away. All these people are under my protection, this my theatre," he said with the patience of someone explaining the obvious truth to a fractious child. The officer swallowed and holstered her gun. Max grabbed Abby and pulled her towards him, wrapping his arms round her torso and holding her tight. He felt her heart pounding through her back.

"Calm down," he hissed. Her breathing slowed.

Odilon spoke quietly and urgently to the officer. She nodded and the Watcher came over to Max. He lifted Abby to her feet.

"To save everyone's dignity, and to prevent any further confusion," he said in his sing-song voice, "I will accompany you two to the Tower and act as an intermediary, and the theatre will stay open."

Max seethed, but saw no other option. Abby unleashed was a major incident waiting to happen but even in her wildest enthusiasm she couldn't take on four trained soldiers from the Carceral Archipelago - plus whoever else his father might send if he still refused to go. Max nodded and thumped Abby discretely in the small of her back. She wiped the plaster dust from her face and, eyes on the officer, spat on the carpet.

Outside a squat shuttle sat on the road, rumbling and hissing steam into the night air. It was only then that realisation dawned on Max. A few hours ago his father had pointedly told him he didn't need his help. Yet now he'd sent soldiers to bring him back to the Carceral Archipelago, with orders to arrest him if he refused. *What's changed? Why is Father suddenly so desperate to see me?* He looked at Odilon. *What did you tell him?* The Watcher sat with his back to Max, his knees drawn up under his blue robes as he crouched on the bucket seat and stared at the city sliding beneath the vessel.

He must have been only four or five. He stood in a bright room, the steel walls, floor and ceiling a matt smear of scratches. His reflection tracked him as his father led him past rows of cages, each a different size and shape, though none was bigger than a packing case. Beneath the overpowering smell of disinfectant lay an undercurrent of foulness - a hint of blood, fear and shit. Some of the cages hung down from rails set into the ceiling. One opened over a dissecting table on which lay two shapes under a sheet. A woman dressed in white waited for him. She pulled the cover back and his father looked at the dead men. A deep grid of bruises scored their flesh and they stank of blood and excrement.

"Enemies, Max," said his father. "Enemies of the Carceral Archipelago."

The woman gave Max a smile of pleasant evil.

"Two in one," she murmured, pointing at the cage above, "and you couldn't even fit a little boy in there." She reached down and pinched his cheek.

Max sat in that very same room, struggling to push away his memories. The cages had gone, only the tables remained and the wooden chair he sat on. What in God's name did his father think this would achieve? Did he seek to intimidate him, to make a point by asserting his authority in as crass and strident a way as possible? The whole situation was a joke. He thought of Abby. The guards had split them up, but Odilon told him that he'd personally ensure she came to no harm. He knew the Watcher carried enough authority in the Tower to be true to his word.

A door opened in the wall and a woman came in carrying a doctor's bag. Max recognised her as his father's personal physician. What was her name? Euphrosyne? She looked around nervously. *Well she's not acting like a torturer, this room spooks her more than me.*

"Your father asked me to examine you, it seems you had an accident in the Wasteland?" she said apologetically. *So that's it. Odilon told him about the giant.* His interest awakened, Max decided to play along. The medical consisted of nothing more than Euphrosyne peering into his eyes with a variety of lenses. She clearly hadn't a clue what to look for. After fifteen minutes she gave up. Herman entered the room. The doctor exchanged a few muttered comments, shaking her head, before leaving them alone. Max gestured around him. He couldn't think of any words to express the stupidity of the situation.

"The walls are a metre thick; steel and iron. No Shadows run nearby, no speaking tubes or mirrors. It's useful for private conversations," said his father, perching on the edge of a table. Realisation hit Max like a blow. *We're entirely cut off from the rest of the tower.* No-one could overhear. Why had Herman chosen this room to speak to his son? Who did he think would spy on the Lord of the Carceral Archipelago himself?

"Odilon told me you met a giant in the wilderness," continued Herman. He wore a searching expression that Max hadn't seen before. He decided to gamble all.

"The giant built a house, like a trap. Inside it showed me my mother, it must have made her as well. Somehow it got into my head, at my earliest memories, and used them to give her life. She looked just like the portrait in the breakfast room." He stopped, appalled. His father's eyes filled with tears. Max had never seen him moved with any emotion other than anger. He instantly regretted what he'd said. He'd blurted it out in an act of defiance, but saw his words wounded his father deeply and now he felt oddly ashamed.

"It was a monster, it just recreated these illusions out of the past to trap me," he said, trying to think of some way to comfort his father, who suddenly looked so old. The man's grief frightened him. After a long silence Herman stood up.

"I want you to stay in the Carceral Archipelago. Spies and assassins roam the city, and you're an easy target," he said.

"That's ridiculous," replied Max, "how would spies from the Empire of the Ear end up in Metacarpi? This city has nothing of value whatsoever." It sounded like an excuse to keep him in the tower. He could understand if his father didn't want to lose him, no matter how distant and cold their relationship. Why not just say so? Why invent imaginary enemies?

"You'll stay here, as will your friend from the theatre. She can ensure your cooperation," said Herman. Max swore. He was tired of the bullying and the bitterness.

"Aren't we too old for this, both of us?" he asked wearily. "I know I'm the universe's greatest disappointment to you, but can't we work together to meet this enemy? Or are you so used to playing the angry father you don't know any other way?"

Herman studied him for what seemed an age.

"Very well. If you want to help, make friends with Ruth an Vircana," he said. "Learn anything you can about the dreadnoughts and if there's a way of stopping them, other than this ridiculous fantasy of rescuing her father. But don't leave the Carceral Archipelago again."

Herman turned to leave. *OK*, thought Max, *I'll stay, for Abby's sake. But there's something you're not telling me, I can see it in your eyes.*

"In the giant's house I saw a room with wooden walls and a fire. A man stood in a passageway, just out of sight. Was it you? The room's not here, I know that, where is it?"

Max saw an expression in his father's eyes he'd never seen before. Fear. The old man's hands trembled. Max saw him place his fingers on the edge of the table to steady himself. He stared long and hard at Max.

"If you value the life of your friend Abby Fabrice, you will never speak of that again. Ever," said Herman, and left the room.

Max returned to his quarters. Sleep deserted him. A thousand questions roared through his mind like a storm. He tried to make sense of what he'd learned, what he'd seen in his father's eyes, but exhaustion made it impossible. He ended up sitting on the end of the bed staring numbly through the window at the Thumb as the hours crept by. No matter how tough his relationship with the Lord of the Carceral Archipelago, the old man represented an axis of unyielding certainty in his life; always there, always in the tower, always watching. If the stone judge turned out to be weak and fearful, where did that leave his son? The idea terrified him, made him giddy with its implications. He realised he couldn't face this alone, he needed to talk to someone.

At first light he went looking for Abby. Maria told him they'd locked her in a cell thirty floors below, but refused to let him see her. When he pleaded, she held her hands up.

"Don't ask Max, you know the consequences," she said, "she's to be treated as an honoured guest, I'll make sure of that, and Odilon's put the fear of God himself into those guards because they're running round her like fawning idiots. Do something to win your father's favour if you want her out of there."

"I asked him about my mother, and where we used to go," confessed Max.

"You're a fool, Max. Some things are better left alone. Especially after all these years. He's enough to deal with without you rubbing his face in his loneliness," she said, genuinely angry. "If you want to help, find out from that princess upstairs how we can stop those battleships, because I don't think anyone else here has any clue, despite your father and Odilon's incessant whisperings."

He climbed up through the empty stairwells of the Shadows, replaying the conversation with his father over and over in his mind. The mere mention of his mother caused Herman pain, and when he'd asked about the room and the man in the passageway he'd witnessed more fear and danger in his eyes than he'd ever seen before. A rogue thought stopped him short. What if his mother had found a lover, fleeing this tower into the arms of another and taking Max with her? That would explain his father's reaction. Could it be simple jealous rage? If so, who was the man? Had he died too? At the hands of the Lord of the Carceral Archipelago? Was there more to his mother's death than a simple fever? The landing swayed under his feet. Wild speculations piled into his mind, each more lurid than the last. He steadied himself against the rail, suspended on a thin frame above a fifty yard drop between the inner and outer walls of the fortress. In the name of God himself, had he uncovered a murder? He mastered himself. *This is stupid imagination, playing with false memories from thirty years ago.* Yet a horrible doubt lingered. Whatever happened to his mother, wherever she took him as an infant, he had to find out more than ever.

He reached the top of the tower. *Cooperation will buy me time, do what he asks for now.* He made his way to Ruth's room. Outside he steeled himself. *She'll probably try again, drape herself all over you as she begs you to take her back to rescue her father.* If he was honest he looked forward to it, despite the warning klaxon in his mind.

He found her dancing with her eyes closed, a strange, high-stepping pavane. Max saw from the way she moved her hands that in her mind she danced with another. Max watched entranced. When she jumped her dress flared around her waist to reveal the muscled legs of an athlete. After the final leap she came to rest, crouching by the window. She opened her eyes and looked directly into his. He caught his breath. *Damn you.* She stood, panting heavily.

"You're better then," said Max drily. She'd made a remarkable recovery from helpless invalid to ballet dancer. She shrugged.

"The Spear Tip Dance. Leaping across the tips of our enemies' lances, we pirouette from spear to spear in a gorgeous display of power and the joy of conquest."

"You perform it beautifully," conceded Max.

"It's really a dance for two."

She unfurled her hand and studied the palm. Max saw a flash of sadness cross her face. He wondered how many etiolated princes from the AntiHelix had thrown themselves out of God's ear for the love of this enigmatic woman.

"I've only the memory of the fingers that once rested here," she continued.

Max didn't think it wise to ask whose. Ruth sat on the end of the bed.

"This is a luxurious prison," she said.

"These are some of the best rooms in the tower, apart from my father's." Abby languished in a stone and iron cell with a stove, a couple of furs and a cot if lucky. He fumed at the thought of his father's stone-headed attempt to bully him.

"What'll happen to me?" asked Ruth.

"We have to think of a way to stop those dreadnoughts. The AntiHelix is too far to ask for help, and it'd be suicide to try and rescue your father," he added, to pre-empt any more pleading. "If there's anything you can suggest, please tell us."

"Metacarpi will be destroyed," said Ruth.

"That's not helpful," he said. He doubted she'd any special knowledge to aid them. She might be the daughter of a defeated General, but he thought it unlikely he'd shared his strategy with her.

After ten minutes conversation Max realised he was wasting his time, but he was happy to keep going. Ruth's slender beauty fascinated him. Talking to her provided him with an excuse to look into her purple eyes, and lust gave him a brief respite from the nagging question of his mother. He wondered how far she'd play this game, and toyed with the idea of finding out. Lingering reason warned him that the consequences of bedding the daughter of a general from the Empire of the Ear would be appalling.

"Is this your home?" asked Ruth.

"Yes I was born in the Carceral Archipelago," he said.

"I come from Long Lock, deep amid God's hair. Each strand's a hundred miles wide. Piled on each other they form huge canyons. Castles, citadels, whole cities cling to a single filament."

Max found her words intoxicating.

"What's it like to live so far above the air, in space itself?" he asked. He only ever saw it from the ground, dark purple fading to black overhead, utterly empty.

"Far below you see the atmosphere spread across the floor of the universe," said Ruth, "it looks like water. Sometimes you think you can reach down and touch it and watch the ripples spread."

Ruth smiled at him and Max's mouth went dry. He realised he looked like a love-sick idiot, and forced himself to turn away.

His father stood in the doorway. Max froze. The memory of their conversation in the Steel Room flooded back into his mind. Herman's face wore the impassive mask of the Lord of the Carceral Archipelago. He bowed to Ruth.

"We think we've successfully made contact with the AntiHelix," he said. "Does the name Crysanthe Uella mean anything to you?"

Silence filled the room.

"What of her?"

Ruth's voice carried a tone of menace that caught Max off guard. If Herman detected any threat he didn't show it.

"Odilon the Watcher succeeded in activating a Speaking Lens," he continued. Max stared at him in astonishment, he'd only ever heard of such devices in stories.

"She talked to you?" Ruth's voice shook. The anger vanished in a flash. Now she looked desperate.

"Yes. If you want to see her I suggest we hurry, the machinery's ancient and Odilon isn't sure how long he can hold the connection," said Herman. Ruth walked out of the room, her head bowed and her face unreadable. Two guards flanked her and his father followed.

"You've spoken to the Empire of the Ear?" asked Max. Herman nodded.

"If they see she's here they might be more helpful," he said.

"You're holding her to ransom?" Max had to admire his father's arrogance.

"She's a bargaining chip, that's all." Herman avoided looking his son in the eye and Max found it unnerving. Perhaps the old man felt ashamed of the vulnerability he'd displayed in the Steel Room. Max dropped behind and watched his father as they made their way through the Carceral Archipelago. He tried to see a jealous murderer in the gaunt man striding ahead of him, but couldn't. He'd witnessed more emotion in Herman in the last two days than at any other time in his entire life, but Max wasn't used to reading his father. He could recognise anger and threats, but sorrow and guilt? This unyielding ogre had shut himself off from human feeling when his wife died. Emotion sat on him like ill-fitting clothes.

Men and women in wool and steel uniforms stepped aside to let them past, bowing their heads and murmuring salutations. Herman ignored them all. They threaded their way down in a corkscrew through the centre of the tower, passing dormitories, schools, libraries and halls crammed with desks where clerks laboured at stacks of paper taller than a man. Max spotted a ladder leading down to the deeper prisons. Far underneath their feet, rotating cylinders of cells ground against each other day and night until their occupants went mad in a rumbling chaos of noise and grit. Max thought of Abby and swore under his breath. He'd get her out as soon as he could.

They came to a copper-lined corridor. It opened onto a circular room. In the centre, two marble angels held up a coin of glass. A net of fine wires ran down from a frame above, brushing at the upper rim. Half a dozen lamps lit the space, turned down so the shadows crowded in. Max looked around in wonder. He'd never seen this room before. As far as he knew Metacarpi and its tower were isolated from the rest of the kingdoms of God, yet he stood in front of a legendary machine capable of sending voices and images to the furthest realms. Furthermore, the lens worked. He noticed his reflection. It rippled and flowed like the surface of a stream.

Odilon, wearing overalls and protective glasses, busied himself at a row of dials and switches. He looked up and gave Max a smile and a wave, as if he'd spotted him in a bar. One of Maria's clerks sat beside him, taking notes. She stood up at the sight of Herman and saluted.

"Are we still in contact?" asked his father, inviting Ruth to take a stool opposite the screen.

"I believe so, though the signal's fluctuating," said Odilon. "The valves in this machine could go any minute." He turned to Ruth. "I advise brevity and haste in your communications, my dear." Max saw her fix her gaze on the mirror, her body taut.

The glass blazed white. Max, startled by the light, cried out and flung up his arm. The brightness faded, leaving after-images in his eyes. A picture formed, of granulated shadows and angles like a photograph projected onto shifting sand. Max saw a woman in the centre of the oval. She looked older than Ruth, and far crueller. *If that's what they're all like*, thought Max, *God help us*. Thin eyebrows arched up from heavy-lidded eyes. The full mouth was dark, the bottom lip pouting. Pale curls tumbled over bare shoulders. Ruth gave a sob and Max saw hope in her eyes for the first time.

"This is her Puissant Worship the General Crysanthe Uella, Ancient to the Condottiere Alaric, Vavasour of the Council of the Nine Kingdoms, Second in Command of the Dogs of the AntiHelix, Princess of the House of the Long Lock, Loyal servant of the Emperor Demetrius of the Empire of the Ear, speaking to whomever style themselves the rulers of the Carceral Archipelago in the City of Metacarpi by the left thumb of God," said the image. Max didn't think she was trying to impress. She rattled through the list of titles as if everyone understood their import. *She's probably expecting us to fall on our knees and bang our heads on the floor.* Odilon and Herman exchanged glances and his father's lips twitched in amusement.

"I'm Herman Ocel, Lord of the Carceral Archipelago. I have with me Odilon the Watcher and my son and heir, Maximilian Ocel. Also present is Ruth an Vircana, a refugee from two dreadnoughts who lie six weeks north of us." Herman gestured to the girl beside him.

Crysanthe Uella's face loomed and shifted, craning to see their image in her own viewer.

"Ruth an Vircana?" she asked. Did Max catch a hint of anxiety in her voice?

"General Uella," said Ruth hesitantly. *That's not how she usually speaks to this woman.*

"What happened?" asked the general.

"Quickly, the connection's fading," said Odilon.

"Captain Hathus took over the ships. My father, if he's alive, is trapped inside the Iron Core. I have to get him out of there, they won't help me rescue him, we have to save him," Ruth pleaded.

"Did he open his orders?" asked the woman in the mirror.

"General Uella, we need your help in stopping these renegade dreadnoughts," said Herman, stepping between Ruth and the lens. "They've destroyed Abductor Pollicis Brevis and they'll do the same to Metacarpi. We'll all perish, including Ruth an Vircana, unless you help us."

"Did he open his orders?" repeated General Uella, ignoring Herman. Max saw Odilon struggling with the machine.

"Yes, and straight afterwards Hathus rebelled," said Ruth. She got to her feet, walking past Herman towards the lens with her hand outstretched. *What's she doing?* thought Max. The seconds ticked by. He tried to read Crysanthe Uella's expression but the shifting waves of light made it impossible.

"Ruth an Vircana is to be returned immediately to the AntiHelix by personal order of the Emperor Demetrius himself," she said eventually. "Do I make myself absolutely clear? Her person is inviolate and she's to be treated with the utmost respect. This command is to be obeyed or the people of Metacarpi will be subjected to the harshest penalties. Captain Hathus is a renegade and a traitor to the Emperor. He's renounced all loyalty to the AntiHelix. All who aid and abet him will be punished. Obey this command or risk the total destruction of your city."

Herman laughed, an astonishing sound that turned every face towards him.

"With all due respect, madam, this posturing gets us nowhere. Two of your battleships head towards this city intent, it seems, on wiping us out anyway. No-one's going anywhere until I know why this is happening, and what the Anti-Helix intends to do about it." Max had to admire his father, it was a desperate call to a woman who'd clearly never bargained in her entire life.

"Crysanthe Uella, please help me," said Ruth. The eyes in the screen fell upon her. Did Max see longing in that gaze? General Uella looked up.

"We're all in great danger," she said.

We? The Empire? Metacarpi? God help us, does she mean the entire human race?

"For the sake of every living person on the body of God, what I'm about to tell you must be kept in utter secrecy, do you swear to this?" she said, her voice softer, but still urgent.

Herman placed his hand on his heart and bowed.

"The Condottiere Alaric is on a mission to find someone whose very existence is vital to the future of humanity." Max saw his father and Odilon exchange glances.

"Who's this person?" asked Herman, "Are they in Metacarpi?"

"No," said Crysanthe, "but we think..."

The screen went blank.

Ruth howled, the sound sent a shiver through Max's spine.

"Get it back," shouted Herman. Odilon struggled with the machine, but Max saw the wisps of black smoke rising from its vents. For long seconds the Watcher switched cables and twisted controls. In the end he shook his head. Herman glared at Ruth, then Max.

"Take her to her room," he said angrily.

CHAPTER TEN

LEAVING HIS FATHER with Odilon in the room of the Speaking Lens, Max followed the guards up through the centre of the tower. Ruth walked with crisp, silent steps. When they reached the top of the Carceral Archipelago Max sent the soldiers away and closed the door behind them. She stood in the middle of the room. Her shoulders began to shake.

"Ruth."

She turned and pressed herself against him, her fingers clutching at his shirt. She buried her face in his chest and wept. Appalled, he stared at the top of her head. At last he put his arms around her, feeling hard muscle beneath her dress.

"Please help me, Max, please help me rescue my father," she said. He knew this was coming but, God, she was beautiful. He didn't care if it was all an act. Despite himself Max desired her. When he closed his eyes he could smell her hair. It would be so easy to take her face in his hand and tilt it up towards him, bend down to kiss those pale lips.

Oh no, you're not that stupid, he told himself. He stepped back, his hands on her shoulders, fighting the lust welling up inside him. It took all his strength, especially when she fixed him with those eyes, bewildered and filled with tears. He wondered whether she possessed psychic powers like the giant's, capable of turning his brain to mush.

She stepped after him, but when she recognised the look in his eyes she halted, and he saw contempt on her face.

"You won't help, any of you," she whispered, "you'll just wait for your end, huddled in this stinking peasant tower. I'm on my own."

She sat on the edge of the bed with her back towards him. Outside, rain lashed against the windows. Max hesitated, fighting the urge to take her in his arms. He forced himself to leave the room.

He threaded his way through the Shadows. Crysanthe Uella had confirmed what they already suspected. The Empire offered no help. Whatever orders Alaric opened no longer mattered if he'd been overthrown and this mad Captain Hathus controlled the fleet. She'd said the dreadnoughts searched for someone vital to the future of mankind. Was it bluster? Judging by her string of titles, the mighty Crysanthe Uella was no stranger to grand gestures.

He stepped out of the Shadows into a corridor. A breathless Level Runner collided with him, pressed a book into his hands, and sped round the corner. *What the hell*? thought Max. They got on his nerves, cocky little buggers the lot of them. He flicked through the pages. Tables of dates and numbers. *What's this*? Understanding dawned and he laughed out loud, promising to hug Maria next time he saw her. He held a ship's Charge Log. It listed records of flights from twenty-eight years ago, detailing where and when the tower engineers had replenished the vessel's capacitors. He guessed it contained data about his mother's flights. Despite her misgivings, Herman's secretary had helped him after all. Given time and a chart he could calculate the distance his mother travelled on each trip and, with luck, her destination. A return to the room of his childhood lay in his grasp.

Voices came along the corridor. Not wanting to be seen with the book, he stepped back into the Shadows and waited for the newcomers to pass. His mouth went dry when he recognised who spoke.

"We should at least prepare," came Odilon's voice, "if we leave tonight we can be across the sea by tomorrow evening. We need to explain what's required to plant the idea. It'll take time to gain hold. We need to start out now."

"And what if we only unleash more destruction?" His father's voice, but so tired it he barely recognised it.

"I know it's dangerous but we've no other way of meeting the threat. Even if the empire wanted to help, their ships are months away. This is what we prepared for, it was given to us for when this day arrived."

"Nobody gave us anything," said Herman. "I found it by accident on the edge of the sea. God only knows what'll happen when we use it."

You bastard, thought Max, *you've got a weapon after all. Where? Across the sea? The Forbidden Sea?*

"Max asked about Yvette." The sound of his mother's name, so strange in the Lord of the Carceral Archipelago's mouth, made Max gasp. He wondered if he'd given himself away, but neither man heard him.

"It's understandable, after his encounter in the Wasteland," said Odilon.

"I should've gone with them, made sure we spent those last months together. Why didn't I pay attention to her? She was about to tell me something important. But I didn't have time, I was arrogant and wouldn't listen. Now it's too late and I hate myself for it." There was a pause. Odilon's voice filtered through the walls, indistinct, comforting. The voices receded.

Max didn't know whether to feel sorry for his father, or angry that he only confided his sorrows to Odilon. For over an hour he hovered in the passageways and stairwells of the Shadows, the Charge Log forgotten. Occasionally other people crossed in front of him, entering and exiting secret doorways or hatches fringed with rust. The Carceral Archipelago still stood, even after its Lord laid bare the guilt and misery that haunted him for over thirty years. *You're another cog in this stone and metal machine, Father, nothing more.* For as long as he could remember Herman Ocel had been as stern and implacable as the tower itself. Now he saw that all the laws, the lectures and the reprimands didn't come from the universal truth of strict government, but from the personal misery of a man unable to come to terms with the death of the woman he loved.

Above him the walls lofted into darkness. Below the stairs disappeared into the gloom. He realised why he hated this place. It made all who dwelled in it peripheral, unimportant, with no control over their lives. It reminded him of a game he'd played as a boy, coaxing a ball through a labyrinth towards a pit. Now he understood he wasn't alone; Max and Herman, rolling towards the same conclusion, through corridors of stone built millennia ago. He and his father, one after the other, trundling towards meaningless deaths. *No thanks.* The reason he left the Carceral Archipelago in the first place was to be master of his own life. He turned over the Charge Log in his hands. Who could he rely on? Odilon was his father's confidant. Despite this book Maria would only help him so far. Her first and foremost loyalty lay with the tower. He'd seen enough in Ruth's face, and Crysanthe Uella's, to understand the utter contempt they felt towards Metacarpi. He'd trust only one person in this whole city with his life, Abby Fabrice.

The guards tried to stop him, but he impersonated his father's fury with disturbing accuracy and they retreated in confusion. Abby sat in a pile of furs with her knees drawn up under her chin, staring through a narrow hole at the grey sky outside.

"Having fun?" she asked. She gestured around at the cell.

"Nice isn't it? Let's hear the excuses then, they'd better be good."

"Odilon told my father about the giant and it's rattled him. He wants to keep me in the Carceral Archipelago, says my life is in danger from spies from the Empire," said Max. Abby snorted.

"And that's why I'm here?"

"You're his insurance against my co-operation," said Max. Abby shook her head and looked out of the window.

"And what about the dreadnoughts and that pilot?" she said eventually.

"My father and Odilon have a weapon. I think it's across the Forbidden Sea. The way they spoke, it sounds like it's dangerous enough to take the city with it as well as the enemy."

"So we're all to be sacrificed to their stupidity," said Abby. Max hated seeing her trapped like this, her voice filled with sadness and contempt.

"Ruth wants us to rescue her father. She thinks that if he's free he can take back the ships. My father said no," he continued.

"Why not? Give her a ship and a couple of spare idiots and send her on her merry way. If she succeeds, wonderful, if she winds up dead nothing changes," said Abby. *The only idiots going spare are sitting in this room.*

"The Empire of the Ear contacted us. We're to send her back to the AntiHelix or risk the wrath of the emperor himself," he said, "my father's keeping her as a bargaining chip to get them to help us, but it's hopeless. Their fastest ships are months away."

Abby sighed and rested her chin on her knees.

"We have to get the people out of the city, out to the warehouses, into the wormholes, even to Thumb", she said, "tell your father that's the only way we can save ourselves. He hasn't seen those ships, we have."

Max remembered the dreadnoughts, vast and dark in Odilon's mirrors. She was right.

"I'll speak to him, I'll try and get word to your sister as well. I expect she's talking to the Anarchists."

"They'll be organising an evacuation, just don't let your father's goons mess it up." Abby looked at Max, searching his face.

"What is it, Max? What's happened?"

"That memory of my mother and the room the giant created, I think it's real," he said after a while, "it exists somewhere. My mother took me there as part of an experiment into the human mind. When I asked my father about it he told me never to mention it again."

"Where is it?" asked Abby. Despite her mood he could see he'd woken a spark of interest. He showed her the Charge Log.

"If we know how often they charged her ship, and by how much, we can calculate the distance," he explained, "even better if she used another station as well as the Carceral Archipelago, we can triangulate the destination."

"Then what?" asked Abby. She flicked through the book.

Got you. Mysteries were like drugs to Abby Fabrice. He saw her thoughts as clearly as if she yelled them in his ear. Steal a flyer and go have a look. She gave him her lopsided grin.

"I've got bugger all else to do in here, but I'll need a map."

That shouldn't be too hard, he could get charts from one of the ships on the Landing Field, on his way to confront his Father.

"Give me a day, I'll get you out of here," he told her. Abby said nothing. She thumbed through the Charge Log. He wasn't sure she believed him. He hated leaving her there. Soon he'd put a gun in her hand and stick her on the deck of a flyer. That'd snap her out of it.

He made his way up through the tower, intent on confronting his father. Perhaps he couldn't help protect the city, perhaps he was only fit to baby-sit Ruth. It was arrogant of him to think he could return after five years and slot easily into the upper echelons of the Carceral Archipelago, and his father was right to slap him down. But the old bastard knew the truth about his mother and conspired with Odilon to keep it from him. That was unforgivable. Whatever it took, he'd force the pair of them to tell him everything they knew about the room, the stranger in the corridor, and the woman who'd loved him like no-one else.

He climbed to the roof. He needed air after the damp gloom of the tower. His father's ship the *Zephyr* kept spare charts and no-one would ask Max awkward questions if he went on board. He'd find what Abby needed, and then seek out Herman and the Watcher.

To his surprise he couldn't see the flyer. A woman with a lieutenant's cap directed the ground crew as they cleared the space on which the sleek copper-sheathed vessel usually sat. She turned and gave him a cursory salute before returning to her ledger.

"My father's ship?" asked Max.

"The Lord of the Carceral Archipelago and Odilon the Watcher took it."

"Where?" He'd already guessed.

"Don't know, sir, it's just the two of them, no-one else. That ship's built for six. You can run her with two, but it's bloody hard work," she said, looking accusingly at Max as if it was somehow his fault. Max walked away, bitter and frustrated. The universe seemed to conspire against him. Rain fell and the clouds descended. He drew his coat about him and cursed. Following them was out of the question.

Flyers sat crammed together on the wet stone. Every few minutes one rose into the air to be replaced by another drifting down from a sky of roiling cloud. Officers and clerks ran from ship to ship, handing out sheaves of documents or lifting up boxes to the crew, faces grim, purposeful, frightened and tired. *They're preparing for war.* He counted thirty vessels. *This is our entire fleet, going through the motions. I give it a lifespan of five seconds if we're lucky.*

He walked to the edge of the roof. A defensive wall pierced with embrasures ringed the perimeter. Smaller ships sat untended in its shadow. *One of those might have a chart.* On a whim he climbed onto the wall and made his way to where the chain *Joy* met the tower. Inside the iron beneath his feet a corridor ran the circumference of the Carceral Archipelago. Hatches led down to the four staples. He looked out over the city. Another flyer rose over the wall to his right, its dynamos crackling in the damp air. *If Father's out of the way I can search his rooms, see what I can find out about this hidden weapon.* He looked over the edge of the parapet. He saw the lights of the city through rents in the clouds below. It might also give him a chance to learn more about his mother.

He climbed back down onto the landing field and entered the wall through one of the access doors. The corridor inside threaded the circumference, punctuated every fifty yards by more gun ports and supply alcoves. Max located a manhole in the floor. He opened it and the cold air hit his face, bringing with it flecks of rain tasting of soot. He lowered himself down. A ladder finished at a platform slung underneath the stone. Metal stairs led to a walkway that hugged the side of the tower. It ended at the staple. Beyond that lay his father's rooms. He stepped onto the gantry. It looked older than the walkway he'd used last time, he could see a few of the bolts pulling away from the stone. Debris littered the metal under his feet. He walked carefully, his heart pounding as the footbridge shifted and creaked. The streets lay two miles down - if he fell they'd have to mop him off the cobbles with rags. He focussed on a house-sized bolt projecting from the wall ahead.

He reached the foot of the stairs leading up to the top of the plate when the gantry gave way. The pins securing it to the wall yanked free in an explosion of dust. The metal under his feet tilted. Max instinctively leapt upwards, grabbing at the staircase. He managed to hook his elbow around the steps as the walkway behind him twisted down into the clouds. The edge dug into his side. He saw the corroded rivets anchoring the stairs. *They're going to break any second,* a voice yelled in his mind, *you idiot Max, why won't you let things lie?* He fought the urge to charge up the staircase. If he did he knew the metal would snap, pitching him into the clouds below. He forced himself to crawl upwards on his hands and knees, concentrating his whole attention on every rung, trying not to think about the void beyond. At last he reached the top of the plate. He lay on his back. Rain soaked his clothes, but he couldn't move. *This tower'll be the death of me yet.*

When the seeping cold grew unbearable he stood up. Ahead another set of steps led down to the gantry he'd used when he first arrived. He spotted the window of his father's study. No lights shone and the glass reflected the nightscape. As expected he found the door bolted, but he'd dealt with enough locks to make short work of it with his knife. He stepped through and closed the door behind him. After drawing all the curtains he lit the lamp on his father's desk and looked around.

It's like the inside of his head, grey and miserable. He saw a wooden ceiling, creaking floorboards and curving walls. His father's only concession to comfort was a leather chair next to a dead stove. On the desk a pewter mug sat next to a piece of half-eaten black bread. *Lord of the city and he eats like a pauper.* The entrance to the dining room and outer offices stood on his right. To the left he saw doors leading to his father's bedroom and a library.

The desk and bookcase yielded nothing but ledgers and reports, the petty day to day workings of the tower in all their relentless tedium. He turned his attention to the bedroom. The Lord of the Carceral Archipelago slept in a double bed. That surprised him. He'd expected a wooden cot at best. Sharply-ironed suits hung in rows in the wardrobe, shirts and collars lay stacked with geometrical precision in the drawers. They reminded him of the piles of reports on Maria's desk and he smiled. He doubted she pressed these herself but she'd make sure the servants were just as meticulous. He also sensed the lingering ghost of his mother in the dressing table with its silver-edged mirror, the inlaid mother of pearl insects decorating the tall wardrobes and the rugs strewn over the boards at his feet. He searched the room, desperate to find clues. At the bottom of a shirt drawer he touched the edge of a framed photograph. He held it up to the lamplight.

He nearly dropped it. The tower swayed and terrified of falling he backed up against the bed and sat down. He placed the picture on the blanket next to him and stared at it. The sound of his breathing filled the air and blood pounded in his ears. The sepia image showed a room with wooden walls and a large fireplace. He recognised it immediately. In the room built by the giant it'd been impossible to focus on details. They'd skittered across his mind like mercury. This photograph showed everything in precise clarity and he drank it in, from the iron decorations of the fireplace, to the grain of the wood in the panelled walls. His mother sat in a chair with a book open on her knee, her head leaning thoughtfully on her hand as she read. He wished she'd faced the camera, but even her profile blurred his vision. He wiped his eyes with his sleeve and looked again. Beside her, on the carpet in front of the fire, stood a toddler. He'd only just learned to walk, because he steadied himself with one hand on the roof of a doll's house, while in the other he held out a wooden cutout animal for his mother.

"It's my doll's house," whispered Max to himself.

Four windows, all different sizes. The house, his mother and the room. The giant had built them from his mind. It had to be a message, not a trap. What did his ghost mother say? *Where is this Max, where is it?* Not in the Carceral Archipelago. Was the giant searching for this place as well? Why? What would a monster from a wormhole want with this room? None of it made sense. He looked again at the photograph. He saw the entrance to the corridor, but no sign of the white haired stranger.

He undid the frame but there was no writing on the back. He replaced it and searched through the rest of the room. He found no other mementos of his mother and in the end admitted defeat. That left the library. He worked his way through the bookshelves. His father's collection consisted of more reports, too old to be relevant and too new to throw any light on the past. Finally, at the bottom of the last case, Max found a dozen volumes of poetry. His heart jumped. Could these be his mother's? He leafed through a few. They contained sonnets and essays on love, sorrow, happiness, in simple verse, like primers for children.

In the last book he saw comments written next to the poems in precise writing. He ran his thumb over the lines, trying to feel the indentations of the pen. *When I appear holding Max in my arms it speaks of motherly love, when I play with Max and sometimes chide him, it speaks of patience and loving kindness.* Her voice spoke to him across the decades. Unable to contain himself any longer he wept as he read page after page. On one a picture showed two boys sitting on a beach next to a man who pointed across the waves. *I took Max to the shore and while he played I looked back towards my home and my dearest husband and wished he was with us, taking part in this great endeavour. He doesn't yet realise what we have found, and what it means to the future of us all. I will tell him soon.*

The outside door banged open. Max nearly dropped the book. He replaced it on the shelf and dimmed the lantern. He listened for a few moments. Silence. He'd hear if anyone came in. Not even a cat could walk across those squeaky boards. He peered out of the library into the empty apartment. Rain hammered against the windows and the lights from the city below cast patches of light across the floor. The door to the gantry stood ajar. Max went to close it. As he did so a ragged shadow rippled briefly across the room.

CHAPTER ELEVEN

MAX STEPPED OUT onto the gantry. Perhaps he should have shut the study door and left by the main entrance, but that cruel taskmaster curiosity dragged him outside. He knew he hadn't imagined the shadow, even though he'd seen it for barely a second.

No birds flew this high. In the bottom quarter of the tower a few scraggy sparrows nested by the windows of the kitchens, but Metacarpi itself held better food. Most of the city birds were crows; black-beaked and the size of cats. They foraged in the rubbish or soared over the tram lines, shrieking loudly every time a wheel threw sparks into the gutters. Unlike everyone else in the city, Max admired them. He recognised fellow scavengers, hunting their own wasteland.

Max looked around. Perhaps an up-draught caught a crow and flung it to the top of the tower. He also wanted to make sure none of his father's spies hovered nearby, ready to report back to Maria or the Lord of the Carceral Archipelago. He didn't fear them. He'd plenty of questions to ask, especially of his father, but not yet. The shock of seeing the photograph, and reading his mother's notes, still smarted. He needed time to think.

The lower cloud bank dissolved into threads and the lights of the city spread out beneath him. The rain slackened off and a cool wind blew across his face. He closed his eyes, trying to soothe his troubled mind, seeing if he could catch a sound or scent from the streets below. Nothing. Too high up. He opened his eyes and spotted a movement on the chain.

At first he thought it was the bird, perched on the inside of the second link. He walked along the gantry to get a better look. *Too big for a crow. That's the size of a human, shaped like one too.* He made out a pale circle on top of a pile of black and purple feathers. *Good God, that's a man in costume.* Where'd he seen him before? Of course. He recognised the actor from Rebecca's theatre, dressed as a Black Rose. What in God's name was he doing on a chain two miles above the city, and how had he got there? You could easily stand on the inside of a link, but there was no way to climb onto it without help. He couldn't see any ropes. Had the man arrived by flyer? Max would've spotted the lights or heard the crackle of the dynamos. Maybe he'd missed it, but none of this explained why the actor stood there. He shouted out. The man didn't react. Perhaps the wind snatched his voice and the actor hadn't heard him. He walked further along the gantry and called again. The man swayed back and forth. *He's drunk, or drugged.* His instinct kicked in and he hunkered down, checking around for any other movement. Wrong things kill you, and this was very wrong.

The man took a step forward. Max called out without thinking, standing up against the rail so his voice carried. The actor looked towards him, froze for a second, then lifted his arms and shrieked. *What in the name of God?* thought Max. Something picked him up and hurled him at the chain. Max screamed and struggled. Amid the mindless panic he realised he wasn't falling. He collided with the actor and the man tumbled backwards off the link. Max slid down the inner surface in a shower of rust and filth. He scrabbled for his knife but a weight planted itself on his chest, pushing him down against the corroded metal.

Above him boiled a column of black feathers. Arms span out like flames from a core of seething darkness. One pressed down on him and he felt it writhe through his shirt, like someone grinding a handful of worms into his chest. Max whimpered, struggling against paralysing terror. He tried to force his hand behind his back. If he could get his knife he'd be able to defend himself. He grabbed at the tendril pinning him to the link. His fingers disappeared into a mass of petals. He instinctively snatched his hand away in revulsion. The pressure increased and his ribs creaked. He saw a glint of something silver amid the roaring motion. The creature bent down towards him and he squirmed frantically, trying to get away. He pushed up with his hands and his arms sank into its body. He couldn't get a purchase on anything, it was like trying to grab a cloud of soot. A hideous wind poured over him, a vapour hinting at infinities utterly alien, utterly inhuman. Max screamed defiance as the shadow moved down over his arms. He felt a blazing pain in his side and cried out in agony. Fluttering shreds of darkness filled his eyes and mouth. He choked, unable to breathe. At the periphery of his vision he saw flashes of colour. A deafening wind filled his ears. Someone shouted. He passed out.

The room looked clearer now. Instead of hints of textures and fragments of detail he could see the grain in the walls, the light from the fire playing across the carpet. His doll's house sat in front of the fireguard. The empty chair from his father's study looked newer, the leather rich and unfaded. *Where's mother?* There she stood, by the entrance to the corridor.

"I think this lies across the Forbidden Sea," said Max.

"Are you sure?" asked his mother.

"Abby's got your Charge Log," he said, "she'll find it."

"Good boy."

Her voice soothed him. He remembered a black bird, or was it a moth? He looked at the ceiling in fear.

"It's gone," said his mother. "We chased it away, but you must hurry."

"What do you mean?" asked Max. He wanted her to hold him in her arms. A nasty creature had tried to hurt him. Were those voices in another room, shouting, the banging of steel doors? Was that gunfire?

"You've got to find out where this is," his mother said. She looked calm, but her hands writhed over each other.

"What were you doing here? Why did you write those notes in that book of poetry?" asked Max.

"I don't know Max," she said. "I'm not your mother, I'm just a memory."

She stepped forward, towering over him.

"Why don't we find out, together?" She held out her hand. "Discover the whereabouts of this room and you'll have the answers to all your questions." He took her hand, warm and solid. *No shadows here*, he thought. She stooped to kiss him on the forehead.

He woke in the Steel Room. *Not again, what have I done this time?* He tried to stand up but had no energy. White sheets pressed him down. His chest ached. He lifted his hand, it felt so heavy, and touched the bandage swathing his torso. He remembered hurtling towards the chain, the actor falling to his death, his own hands disappearing in a seething cloud of darkness. Despite himself he cried out, panting hard, looking wildly round for his attacker. Scratched steel and white plastic. Not a single shadow, except for his father in his long black coat, sitting on a stool, watching him. Beside him stood the doctor, a syringe in her hand. *She's just woken me up, how long have I been out?*

"Three days," she said, answering his unspoken question. "A poisoned knife cut. Luckily we got to you before it took a hold in your system. You're very lucky to be alive." She left the room. Herman continued staring at Max, an all-too familiar expression of cold anger on his face.

"You will leave Metacarpi," he said eventually. "Take the *Zephyr*. Accompany Ruth an Vircana back to the AntiHelix. You will never return here. If your ship comes within a hundred miles of Metacarpi I will have it blown out of the sky. If I hear word of you again I'll take everyone in the city you hold dear and hang them from the chains of the Carceral Archipelago."

Max couldn't believe his ears. *This is completely ridiculous. Is he capable of nothing but this endless pompous bullying?* He heard his father's voice crack as he intoned the terms of his exile.

"I broke into your room, that's all," he said, "and if you haven't noticed, I got stuck by a monster in the process. Surely that's punishment enough."

Herman stopped, his face working. He looked ready to hit his son, but under the fury Max saw a hint of real fear.

"A Black Rose stabbed you," said Herman. "A patrol ship spotted it before it finished the job."

"No you're wrong, it was an actor from the Theatre of Angels, dressed as a Black Rose. They'd just performed *The Gate of Light* for Odilon." He stopped. *But you were stabbed after he fell from the chain, you collided with the actor and saw him go over the edge. Then the creature attacked you.*

Max felt the room's temperature plummet. The bed swayed, forcing him to lie back, gripping its edges. His vision filled with shreds of darkness, boiling from a core as black as midnight. His father meant the aliens responsible for the singularity itself, beings from the outer darkness, utterly different in every way and complete masters of sciences incomprehensible to humanity. Why in God's name would a Black Rose journey to the Carceral Archipelago to stick him with a knife? He remembered shouts and the sound of something mechanical chattering away, machine guns? It brought the actor up to the chain as a decoy, to distract him.

"Why?" he whispered.

"Odilon thinks it's in league with Captain Hathus, that he's captured and tamed the alien to his will," said Herman. He didn't sound convinced.

"What do you think?" asked Max.

"It doesn't matter. You will leave here in the next twenty four hours," Herman stood up. *Doesn't matter?* Max felt his temper rise.

"Forget your stupid punishments for once," he shouted. Pain stung his side.

"I'm not punishing you, you cretinous little shit," bellowed his father, "I'm saving your worthless life."

Herman Ocel had never once lost his temper in the thirty years he'd known him, he didn't have to. A stern word in that rich voice sufficed to send the hardiest souls scuttling away in fear. As he towered over the bed, incandescent with fury, it seemed as if the fortress itself was about to fall on Max.

"What do you mean?" he managed to ask. With a great effort his father brought himself under control.

"Enemies are everywhere," he said, turning away to hide his face, "in the city, even in the Carceral Archipelago itself. Your meddling marks you as a target. You know too much." His voice sounded hoarse, defeated.

"I don't know anything," said Max, "you have a weapon somewhere across the sea, that's it." He saw the muscles in his father's jaw bunch. *There's something else you're not telling me, there's more to this than military intelligence and alien spies.*

"What's going on?" he asked. Herman said nothing. *You think I'm a stupid child who can't be trusted.*

"God's cock, who do you think you're talking to? I'm not an idiot," yelled Max. Pain lanced through his body and he collapsed back on the bed, gasping in frustration and anger.

"The more I tell you, the more your life is in danger," said Herman, it sounded as if he was almost pleading with Max. "Every scrap of information in your head, no matter how trivial, marks you as a target."

"Every scrap of information about what? Father, I'm just a Time Scavenger."

The Lord of the Carceral Archipelago's gone mad, or he's playing whatever passes for a practical joke in his miserable world.

"What is it you used to call me," he continued, "a worthless piece of shit? Good for nothing? A disappointment to all whoever cared for me? God, the list is so long I can't even remember all my titles. What can I possibly know that's of interest to anything? Stop speaking in riddles."

A thought struck him.

"Is this something to do with mother?"

Herman Ocel froze, his profile a craggy shadow against the steel walls. Max saw a glint on his cheek. He struggled to comprehend the sight of his father in tears. He finally understood the old man's motives.

"You lost her, and now you fear you'll lose me, that's why you're sending me away," he whispered. Herman pulled out a handkerchief from his coat pocket, an immaculate white square, and wiped his face.

"You will leave in the morning," he said in a voice of iron.

So be it, if that's how you want to play it. He had his own plans. A ship and two spare idiots on their merry way.

"Only if Abby Fabrice comes with me." His father nodded and left the room.

He couldn't sleep. He lay on his bed, searching for answers and going mad with frustration. Nothing made sense. The pain in his side gradually subsided to a dull ache. Two guards came for him. One helped him dress, the other carried his few possessions in a duffle bag. They escorted Max through the Shadows to the roof of the Carceral Archipelago. He'd no idea of the time and it was dark when they emerged on the wind-swept concrete. Ruth and Abby waited for him next to his father's ship, the *Zephyr. This is the flagship of the fleet*, thought Max, *it's useless against those dreadnoughts from the Ear so he can afford to give it to me.* Abby couldn't resist a surreptitious 'here we go again' thump in the ribs, whispering a sorry when he winced. Ruth stood to one side, pale and silent like a ghost. Max saw Maria conferring with a huddle of officers near the prow. She strode over to him.

"Does it hurt?" she asked, poking his bandage with a bony finger.

"Ow," said Max.

"Good," said Maria. She looked him up and down and shook her head. Her face crumpled for a second but she swiftly brought it back under control.

"Captain Peltro and his crew will go with you. Take Ruth an Vircana to the AntiHelix. Aim for the Thumb, then strike north. That way you'll avoid the enemy dreadnoughts."

"Where's my father?" asked Max.

"Don't ask," said Maria icily. She took him by the arm and led him away from the ship. The crew escorted Abby and Ruth on board.

"It seems the city will evacuate," she said. "Your father and Odilon prepare to surrender in the hope that Captain whatever-he's-called will spare us."

Maria walked to the edge of the parapet and looked out across the Forbidden Sea. Max followed her. They stood side by side, out of earshot of the others. He tried to read her expression but the woman's severe profile told him nothing, he could have been looking at a statue.

"Your mother loved the sea, its stillness and its purity. When you were a baby she would take you to play in the shallows. She saw warmth and beauty in simple things. It's hard to be an exile, but there's nothing left here for you, Max. Journey to the body of God, find new wonders." Maria nodded towards the wall of the Thumb. She grabbed him and hugged him tight. After a second she pushed him away.

"Go." She turned her back on Max and strode swiftly across the landing field towards the entrance to the tower. Max looked around. He knew he ought to feel bitter, leaving the Carceral Archipelago with no father to bid him farewell. Instead he just felt pity for the old man. The stone-faced bullying was an act to mask his loneliness and sorrow. *Let him go, you've got more important things to do. Find your mother's room and the answers to all these riddles. And while you're at it, see if you can't discover a way to stop those fucking dreadnoughts.*

He walked back to the *Zephyr*, climbing on board without a word. The crew pulled the steps up and the ship lifted into the air, angling away from the roof. Max went into his cabin and sat on the bunk, staring at the Thumb, waiting for its immensity to wipe his mind clean.

Abby woke him up. He looked out of the window. They still hugged the edge of the sea.

"Where are we?" he asked.

"Half a thousand miles west of the city. You've been asleep for three hours. This ship's fast." she said. "Is it true you got stuck by a Black Rose?"

For some reason the anxiety on her face embarrassed him. He grunted.

"Why?" asked Abby.

Max shrugged. "I've no idea. Maybe it's in league with this Captain Hathus. My father thinks I'm a target for some reason, that's why he's sent me away."

"A target? You mean it hunted you out?" Abby's voice filled with fear. Max thought the idea stupid.

"I think it was just spying for the enemy, saw me on the roof and fancied its chances."

"A Black Rose?" asked Abby incredulously. Max knew it sounded ridiculous. Creatures who gave man the chance to build his God had better things to do than stab the son of a petty tyrant on top of his stone tower.

"I don't know, Abby, I don't know why it happened," he said helplessly. Her mouth twitched. He recognised her tell.

"What?" he asked, dreading what might come next.

"Are you ready?"

What's she talking about, ready for what? She waved the Charge Log under his nose.

"I worked it out. I know where your room is," she sang with a grin.

He jumped off his bunk in elation and instantly regretted it. Pain lanced through him. He touched his side, it hurt. He could see a yellow line in the bandage marking the cut. Swearing at the discomfort, he took the book from Abby and flicked through it. She'd marked a dozen pages in her swirly handwriting.

"Anything you want, from anywhere in space and time, it's yours, just name it."

"Really?" she laughed and blushed. He'd never seen that before.

"Where is it?" he asked.

"Across the Forbidden Sea, about three hundred miles south-east of here."

Her words caught him off guard. Could there be a connection between his mother's project and Herman Ocel's hidden weapon? He dismissed the idea, high grade military research didn't involve studying the mind of a two year old; coincidence, nothing more. Even so, perhaps he'd also get a chance to find Father's secret, though the sea stretched for thousands of miles and it might be anywhere on the far shores. First they needed this ship.

"There's four crew," he said, pulling on his trousers.

"Three, I locked one of them in the lavatory," she said. He grabbed her face and planted a loud kiss on her forehead. He noticed her eyes glistening with genuine happiness for the first time in ages.

He followed her to the bridge. They'd done this before, on different worlds, in city bars, once or twice on other ships in the Wasteland. Two men operated the controls under the eye of the captain. Max stood between them and stared out of the window, trying to look innocent. Abby approached Peltro to ask an inane question about the ship. Max watched the cracked land flicker under the prow. Ahead rose the Thumb, four days away at this rate. Wreckage littered the plain. Ragged clutches of girders bigger than houses whipped past. Max counted them; *one, two, three,* and turned round.

Abby was pointing Peltro's gun at his head. In her other hand she held her poisoned hairpin to his neck. The man's head strained up and his eyes rolled like a panicked animal's. *Poor bastard, meet Abby Fabrice.* The man to his right turned round and swore. Max elbowed him on the jaw and snatched his revolver out of its holster. His chest flared in pain. He moved next to Abby, covering the startled crew.

They forced the ship down on the shore. Abby fetched the remaining crewman from the toilet while Max kept an eye on the others. They came back with Ruth in tow. The girl looked wide-eyed and frightened.

"Two options," said Max, "I take command and you do what I say or I drop you off here and you make your own way back to Metacarpi."

Enough warehouses dotted the route to keep them alive until they reached the edge of town. Captain Peltro, thin-lipped with embarrassment, lifted his chin.

"And where do you propose to fly?" he asked stiffly.

"Across the Forbidden Sea," said Max.

The men exchanged frightened glances.

"You can't," said Peltro. Max saw that the idea rattled him, fear replacing pomposity in the man's eyes.

"Why not?" asked Abby.

"It's forbidden," said Peltro. Abby laughed and the captain turned bright red. In the face of the man's bone-headed stupidity Max decided he'd no choice. The other crew members stared at Max with their mouths open. His chest hurt and he still felt fragile after his fight on the chain. Two could fly the *Zephyr* and he couldn't be bothered to argue with these idiots any longer.

"Alright, five minutes to gather supplies then off the ship," he said. "Blame me when you get back."

"Sir, I really must protest in a most emphatic and robust manner!" started Peltro. Abby fired in the air and the crew jumped. Ruth gave out a whimper of fear. Realising the futility of argument, the captain and the others gathered what they could and climbed down onto the shore. Behind them the surface of the sea reflected the Thumb.

"You too," Abby said, gesturing at Ruth with Peltro's gun. The girl shook her head in mute fear.

"What're you doing?" asked Max. She wasn't thinking of forcing Ruth off the ship, was she? He didn't doubt the men could make the trek back. They might be tired and thinner at the end but they'd survive. Not Ruth, he wasn't prepared to abandon her five hundred miles away from the only nearby city, one facing imminent destruction. After finding the room he'd planned on continuing north. She might be the only chance they had of saving the city. He'd even mulled over the possibility of rescuing her father, and he needed her for that.

"No," he said.

Abby shot him a filthy look.

"We don't need her, the men'll get her back to the city safely."

"No, she stays with us," said Max. "I'm not dumping her out here." He meant it and Abby could tell. For a second she looked ready to argue, then she shrugged.

"Whatever you say, Max," she said, her voice filled with a weary disappointment that surprised him. She could be thoughtless, but he'd never thought her cruel.

"Go back to your cabin and wait there," he told Ruth. She nodded fearfully and drifted back into the ship. Abby and Max powered up the engines and turned the prow southwards. In seconds they swept over the water, the figures of the crew dwindling behind them.

CHAPTER TWELVE

AS THEY FLEW across the sea Max ran through the last couple of days in his head. The more he thought the less he understood. His father said the Black Rose tried to kill him because of what he knew. But he knew nothing of any worth. His father hid a dangerous weapon that might defeat Hathus, or blow up in his hands. Thirty years ago his mother did research into the mind of her infant son, playing games with him in a room beyond the sea. That was it. Disconnected scraps of knowledge, meaningful to no-one but himself, certainly of no interest to aliens from the depths of space.

He wanted to talk to Abby but she sulked about his decision to keep Ruth on board, working the controls beside him with a permanent scowl and answering every question with a monosyllable. They found the *Zephyr* had a simple autopilot to keep it level in one direction so, after enduring Abby's mood for half an hour, Max left her on the bridge and went in search of Ruth. She'd be terrified after they kicked the crew off the ship, the second mutiny she'd lived through. Max winced at the thought.

Ruth sat on her bed, staring out of the porthole. He remembered the feel of her body pressed up against him in the tower. He could just detect the scent of her hair in the cabin. Momentarily thrown by his own desire he struggled to find words. He managed a smile.

"Where are we going?" she asked.

"South for a few days."

Ruth bowed her head and cried. *Here we go again.*

"I want to save my father, please," she said. Against his better judgement he put his arm round her shoulder, feeling the weight of her head against his cheek.

"There are three of us, flying a tiny ship. Your father is in one of two dreadnoughts, each with thousands of crew and their own fleets. We wouldn't stand a chance."

Ruth wiped her nose with the back of her hand.

"There're ways, there are always ways, if you're so small that no-one sees you," she said. *You're talking from experience*, Max thought. On an impulse he took her hand in his. She didn't pull away. Her skin felt cold.

"Max."

He looked up. Abby stood in the doorway.

"When you've finished you might want to come and have a look at this," she said and went back to the bridge.

He joined her. She nodded into the distance.

"What in God's name is that?" asked Max.

Dark rectangles cut holes in the seascape ahead. Max studied them through binoculars. They looked like a row of teeth rising out of a jawbone. With a shock he saw some moved, sliding imperceptibly towards each other. He thought of the outer wall that ringed Metacarpi.

"Automatic defences, and they're active," he said.

"Your room's on the other side."

"Are you sure?" he asked. Abby nodded.

This didn't look like the location for a family excursion. He found it difficult to reconcile the memory of his mother and the room with this sinister hardware.

They slowed the *Zephyr*. As they approached Max saw machines on rails, blocks of metal with spoked wheels hundreds of yards high. Max realised that only a few of the mechanisms still worked, the others lay in pieces, their wheels buckling under the weight of the broken fortresses. *This is the place.* The thought popped into his head, taking him by surprise. *Why do I recognise it?* He had no memories to go on, just a disturbing familiarity lurking at the edge of his consciousness. His palms itched and his mouth felt dry. Elation and fear jostled in his mind.

"Take her closer, but slowly," he said. He knew Abby well enough, she'd cheerfully keep flying till the shells whistled round their ears. The *Zephyr* crept forward. Max heard the grinding of cogs and chains inside the hulks as they inched back and forth.

"Max," Abby said. He heard the worry in her voice. A light winked on the panel in front of her.

"Someone's hailing us from those forts," she said, "there're people inside."

Max hadn't expected this. He assumed only his parents and Odilon crossed the Forbidden Sea. Who in God's name lived out here? If Metacarpi's long isolation made its inhabitants decadent and perverse, what monsters dwelled in these metal boxes? Abby held the radio headset to her ear and shook her head. Max lifted his binoculars. Two of the hulks stopped. Doors slid apart in showers of rust and clusters of gun barrels swung towards them, polished metal shining in contrast to the dark interiors.

"Get us out of here," yelled Max. He'd made a stupid mistake and killed them all, they'd never outrun those guns. In a second they'd be pounded into the floor of the Forbidden Sea.

"Wait," said Abby. Three more lights flickered in the cabin. The guns swivelled back into the forts. The iron doors shrieked closed.

"They recognise us," said Abby in wonder. A thought struck Max. His father had given him the *Zephyr* because it was the fastest ship in Metacarpi. Was it also because he knew it could pass these defences? Did he want his son to find whatever lay beyond those wheeled wrecks? They moved forward again, the ship rising high above the sea as it approached the wall.

"God's cock, now what's she doing?" muttered Abby.

Through the window Max saw Ruth emerge on the forward deck. She walked to the rail and stared across the sea at the fortresses. They'd stopped moving, becoming shapes against a wall of cloud once more. The wind blew Ruth's hair sideways in a fan. The dress pressed against her body. *God she's beautiful*, thought Max. Would she really be interested in raggedy scavenger from the Thumb?

"Get your girlfriend back inside," said Abby, "we don't need any more distractions."

Max snapped out of his reverie and went on deck. Perhaps Abby was right, they should have left her on the shore with the others. They couldn't have her wandering about playing the lost waif while malfunctioning machines waved cannon in their faces. He'd lock her in her cabin until they were somewhere safer. *Maybe I should let Abby look after the key*, he thought as he looked at her slender body leaning against the rail.

"Ruth?"

She either didn't hear or chose to ignore him. The thin material showed the muscles on her back. *You're not a delicate lady of the court are you?* Ruth turned and kicked him in the chest.

It felt like a sledgehammer. He flew back across the forward deck, banging against the cabin wall before sitting down in heap. He couldn't breathe, his whole torso blazed with pain. As well as the thundering ache in his ribs a line of fire from the wound burned his side. He clawed at his throat, trying to suck in a breath. When he succeeded pain flared again. *The bitch's cracked a damned rib.* He got onto his knees, scrabbling for his gun while staring at Ruth in baffled horror. She faced him now, pacing sideways on tiptoes with her arms stretched out. *She's gone mad, she's doing that ridiculous dance.* He clambered to his feet. She'd taken him by surprise, he just needed to subdue her and get her back to the cabin till she calmed down. He took a step towards her.

It's not a dance, he realised as she kicked out again, sweeping him off his feet. He fell onto his back and cried out as more pain swept through his body. Ruth stood over him, her face expressionless, and punched down towards his heart. He managed to roll out of the way and wood splintered under her fist. She pulled her hand back ready to strike again, this time her fingers were rigid daggers. He didn't doubt she could rip his throat out in a second.

Abby kicked her in the side. Ruth cannoned into the deck rail. In one flowing movement she rebounded, twisting to aim a blow at the other woman. Even through his pain and anger Max still thought she looked beautiful as her hair streamed out behind her. Her face stayed calm, only her eyes burned with fury. *She's a trained fighter, all that frightened waif act was a ruse*, realised Max, *she's the daughter of a mighty warrior, you moron, what did you expect?* She could fight but so could Abby. She moved back and forth, the measured pacing of a cat against Ruth's wild leaps. Ruth kicked, Abby deflected it and socked her on the cheek with an eye watering punch. The girl's head snapped back, but in a second she attacked again. Abby retreated across the deck, dodging the blows. Her nose bled and her red hair hung round her shoulders. Max moved in behind Ruth, looking for a chance to grab her, or kick her feet away. She moved too fast.

She slipped in a puddle on the deck. Abby ducked under her arm, grabbed her wrist, twisted and threw her over the side of the *Zephyr*. Max roared and ran forward. A fall from this height would kill her. Abby simultaneously pelted to the edge, yanking a pin from her hair. Max saw Ruth hanging from the rail by one arm. She'd managed to hook it over the bar to stop herself falling, but she was stuck facing outwards. No matter how hard she tried she couldn't bring her other arm round. Abby took the skewer in her hand and held the point to the other woman's cheek. Max felt sick when he recognised the poisoned one.

"Abby, put the pin away," he said as calmly as he could.

He'd never seen her like this. She could be mad, yes, a wild, yelling force of nature plunging into stupid situations with her mile-wide grin. Abby got drunk on adrenaline in a second, but never lost control. This was totally different and it scared Max. It frightened Ruth too, her head strained back, her eyes wide as her glance flickered from Abby's face to the end of that fatal spike.

"Abby, put it away," he repeated. He struggled to keep his voice even. He wanted to yell in her ear to stop being so stupid. Her eyes locked on Ruth's with a hatred so powerful Max was surprised the girl didn't burst into flames. The smile on Abby's face turned his stomach.

He had the sense to grab her wrist with his left hand so when she swung her other fist at him he could catch that too. It still hurt. She'd put her whole weight behind it and would have easily broken his jaw. They stared into each other's eyes. Max saw her expression flicker through surprise, rage and finally sadness. He didn't have time to argue, he twisted the pin out of her hand and threw her across the deck. He reached down, grabbed Ruth's arm and pulled her onto the ship. He pointed his gun at her and jerked his head in the direction of the cabin. He could see her weighing up the chances of another attack and realised he'd probably need to shoot her. He couldn't do that. In his head he begged her to surrender. To his utter relief she gave a small shrug and padded silently back inside.

He locked her in her room and returned to the forward deck. Abby sat with her hands wrapped around her knees. She took her pin without a word and threaded it back through her hair.

"What in God's name was all that about?" he asked, "were you really going to kill her?"

She said nothing. She just sat slumped on the deck of the *Zephyr*, looking empty and exhausted like an unstrung doll. All his anger at her stupidity deserted him. He looked around. The ship flew on autopilot between cliffs of corroded metal. He sat down next to Abby and watched the walls of a ruined fortress drift by. A lacework of holes punctured sheets of rust.

"She wants to rescue her father," said Max. "The little-girl-lost act didn't work so she tried to take over the ship." He should have seen it coming. Despite all his misgivings he'd still fallen for those purple eyes and that elfin face.

"We need her alive, Abby, she's the only link we have to the Empire of the Ear, possibly the only chance of stopping those ships."

"Is that you or your dick talking?" she asked wearily.

"For God's sake," he said, "what the fuck's got into you?"

"Do you remember when we first met?" she asked, dabbing at her nose with her fingers. The question brought Max up short. He racked his brains.

"Odilon told me there was a man, a good man, who'd lost his way, and he asked me if I'd help him find some joy again," said Abby. "It was just after you'd had your last argument with your father and you'd turned your back on the tower. It was in the Jazz bar on Berthold Street."

Max remembered gazing across the narrow brick vault at the top-hatted musicians. Their masks were as grotesque as their songs, and they bent their arms and legs into disturbing postures as they played. Waiters pushed frosted glasses of absinthe and beer towards him, a sad, battered drunk. In all the faces that swam into his memory he couldn't see Abby's.

"I fell in love with you as soon as I saw you face down in a puddle of beer. You tried to pick a fight with the violinist because he looked like your father. You were a mess. And I adored you for it."

It took a few seconds for her words to sink in. The ship flew through a rusted wheel. *There's more than an autopilot guiding this ship*, he thought as the spokes cast their shadows across the deck, *it's as if it's following its own path*. He daren't look at her. *What do I say?* Abby Fabrice, wild-eyed maniac, how many times had she nearly got him killed? How many times had he saved her life, or she'd saved his? She always gave him that mad look of triumph, that insane grin. Just before they kicked open the door, and just after the last enemy died in a pool of blood or slime.

"No, you can't. Not you," he said without thinking.

Abby laughed and the sound carried such sadness it cut his heart.

"I was always there, by your side, always, fighting against the desperate hope that one day I could make you love me."

That's why she hated Ruth. She thought he'd fallen for her. But he'd taken other lovers. He'd spent a year with one of the actresses from the theatre, what was her name? Amelia. Rebecca fired her, sent her off somewhere and that was the end of that. He stopped. Abby's sister's words rang in his ears. *You're an idiot Maximilian Ocel, just like your father.* No wonder she treated him with such scorn, Abby meant the world to her. *God she's right, I am an idiot.*

"Why now? Why are you telling me this now?" he asked.

"It's the end, Metacarpi will fall, the city will die. What have we got left except each other?"

"Why did you never say anything?" he asked.

"What was I supposed to say?" she said. "I can see it in your eyes. You're the son of the Lord of the Carceral Archipelago and I'm just a pain in the arse."

"That's not true," said Max.

"So what is true?" she asked. She sounded so tired. She stood up.

"Ruth's people will wipe out everything we know and love," she said. "They're evil, treacherous and vicious. Surely you can see that now. They won't help us against the dreadnoughts. How long do you think you and I will last in the AntiHelix once we've returned that bitch to her masters?"

She wiped her eyes with the heel of her hand. Blood caked her shirt. A bruise stained her temple and her hair fell in a cloud of tangles. Stunned, he tried to understand his feelings for her. *Now what?* If he stood up, held her in his arms and kissed her what would it mean? He didn't know. It seemed as if the entire singularity beneath him had vanished and he floated in empty space without a single frame of reference. He got to his feet. Abby looked into his eyes. *She's doing it again, she's searching for something in my face, and now I know what she's looking for.* He tried to gather his thoughts and looked beyond her at the distant landscape.

"God almighty," he said.

The inner side of the defensive wall sloped into a wilderness of concrete speckled with pools of water. On either side the battlements curved away into the distance, the walls of an amphitheatre a thousand miles across. Ahead lay a bank of mist. Above this rose the spires; shards of stone and metal lifting above the atmosphere, their tips plunged into darkness. *They must be a hundred miles high*, thought Max. Abby gasped and grinned despite herself. Max saw the excitement cut through the tiredness and disappointment and briefly felt less guilty. *This is where we belong isn't it? Two spare idiots on their merry way.*

They flew between the towers, passing ten in half an hour. One lay in ruins, its debris forming mountains between the remaining spires. Max couldn't see any doors or windows. They just looked like blades of stone banded with strips of metal half a mile wide. They made him think of the copper blades that ringed the dynamos on their ship. *Is this the weapon?* If so, what did it do? How could it help Metacarpi? These towering vanes were rooted in the concrete plain, they clearly couldn't move. Abby grabbed his arm and pointed. In the past he'd have thought nothing of it, but now the touch of her fingers made him jump.

A second wall appeared in front of them, punctuated by an archway and capped by the ruins of innumerable stone towers. To Max they looked like more ancient defences. The *Zephyr*'s autopilot guided the ship into a tunnel. Its roof curved a mile above their heads. The bottom sloped upwards and when they emerged on the other side of the battlements he saw the floor of the passageway formed a ramp rising towards a cylinder standing in the centre of an arena. The slope ended at a set of doors taller than the Carceral Archipelago. He looked at Abby.

"This is the place," she said, but he saw the doubt in her face.

"Are you sure you didn't make a mistake?" he asked, struggling to keep the disappointment out of his voice. The citadel didn't look like it housed the room of his childhood, though it did look a fitting location for a weapon.

"I checked and checked again," Abby insisted. "When you were two years old your mother flew here from the Carceral Archipelago once a month for almost a year. It's in her Charge Log."

They landed on the ramp a mile away from the structure. Through binoculars Max saw a featureless stone cylinder without windows or any other doors. Nothing moved on the plain around them. Behind, the blades rose into Trans-Atmospheric space. Silence reigned, apart from the hissing of a faint breeze over the concrete. Despite Abby's assurances it looked to Max as though no-one had set foot here for thousands of years. He scanned the arena, its walls and the distant blades beyond, trying to understand what it meant. *Nothing, just more incomprehensible junk left over from the Great Task.*

"Let's take her up," he said.

They stopped again at the foot of the doors. They were fashioned of a dark metal Max didn't recognise. He couldn't see any way to open them, or to communicate with whoever or whatever lurked inside the citadel. He toyed with the idea of using the *Zephyr*'s rear cannon to try and blast a hole in the wall. That's what Abby would do. He glanced at her. She sat cross-legged on the floor, leafing slowly through the Charge Log. *She thinks she's made a mistake, let me down.* She looked so unhappy he couldn't find it in his heart to be angry with her.

"Let's scout the cylinder, see if there's another entrance," he suggested.

They found nothing. The smooth walls rose out of the concrete without a break. The ramp and the titanic doors marked the only entrance to the cylinder. They flew over the top. The altimeter showed three and half miles above the singularity and the dynamos strained in the thin air. Night fell, turning the landscape purple as the light faded. They set the *Zephyr* down beside the defensive wall and powered down the engines.

"We'll look again in the morning," said Max as they sat either side of the navigation table, eating straight from a pair of supply cans. Although Abby nodded in reply, her expression was far away, as if he didn't exist any more. In confessing her love for him had she written him out of her life? Was her declaration nothing more than a final cry of desperation in the face of failure? He didn't know what to say. Forget the room and his father's stupid wonder weapon. He wanted the old Abby back, but his own feelings were a jumble and the idea of taking a step he couldn't retract terrified him. Without the usual jokes, the mad banter and the sarcasm the meal became a miserable ordeal. In the end he couldn't bear the tension and the unsaid accusations any longer so he found another can and took it to Ruth.

She sat on the bed in the dark looking through the porthole at the citadel. He gave her the food and sat down on a stool in the corner. He rested a revolver on his knee, its muzzle in the girl's direction, and turned up the lamp. He wanted to make sure he could see her. She looked as delicate as before, large eyes watched him from a face so slender and pointed it made her look like the ghost of a predatory animal. His chest still hurt every time he breathed.

"Have you found what you came for?" she asked.

"What did you hope to achieve? This flyer needs a crew of two at least. Kill us and you're stranded."

"I want to save my father."

Stubborn as well as cruel, we should dump you here and have done with it.

"Even if we got within a hundred miles of those ships, you're one stupid girl against an army."

Ruth smiled.

"How's your rib?"

And you're insane. Gloat as much as you like but you were still defeated by two scruffy peasants.

"OK then. Tell me how you'd rescue your father," he said. She paused and he saw hope in her gaze, just for a second. She mastered it well and started to eat.

"Get me on board, that's all I need," she said between mouthfuls, "the *Beatrice* is riddled with hidden paths. If I can get to the Iron Core I can release my father."

Hidden Paths, like the Shadows. Every tyrant's got them.

"What's the Iron Core?" he asked.

"A fortress within a fortress, completely separate from the rest of the ship. It's a self-contained command centre and refuge for a fleet's supreme commander. It has enough supplies to last a month," said Ruth.

She leant forward as eagerness got the better of her.

"There are loyal people on both ships, I know. If I can get my father out we can retake the *Beatrice*," she said.

"I'm sure you can," said Max, "but how do we get you onto the ship in the first place? They'll blow us out of the sky. Even if we did get past, and the only way would be if they captured us, you'd be walking straight into the arms of the enemy."

"If you're small enough there are ways," said Ruth.

"Well neither I nor this ship qualify as small," said Max. The idea was ludicrous and after her performance on the forward deck there was no way he'd trust her. Something caught his eye. He looked out of the porthole. Halfway up the cylinder an orange light shone in the gloom.

CHAPTER THIRTEEN

THEY MUST HAVE missed it the first time they circled the tower. The fight with Ruth and Abby's confession had rattled Max and he'd lost focus. He cursed himself as the *Zephyr* drifted up towards the light. He'd locked Ruth in her cabin just in case she tried to take over the ship again. He and Abby each stuck two revolvers in their belts and placed loaded carbines on the floor at their feet.

Max soon realised why they hadn't spotted anything during their first pass. The light came from an indentation in the side of the cylinder. From below it blended into the featureless surface. Now, as the ship drew level, he saw a flat space dozens of yards across with a structure set against the inner wall. Abby angled the *Zephyr* so its own lamps shone towards it. If anyone objected to their presence, they'd know soon enough. Nothing moved. They set the ship down and Max clambered down the ladder. Abby made to follow. He stopped her.

"Keep an eye on Ruth," he said.

"What? To hell with that. I'm coming with you."

"No," he said. Her eyes filled with tears. He saw the hurt in her face and felt wretched. They always faced danger together. Forcing her back on board felt like another betrayal, but Max had to do it. He'd seen echoes of his past in those shapes, in the wood and glass lit by a single orange lantern set above a door. He stood on the threshold of a discovery he wanted to face alone.

"I know this place," was all he could say, his voice shaking. "I know this place."

Abby turned without a word and scrambled back up the ladder. *God help Ruth if she tries anything now.*

He stood in front of a single story building. He unhooked the lantern from the arch above the entrance and tried the handle. The door swung inwards. He couldn't see inside. He called out, but no-one answered. He stepped over the threshold.

The first room looked like a chandler's office, with desks set against the walls beneath shelves and cases of equipment for a flyer; lanterns, rope, tools, a stack of supply tins, bulbs and radio valves, replacement gears and fuses for dynamos. He searched for anything that might give him a clue to the nature of the cylinder, but found nothing but a quartermaster's ledger and books of circuit diagrams for a ship. A cursory glance told him it was the *Zephyr*. Realisation hit him, this must be the place his father and Odilon had visited. His heart pounded. That meant the weapon they planned to use in the defence of Metacarpi had to be nearby, probably inside the citadel itself. But Abby also swore his mother came here all those years ago. Did that mean a link existed after all, between her project and his father's dangerous secret? He thought of his mother. She hadn't made weapons, she'd played with her son and a pale stranger, and annotated poems with naive comments on the nature of love and kindness. None of that would be much use against a fleet of dreadnoughts.

He entered the next room and almost dropped the lamp. It looked like the parlour of a town house. Four chairs surrounded a dining table. A long sofa faced an empty stove. It was everything the Carceral Archipelago wasn't; homely and inviting, and yet he saw echoes of his father everywhere. A coat hung from a hat stand, an empty beer bottle sat next to a pewter mug. But he noticed signs of someone else, the same woman's touch he'd seen in Herman's bedroom. A guitar leaned against a corner. Had his mother played? He searched his memory, but heard no music. A black fan lay on a small table. He picked it up, opened it and breathed in, searching for a scent. Nothing. Another door lay ahead. He lifted up the lamp and in the corner of his eye saw the spark of its reflection in a framed photograph above the stove.

His father and mother stood side by side. Herman looked stiff as a door and he had one hand thrust into his waistcoat but, God almighty, he smiled with the easy happiness of a man in love. His mother also faced the camera, even more beautiful than his memories or the portrait on the dining room wall in the tower; beautiful because she was less perfect than either and infinitely more real. Max gasped like a man who'd just escaped drowning. He wanted to sit down and study the photograph, drink in the image of a family he'd never known - not least because of the toddler who stood between the adults, his hands grasped in theirs. But another door waited and he knew what lay on the other side.

Darkness. He didn't want to look around; too much too soon. He busied himself with the fireplace, stacking coal with trembling hands. After a while the fire burned, spitting embers onto the thick rug. He knelt down and ran his fingers over the pile, remembering the feel of the wool. Toys lay scattered on the floor, wooden animals with pegs, and next to the grate he saw a board with shapes cut out. He could scarcely breathe, he thought he was going to pass out.

Max looked up. Exactly as he remembered it, as he'd seen it in the giant's house, but the clarity of detail hurt his mind. With surprise he saw that from where he knelt everything looked right. *Of course, my memories are those of a toddler, and so it all towers over me.* He closed his eyes and breathed in deeply, could he sense faint perfume?

"Max?"

He looked up. Mother stood in front of him, wearing the same smile he'd seen in the photograph.

"You found it, you're so clever," she said.

"What happens now?" he asked.

She knelt down and gathered the wooden animals together.

"We're going to play a game," she said and his heart filled with joy, "look, someone's here to see you."

The man stepped out of the corridor. *You're not my father*, thought Max, *or my mother's lover. Who are you?* The newcomer looked terrified, large eyes stared at him from a pale face. He wore a badly-fitting black suit, and his fingers plucked at the sleeves. Hair so blond it was almost white fell over his shoulders. Something about him frightened Max and he reached out to his mother. *I have a baby's hand again*, he thought, *is this a dream?* His mother took his fingers and kissed them reassuringly. Gathering her dress around her she knelt beside him and set out the game, putting the animals in a ring around the board. The man sat cross-legged on the carpet opposite. *He looks more frightened than me.*

"Max, you go first," said his mother.

He picked up the dice and rolled it.

"A sheep, where's the sheep Max?" Max found the wooden animal and slotted it into the hole on the board. He laughed and clapped his hands. The white-haired man gave a shout of alarm and scrabbled backwards across the floor. Startled by his reaction, Max began to cry. His mother gathered him in her arms and soothed him. He couldn't begin to describe the feel of her touch on his brow.

"It's alright, it's alright," she whispered, before turning to the man, "Max was happy," she said. The stranger listened to her with wide eyes, "and so he laughed. But then you surprised him, and that made him scared. That's why he's crying, but soon he will be comforted."

Deep inside the toddler, Max the raggedy scavenger tried to make sense of what happened. Why were they playing a game with a man who acted like a child himself? He looked at his hands and saw the scarred fingers of an adult. He glanced up and the newcomer had vanished, but his mother still knelt beside him. She looked intently into his eyes.

"Is this how it was Max? Is this what used to happen?" she asked.

"I think so," he replied, struggling with his memories, "but who is he?"

He opened his eyes. Abby stood in front of him, her expression anxious. Beyond her the room was empty.

"Bad dreams?" she asked. *Why aren't you on the ship?*

"I waited for hours," she said, "I started to worry. I found you here in a trance again, like in the giant's house."

I only slept for a few minutes. He looked at the fire and with a jolt saw the cold grate.

"This is the room in the giant's house. The monster used my memories to build it, and to show me my mother. She brought me here as part of an experiment, I think. I used to play children's games with a man. He wasn't right in the head, he acted like a lunatic or a simpleton." It sounded so ridiculous, so trivial. His mother cured the mentally ill? Was that the great mystery? Why here? Why did the giant choose this place out of all of his memories?

"Max?" said Abby in a choked voice. She stood next to a doll's house. Four windows, all different and a single door that opened onto darkness.

"It's the giant's house," whispered Abby. "It built that from your mind as well."

"It's trying to tell me something," said Max, "it's not just a monster from a wormhole."

He saw the entrance to the corridor. He drew his revolver and picked up the lamp. As the shadows moved across the room he had the brief impression of a man standing just inside the passageway, but when they approached they found no-one. *Imagination, stirred up by too much mystery.*

The corridor headed into the interior of the cylinder, a featureless tunnel through the stone. Max was disappointed, he'd half expected an astounding revelation. They walked along the passageway. After a few moments Abby put her hand on his arm.

"Listen."

It sounded like the wind, but the air here was still. Perhaps other chambers and tunnels surrounded them. Behind, the room shrank to a square of light no bigger than his thumbnail. Ahead he thought he saw a glint of reflected light. After another quarter of an hour a bulkhead door blocked their way. The wheel refused to budge, even with both their weights behind it. Max lifted the lantern and peered through the panel in the top half. The light barely penetrated the thick glass. He pressed his ear to the metal and heard the ebb and flow of the wind beyond. He realised a vast space lay on the other side of the door.

"We've got explosives on board," said Abby, "that might shift it."

For God's sake Abby, what if the biggest bomb known to man is on the other side?

"If we missed this entrance we might have missed others," he said.

They returned to the room. A new day approached and weak light filtered through the outer door. Max looked around. He'd found the room at last but had no idea why it was here of all places. He guessed his father's secret weapon lay on the other side of the sealed valve, deep in the citadel. What possible connection did it have with his mother and a simpleton scared of toddlers? He'd go through this building inch by inch to find the answer. He knew it was here, the missing piece of information he needed to complete the puzzle. But first he had to find another way into the cylinder.

They climbed into the *Zephyr* and span up the dynamos. Max looked out of the cabin at the wooden buildings, so flimsy and out of place in the shadow of the wall. He guessed the fortress must be at least a thousand years old. Those vanes reaching into space were far beyond the capabilities of anyone still alive. His father must have added the cabin when he and Odilon found their super weapon. Max seethed with growing impatience. The lack of any answers maddened him. If he couldn't find another entrance he'd return to Metacarpi and demand the truth from the old bastard. He didn't care what danger his father thought he was in. He signalled for Abby to take off.

A shadow sped over the stone in front of the ship, followed by a line of ragged holes. The house blew apart in a shower of glass and wood. Stunned, Max watched an iron beam spin lazily towards him through a cloud of smoke. It clipped the forward rail with a loud clang and flew over the bridge, bouncing off the roof.

If that'd hit me, I'd be dead. Instinct kicked in, he slammed the ship into reverse, trying to swing the nose around. The *Zephyr* was fast, but it manoeuvred like a brick. He heard the copper bottom scraping along the stone.

"Where is it?" screamed Abby above the din. The ship sped forward in a cloud of blue light as arcs from its engines played across the ground. They shot over the edge of the shelf and plummeted in a nose-dive towards the amphitheatre floor. Max yanked back on the flight controls, pulling her up just a few yards from the ground. *What did that woman on top of the tower say? This ship needs a crew of six and there's only two of us.* They could barely point her in a straight line and speed her up or slow her down, but now they were under attack, with no-one on the cannon. Max swore viciously.

After a few heart-stopping seconds of cursing and hitting levers Abby managed to line the ship up with the tunnel in the defensive wall. She opened the dynamos and weaved the ship from side to side as they raced away from the cylinder. Max heard a sound like gravel thrown at a metal plate and half a dozen holes opened up in the deck, each as large as his fist. Panic gripped him. A couple more salvos like that would finish them off.

Leaving Abby wrestling with the steering he stuck his head out of the cabin and scanned the sky. There, about a mile away, floating in an arc between two of the immense towers. He'd expected a warship of some kind, but instead he saw a rust-coloured cube. It turned towards them. *God, it's as big as a house.* He could make out a horizontal slit above a grill. Lights sparkled and a few seconds later gouts of dust threw chunks of stone into the air to their left. The shell holes raced towards them but Abby swung the *Zephyr* into a hard turn and the salvo passed behind.

The tunnel closed over them and to Max's relief the cube didn't follow, though he knew it'd be waiting on the other side.

"It's got to be the old defence system," he shouted as he joined Abby at the controls, "we'll have to outrun it."

Max cursed. The flyer needed both of them at the helm, neither of them could manoeuvre this pile of crap by themselves. With Ruth locked in her cabin there was no-one to man the gun. In any case it would be sheer madness to put a cannon in her hands after her attempt at mutiny. For all its speed and beauty, the *Zephyr* would end up being the death of them.

Abby lowered her head, her eyes fixed on the daylight ahead. The *Zephyr* emerged on the other side of the wall. A volley cut straight through the middle of the ship. It lurched beneath them. Together they managed to right the ship before it slammed into the side of a wheeled fortress. Through the window Max saw the iron box speeding towards them. *We're directly in its line of sight.* He heard a rhythmic chatter above the shrieking dynamos and the enemy tilted away, weaving to avoid a line of tracers arcing towards it from the back of their own vessel. *What the fuck?* Flashes of light erupted where the shells struck the cube. Somehow Ruth had escaped and now she returned fire at a murderous rate. She was worryingly good, every shot thumped into the side of the enemy vessel and Max saw it shudder under the impact. He doubted they'd do much damage, but it might buy them enough time to outrun their attacker.

They hurtled over the Forbidden Sea. Another line of shells kicked up fountains of water around the stern and the *Zephyr* faltered. Miraculously the engines continued to shriek and a few seconds later Max heard their own gun hammering a reply. Ruth still lived. He thought of the helpless waif act in the Carceral Archipelago and couldn't help smiling.

"I don't know how long we can keep this up," yelled Abby. Red lights flickered on her console. Max heard no shots for several minutes so he left her at the helm and made his way to the rear deck, clambering through the wrecked interior. The shells had ripped through the cabins and he could see purple sky through the ruined ceiling. Jagged holes ended at Ruth's door. It hung from the frame in a tangle of wood and metal. *That's how she escaped.*

He pulled out his revolver. The cannon's arc of fire lay to the rear of the vessel, Ruth couldn't aim in his direction but she was deadly enough unarmed. The splintered chaos around him gave plenty of opportunity for ambush. He realised he'd no choice but to shoot the minute she popped out of the shadows. He crept forward. There was no sign of her. He emerged onto the rear deck and gasped in shock. The stern ended in a ragged mess of iron and wood. A trail of black smoke from an internal fire drifted in their wake. Ruth sat on the cannon saddle, naked from the waist up and caked in soot and dried blood. He walked slowly forwards, gun trained on her head. She watched him with amusement.

"We're outracing it," she said, her voice matter of fact. Max wondered if all the women of the AntiHelix were as steel-hearted as this. He admired calmness in the face of death but this seemed inhuman. He felt a wreck and put one hand on the back of her seat so his shakes weren't too obvious. He risked a glance back across the sea. The cube no longer swept from side to side but followed them in a straight line. They'd dropped out of range of its guns, but it looked a remorseless bastard and Max guessed it'd follow them to the Ear if it had to.

"Is that one of yours?" he asked.

Ruth laughed.

"No, our ship design is a bit more sophisticated," she said.

"It must be from the fortress defences. A machine mind's controlling it," said Max. If so they were in trouble. Machines didn't give up.

"No it's not," said Ruth, "a living creature's flying that thing."

Max absorbed her words. It couldn't be guards from the Carceral Archipelago. He was flying his father's ship and they wouldn't open fire on it. Who else would want them dead? He shuddered, remembering the seething cloud of petals on the chain above Metacarpi.

"It's a Black Rose," he said, rubbing his hand over the bandage covering his wound. Ruth looked at him as if he'd gone mad.

"One of the bastards stuck me the other night," he added ruefully.

"Well, whatever it is we're down to our last case of shells and it outguns us. If it catches up it'll destroy this ship in seconds."

Max watched the pursuing craft. It still followed them, but was noticeably smaller. *Better not let it catch us then.*

"Now what do we do?" asked Ruth.

He looked at her sitting half naked in rags on the gunner's seat. He couldn't lock her up, the cabins were wrecked, and they might need her on the cannon again. Abby wouldn't like it but he had no option but to trust her. He couldn't stand pointing a gun at her for the rest of the journey.

"Come anywhere near the bridge and I'll shoot you," he said.

"Of course Max," she said softly, "whatever you say."

They flew north across the Forbidden Sea. Abby grew anxious about the power left in the capacitors and slowed the *Zephyr*, but the box gained on them. They had no choice but to keep heading north at maximum speed. If they returned to Metacarpi they'd drag the other ships into a firefight the town's defences could ill-afford. Max decided they'd have to lose it in the Wasteland.

They crossed the shore at nightfall, their pursuer now nothing more than a speck far to the south. Max watched it through binoculars. Did it contain a Black Rose? What in the name of God did the aliens want with him? A few days ago he thought of them as creatures from story books and legends, mankind's guardian angels bestowing one last chance of survival on the human race. He remembered the performers tumbling over the audience in the Theatre of Angels, the actor falling from the chain just before the alien tried to kill him. *We're just a little town next to the left thumb of God, what do you want with us, with me?*

They took it in turns at the controls. When Max took food to the stern Ruth offered to help but Abby still didn't trust her, and so it was just the two of them. Exhaustion hit them both and Max realised they couldn't carry on for much longer. Once in a while he saw tears running down Abby's cheeks. *We're all worn out, teetering on the edge of collapse.* They needed rest and food. *God only knows what state this ship's in.* At this speed he reckoned they'd be deep into the Wasteland by morning. He racked his brains, trying to remember what lay out there. He knew a few open wormholes, but whether they led to useful worlds or not he couldn't tell. He hadn't been out this way in years. He prayed that the ship needed nothing more esoteric that copper wiring and a bunch of nails. Other than that, all he wanted right now was food and a place to sleep. Abby's head nodded forward. He put his arm across her shoulder and she woke with a snap.

"I'll take over," he said.

She paused and closed her eyes again. He drew her closer and she rested her head on his chest. He smelled smoke in her hair. She clutched at his shirt, balling the material into a fist. It amazed Max how natural this felt, how right. Abby slowly pushed herself away, wiping her face with her sleeve. She left the room without a word, picking her way over the debris littering the floor of the bridge. It took Max five minutes to remember he was supposed to be flying the ship.

CHAPTER FOURTEEN

IN THE MORNING Max couldn't see the iron box. Just to make sure he slowed the *Zephyr*. After an hour the sky behind remained empty. He'd no idea where they were, but guessed they flew far north of Metacarpi. The ship hummed over forests of massive girders set in concrete, scattered wheels the size of the Carceral Archipelago, trenches stretching for hundreds of miles in serried rows. Mile high sheets of mesh, canted at odd angles, lay scattered across the landscape. Wheels poked out of the ground, their spokes draped with chains and hawsers. Always the Thumb lay on their left, cutting the sky in half. Max went on a hunt for maps but found the chart room a shattered mess. They'd have to keep going and hope they ran into a wormhole, or at least a place to shelter. When Abby came up from the engine room she looked grim.

"We're an inch away from blowing apart."

Max could barely stand. He tried to concentrate on the meaningless chaos of shadows ahead; red land, purple sky, fragments and debris. Abby coaxed his hands away from the console. Too tired to walk he slumped down against the wall.

"What do you think's in that cylinder?" she asked, taking over the controls.

Max shrugged.

"It's the weapon my father and Odilon plan to use against the fleet. God knows where it's from . . . maybe a wormhole, a long-dead planet, an ancient war. They're not sure they can control it. I don't understand why my mother took me there. Why bring a toddler to a weapon silo to meet a mad man?"

He saw Abby peering intently out of the cracked window. Max managed to get to his feet. In the distance a cluster of buildings emerged from the haze. Warehouses, and that meant a wormhole.

The storage silos spiralled out in concentric rings. The shaft sat beneath a domed building at the centre. They landed outside. Max fetched Ruth and the three of them disembarked. The damage to the *Zephyr* horrified Max. *How in God's name did we stay aloft*? Shell holes peppered the hull, several leaked oil and smoke. A third of the stern had gone. He doubted they'd ever get the ship into the air again. Abby scribbled down a list of materials they needed for the urgent repairs, but he could see his own worry mirrored in her face.

They didn't bother hunting through the warehouses. Max knew they'd been stripped bare centuries ago. They headed straight for the mouth of the wormhole. One of the immense doors stood ajar. They squeezed through the gap into a cavernous hall. Max looked around, trying to gauge how long ago since the last Time Scavengers abandoned this shaft. The more recent, the better the chance its stairs might still be intact. Light filtered down from high windows. *That's good, there's glass up there*, he thought. That put the installation within the last hundred years or so. Rail tracks for supply wagons ended at buffers halfway along the hall. The entrance itself lay in the centre, covered by a lid fifty yards from side to side. Rust sealed it to the floor.

Max rubbed his hands, some of his old energy returning. This felt like familiar territory. He and Abby could plunder the distant past in their sleep. He even saw a hint of the mad grin on her face as they walked across the floor. Max spotted Ruth lagging behind. She looked nervous. *She's not putting on that helpless princess act again, is she?* he thought with a burst of irritation. *You're surely not thinking of staying behind and stealing the ship?*

"I've never been in a wormhole," she said. Max realised he was seeing real fear.

"We're not leaving you on the ship," snapped Abby. She gave Max a *you're kidding me* look.

"You'll be OK," said Max. "If you can look down at the floor of the universe from God's ear hole, you can cope with this."

They found an office in the corner of the hall. He and Abby started to pull the room apart.

"What are you looking for?" asked Ruth.

"The catalogue," said Max. "Every wormhole's got one. It lists all the explored worlds, what they contain, what the dangers are."

"Found it," called Abby. The previous occupants had etched it on a steel wall along an access corridor. Max saw steps at the end, leading down to the shaft itself. He started to run his fingers along the list, mouthing the names as he went.

"Are each of these worlds?" asked Ruth. The wonder in her voice surprised Max. He kept forgetting she'd spent most of her life in Trans-Atmospheric space, thousands of miles above the singularity.

"Uh huh," he answered, "most are worlds, some aren't, but we tend to avoid those." Abby gave a short laugh. She sounded more like her old self. A surge of affection caught him by surprise. *Is that love*? He didn't know.

"How far down does it go?" asked Ruth.

"Nine-hundred and twenty-six levels mapped, four thousand doors," said Abby from the end of the list.

"God," whispered Ruth in awe. It was Max's turn to laugh.

"It's a small one."

"Got it," shouted Abby. She pointed at two names. "Spares for the ship, and there's one of our temples here. We can get food."

"Temples?" asked Ruth.

"On some of the older worlds we're divine beings," explained Max. "Secret cults worship us. We turn up and they give us offerings. That way we don't have to fight for what we want."

The stairs zigzagged back and forth to the wormhole. They stepped onto a landing above a square brick-lined shaft. The steps continued, hugging the side as they dropped into the past. Ruth leaned over the rail and looked down. Despite himself Max grinned at the disappointment on her face.

"What did you expect, a vault of stars?" he asked.

The walls dwindled into a single point far below. The glowing mist that filled all wormholes cast a uniform light. It looked to Max as though the pit had no depth at all, and they stood over a geometric pattern painted on the floor.

"It's infinite?" asked Ruth.

Abby nodded.

"If you fell into that you'd fall forever," she said with disturbing relish in her voice. Max could almost hear the thoughts running through her head. If Ruth caught any hint of menace in the other woman's words she chose to ignore it.

"And this staircase goes all the way down, with millions of doors to ancient worlds?"

"Yes," answered Abby. "Odilon told me the Black Roses built these using alien mathematics."

"Come on, we're wasting time," said Max. The mention of the Black Roses reminded him of the iron cube.

They continued their descent. The mist thickened around them. Faint sounds filled the air. Max couldn't tell whether they came from the myriad tunnels leading from the stairs or somewhere deep in the wormhole itself. He remembered the tales of escaped creatures making their way up the shafts, and shuddered. They passed by a hundred tunnel mouths before Abby left the steps and disappeared into a stone passageway. Ten minutes walking brought them to a plasterboard door covered in peeling yellow paint. Abby and Max took out their guns.

They stepped into a white room with a bunk bed in one corner and a stack of plastic boxes by the entrance. Arches leading to a balcony punctuated the opposite wall. Beyond, a blue sky spilled light across the cracked whitewash and orange carpet. To their left a door opened onto a corridor stretching away into infinity. Ruth gasped as she followed them into the room.

Max checked how long they had. He held his hand up to the light, looking for any haze coming from his fingers. *Nothing. Good.* He rubbed his palms together. They tingled more than usual, but not too strongly.

"What are you doing?" asked Ruth.

"The further back in time we go the more the universe is saturated with energy," explained Max. "In our age there's almost no energy left. Here we're like ice cubes in tea. We melt. Our atoms start to unravel, so we can only stay a short time. I'm guessing this world is just over a billion years ago, so we could live here for days."

"This looks like a hotel," said Abby. "I could murder a bath." Max shook his head. Abby had no concept of place. She could be in the middle of an all-out battle and still act like it was Saturday afternoon in a park, cheerfully wandering off during a lull in the fighting to grab a coffee or take a nap.

"We haven't time," said Max, "that ship could still be hunting us."

Abby swore. She walked over to the other side of the room and stepped onto the balcony. Max followed. He couldn't see any land beyond. He guessed they were in a high building. He peered over the parapet, then jerked back, the walls around him reeling as he fought the vertigo. Every frame of reference had been pulled out of his mind and he felt he was falling. Up, down? He'd no idea. He knelt down on the carpet until he'd recovered, then stood up again and forced himself to look over the edge. Abby watched him with an infuriatingly smug expression.

The section of the building they stood in projected over sky that stretched around them, as blue below as it was above. Max saw lines of cloud, like ribs, dwindling away on all sides. White rectangles floated in the abyss, each as big as an island. With a shock he realised they were studded with buildings of white stone, silver and glass. Some of the sheets floated close together, the roofs of their houses passing within a few yards of each other. The mere thought of living in one of those buildings gave him the shivers. Other rectangles lay scattered at different angles throughout the sky. Max tried to count them, but there were too many.

The terrifying scene repeated itself above. Max saw, with a gut-wrenching feeling of vertigo, two of the islands collide. The corner of one plane sheared through the buildings of the other, crumpling them like eggshells. Motes of silver buzzed between the sheets as debris broke away and drifted through the air in a halo.

Is this a war? Max flinched, expecting the rubble to cascade down upon them, but the shards stayed clustered around the broken cities.

"Forget the bath," murmured Abby, looking up at the battle. "Let's find the stuff we need."

They left the balcony and turned into the corridor. After half an hour they came to the first of many doors set in the wall to their right. Max opened it onto a cubicle with two white curved chairs and a window that showed nothing outside save for more sky. They continued along the passageway, looking into rooms at random. Every one had exactly the same chairs and window. The monotony and the endless doors woke disturbing memories in Max's mind. To him it looked like a negative image of the corridor in the giant's house. He fought the urge to run back to the landing and the wormhole shaft.

After another hour they came to a crossroads.

"This is a waste of time," said Ruth.

"Really?" said Abby scathingly.

Max forced himself to open yet another door. To his surprise he saw rows of shelves stretching into the distance, piled high with plastic cartons, boxes and barrels. In one wall windows opened onto more rooms. *Are those operating theatres?* Walls of pristine metal and plastic reminded him of the Steel Room in the Carceral Archipelago. *Perhaps not.*

"Perfect," said Abby. She planted a kiss on his cheek.

They collected a stack of boxes and eventually Abby said she'd enough materials to keep the *Zephyr* airborne a little longer. Max was glad to leave. Despite the unearthly quiet and the absence of any life, the memory of those floating cities ripping each other to shreds lurked in the back of his mind. Besides, they still needed food, and he couldn't see any in this sterile world. That meant journeying deeper into the wormhole.

They piled the boxes on the landing outside the door and continued their descent.

"This one's older, much older," said Abby, keeping her voice low so that Ruth wouldn't hear her. "An hour or two, maximum."

"Let's leave her on the stairs," said Max. He and Abby had spent years exploring wormhole doors. He knew what to expect. Dropping Ruth into the furnace of deep time would be too cruel.

"I'm not letting that treacherous little whore out of my sight," muttered Abby.

"I'm coming with you," said Ruth loudly behind them, "wherever you go, I go."

"Fine," said Abby, with evil relish, "we're here."

They walked down a muddy corridor. After a hundred yards it ended in a curtain. Behind that they passed another filthy drape, and then another. Max counted twenty before he sensed a warm breeze drifting under the edges. Sounds filtered through the weave; the babble of voices, the soughing of wind over sand. Were those cymbals in the distance? They emerged in a room with adobe walls and a floor covered in rushes. A fierce beam of light poured through a high window. The air was thick and heavy. Every detail in the surfaces around him abraded Max's senses. This was deep time. They would die in hours if they lingered.

A rug covered the opposite door. It moved aside and a young woman stepped through. Beyond her the light shone so fiercely Max flinched and turned his face away. Ruth gave an involuntary cry of pain. Through watering eyes Max saw the girl wore nothing but a linen skirt and a necklace of oyster shells. She'd shaved half her head and a thin plait of black hair hung from the other side down to her hip. Max reckoned she looked about sixteen. Her skinny rib cage rose and fell rapidly but she mastered her fear with a courage that impressed him. Like everything else on this world the girl's skin shone with a radiance that made her whole body shimmer like an image painted onto silver. He stepped towards her. She placed her fingers on his chest. Max winced and stumbled back. It felt as if she'd thumped him with a red-hot hammer. She smiled and disappeared outside.

"She looks just like us," said Ruth in wonder.

"If it's monsters you're after, I'll take you to monsters," muttered Abby. She doubled over with her hands on her knees, trying hard not to be sick.

They waited. The intense heat and constant susurration from outside scraped at Max's nerves. Ruth's face turned grey. She looked terrified. The air around each of them shimmered. *We're dissolving*, thought Max, *we can't stay here, we'll die.*

At last the girl returned with a woven basket and a jug. Max took them. He looked around. Everything blurred. He couldn't see his companions. He looked intently at the girl, trying to piece together words in his exhausted mind. She crossed her hands on her breasts and bowed. *I'm a divine spirit*, he thought, *I can't pass out.* Somehow he made his way back through the corridor. He found Ruth and Abby on the landing. Ruth leaned over the banister, her head between her hands. Vomit spattered the edge of the stairs. Abby sat on the stairs, panting heavily.

"Too ancient," Max said.

They shouldn't have gone in there, a few more minutes and they'd be dead on the muddy floor of the temple. Some gods.

"What did we get?" asked Abby.

He looked in the basket and grinned despite the pain and dizziness.

"Pomegranate seeds," he said, holding up a leather pouch. Abby held her hand out but he shook his head.

"Not yet, you'll be over the rail if you have one here." He tucked the bag into his back pocket. "Wait till we get to the top."

"Come on Max, it's going to take hours," pleaded Abby. He shook his head. She gave him a look of weary disgust and climbed back up the stairs.

"What seeds?" asked Ruth.

"Pomegranate seeds. It's an old scavenger secret. Think how much energy filled the universe billions of years ago," said Max. "Think how much is packed into just one of these seeds. One will keep you alive for a week, two and your head explodes."

His partner clumped up the stairs ahead, eyes on her boots.

"They can send you mad, we can't eat them here, too risky." said Max.

The return climb took forever. Ruth stumbled a few times and Max had to grab her in case she went over the rail. The boxes from the landing of the white cities felt twice as heavy as before. Max toyed with the idea of trying another door, finding a world close enough in time so they could rest without falling ill. Memories of beautiful landscapes he'd visited plagued him; beaches of white sand, the cozy warrens of abandoned monasteries, meadows of alien flowers. He resisted temptation. That iron box might still be following them. They needed to fix up the *Zephyr* and move on. Returning to the mysterious cylinder or Metacarpi was out of the question. They had to push on north.

He halted yet again to catch his breath. Ruth stood below him on the step.

"What would be the chances of your father stopping the fleet if we freed him?" he asked. Hope flared in her eyes again.

"There are people still loyal," she said, "but the brave ones died fighting and the others may be too scared. Our best hope is Andagis, captain of the *Geryon*. I can't understand why he fell in with Hathus. He hates him."

Max saw bitterness in her face.

"Hathus may have concocted a tale of treachery, accusing my father, but Andagis wouldn't be fooled. Just get me on the *Beatrice*, Max, I don't care what you do after that."

How? How in God's name could they get close enough to the dreadnoughts? He shook his head and carried on climbing, scenarios playing through his head while Ruth trudged silently behind.

When they got back to the wormhole office Abby raised her hand, signalling them to stop. She crouched down, looking through the cracked glass in the door.

"We've got company," she said, nodding towards the entrance. Max saw the prow of the *Zephyr* in the plaza beyond. A figure with a bulbous, featureless head walked up to the flyer. Another joined it.

Max swore. Why the hell had they stopped? Were these the pilots of the iron box? They looked nothing like the Black Rose that had attacked him on the chain, but they appeared alien enough with those deformed heads. Abby pulled out her gun and cat-stepped through the door. He hissed for her to stop but she ignored him. When would she ever, ever listen? He looked round to tell Ruth to stay while he hauled Abby back inside. With a gut-wrenching lurch of panic he saw she'd also vanished. *She must have gone back into the wormhole, the idiot.* There was no other way out, unless you wanted to spend your last days watching your spirit bleed through your skin in pretty auras.

Cursing all disobedient women past and present Max followed Abby. Another mistake. The instant he stepped into the main hall a voice called for him to freeze and drop his weapon. Five figures padded out of the shadows, slender guns trained on them both. Abby put her hands on her head, Max could see her fingers resting on her poisoned hair pin.

"God's sake Abby, enough is enough," muttered Max, inching next to her. She had an insane look in her eyes. Usually she knew just how far to push her luck, but he could see she was exhausted and emotionally un-strung. She'd get them killed in seconds.

"Don't be pathetic Max, there's only five," she hissed back. In desperation he floundered for something to bring her to her senses.

"I love you," he whispered. Her eyes went wide and her fingers relaxed. "Now put that fucking pin away."

The featureless heads were helmets, sleek and black. One of the figures removed hers to reveal a sharp face surrounded by a torrent of platinum curls. By now Max realised he stood before a pilot from the Empire of the Ear. Of course these were Ruth's people, pale and evil-looking, the red whorl sigil on their uniforms. His mind raced. If the bastards didn't kill them outright here and now did that mean they'd get a chance to go onboard the dreadnoughts? But where was Ruth?

"A ship from an ancient defence mechanism chased us, looks like an iron box," said Abby. "It might still be following."

"Are you alone?" asked the woman who'd taken off her helmet, clearly in charge.

Max nodded. The leader stared into his eyes. Max met her gaze. *God almighty they're all the same*, he thought, *porcelain statues from airless halls*. The woman nodded towards the office and two of her companions headed that way. They wouldn't find Ruth. She had infinity to hide in, but if these troops took he and Abby prisoner she'd be trapped in the middle of the Wasteland, hundreds of miles from anywhere.

The pilots escorted Abby and Max back to the *Zephyr* at gunpoint. Max's jaw dropped when he saw the five ships surrounding his father's flyer. Four were variations on Ruth's machine; bubble-canopied with raked dragonfly wings, only these bore collars fringed with weapons. They reminded Max of the delicate quills used by scribes in the Carceral Archipelago, but he guessed each one could outgun the entire *Zephyr*. The fifth vessel was a squat wedge sitting on three legs, some kind of command ship. Max did a head count. Altogether he saw eight soldiers on the ground. Others moved in the cabin of the larger airship but he couldn't tell how many. *How the hell did they find us*? Was it just a routine patrol scouting ahead of the fleet, or had these flyers come looking for them?

"Can it fly?" asked the leader. Abby told her yes. Max kept thinking about Ruth. Every second he expected to hear the sound of chattering guns. What could he do? If they found her, and these soldiers came from the *Beatrice*, they might even kill her. Should he and Abby run for it? They'd never succeed, they were still too weak from the temple world. These bastards would cut them down without blinking.

"Accompany our fighters. If you try anything, we will blow you out of the sky, am I understood?" the lead pilot said crisply. Abby muttered something under her breath. Max thumped her in the small of the back and she gave the commander an icy grin.

"Perfectly," she said.

The two soldiers returned from the wormhole office.

"Nothing," said one. *They didn't find her*. He tried not to show his relief. Now what? He had a few moments at best to try and help Ruth. Could they leave the *Zephyr* behind, claiming it was wrecked? Then at least she might have a ship she could use. But his father's flagship needed a minimum crew of two. Too late, around them the squad prepared to leave. Before they climbed back on board the guards searched Abby and Max. They took Max's knife and the derringer Abby kept down the back of her pants, though they missed her hairpins. The bastards would take their pomegranate seeds as well. He hoped they'd try a few and die screaming and frothing in their own blood. But when they went through Max's pockets the bag was missing. *The bitch stole it*, he thought, half in admiration, half in anger, *when she stumbled against me on the stairs*. He only hoped she was sitting somewhere quiet and safe when she ate her first seed.

Their captors all looked the same to Max, lithe, arrogant and murderous. Abby must have spotted something in his eye because now it was her turn to shake her head. It wasn't worth it, Ruth wasn't worth it. That's what she was saying. Seething with anger Max returned to the bridge. In a few moments his father's ship rose into the sky while the imperial flyers hovered around it like wasps. Ruth remained in the wormhole, perhaps a billion years in the past, dissolving in a storm of ancient energy, and there was nothing Max could do to help her.

CHAPTER FIFTEEN

TWO FIGHTERS TOOK position in front of the bow of the *Zephyr*. The rest of the ships from the Empire of the Ear followed in their wake. Max and Abby worked the controls. Exhaustion made them automatons. The simplest course corrections took all Max's concentration. He was grateful because it meant he didn't have to think of Ruth, or Abby standing beside him, though he knew it would hit him soon. Ruth could survive in the wormhole, he didn't doubt that, but she'd be stuck there.

They left the warehouses behind and within an hour came to a range of mountains. Peaks like knives rose out of the ground. Max saw they ended far above the atmosphere, their tips glittering in Trans-A space. They reminded him of the blades surrounding the hidden weapon across the Forbidden Sea, but these were ominously different. No-one fashioned these, they'd been kicked up from the singularity when the Black Roses first unrolled it. He saw holes bored deep into the cores of the mountains. They frightened him. They looked too regular and glistening stains the size of rivers marked the slopes below them. He didn't relax until the scouts guided them into a pass and the tunnels disappeared from view.

"Look," said Abby. Max saw a warship hovering at the end of the valley. It looked like a spinning top made out of black metal, ringed with turrets and countless guns pointing in every direction. They had no option but to follow the scouts into its shadow. Max cut the engines and stood next to Abby. She grabbed his hand and he gave her a smile that said *how many times have we been here?* Rope ladders clattered onto the deck outside. In an instant the cabin filled with soldiers in uniforms, training carbines on Abby and Max. Max realised that twice as many guns pointed at his companion as at him. These people weren't stupid, they spotted straight away which one of them was the most dangerous.

An officer stepped through the ranks. Despite his youth a white beard spilled over the front of his uniform and halfway down his chest. To Max's amazement he saluted.

"Maximilian Ocel, I'm Captain Beremud of the Imperial Monitor *Mab* at your service," he said. "I'm afraid I must put you under arrest and escort you back to the *Beatrice*."

So that wasn't a random patrol. You were searching for us. How did you know where to look? Spies in Metacarpi? That Black Rose? His father said enemy agents roamed the city and he'd laughed at the old man's paranoia. The Lord of the Carceral Archipelago was right after all, but what made Metacarpi so important that the Empire of the Ear bothered infiltrating it? Habit? Father always told him power needed to be ever-watchful. The next question took him completely by surprise.

"Where's the Lady Ruth an Vircana?" Of course, if they recognised him then they also knew he'd been taking Ruth back to the AntiHelix. Any thought of sneaking aboard the dreadnoughts and releasing Alaric vanished. They'd never stood a chance.

"We dumped her and the crew of the *Zephyr* on the shores of the Forbidden Sea," said Abby. "It's a long walk back to the city."

The officer glanced at the squad leader who stood nearby, her helmet under her arm.

"We didn't find any sign of her. She might be hiding in the wormhole," she said. Max stifled a sigh of relief. The captain watched him for a few seconds. Max didn't want to know the options running through the man's head. He felt sure the Empire of the Ear had many entertaining ways to extract the truth from liars.

"Send a platoon back and search the area. Put a watch on the wormhole," said Beremud. "Bring these two and destroy their ship."

The soldiers took them on board the monitor. Inside Max saw nothing but shadows, cogs and plate armour, a purely functional war machine. They ended up in a metal cell with a narrow window running from floor to ceiling. Max watched the hills drift past as the monitor lifted out of the valley. He calculated they headed north east. The ship trembled for a second. Max heard the sound of a cannon. In his imagination he saw the *Zephyr* disintegrate as shells from the *Mab*'s guns tore into its copper-sheathed hull. The flagship of the fleet, his father's own personal warship and the quickest flyer Metacarpi could field, gone in an instant.

Max and Abby slumped down on the floor. Max was conscious of her body beside his, her bony elbow pressed into his side and the weight of her head on his shoulder. It felt so strange. They'd probably sat like this countless times before; in bars, after firefights on distant worlds, friends in the grip of exhaustion using each other as handy props, yet now it seemed so new. He held her hand in his and looked at the scar on the back. Where was that from? He remembered an assassin's stiletto nailing her to a door. Despite being pinned to the wood she'd kicked the man in the balls and shot him with the ray gun Max tossed to her across the tavern.

"We'll come out of this, we always do," he whispered into her hair. She didn't hear him, she was fast asleep and snoring.

Max woke to see Abby standing at the window, looking out at a plain mazed with cracks. Beyond her, mountains curved round to form an amphitheatre. In the centre the fissures bled into a canyon. The two dreadnoughts hovered over the gulf like fish floating in a pool of blood.

The images in Odilon's mirrors had been bad enough, but this was far worse. *They're not ships, they're flying cities*, thought Max, *no weapon can stand up to this, my father's mad to even try.* The absence of any sound from their engines made them all the more sinister. His companion didn't say a word, but he could read her thoughts in her face. Crazy, stupidly brave Abby Fabrice wore the expression of a child cowering in a dark corner. *God, I only hope they get everyone out of the city before those monsters turn up.* Had Ruth really thought she could get inside the *Beatrice* and free her father? Lead a counter-insurrection?

"What do we do, Max?" asked Abby in a whisper.

"They know who I am and we're alive for a reason," said Max, not wanting to imagine what that reason might be. He took her face in his hands. She looked like a snotty-nosed urchin, all wide-eyed terror.

"We've been here before," he said.

"No we haven't, not like this."

"Yes we have, they're big ships, that's all," he continued, "just don't do anything stupid."

The *Mab* flew across the plain towards the nearest of the two dreadnoughts. Max guessed it was the *Beatrice*.

Somewhere inside that fortress the deposed Condottiere hid in his Iron Core. Max tried to make out detail but his eye soon tired of endless cannon, gun blisters, weapons pods, observation ports, smoke ejectors, turrets and cupolas. He gave up trying to count them all. Vast wings raked back from the ship's hull, each carrying four engines as big as factories. Now he heard them roaring in the wind. A ship this size scoffed at camouflage, the skin was black striped with silver, except for the tail fins where Max spotted the now-familiar glyph of a stylised ear in red. A few miles behind, the sister ship the *Geryon* lazed over the landscape.

Abby stepped back into the cell when the shadow of the *Beatrice* fell over them. Max held her in his arms as ropes and chains snaked down from the belly of the vessel above. They staggered as the ship rocked from side to side, hurtling up into the darkness. The *Mab* came to a halt. Max heard soldiers and crew clattering along the corridors outside. Silence fell. Abby stepped away and stretched. Max realised she was priming herself, chasing away the fear. She fiddled with the head of her hair pin.

"Don't even think about it," warned Max.

The door to their cell opened and two guards escorted them to the top deck. Max looked around, memorising the layout. Abby did the same, hiding it behind an expression of fearful awe. The *Mab* sat at the opening of a cone that disappeared up into the dreadnought. They stepped onto a walkway curled around the inside of this funnel, lit at intervals by lanterns hanging at calf height. Max could make out figures standing along gantries that ringed the bay, silhouettes brushed with gaslight. Some leaned against the rail and looked down at the monitor.

"Evil looking bastards," muttered Abby. She had a point. They reminded Max of Ruth and her friend Crysanthe. Their faces bore the same stamp of cruel diffidence.

At the top Max and Abby found themselves face to face with a short man in a grey uniform. He had a shock of brown hair and an open, genial expression. To his surprise the man smiled and offered his hand.

"You must be Maximilian Ocel, am I right? And Miss Abigail Fabrice? You are most welcome. This is the Imperial Dreadnought *Beatrice* and I am Captain Hathus, at your service."

It was all he could do to control himself. Some of his shock must have seeped through because Captain Hathus's mouth twitched in a brief smile and a bushy eyebrow went up. Max tried to think of what to say. He stood opposite Ruth's enemy, the man who'd obliterated Abductor and who now bore down on Metacarpi with two invincible battleships. He'd expected a cruel etiolated warrior, all sneers and an unslakable appetite for death. Hathus looked like a fat uncle. He knew what Abby thought, stick the bastard and damn the consequences. He was too stunned to think of intervening if she tried.

"How do you know my name?" asked Abby softly, her voice filled with cold menace. Hathus laughed with pleasant embarrassment.

"We do our homework," he said, tapping the side of his nose like a pantomime cad.

This was surreal, he was speaking to them like guests, not prisoners.

"First of all I must apologise most sincerely," he continued, "as the Commander of the fleet - the most noble and esteemed Condottiere Alaric an Vircana - would have met you in person but is unfortunately indisposed. You'll have to make do with me."

He's mad. What purpose does he think this charade serves? thought Max. Hathus opened his arms with a chuckle.

"But I'll do my best. I'd like to invite you to dinner, where I hope to present you with a delightful surprise." He took Abby's hand and kissed it. Max's first thought was she'd have his arm off at the shoulder if he didn't watch himself.

"I have quarters prepared for you," said Hathus.

Two guards stood behind them with thin-barrelled rifles at the ready. Abby and Max had no choice but to follow the captain up the ramp as it curled around the funnel. Max saw other ships suspended in the blackness. He tried to count them but soon gave up. The daylight faded, leaving only lanterns to light their way.

The inside of the ship reminded Max of the Carceral Archipelago. He walked through a familiar warren of ledgers, whispers and brutality, though it seemed deceptively comfortable compared to his home. He saw mahogany panelling reflecting light from doorways. Men and women in grey and blue uniforms huddled over dials, telephones and radio receivers. In one room he caught a glimpse of a map covering the wall. It showed the eastern length of the Hand, from the Wrist to the fingertips. Max tried to spot Metacarpi but could see nothing in the network of navigation lines spreading out from the Palm. He'd always disliked the city for its lonely introspection, now he regretted its loss of anonymity. Soon it would be very much part of that map, or simply no longer there.

It became clear to Max that Hathus was taking them on a tour designed to impress. He saw the atomic generators; a network of house-sized spheres filled with light. In a room bigger than the Theatre of Angels, banks of accumulators rose on either side in tiers. Hathus gleefully pointed out the delicately sculpted cannon next to portholes, and projecting from clusters of glass and steel blisters attached to the fuselage. To Max it seemed pointlessly theatrical. The ship spoke for itself. Abby on the other hand, took it all in with a convincing expression of round-eyed awe. He dreaded to think what went on in her head. Knowing her she was calculating how easy it would be to wrench one of the weapons from its mount and turn it on its owners.

He looked round for signs of a mutiny. Nothing. Crew scuttled back and forth; purposeful, efficient, speaking in whispers, pausing briefly to salute Hathus. Max watched them closely. Ruth claimed many of the crew had stayed loyal to Alaric, but he saw no resentment in their faces. *Wish fulfilment*, he thought. *Of course she wants to think that everyone's just waiting to return the Condottiere to power. Looks like none of them care. I bet usurpation and treachery's meat and drink to this lot. Even so, it's our only chance to stop the ships, even if it's just the desperate fantasy of his daughter.* While he half listened to Hathus's genial boasting he tried to get a sense of the geography of the interior. Ruth talked about hidden walkways, like the Shadows in the Carceral Archipelago. In boyhood Max had soon developed the knack of spotting ways within ways, secret passages and cunningly hidden alcoves. He started to notice a pattern beyond the main corridors; shadows between lamps concealing a sliding door, or hatches opening onto the gantries that led from the ammunition stores to the turrets. *There's a maze on the other side of those walls*, he thought.

At last Hathus took them to a suite of cabins in the upper levels of the ship. The guards locked the door behind them, leaving Abby and Max alone in a network of rooms. Instinctively they split up and hunted for another exit. Five minutes told them they were prisoners. Max sat on the end of a bed and tried to gather his thoughts. *I'm in the belly of the enemy ship, the one place impossible to reach, but Ruth's not here.* She'd said that once her father was freed from the Iron Core he'd re-take the ship, but how could Max and Abby get to him? They were trapped themselves. Even if they overcame the guards and escaped into the corridors of the *Beatrice* they'd no idea where to find Alaric. This behemoth was as big as a city and filled with enemies. Frustration and anger brought with it a wave of desperate tiredness. He fell back onto the bed and closed his eyes.

He woke with a start when Abby yelled in delight.

"Bath," she said, opening a door onto an iron tub with taps the shape of demon heads. She undressed, dumping her clothes on the floor, the last thing Max needed. He'd seen her naked before - on the few occasions when they took a rest from adventure with a quick jump into an alien sea, or when they found a working shower in the remnants of a godforsaken warehouse out in the Wasteland. But all that came before she told him she loved him. He still couldn't fathom his own feelings. Had the desire he now felt always been there, buried under his own stupidity? Just looking at her gave him an erection and a headache. He saw her freckled back laced with scars, the flare of her hips, her muscled buttocks and thighs tensing as she stretched. Her hair looked as if someone had dropped a grenade in it. It cascaded over her wide shoulders like a red shell burst. He groaned, unable to cope with the sight, put his hand over his eyes and turned away. In a second she'd disappeared and the room filled with the sound of tumbling water.

Abby shook him awake. Two piles of clean uniforms sat on the end of the bed. The bastards came in while he slept and she bathed. Abby panicked, hunting for her hair pins, but Max found them side by side on a shelf along with her old gear, which was still caked in blood and grime. He washed himself and dressed in the cobalt fatigues. They itched. The collar dug into his neck. He hated uniforms anyway, so he put his lizard waistcoat over the shirt. He reached into a scaly pocket and touched something like a tiny pebble. He withdrew his hand and looked at the object sitting in his palm; a pomegranate seed. How in God's name had that found its way into his waistcoat? He'd stowed the pouch in his back pocket and Ruth had stolen it on the wormhole stairs. Realisation dawned on him and he sat down suddenly on the end of the bed.

"What?" asked Abby. He showed her the seed.

"Ruth's on the ship," he said, unable to believe his own words. "Before we boarded the *Zephyr* they searched us, remember? She swopped places with one of the pilots sent to find her and planted this as a sign. If she's aboard we might have a chance of rescuing her father and stopping the fleet."

Abby shrugged.

"They might have found her already," she said. "In any case, I doubt she gives a fig for you or I. I wouldn't bother wasting any more time waiting for her to turn up."

"Just prepare yourself, it doesn't look like it's over yet," he said.

Guards came to lead them through the ship. They seemed to walk for ages down gloomy corridors before finally stopping in front of a pair of doors fashioned from wood the colour of bone. They opened into a dining hall. Max heard Abby gasp. On one side oval windows arched from the ground to the ceiling high above their heads. Outside he could see a jagged wall of mountains. Gauze curtains trailed out across the floor. Max thought they looked like dead women's hair. A table set for a meal stood in the centre. His father, Odilon the Watcher and a man who Max recognised as Theodore, the fleet commander from the City of Metacarpi, sat in three of the chairs, staring back at him.

Max froze. *I've failed you again, Father*, came his first instinctive thought as familiar voices of shame and self-doubt filled his mind. He batted them away, and then realised that the three most important men in Metacarpi sat in front of him, all stiff and pompous with napkins on their knees. If Hathus tossed them out of the window the city would be headless.

Hathus jumped from his seat at the end of the table.

"Honoured guests, forgive this surprise. At the very point we reach an impasse you arrive to save the day. Your father, the Lord of the Carceral Archipelago came yesterday, intending to throw himself at our mercy, bravely seeking to save the City of Metacarpi, but we have inevitably bogged down in the complexities of diplomacy that quite frankly elude me."

Herman watched Hathus, his expression blank. For once Max admired the grim resolve stamped over his father's face. Next to him glowered Theodore, clearly incensed by Hathus's comments. Odilon's plastic face displayed worried solicitude.

Max realised he'd become the joker thrown into the game. *Hathus is using me to make a play*, he thought as he took the seat opposite his father. A servant led Abby to Odilon's side. When she sat down, Max saw the Watcher pat her hand and give her a reassuring wink.

"All those heated words and threats we began with, well, let's start afresh," continued the captain of the *Beutrice*. "But before that, we must eat. I am simply starving."

Concealed doors opened. More crew members emerged and started to serve, spooning soup into bowls. Rich aromas filled the room. Max noticed a young girl in a black dress sitting in the corner of the hall. She held a cello between her knees. Her face looked down and the bow rested unused in her hand. For an instant he thought it was Ruth and almost called out to her, but a second glance told him he was mistaken.

"Tell the guests your name," called Hathus.

"Bryony, my Lord." murmured the girl. It seemed to Max that her voice was filled with sorrow.

"Play some more music for us," said Hathus grandly, "something to aid digestion."

Max saw her wipe away tears with the back of her hand and lifted up the neck of the instrument. The first few notes drifted across the room. *She's here against her will*, Max realised, *she's a prisoner like us*. That made her a potential ally.

"And what is this called?" asked Hathus.

"*The Tomb of Regrets*, my Lord," answered Bryony.

"An interesting choice," said Hathus, nodding approvingly at the tune. Max noticed how the man's eyes lingered on Bryony for a split second before he returned to the food. *He wants her*, thought Max.

"The General's Lieutenant, Crysanthe Uella, is not with the fleet?" asked Herman. Hathus's head bowed over his meal, he slowly took a spoonful of soup.

Father's letting them know we've spoken to the Anti-Helix. He admired the old bastard's nerve.

"The Honourable Crysanthe attends upon our Emperor," said Hathus without looking up. "In these auspicious times it would be a luxury for her to accompany the General."

"These must be auspicious times indeed if the General is bereft of his Lieutenant," said Herman. Hathus looked up, burst out laughing, and rubbed the back of his head.

"I can't do this, gentlemen. I'm a simple pilot," he said. "These diplomatic subtleties are beyond me."

"There are rumours," continued Theodore. Max saw his father wince. The head of the fleet clearly posed a liability. He tried to catch Abby's eye but she looked down at her plate as Odilon whispered in her ear, his hand clamped firmly over hers. He began to realise the Watcher was the only one here he could trust. Herman acted like an inhuman statue and Theodore a blundering idiot. Odilon sailed on like a ship floating serenely through a shoal of battling monsters. If he got out of this alive the first thing he'd do was ask the Watcher about the cylinder and the rooms. Confrontation with his father about the hidden weapon could wait.

"Rumours? Really?" said Hathus.

"Rumours concerning Abductor Pollicis Brevis," continued Theodore, oblivious to the rising tension.

"And they are?" asked Hathus. Theodore finally realised he'd overstepped the mark and dropped his gaze to his plate.

"Rumours aside," said Herman pointedly, "we're delighted to invite you to our city as guests. Compared to the Empire of the Ear we are tiny but would be happy in the knowledge that the Emperor and his servant, the Condottiere Alaric, regarded us as a friend and - for what it's worth - an ally."

Hathus grunted and popped a lump of bread into his mouth.

"As I said, I'm not a diplomat," said the Commander eventually. He leant back in his chair and looked quizzically at Max.

"Where's Ruth an Vircana?" he asked.

CHAPTER SIXTEEN

MAX FELT ALL eyes swivel towards him. *Ruth an Vircana is on this ship, waiting to tear your heart out.* He mastered himself.

"On her way back to Metacarpi in the company of a troop of our elite guards," he said carefully. His father didn't move a muscle, but Max sensed the temperature around the old man dropping several degrees.

"When we arrive at Metacarpi please deliver her to us. She is a scion of a noble house and should be safely cared for," Hathus said, looking across the table. Herman nodded.

"I apologise for my son's careless disregard for her safety," he said. *You didn't see her try and kick my ribs in,* thought Max, but kept his mouth shut.

Hathus grunted, rang his nail against his glass and waited for it to be filled. He sniffed the wine, tasted it and nodded pleasantly at the officer who'd served him. Max noticed a slight shift in the room. Vibrations filtered up through the floor beneath his feet. Hathus rolled up his napkin and dropped it on the table.

"We're moving at last," he said. "This is worth seeing, if you please gentlemen."

He led them to a glass door. Max saw that it opened onto a balcony that ran the length of the room. He felt Abby furtively touch his hand and Odilon gave him a quick *don't worry, we're all going to get out of this* smile. His father sailed past him without even a glance. *No surprises there*, thought Max, *just add another page to that immense book of Max's failures that you keep in your head.* He stepped out of the room and looked over the ornate railing. The hull of the *Beatrice* curved steeply down to the jagged prow several hundred yards below. He shuddered at the sight. The metal landscape below him spoke of nothing but relentless destruction. On either side cannon projected from bearings as big as houses. Inside bubbles of glass men and women checked flickering lights and chattered into speaking tubes. *This isn't a dreadnought, it's a whole damned world, like those metal planets that used to float in space after the real ones died.* In the face of such overwhelming power Hathus seemed to be having some kind of religious epiphany. He gripped the rail with both hands and breathed deeply.

Max looked beyond the ship to where the ring of mountains stamped red shapes on the horizon. As he ran his gaze up the edge of one peak he saw the sky fade to blue, and then to purple where the atmosphere softened the emptiness of space. To his right the wall of the Thumb rose into the darkness, a second landscape resting on its side, the skin a patchwork confusion. Max would have given anything to grab Abby, leap into a ship and flee to the Hand. They would hide forever in the body of God, away from these evil men with their empires and their dreadnoughts. His mind flickered through countless tactical options, running through a catalogue of all the firefights they'd ever been in. He knew Abby did the same but the odds were overwhelming. Better to bide their time and learn more about their captors and their dreadnoughts.

Hathus gave a sigh, turned round and looked at Theodore.

"You asked me about Abductor Pollicis Brevis."

He jerked his head at a guard. Before anyone could react the soldier stepped behind Theodore and ran a dagger across his throat. Max watched in horror as blood poured out of the gash, splattering the man's hands. He held them up, staring at them in confusion as if he'd just spilled soup down his front. The soldier put a foot in the small of Theodore's back and pushed him over the rail. Abby started shouting, but to Max's relief Odilon grabbed her hands and held her fast. The guards moved towards Max and his father. Max crouched ready to fight, calculating the options furiously in his head. Hathus raised a finger and the men paused.

Out of the corner of his eye Max saw Theodore trying to scream as he slid along the hull. All that emerged from the man's ruined throat was a slobbering grunt. His hands slapped at the metal but the trail of gore he left behind him made the iron slick. He gathered speed, his body turning as he fell. His head caught the side of a glass bubble, snapping back in a spray of blood as the weakened ligaments tore. Finally he disappeared, his head flopping back and forth like a puppet's. Sick fury enveloped Max. He wanted nothing more than to leap at Hathus and rip that grin from his face with his hands. Abby yelled her way through a lexicon of abuse. *She's next if she doesn't shut up*, thought Max. Odilon tapped her on the base of her skull with his knuckle. She slumped unconscious in his arms. *He's saved her life.* In the sudden silence he gathered himself, fighting down the terror and the fury, pushing it into a point of focussed courage. *Make it your guide, it always brings you through.* Max turned to his father. Herman's face looked like a mask of stone. He said nothing.

"The Lords of Abductor had this odd idea they possessed weapons from ancient time to match our fleet," said Hathus. "They were sadly mistaken. Take the Lord of the Carceral Archipelago, Odilon the Watcher and Abby Fabrice, give them a flyer and send them back to Metacarpi. When I arrive I expect Ruth an Vircana to be delivered to me in return for my mercy towards the city and its people."

He's going to kill me too, thought Max, battling his desperation. He looked at Abby, unconscious in Odilon's arms. *This is the last time I'll see her*. He had to speak to her, if only to see her search his face with those crazy green eyes once more. His vision blurred. Hathus's next words took him completely by surprise.

"Take Max Ocel back to his room, he's still our honoured guest."

The soldiers looked puzzled. Hathus waved his hands at them like a farmer shooing geese.

"Go on, go on."

They stepped back into the room, the muzzles of the carbines trained on the four of them. Max saw the girl with the cello staring down at the floor. He'd completely forgotten her. Her body shook uncontrollably.

"Bryony," said Hathus. Her knuckles whitened around the neck of the cello. "Thank you. Captain Andagis must be very proud of you."

The guards took him back to the guest quarters. To Max's surprise Hathus hurried after them. He stopped in front of Max and looked into his face. Max stared back. *I'm going to kill you, and slowly. I will visit such horror upon you, you fat shit, that all your arrogant compatriots will look on your remains and flee shrieking back to the AntiHelix forever.* He stopped, puzzled. As Hathus stared into Max's eyes he moved his head from side to side like someone trying to see through a misted window.

"Are you really in there?" said the captain. "Can you hear me?"

218

He's mad, he's completely insane.

"If you're there, I'm so looking forward to meeting you," continued Hathus.

"You're a filthy murderer," said Max, the words tumbling out of him despite his fear. "Why don't you just kill me like you did Theodore and have done with this pantomime?" Hathus looked at Max as if seeing him for the first time. He gave a good-natured laugh.

"I've no intention of killing you," he said, "you're going to help me find a giant."

Before his words had sunk in the guards pushed Max through the door and locked it behind him.

Max stood in front of a mirror in the room where he and Abby had been imprisoned. He couldn't stop shaking. He ran through the things he knew for certain. They were precious few. The *Beatrice* and the *Geryon* were bearing down on Metacarpi. His father kept a hidden weapon in a place where his mother took him as a child to play with a mad man. Hathus wanted him to help him find the giant, and spoke to him as if someone else lived in his head. He peered into his own eyes; grey ringed with gold, like his father's. *Odilon also looked into my eyes after the encounter with the giant, what did he see that frightened him?* He remembered the doctor Euphrosyne in the Steel Room, examining them with her lenses. *What are you all looking for?* His reflection looked completely ordinary, the face of a thirty-year-old Time Scavenger, craggy face lined with bewildered fear.

None of this makes any sense. He pressed his fingers to his forehead. *But it must. It's like the Shadows, a maze of paths threading in and out of my life, and somehow they're returning, coming round in a circle. I'm missing something, the link in the chain that binds it all together.* He battled against panic, trying to force his mind to work through the facts. It felt like piloting a flyer through a storm. In his mind he saw Theodore sliding down the skin of the dread-nought like a dying slug. He remembered Odilon walking out of the banquet room with Abby unconscious in his arms. Each image brought with it a fresh surge of fear. He tried to focus again and this time saw the giant rising up in the mist above the doll's house. *That's when all this started.* He'd assumed that his search for the truth about his mother was just an obsession triggered by the illusions the giant plucked from his childhood memories. Now he wasn't so sure. Who told Hathus about the giant? His father? Odilon? He doubted it just popped out during dinner before he and Abby turned up. Was it the gleaning of spies in Metacarpi? Who did Hathus look forward to meeting? *I'm going mad.* His reflection frightened him. He couldn't stay in the room. To calm the fire in his head he went exploring, searching the network of rooms in the hope he could find a way out. If Ruth was on the *Beatrice* she wouldn't bother with him. She only wanted to rescue her father. He'd have to escape on his own.

After an hour tracing his way through a labyrinth of corridors he admitted defeat. The only exit he found was the door he'd entered through, and none of the rooms had windows. Exhaustion crept back, born of anger and fear. He needed to sleep, if he could. When Hathus came for him he'd want his strength and a clear mind.

A face beyond a half-opened door stopped him in his tracks. His heart thundered in his chest at the thought of someone else in this silent maze. Getting ready to defend himself, he padded into a vaulted chamber. He realised with surprise that he was still alone. *Imagining things again, God help me.* He sighed. *I've got to get a grip.* He felt his boots sink into thick carpet as he walked up to a table flanked by chairs. What made him think someone else was here? He looked around and almost yelled out in alarm.

The face filled the entire wall. *God, it must be ten yards high.* Once the shock passed he saw that the features shone with the lustre of carved wood. Who was it? Some lord of the AntiHelix, the Emperor Demetrius himself? It did look like one of the sadistic monsters on this ship. He recognised the pointed chin and slanted cheekbones of Ruth and the others, exaggerated by the artist into the head of a demon. The eyes were half open. He'd seen that expression on the faces of the opium eaters in the cellars of Metacarpi's cheapest hotels. *He's an evil looking bastard.* The hair spread out in stylised daggers. Max spotted writing on one of the blades. Peering up he read the words. *Long Lock.* Understanding hit him like a blow. *It's God. This is what they think God looks like, a mirror of their own evil.* Max hoped it was just an artist's fantasy. The face of God lay far above the atmosphere. Mankind no longer possessed a ship capable of flying so high above the body of the Deity. The people of Procerus, Zygomaticus, Mentalis, each of the hundreds of nations working in the darkness of Trans-Atmospheric space, busied themselves with their own task, heads down, caring little for the whole. As far Max knew, no-one actually knew what God looked like. Perhaps he wore the face of this monster after all. He shuddered as he remembered the Black Rose he'd fought on the chain of the Carceral Archipelago. They could fly through space, they'd know what God looked like. Unable to bear that half-smile any longer he left the room. Eventually he came across an empty apartment with a bed and crawled under the covers. He fell asleep in seconds.

Max awoke to find a shadow standing over him, shaking his arm. For a second he thought it was Abby, then he saw the face of the young cellist, her eyes filled with tears. Fighting against disappointment he trawled through his memory. What was her name? Bryony.

"How did you get in here?" he asked. She hadn't been in any of the rooms when he'd searched before. That meant there must be a way out of this labyrinth. He stood up and she stepped back with a whimper. *She's terrified of me,* he realised.

"I won't hurt you, all I want to do is escape," he said.

"You can't. I'm a prisoner like you," she replied, her voice cracking with sadness. "There're paths in the walls for servants. They run between the guest floors, but they don't go anywhere, just to kitchens and storerooms."

Like the Shadows again, thought Max, *hidden ways, just as Ruth said.*

"Why are you here?" he asked.

"So my father will do what Hathus tells him," she answered. Max remembered the captain's comment at the end of dinner.

"Your father's Captain Andagis of the *Geryon*?" he asked. She nodded.

"What happened when Hathus took over?"

"I don't know. I came to the *Beatrice* with my father, to visit the Condottiere and his daughter. I heard fighting."

From her voice Max realised she and Ruth were friends. It made sense, the Condottiere's daughter and the loyal captain's. He wouldn't tell her Ruth might be on the ship. He didn't want to give her any false hope till he'd decided his next steps.

"Ruth left with some of the Dogs," Bryony continued. "She told me to stay in the rooms. I waited. Hathus came and said that he was in charge and that Ruth and her father had gone. He said I must stay here because it was the only way he'd guarantee my safety. Traitors were everywhere. I begged to go back to the *Geryon* but he wouldn't let me."

Now Max understood why Andagis hadn't helped Alaric. Ruth had asked why a once-loyal friend did nothing to aid the Condottiere. The reason stood in front of him. One false move and Hathus would kill Bryony, or worse.

"You're a hostage," said Max. Bryony's gaze dropped and a tear ran down her cheek. *Not just a hostage, are you*? thought Max. He remembered the way the captain looked at her at dinner. How old was she? Fifteen, sixteen? Another reason to loathe Hathus, as if he didn't have enough already. A sudden thought struck him.

"If you got back to the *Geryon*, what would your father do?" he asked. Bryony stared at him. He saw desperate hope in her face.

"He'd hang that monster by his stones from the hull till nothing remained but the shreds of his stinking corpse," she spat. She displayed the same imperious fury he'd seen in Ruth when she dropped her guard. He suspected Bryony was no more the helpless waif than Ruth. His ribs still ached from her kick.

For the first time since his capture, Max had the beginnings of a plan. Ruth thought if she released her father from the Iron Core it'd spark a counter-revolution on the ship. Having seen nothing but dutiful obedience on the faces of the crew, Max thought she deluded herself. Bryony might actually help him stop the fleet in its tracks. If he got her to the *Geryon* and her father, Hathus's hold over the other captain might break. Free her and steal a flyer. God, if only Abby was here, her plans were harebrained, but they always seemed to fall together at the end. He stopped, startled at the sudden urge to see her. *Damn, am I really in love with her*?

"There's windows in the servant's rooms," said Bryony. "I wanted to try and climb out that way, the hull is not so steep, but the black bird frightened me."

Her words snapped Max out of his reverie. The room suddenly seemed colder, the shadows longer.

"What black bird?" asked Max. Something in his expression made Bryony take a step back.

"It crawled across the hull," she said, her voice trembling. "I saw it out of the window. It disappeared into the command centre. I wanted to climb up to the turrets. They're only manned in battle and you can get into them from outside, but I thought it would see me."

If only he had a weapon. He gave a sour laugh. That wouldn't help him against a Black Rose. What else could it be? Had it followed him here? Did it still hunt him? He remembered his hands sinking into a seething cloud of petals and swore viciously. What could he do? Stay here and wait for Hathus or the alien to come and get him? He'd no doubt that once he'd done whatever the captain wanted he'd end up like Theodore. Or he could try to escape, chancing a climb to the turrets and a possible encounter with the alien creature on the hull. *I've no choice.*

"Show me where I can get outside," he said to Bryony.

"You need a rope," she answered, pulling sheets from the bed. After an hour they'd fashioned a cord from torn strips. She led him to a panel in the corridor wall. She pressed the corner. It swung back to reveal a passageway curving into the darkness. They followed it to a chain of service rooms, ending in a kitchen with a porthole. Deep gouges ran around the frame. Max was impressed, she must have spent hours working at the wood. He spotted carcass hooks in the ceiling. He jumped up, grabbed two and kicked at the window. On the second blow the glass popped out and the night wind roared into the room. Max turned to Bryony.

"I'm going to get you back to your father," he shouted above the noise, "wait here. I'll steal a flyer and bring it to the window." She nodded furiously, wrapped her arms round his neck and kissed him for luck. *I'll need more than a peck on the cheek from a sixteen-year old cellist to get through this night.*

He tied the end of the rope around one of the hooks. They both pulled hard, putting all their weight onto the sheet. To Max's relief both the cloth and the hook held. He kicked off his boots and sat on the porthole edge. The wind tore at his shirt as he leant back into the night, letting the makeshift rope take his weight. Bryony watched him wide-eyed. He stepped carefully out, bracing his feet against the hull of the ship. He glanced left and right but the windows and portholes nearby were black. He took another step, and the hook in the galley broke away from the ceiling. Bryony screamed as Max fell backwards into darkness.

His fall was arrested by a sudden jolt that snapped his head back, banging it painfully against the hull of the *Beatrice*. He looked upwards. The sheet had snagged on a row of smoke mortars running over the top of a gun blister. The turret itself formed a hill of metal and glass rising out of the fuselage. Four repeating cannon projected from slots along its axis. What had Bryony said? The turrets could be accessed from the outside. He couldn't see the galley window he'd fallen from, but he imagined her anxious face searching the darkness, hope draining out of her as she peered into the night.

He hung with his back to the ship, looking out at the Wasteland. Below him jumbled shadows drifted past. Raw terror overwhelmed him. He struggled to turn his fear into an anger he could use. *You've been here before, a thousand times before,* he chanted to himself, *you know what to do.* He forced himself to relax and twisted around to face the vessel. The turret glass proved too smooth for a foothold, but further up one of the panes was missing. He focussed all his mind on that gap. If he could climb up the surface of the sphere he might be able to worm his way inside. The armoured frame projected out from the glass by a few inches and it had enough of an edge for him to get a grip.

He raised his knees until they pressed against the surface of the blister, then pushed himself out and straightened his legs so that the soles of his bare feet were on the glass. His body shook with the effort. He started to walk up the surface, concentrating on each step. He saw a movement along the hull to his left. A hundred yards away something black crawled through a window, shimmering arms reaching out for purchase on the armour plating. In the onrush of terror he nearly lost his grip there and then. It was dark, but the Black Roses lived in eternal night and if it looked his way it would see him immediately. With horror Max remembered the thing had no face. It could be staring at him right now. The creature paused as if sensing the air. It launched itself into the sky. Max closed his eyes and waited for the blow. Nothing happened. He looked again. A shadow flickered across the distant mountains. It hadn't seen him. He almost wept with relief. *For God's sake let there be only one.*

The sheet ripped and he fell a few inches. He yelled out in fear as he swung away from the turret, his fingers scrabbling at the rivets in the hull. The wind carried his voice into the darkness. Flailing in terror, he turned back to the blister as it raced towards him. His side banged painfully into the frame and he swung out into the air once more. This time the sheet ripped away from the smoke projectors. As he fell his forward momentum caused him to smack into the side of the turret. He clutched at the surface, slipped, grabbed again and managed to hook three fingers into the gap between the frame and the glass. A lance of pain shot through his arm as a fingernail ripped free. He dangled by one arm from the side of the ship.

Exhaustion crept over him. It would be so easy to open his hand, to give it all up and let the Wasteland claim him. His head sagged, his thoughts dissolved into mist. *Just let go, just let go, fall for a few seconds and then sleep.* In those last few moments before he lost his grip he thought he heard his mother's voice at the back of his mind. *Eat up Max.* Without thinking he reached into his waistcoat pocket with his free hand, pulled out Ruth's pomegranate seed and put it into his mouth.

Of all the idiotic things he'd done in his life, this was up there with the best. The food of the past held concentrated energies unheard of at the end of time. Eating fruit as ancient as this usually involved sitting in a chair bolted to the floor while your friends held you down. Even then you'd probably injure one or two by accident, under the belief that you too had become a god. Consuming one while dangling by an arm from the side of a dreadnought thousands of feet in the air was beyond insane. Not even Abby would be so stupid.

A bomb went off inside Max's head. Energies from billions of years ago coursed through his body. He convulsed, hanging on to the turret only because his hand spasmed shut with a grip that could easily have bent weaker metals. He let out a joyous roar loud enough to topple mountains. As his mind went into overdrive he convinced himself he'd made the *Beatrice* lurch sideways with the power of his shout. Fighting against the white fire filling his limbs he flicked round and grabbed the frame with his other hand. With one yank he'd hurled himself up the face of the turret, grabbed the edge of the gap and somersaulted into the blister, giggling all the while. He fell in a heap among a pile of used shells, clamping his hands over his mouth to stop any more noises escaping.

After what seemed forever the initial rush subsided, though he still believed he could rip open the hull of the ship with his bare hands. He got to his feet and, humming quietly to himself, searched around the gunner's seat. Using a shell casing he broke open a locker. Inside he found a single-shot derringer and a handful of bullets. He tucked the pistol into his waistband and stuffed the shells into his pocket. Opening the hatch, he stepped quietly out into the corridor. Maximilian Ocel was ready to take on the entire ship.

CHAPTER SEVENTEEN

MAX NOTICED ENTRANCES to the passageways hidden in the walls on the *Beatrice* during their tour with Hathus, and later when the guards brought him back to his prison. It only took him a few moments to get out of the corridor and into a gantry linking the turrets with the ammunition stores deeper in the vessel. Years of creeping through temples, palaces, office blocks, tenements, labyrinths, prison pits, warrens and alleyways in the wormholes left him with the skills to evade capture. He saw few of the crew. He guessed that out here in the Wasteland they'd become over-confident and lazy. These slender warriors from the Empire of the Ear exuded contempt in everything they did, but arrogance made them blind. His biggest problem was the pomegranate seed. Energy surged through him like an ocean breaking on rocks, frequently catching him by surprise. It took a massive effort of will to stop himself shouting out or suddenly laughing. At the same time it heightened his senses, making him acutely aware of every change in the light, every new sound no matter how soft. He felt the ship vibrating through his feet, and found to his amazement that he could detect shifting patterns in the hum as the dreadnought flexed and twisted under the force of its engines. *This is a dance,* he thought in one crazy moment when the pomegranate seed caught him unawares. He remembered his old tutor sneering at the men of Tip and their fantastic tarantellas. *They're all mad in Tip*, he thought as he hopscotched through a pattern of shadows, *mad and arrogant. Are they next after Hathus finishes with Metacarpi?* He stopped and gasped in astonishment.

The gantry finished at steps leading down to a junction. He saw two figures immobile like statues. A soldier stood with his back to Max, unaware of his approach. He pointed his carbine at the face of the woman kneeling on the floor in front of him, her hands behind her head. He recognised Ruth immediately, dressed in the uniform of a pilot. She saw him, but her face gave nothing away as he stepped quietly into the passage. A quick glance told him they were alone. He drew his derringer. Ruth saw the gun. She shook her head and the guard, noticing her movement, started to turn. Ruth leapt to her feet and slammed the heel of her hand into his face. Max heard the sickening crack of bone and the soldier fell, his limbs jerking as blood fountained from his ruined nose. Ruth snatched up the carbine.

"Hide him," she said. Max dragged the body into the darkness under the gantry stairs. He turned to ask Ruth how in God's name she'd escaped from the wormhole, but she'd gone. *She's deserted me*, he thought, *I just saved her life again and she's disappeared.* Taking a wild guess he ran down the corridor opposite. He turned a bend just in time to see her slip through another concealed door. He followed her into a crawlspace that angled up into the hull. She stopped when he caught up, irritation plain on her face.

"How did you escape?" he asked.

"I swapped uniforms with one of the pilots who came after me. She was loyal to my father."

Max noticed her gaze flicker away for a second. He had a sudden image of a screaming woman tumbling for eternity down a wormhole. *Loyal my arse*. Theoretically you'd die of thirst or starvation or even madness as you fell, but air currents in the shafts usually slammed you into the stairs or walls further down and you died a broken heap at the entrance to an ancient world.

"Why're you still alive?" she asked. It sounded like an accusation.

"Hathus wants me to help him find the giant," he said. Her expression said it all. Max hoped she'd cast some light on the captain's motives but she clearly thought him deranged as well. His interest in Max held no meaning for her.

"The daughter of the captain of the *Geryon* is on board this ship, Bryony," he continued. Ruth gasped at the name.

"She's a hostage. That's why he won't move against Hathus. If we can get her back to her father, can you persuade him to stop the fleet?" asked Max.

He could see her mind working.

"I'm on my way to steal a ship," he continued, "there's a broken window in the rooms where she's held prisoner, we can get her out that way." Ruth shook her head as she strode along the corridor. Max hurried to keep up.

"I have to release my father," she said.

"He's one man in an enemy ship of thousands. Andagis commands his own dreadnought," said Max, "take Bryony to the *Geryon* first, then we can rescue Alaric."

She turned to him and Max felt the point of a knife under his chin. *Where the hell did that come from*? She stared into his face, her eyes two violet shards. She'd kill him in a second, of course she would, she came from the same mould as the rest. Max wished Abby was here, they'd be on the flyer by now with the rescued girl, saving Metacarpi from destruction.

"You can help me rescue my father. You can get out of my way. Or I can gut you like a fish," she said in a voice of pleasant cruelty.

The pomegranate seed enhanced his reflexes. He whipped the knife from her hand, thrust the blade between two pipes and snapped it. Her eyes went wide with shock and she stepped back, suddenly uncertain.

"I'll help you release him, but in return you help me get a flyer to take Bryony to her father." The fading energy must have added something to his voice for now he saw fear in her eyes. She nodded.

She took him through a network of tunnels that led ever deeper into the ship. Finally they stopped at an open hatch beside an alcove in a corridor decorated with mirrors and lacquerwork. Four guards stood in front of a polished iron disk twice the height of a man. Max's heart sank. They carried machine guns and he couldn't see any way to approach them without being spotted. Ruth's eyes glistened and she panted like a wolf about to strike. *This must be the Iron Core*, he thought, *somewhere on the other side of that entrance is the Condottiere Alaric.*

"Now what?" he said, turning to Ruth. She'd gone. He looked back at the alcove and a chill ran through him. Ruth walked towards the metal disc. *There's bravery, there's skill and there's utter stupidity*, he thought, *she's worse than Abby. There's no way she can handle four heavily armed sentinels*. He prepared to charge.

The four guards stared at Ruth. Their weapons swung towards her. Max realised he wouldn't make it in time, but he couldn't back out.

"I am Ruth an Vircana of the Long Lock, daughter of the Condottiere Alaric, Admiral of the fleet of the Emperor Demetrius," said Ruth. Max couldn't help but admire her nerve, the easy command in her voice. "Is there any loyalty left on this accursed ship?"

They're going to kill her, thought Max. The guard furthest to Ruth's left moved first, but to Max's surprise he dropped his gun, pulled out a knife from his belt and rammed it into the throat of the woman standing beside him. A second blade shone in Ruth's hand. She whirled in a pirouette and the other two guards crumpled. The metal circle behind them glittered with blood. *God,* thought Max, *they're all as mad as each other. Life means nothing to them.* He'd seen horrors on countless worlds, bloodshed and misery, but these clinical executions, performed with all the measured precision of a ballet, revolted him. Even so, he couldn't stay where he was. He stepped out of the secret passageway and followed Ruth into the alcove. She put her hand on the remaining guard's gun.

"He's with me," she said, "what's your name?"

"Captain Samson an Ulphilas, my lady, from Occipital Vellus."

"An Ulphilas," she said, "how many remain loyal?"

Tears appeared in the man's eyes. To Max he looked in his early twenties, though his precisely trimmed beard was shot with white and up close he saw fine wrinkles patterning the soldier's face.

"I don't know," he said, his voice trembling, "only a few. All the Dogs are dead. They slaughtered them, threw the bodies out of the portholes and the flyer bays." Max thought he saw a shiver of fear pass through Ruth.

"Captain Hathus told us your father was a traitor," continued Samson, "in league with the Steel Queen, but I know it's not true. I hid my heart and they let me stand guard here, but I don't know the way in, I don't know how to set him free."

Max's ears pricked up at the mention of the Steel Queen. He'd heard of her in one of Abby's fairy stories. She ruled a kingdom enclosed in a sphere that floated across God's abdomen on a river of mercury. He'd dismissed it as a fantasy for children. This man spoke of her as if she really existed.

"This door'll open for me, it knows my hand," said Ruth.

She placed her fingers on the metal circle. To Max's astonishment it irised open. Ruth stepped through into the darkness beyond. Samson and Max pulled the bodies into the room. The portal closed behind them.

The first thing to hit Max was the stench. He guessed the pomegranate seed heightened his senses. The room reeked of rotting wounds and vomit. He saw his breath mist in the cold air. Ruth and Samson didn't seem to notice the smell. They glided ahead of him, their silhouettes flickering against emergency lighting. He looked about him. For a fortified refuge the Iron Core appeared ornate, even sumptuous. As his eyes adjusted to the gloom Max saw a collage of textures and materials; oak, mahogany, rarer woods from long forgotten worlds. The walls alternated between iron and sheets of ruby glass scattered with jewels and metals. He spotted onyx, molybdenum, chrysolite, pewter, jade, black marble and lead. Low archways opened on corridors that curved away on all sides. He couldn't see Ruth or Samson. They'd disappeared, but he daren't call out. He felt as if he was in the lair of a beast, an implacable animal force that only he could sense. He listened, drawing on the last remnants of the energy he'd stolen from the past. He heard a sound that filled him with dread. It was

Ruth crying quietly in a distant room. *He's dead*, Max thought, *this is a tomb*.

He found her and Samson crouched over the body of a man slumped by an empty fireplace. He gasped at the sight. When standing he would have towered over Max by at least a foot. Now, clothed in armour and fur, with his long black hair and beard matted with blood, he looked like the corpse of an animal spread out before his hunters. Max's contempt for the people of the Ear and their supercilious cruelty stripped away any awe at their power, but Ruth's father was something else. Even in death, Max found him terrifying.

He heard Ruth begging her father not to leave her and Max realised, with a shock, that the Condottiere still lived. She shook him, stroked his face and pleaded with him, telling him loyal troops waited on the ship and together they could take it back. Samson, grey faced and breathing in ragged sobs, stared down at his master. He looked at Max and his expression said it all.

"Lift me up," Alaric whispered. Ruth cried out in joy and pressed her face to her father's cheek. She motioned to Max and Samson and together they raised the Condottiere into a chair beside a table. He slumped forward, his hands clenched. Max looked at his own fingers. They were wet with blood. In the lamplight he saw a ragged wound where the commander's steel breastplate met the fur cloak. The smell of rot grew stronger.

Alaric looked at his daughter. He smiled and Max saw that his teeth were coated with blood.

"Why did you come back?" said the Condottiere, "I gave the Dogs orders to save you."

"How could you?" said Ruth. "How could you send your own dear one away?"

Despite himself Max's heart twisted in compassion at her words. Alaric gasped out a tired laugh. His head drooped.

"There's little time left," said Alaric to Ruth. "Listen, listen to me carefully, you must finish what I was charged to do."

Every word was a gasp. *It must be agony just for him to speak.*

"My mission is the last step of the Great Task," continued Alaric, "it must be completed."

Max sat down at the table, his eyes fixed on the dying man. Ruth and Samson exchanged fearful glances as Alaric continued.

"Humans built the body of God from wood, metal and cloth," he said. "It's only a doll, hundreds of thousands of miles long, fashioned by carpenters, engineers, metalworkers, welders. Nothing more, a million years of simple engineering. The mind of God is different."

Alaric's head slumped. Ruth stifled a sob. Moments passed. The Condottiere spoke again, his voice a whisper that filled the room.

"We made the Machine Men to work inside the Body, where we can't go. In his heart. Inside his head. They tried to make his mind. But it's too great a task. Nothing can fashion thoughts greater than their own." Alaric's breathing became ragged. Max panicked, he didn't want to think what Ruth would do when the Condottiere died. After a pause that seemed an age, Alaric looked at his daughter. Max saw the love in his eyes and quailed at its intensity.

"The Machine Men discovered a way to make the mind of God. They split it into parts, fashioning eight spirits, each a manifestation of the soul of the Deity," Ruth's father continued, "they gave each spirit sense and feeling, and shape. But they could only go so far. God must understand us in order to save us.

"The Machine Men sent the eight spirits out into the realms of man to learn about his people. They wander the singularity, inside and outside the Body, studying us, trying to comprehend us. When the time comes they'll go back to the Head and unite to form God's mind."

The question burned in Max's thoughts. He had to ask it, even though the Condottiere lay close to death.

"What form do these spirits take?" he asked. He had a horrible feeling he already knew the answer.

"Giants. They're giants," whispered Alaric without looking round. Max place his trembling hands flat on the table, trying to calm the storm raging in his heart. He remembered the shadow in the mist above the house. *You're not a monster at all, you're part of God's consciousness, His spirit.* Alaric's eyes closed. Samson caught Max's eye and shook his head. The Condottiere's strength was almost spent.

"My orders were to search for the giants," he murmured. "In the centuries since they left the Head, the Machine Men lost contact. We have to find them and tell them it's time to return. God is finished."

That's why the dreadnoughts are here, thought Max, *this isn't an invasion fleet. They're looking for my giant.* His own thought caught him unawares. *Why did I call it my giant?* Ruth looked at him and saw the understanding in his eyes. Max wanted to say he'd seen the spirit they searched for, that it tried to speak to him, but he daren't distract Alaric.

"Why the mutiny when you opened your orders?" asked Ruth.

"Enemies afraid of God," whispered Alaric. "They don't want him to wake."

Hathus, thought Max, *Hathus and the Black Roses*. He remembered the creature creeping from the window of the Beatrice's command centre. *Hathus is in league with the Black Roses. Why? Why would the aliens suddenly turn on the God they helped us make? And why do they want me dead? What have I got to do with the mind of God?*

With an effort Alaric lifted his head and stared straight at his daughter. Max saw their gazes lock.

"Ruth an Vircana, daughter of the Long Lock, scion and lord of the greatest house in the Empire of the Ear, listen to me," said Alaric. He reached out and took her hand. Max could see in his eyes that it took all his strength. "Swear on my dying heart that you'll find the Giant of the Thumb and keep him safe from our enemies. Persuade him to return to the Head. Find all the giants, for the time has come for God to wake and carry mankind to the new universe."

Max could see in Ruth's eyes that all she wanted to do was seek out Hathus and punish him for what he'd done to her father. Alaric sensed the doubt in her eyes. Tears gathered in his own.

"Ruth, swear you'll do nothing else until the giants have returned to the Mind, as you love your father and the Emperor."

She opened her mouth, and hesitated. Alaric's grip tightened and she yelped in pain.

"Swear it," said the Condottiere and Max heard the tones that had commanded thousands of troops. He shivered.

"I swear it," Ruth said in a voice so filled with sorrow Max thought it couldn't possibly be hers. Alaric let go of her hand. His own fingers wrestled with each other and Max thought he was having a fit until the Condottiere lifted up a gold ring carved like a lock of hair. Ruth began to cry, the heart-wrenching sobs of a child.

238

She shook her head violently, but Alaric still held the ring towards her. Finally she reached forward and took it. To Max she looked like she was picking up the most loathsome object in the universe. It was too big for her fingers so she placed it on her thumb and held it to the light. In the darkness Samson started sobbing. Max looked at Alaric. The Condottiere's head had slumped forward one last time, his profile still against the lamplight. With a wrench of fear Max realised he was dead. He reached forward and took the man's pulse. Nothing. Ruth snatched his hand away.

"Don't touch him," she said, her voice filled with hatred. She rocked back and forth, keening. Max thought he heard fragments of a childhood song, a lullaby perhaps, long forgotten. The universe froze around him and they sat in a pocket of time beside the dead lord.

Ruth stood up and walked out of the room. Samson and Max swapped alarmed glances and ran after her. To Max she didn't look like someone dutifully following her father's dying wishes. She took a machine gun from one of the corpses and checked the magazine.

"We have to get out of here," said Max. She wasn't seriously thinking of revenge, was she?

"My lady, the guards will be here within the half hour. We must leave," said Samson. Max sensed he was beginning to panic.

Ruth ignored them both. Max couldn't see her face. He didn't want to, though as her silhouette turned he saw her eyes flash. *She's going to march through this ship until she finds Hathus or they cut her down.* He took Ruth's arm, even though he knew he risked his life in doing so.

"If we get Bryony back to the *Geryon*, her father will stop Hathus," he said.

Ruth looked down at his hand until he withdrew it. She gave a chilling laugh.

"Andagis is nothing to me, he let my father die," she said, her voice leaden. It appalled Max.

"What about the giant?" he pleaded. "If you try and kill Hathus you'll perish. Even with your skill and our help we won't get anywhere near him, there are thousands on this ship. We have to find the giant before Hathus does. He wants to destroy it." He started to lose patience, "Can't you understand? If the giant dies then God dies."

Ruth turned and strode through the apartment. *She doesn't care*, he realised, *she'll consign all of humanity to destruction for the sake of revenge.* He'd had enough. Some of the energy of the past still lingered. He wasn't going to let Ruth kill them all.

"We've got to stop her," he hissed to Samson, and leaped at the girl. He was ready this time. Before she could react he twisted the machine gun out of her hands and flung it across the room. She swung at him but he ducked the first punch and blocked the second. Samson grabbed at her from behind but she kicked backwards and he thumped into the wall. Max tried to sweep her feet from under her but she jumped out of the way and drew her knife. It became a deadly dance, Max circled around as she watched him, blade up in front of her face, easing herself from one foot to the next. Samson peeled himself out of the corner and hovered behind her. Max saw he was looking for a chance to throw her but every few seconds she flipped round to face him, so fast she looked like an image in a child's thaumatrope.

"Can you really afford to kill the only two allies you have on this ship?" he asked. He knew she'd slaughter them both without a second thought. Ruth jumped forward. He only avoided the blade by bending backwards so far he nearly lost his balance. She'd turned herself into a machine, as remorseless as the iron box that chased them across the Forbidden Sea. He had to get through to her.

"You swore an oath to your father," he said.

Ruth's violet eyes swivelled up into her head and she shrieked. Samson's head snapped back in a spray of blood as she kicked behind her. Max barely had time to recognise the Spear Tip dance before he landed on his back. Ruth stood on his chest and drove the dagger down, her body like a whip. He felt the splinters gouge his cheek as she buried it hilt deep in the floor.

This is it, I'm dead, thought Max. To his surprise Ruth sat down on his legs, rolled off, curled up and burst into tears. Max stared at the ceiling, trying to stitch the universe back together in his head. He sat up. Samson slumped against the wall, hand clamped over his nose. Blood poured between his fingers.

Max rolled onto his feet and yanked Ruth up.

"We have to go," he said. He saw the demon had fled from her eyes, temporarily at least. She nodded, wrenched the dagger out of the floor and picked up the machine gun.

"There's a hangar two floors above us," she said.

CHAPTER EIGHTEEN

BEFORE THEY LEFT the Iron Core, Ruth made them place everything burnable around the table where Alaric sat with his hands clenched and his head down. They dragged the dead guards and heaped them in the centre of the room. Ruth emptied the contents of all the lamps but one over the pyre. As they left she turned and hurled the last onto the table. It shattered and flames ran swiftly over Alaric's arms and down onto the heads and shoulders of his jailers. Max felt the heat on his face as the rest of the oil caught fire. The entrance to the Iron Core closed behind them.

"Won't it spread to the rest of the ship?" asked Max.

Samson shook his head.

"No-one will ever know, it's completely sealed off."

They still had time if they moved swiftly and stayed out of sight. As soon as they'd stolen a ship Max reckoned they could pluck Bryony from her prison in minutes. After that they only had to fly to the *Geryon*, which trailed behind them through the mountains. He desperately hoped his daughter's return would give Andagis enough reason to halt the advance on Metacarpi. Hathus might be on the hunt for the giant, but Max didn't doubt his city would end up like Abductor if someone couldn't stop the dreadnoughts.

Ruth led them through the ship. Max marvelled at its size. He'd assumed the captain had deliberately showed him the most intimidating sections, but now he realised it was all the same. They jogged past shells as big as trams stacked in cavernous ammunition bays, under gun barrels wide enough to swallow the *Zephyr*. At last they came to a hangar filled with scouts and fighters. Steps led up from the bay floor to a glass fronted office. The lights were on and Max heard voices and laughter. With the hangar staff distracted, taking a ship should be simple. Ruth nodded towards a scout half the size of the *Bricolage*. Max turned to Samson.

"Can you get the bay doors open?" he asked. Of the three of them, the guard looked the least suspicious, now he'd wiped away the blood from his nose. He might be able to fool the ground crew into helping them escape.

Samson nodded. Max turned back to Ruth, but she'd disappeared.

"What's she doing?' asked Samson, his voice tight with alarm. Max turned and panicked as he saw Ruth step into the hangar control room. The laughter stopped. *The idiot, she'll alert them,* he thought, racing to the foot of the stairs. With the alarm raised they'd no chance if they stayed close to the *Beatrice*, all eyes would be looking for them. He cursed the sound his feet made on the steps, hoping no-one else was around.

Three technicians sat next to an upturned crate, playing cards. Behind them winking control panels rose up to the ceiling. *For the servants of tyranny they're untidy buggers,* thought Max, *Maria would have them for breakfast.* Ledgers with flight schedules and reports spilled off the desks and stood in piles in the corner of the room. The three men seemed so young. He found it hard to guess the ages of people from the Ear, but none of these looked older than twenty. Ruth stood in front of them with her arms folded and a smile on her lips. Something in the set of her shoulders chilled Max.

"We have to go now."

"Do you know who I am?" said Ruth, ignoring him. One of the men swallowed and nodded.

"Well?" asked Ruth.

"Lady Ruth an Vircana," said another, "we thought you dead."

Ruth shrugged and smiled as if to say it was easy mistake to make.

"Ruth," hissed Max.

"I'm alive, as you can see. However my father, the great Condottiere Alaric an Vircana and Admiral of this fleet, died half an hour ago," she said in pleasant, measured tones, like a teacher reading a lesson. "Betrayed and abandoned by the crew of this vessel, and left to perish in the Iron Core."

The men looked at each other fearfully.

"Ruth, they're just kids," Max pleaded.

"What did you do to help him?" she looked at each of them in turn, "nothing, nothing, and nothing."

Max lunged for her but didn't make it. Ruth's knife whipped across the throats of two of the men and blood splattered on the floor. They scrabbled at their necks in vain, fell from their chairs and lay twitching at Max's feet. Ruth stared at the knife in her hand as if seeing it for the first time, shivered and dropped it. The third man started to beg for his life. She stepped over his dead friends, placed a hand on each cheek and with a twist of her arms snapped his neck.

Max stared in revulsion at Ruth. In a few seconds of revenge she'd destroyed his chance of freeing Bryony. He knew why she'd killed the men. *She's left a sign for Hathus.* He looked at her face. *She's in a trance, she's shut herself off from what she's done.* Her face stayed calm but her hands shook as she reached across a console and flicked a set of switches. The bay doors rolled open and a cold wind blew in from the mountains. She ran down the stairs and across the hangar to where Samson powered up the flyer's dynamos. Max had no choice. If he stayed he'd be killed, if he tried to take another flyer to rescue Bryony now, the guns of the *Beatrice* would shoot him down. His only chance of survival lay in fleeing the battleship. He joined the other two in the scout. It rose into the night and in seconds the bulk of the dreadnought receded into the darkness behind them.

Max sat at the rear of the cabin wrapped in a black cloud of despair. It might have been an idiotic idea to try and spring Bryony from her prison, but from what he could see it was the only option left. In one act of vendetta Ruth had snatched it away from him. A city would fall just so she could vent her misery on three low grade technicians. It was obvious to anyone with half a brain they'd no hand in Hathus's coup.

He stared at Ruth and Samson while they worked the controls of the flyer. He wanted to wring her neck, shout and scream into her face until those eyes showed even a flicker of understanding at her vindictive stupidity. He knew he'd be wasting his time. Any remaining admiration for her beauty dissolved into contempt. He hated these creatures from the Ear, all of them. They thought themselves above every other living soul on the singularity yet all they had to show for it was arrogance and moronic cruelty.

After an hour Ruth left the controls and came over Max.

"Where's the giant?" she asked.

"I don't know," snapped Max. She flinched. Something in his voice rattled her. Perhaps he still had a hold over her.

"You've doomed the city," he continued, fighting his rising anger. "We had a chance to stop the *Beatrice*. We could have taken Bryony to her father, if you hadn't slaughtered those kids."

"They weren't kids," spat Ruth, but he could see doubt on her face.

"They certainly weren't soldiers."

"Hathus isn't interested in your city, he's after the giant," said Ruth. "We've got to find it before he does."

"I hope to God you're right." If she wasn't and Metacarpi fell, he'd show her the meaning of vengeance.

"Where's the giant?" repeated Ruth.

"I've no idea," said Max, suddenly exhausted. Why did they think he knew?

"I met it once in the Wasteland. Odilon saw the place in his mirrors but the giant wasn't there anymore. I've no idea where it is now. It could be anywhere in fifty thousand square miles." With a chart he could take a guess, but that was all.

"Why did Hathus think you could find it?" asked Ruth.

"Don't know," said Max. He wish he did. He still couldn't understand how Hathus found out about the giant in the first place.

"Tell me what you do know," said Ruth. He toyed with the idea of telling her exactly where to go but held his peace. In reality his options were limited. They flew at speed through mountains. He saw no point goading his companions, they might decide they'd had enough and throw him out of the window.

"The giant built that house from my early memories," he said carefully, trying to piece together what he knew so it made sense, an impossible task.

"It showed me my mother in a room where she used to take me as a toddler. A man lived there, he was either mad or a simpleton and I think she tried to cure him by getting him to play children's games with me.

"After we left the giant's house, I kept dreaming about the room, until we found it in the fortress on the other side of the sea, stuck on the side of a silo that contains a weapon my father plans to use against Hathus. That's all I know. None of it connects. All I can think is that the giant tried to tell me something, and used my memories to do so. It unlocked recollections I didn't know I had, and now they plague me with a thousand unanswered questions."

He saw from Ruth's expression that his story meant nothing to her either.

"Hathus wants to destroy the giant," continued Max, "and the Black Roses want me dead. I saw one of them on the *Beatrice* when I climbed over the hull. Bryony said it came from the control centre of the ship. Is Hathus in league with the Black Roses?"

The look of horror on Ruth's face said it all. He guessed she saw Hathus as a treacherous general grabbing at power. This took his crimes to an unheard level of betrayal. He remembered the fat captain with his affable smile and easy good humour, up to the point Theodore slid down the hull in his own blood. *He'll betray the entire human race. Where's the advantage in that? What reward could the aliens offer to Hathus so he'd condemn every single man, woman and child left alive and all their descendants?*

"He's either completely insane," said Max, "or there's another reason."

"If the giants die, God won't wake up, and humanity will perish in this empty universe," said Ruth, "who'd wish for that?"

"The aliens might not want us in the next universe, our track record in this one isn't so wonderful. But that doesn't explain why Hathus is helping them. Your father spoke of other enemies, human ones?"

Ruth didn't know. She stared pale-faced at the floor. Max saw the waif again and this time he didn't think she was faking the helplessness. In the last twenty-four hours she'd watched her father die and killed half a dozen men. No matter how much she thought of herself as an elite executioner, she couldn't escape the emotional strain forever.

"If Odilon returned to his tower, he can help us," said Max. "He'll know how to find the giant, and why Hathus is conspiring with the aliens to destroy God." Ruth nodded and turned away. Her hands trembled as she wiped her eyes.

Samson agreed to fly the ship while the other two slept. Max squeezed into a cabin no bigger than a cupboard. He wanted to spend time working through plans in his mind, trying to understand his involvement with the giant, and how to rescue the city, but the second his head touched the pillow exhaustion took over and he fell asleep.

Samson woke Max up. He looked terrified. Max realised the flyer no longer moved. Light shone through the hand-sized porthole above his bunk. His first thought was Hathus had caught them, their escape hadn't worked and they were back on the *Beatrice*, or grounded somewhere in the Wasteland, ringed by enemy flyers.

"You have to see this," said Samson, his voice trembling. Not Hathus then, by the look on the man's face he could tell they'd found something far worse. He had a horrible feeling he knew what to expect. He went onto the bridge and found Ruth staring out of the window. He followed her gaze and fear swept over him. Mist rose into the sky. At the foot of this pallid wall of nothing sat the giant's house, the perfect copy of the toy building he'd played with as a toddler.

"When dawn came it appeared. Now what?" whispered Ruth.

"It's the giant," said Max. "It's entered my memories again and built that house. It wants to talk to me."

The raggedy scavenger inside his mind ran round in circles screaming in terror, begging him to turn the ship in the opposite direction, open the dynamos and not stop till he smacked into the Thumb itself. He remembered the corridor, the voices clamouring in his head and the ghost of his mother. He wished he could be anywhere but here. He closed his eyes, forcing the voice of panic to a whisper.

The building's walls and windows seethed as if a multitude of insects crawled over the plaster and glass. When he tried to focus on the details, his vision still slipped away. Four windows, all different sizes. *My God, the door's open.* He could see nothing of the interior, merely blackness. *The longer I stand here, the harder it'll be.* He walked onto the deck. The mist formed a wall around the ship, fading to a purple disc far above his head. Ruth followed him.

"What are you doing?" she asked fearfully.

"I'm going inside," he said, forcing himself to climb down the ladder.

"I'm coming too." He had to admire her bravery, but she was the last person he wanted with him.

"This house is for me," he said. "Abby didn't see anything last time. She said I just stood there in a trance while I talked to my dead mother in my head, it's not interested in you." He trusted Abby, but he didn't trust Ruth. The thought of her hovering around while he communed with the creature frightened him. *God knows what the snotty bitch might attempt. She'll probably try and order the giant about, tell it in no uncertain terms how she's the fifteenth princess of the House of Hair or some other bullshit aristocratic nonsense, waiting for it go ooh and aah and three bags full.* Sure enough, he saw her fling her head back and glare at him with angry hauteur.

"My father charged me with the task of warning the giant," she said. "He made me the voice of the Emperor Demetrius, Lord of the Ear."

"That means bugger all out here," said Max, losing patience with her. God how he missed Abby. She'd be cracking jokes now, playfully thumping him in the ribs and winking before charging at the enemy with a happy yell. He remembered her walking ahead of him the first time they saw the house, gun pointed at the ground, and the memory cut him like a knife.

Ruth followed him onto the surface of the Wasteland. Max rounded on her.

"What's the best way of saying this?" he said coldly. "Your father told us that the giants came out into the realm of man to learn about us and to understand us. You're an arrogant murdering little shit, what can you possibly teach God that would make him want to save us?"

Her face paled and her eyes filled with tears. She looked as if he'd slapped her. *Good, now fuck off*, thought Max. He turned his back on her and stalked towards the house in grim satisfaction. Part of him expected to feel her knife between his shoulders. He stopped outside the door. Maybe she stood behind him, maybe not. He was past caring.

He stepped through the door and someone behind him screamed his name. He fell into nothingness, the rush of air around his face snatching his breath. Panic overwhelmed him. Where were the doors and stairs, the jigsaw of images the giant had used to build the corridor last time? Max plummeted through empty space. He shut his eyes and screamed in fear. A trap, the whole thing was a trap. The giant didn't want to talk to him. It wanted to destroy him, turn him inside out, rip all his loves and fears from his mind and spread them out for the universe to laugh at. They all waited for him. His father, stone-faced, sneering in disappointment. Rebecca Fabrice lighting a cigarette and shaking her head at him in pity. *You're a waste of space Maximilian Ocel*, he heard her say, *you do know that, don't you? The city's going to fall, you haven't a clue why and you can't do anything to save it.* He heard shrill laughter, so high it sounded like his tutor's chalk on the blackboard in the schoolroom on that rainy day in the Carceral Archipelago. *They're all mad in Tip, arrogant and mad.* Above him he sensed millions of Black Roses hovering in Trans-Atmospheric space, mocking his death while they plotted the destruction of God. This was the end, and he'd never see Abby's face again, her green eyes or that red explosion she called a hairstyle.

He opened his eyes. He still hung in the darkness but ahead he saw a plain spreading away on all sides, rust brown in the centre, fading to silver at the edges of his vision. A man lay on the surface. To Max it seemed as if he stood at the edge of a table in the Steel Room, looking at the corpse of another traitor his father had consigned to death. The head was towards him. He could make out the top of the skull, long black hair spread out across the plain around it. He glimpsed the peak of the nose, a jaw, then a pair of broad shoulders.

The rest of the body stretched into the distance, ending in two feet turned slightly outwards.

Max regained some of his sanity. He floated through a void, still conscious. His thoughts were clear and he didn't feel any pain. He lifted his hands to his face but saw nothing. He cried out in fear again. *I'm a spirit, my body's gone. Am I dead?* That constant grinding panic came from somewhere. *Ghosts have no hearts to quail, mine must still be beating.* He looked back at the figure lying on the platform in front of him. *Is that the giant? Is he asleep? How do I speak to him?* He could just make out the man's hands tucked against his legs, palm up. Instinctively he looked at the left thumb.

Realisation hit him with the force of a runaway tram. *It's God. I'm floating in space looking at the body of God.* He shouted out in fear and wonder, intoxicated by the scene. If only Abby were here now, to share this moment with him. He forced himself to calm down, an almost impossible task. If he was dead, or about to die, this formed a hell of coda to his life, no matter how short and pointless it'd been. Was it real? Did he actually look down on the body of the Deity, or was his dying mind merely concocting a desperate vision in its last confusion? At this point he didn't care. As far as he knew, he was the only man in history who'd gazed down at the body of God, the summation of the Great Task, a mannequin half a million miles long from toe to crown.

So that's the singularity, he thought, looking at the plain. *A billion ground-up worlds scattered by the Black Roses.* Where the dirt petered out, the surface shimmered like a mirror. He tried to move but couldn't. He wanted to look at God's face. He could just make out the brow and the nose, but he wasn't high enough to see any more detail. Even so, he realised the stupid bastard who carved the sculpture on the *Beatrice* hadn't a clue. This wasn't the face of an overlord, the echo of all those sybarites in their palaces in the AntiHelix. This was a man, nothing more. God had the face of someone he might bump into in a bar near the Theatre of Angels. Max laughed with joy.

As if in answer to his thoughts he started to move, drifting down towards the head. He tried to change his course but had no control over his descent. He plummeted towards the scalp of God, panicking as his speed increased. He tumbled past hairs a hundred miles thick. *This is Ruth's world*, he thought, glimpsing cities and fortresses clinging to the scaled cuticles. It grew dark. In seconds he would smash into the skull. He closed his eyes and yelled out in fear.

He opened them again and found himself sitting at a table opposite a young woman. Her skin was almost as pale as her dress, and long white hair fell about her shoulders. *I've seen you before somewhere*, thought Max, *you're so familiar*. She watched him with an expression of amused curiosity. To her left sat three more women, the family resemblance struck him immediately. *Of course, you're my sisters, your expressions were always nothing more than variations on a theme.* Four sisters and four brothers. He looked to his right and saw three men sitting in a line beside him, each facing one of the women. They all wore black suits, shirts open at the neck and shoes polished to a mirror gloss. He stared down at his hands, flat on the table. Glittering insects scuttled over his long fingers and across the wood. *This is home, this is where I belong.*

But the time came to leave. Sorrow filled his heart, but they had no choice. They stood up and embraced each other, insects falling from their skin like motes of silver dust. Two sisters and two brothers walked into the darkness. He turned to the remaining three. They smiled at him sadly, knowing they too would soon say their farewells. Hand in hand they made their way across the floor of an immense space. He saw debris littering the ground at his feet; sheets of iron, chains, cogwheels, and shattered wood. Was that a miniature castle on the floor, no larger than his little finger nail? Perhaps it was merely a trick of the shadows.

He noticed a change in the texture of the darkness ahead. A blue radiance, barely visible, rose before them. As they drew closer he realised they approached a ridge, beyond which lay a gulf far larger than the hall they'd left behind. They stopped and he gasped in wonder. A plain stretched far below. It glowed blue, as if it lay under glass, and beneath the light the mottled brown surface faded to silver in the distance. He looked to his left and saw masses of black cables spread out over the land. They rose up in sloping walls to disappear behind a shadow that blotted out the universe. One by one the four of them made their way down the slope.

CHAPTER NINETEEN

"HELLO MAX," SAID a voice behind him. He turned round. He stood next to the table with its battered chairs. It felt colder, more real. *What was I thinking? I don't belong here.* The darkness surrounding him looked unfamiliar. Indistinct shapes moved in the distance. He pulled out the derringer he'd taken from the turret in the *Beatrice*. That brought him up with a jolt. *I'm Max again.* He looked at his hand and saw stubby fingers ingrained with those speckles of gunpowder he could never shift. He checked his clothes; a uniform and a lizard-skin waistcoat. *I never had brothers or sisters, I lived someone else's memory, but whose?*

A man walked out of the shadows and stood at the opposite end of the table. Black suit, pale face, white hair. With a wrench of fear Max recognised him. *He's the dream brother sitting on my right hand side. We stood at the entrance to the Ear and looked out on the realms of men.* But that wasn't the only place he'd seen the stranger. He steadied himself against the table as giddy realisation took hold of him. His heart thundered in his ears. *Surely not, it can't be true.* At last he found the strength to speak.

"You're my friend, we played together when I was a toddler," he said. He couldn't believe it. The newcomer appeared relaxed, assured, unlike like the nervous simpleton scared by a baby's laugh, but they looked so similar.

"No, not I," said the man with a sad smile. His voice sounded like thunder heard from far away. His answer shocked Max. The man gestured around him.

"I built this from my memories, do you know where it is?" he asked. Max shook his head.

"Deep in God's mind," said the man, "in the chamber where we came to consciousness, and to where we will return. It sits in the centre of the Head, a vault forty thousand miles in diameter," he laughed. "That's very big, even for us."

He pulled out two chairs.

"Come on Max, let's talk," he said.

Max didn't want to talk, he wanted to run shrieking in the opposite direction, but he'd no idea where to go. Even if he located the ear canal it lay twenty thousand miles away and God only knew what lurked out there in the darkness. He sensed titanic forms in motion beyond the pool of light surrounding them. *They're God's errant dreams, primitive urges spawned before the giants unite to make his higher consciousness.* He certainly didn't want to meet them. At least here familiarity lingered, if only from the vision he'd just experienced.

"I'm not going to eat you, or turn your mind inside out," said the man. Max forced himself to sit down.

"You're a giant, part of the mind of God."

"Yes, my name is Ragaleis." said the giant.

"But you're shorter than me," Max blurted out. Ragaleis laughed and something in the sound hurt Max's ears. The giant held out his hand.

"See," he said. Max looked. The skin seethed like boiling milk. He fell down into the palm. It grew to the size of a wide plain, the pores gaping like pits. He saw individual cells as big as houses, molecules vibrating in clouds of light. He tore his gaze away, fixing his eyes on the table top. Reeling with the vertigo, he fought the urge to be sick.

"I'm a giant, in fact I'm as tall as that tower in your city," explained Ragaleis. *He means the Carceral Archipelago*, thought Max. *God, he's two miles tall.*

"So why don't I see you as a giant?" asked Max, forcing himself to meet Ragaleis's gaze. He saw eyes the colour of rain on a window.

"Only a few people can communicate with us in this form," said the giant. "Thousands of years ago, when the Machine Men made us, their human allies chose a handful of families and refashioned their children's minds. They taught them how to think like us, so to those of you with this gift we appear as you see me now, human, not monstrous or fearful. They wanted to ensure that only the best of humanity would teach God about the people he'll eventually save. You're a descendant of one of those children."

Max's mind reeled at Ragaleis's words. Images, voices, memories fell into place and the implications terrified him.

"I'm someone who can speak to giants?" he asked. *Mother too. This is utterly insane, for God's sake what did she curse me with?*

Ragaleis nodded. Max didn't know whether to laugh or cry.

"You seek to learn from us, to understand what we are?" he continued.

"Yes," answered Ragaleis. "That's why we left our home to wander the singularity."

Max remembered the words from his mother's book of poems.

When I appear holding Max in my arms it speaks of motherly love, when I play with Max and sometimes chide him, it speaks of patience and loving kindness.

It suddenly all made sense.

That's how she explained humanity to God, using me as an example.

He had to ask one last question. He didn't want to, he was terrified of the answer, but he couldn't turn back.

"The man I played with as a child?" he said.

"My brother," answered Ragaleis, "his name is Bassandis."

The universe fell silent. Time froze. Max sensed every face turning in his direction. Man, woman, child, Machine Man, all creatures known and yet undiscovered in the body of God looked at him. A billion light years away the other gods faltered in their stride and waited. All the scattered pieces in his mind slid into place; the room, his mother, his father's secret weapon, the games he'd played with the simple-minded stranger. *He wasn't foolish, or mad, he just didn't understand us.* His mother tried to explain everything to his father before she died. *I didn't have time to listen,* that's what Herman said to Odilon. *I was too arrogant.*

Max shuddered. *The Lord of the Carceral Archipelago doesn't know what he's got locked in that fortress. It's another spirit from the mind of God. Ragaleis isn't the Giant of the Thumb. He's not the one Hathus and his Black Rose friends are after. It's Bassandis, and my idiot father is about to send him to defend the city against the very ships seeking his destruction.*

"I'm looking for him," continued Ragaleis. "You showed me a glimpse of where he is but not long enough for me to understand. I know it's across a sea, in some kind of citadel, but I want you to take me there."

Max realised what the giant meant. He pushed his chair from the table and jumped back, appalled.

"You've been inside my head all this time," he said. "When my mother spoke to me in my dreams it was you."

Is this how it was, Max? Is this what used to happen? she said to him when he fell asleep in the room. He'd wondered at the time why she asked questions she should already know the answers to. But it wasn't his mother, was it? It was Ragaleis disguised as her. The creature had tricked him. It had looked into his mind and found his earliest memories, showed him the warm room and the loving parent he'd forgotten. He could almost forgive it for that, but the idea that the creature sat in his head like a parasite filled him with nauseous rage. Ragaleis lurked behind his eyes, tracking all his thoughts and actions. Max, the giant's puppet, danced to his tune.

Now he understood Odilon's odd response after the first encounter. The Watcher saw the creature in his head. Euphrosyne and Hathus had also searched for Ragaleis in Max's eyes. When Hathus said he was looking forward to meeting him, he spoke to Ragaleis, not Max. Odilon, his father and Hathus all knew. How? He didn't see anything when he studied himself in the mirror on the *Beatrice*.

"It's not like that, I haven't invaded your mind. Our link is tenuous, and it weakens with distance," Ragaleis said. "I only see your thoughts when you sleep or your guard is down. Even then, it's like a voice played on a distant radio, nothing more."

He wasn't convincing, but Max returned to his seat. He'd hear the creature out.

"I've been searching for my lost brother for hundreds of years," continued the giant. "When your ship passed by me I sensed your mind, and in your memories I found echoes of the games you played together. That's why I chose you to help me find him."

It's too late, thought Max, *we'll never get there in time. My father will unleash him on the dreadnoughts and they'll all be destroyed.*

"You're not immortal, are you?" he asked, hoping against hope. "You're physical creatures and can die."

He saw fear on the creature's face. "Why do you ask?"

"There are humans seeking to destroy you," Max said, "two dreadnoughts from the Empire of the Ear are looking for a giant. At first their leader, a man called Alaric, wanted to make contact with you, to tell you that God's finished."

The giant gasped and Max saw his eyes glitter with happiness.

"I knew it," he said in wonder, "that's why I've been looking for my brothers and sisters, in my heart I realised it's time to return."

Max almost felt sorry for the creature, he saw nothing but naivety and trust in his expression.

"But Alaric's dead, and another man controls the battleships. He wants to kill your brother, to destroy all the giants. They're heading for my city. You and your brother are in great danger."

Even a two mile high giant would be no match for the fleet. Ragaleis didn't look like a warrior. He or Bassandis might defeat one of those flying battleships, but not both.

"Your brother's a prisoner in the fortress where we used to play," he said. "My father thinks he's a weapon and intends to use him to defeat the fleet from the Empire of the Ear."

"Why?" asked Ragaleis, his eyes wide with alarm. "Why do men want us dead?"

He can't have learned much about humanity if he's surprised, thought Max. He realised what he had to do and wasn't ready for it. *So I'm the one who gets to explain man's betrayal to the God we created in order to save ourselves. What do I say?* He could take a stab at Hathus's motives; madness, nihilism, desperation, fear of what they would unleash when God finally awoke. How could he describe the motives of the Black Roses? *They're aliens, for God's sake. I don't know why they want you dead.* It'd take a lifetime to frame even the simplest explanation and he didn't have time.

"We've got to stop my father using Bassandis as a weapon against the dreadnoughts," he said, ignoring the question. Herman and Odilon had no idea what they had, he could see that. The stubborn old man and the dreamer thought the giant a mere monster that had escaped a wormhole and somehow survived.

"Can you take me to him?" asked the giant. Max sensed the creature's desperation.

"How fast do you move?" he asked.

"I walk," replied the giant. Max did the calculations in his head. Too slow, besides Ragaleis would head into the path of the dreadnoughts.

"Get away from here," he said. "Go east, as quickly as you can. Pray that I'm right and the enemy is looking for your brother and not you. If I can get to my father before he unleashes Bassandis then I might have a chance to save him."

I've got to convince the stubborn old bastard, thought Max, *when did he ever listen to me? He didn't even listen to Mother. She was on the verge of telling him what he'd really found, but she died.* The only other option was to get Bryony to the *Geryon*, but he'd no idea how to do that after Ruth's performance in the hangar.

Ragaleis's took Max's hand in his own. *God how much does that weigh outside this house?* thought Max, yet the creature's touch felt light.

"Go, quickly, save my brother," begged the giant. "If he dies God's mind will be incomplete. He'll become a monster."

Max looked up at Ragaleis, but with a shock realised he sat alone. He called out the giant's name. His voice faded in the darkness. He turned and saw a rectangle of daylight.

He stepped out of the house like a man in a trance. He felt the wind stroke invisible fingers through his hair. The plain stretched to the horizon where a range of hills led up to the mountains. Beyond, the skin of the Thumb rose into the sky, its mottled surface muted by the haze.

Yesterday I was a raggedy scavenger hunting for scraps in a few remaining wormholes, dreaming of running away to the Thumb, he thought, *what am I now? I talk to giants, I talk to God's mind and I don't go mad. What does that make me?*

He saw the flyer. He walked towards it. Ruth stood on deck, clutching the rail. He climbed up the ladder and saw the terror and sickness in her face. Red eyes stared at him in wonder. Dried blood crusted her nose. She glanced beyond him as he stepped onto the ship and shrieked, falling onto the deck and burying her face in her hands. Max turned round.

Ragaleis stood in the mist beyond the house, a shadow as big as a mountain.

God almighty, he really is the size of the Carceral Archipelago. Ruth whimpered in terror at his feet. He felt scared, who wouldn't when confronted by that titan? It destroyed any frame of reference a sane mind might use to navigate reality. After their first encounter he'd hidden his eyes and cowered, convinced the giant wanted to kill him. This time his fear felt no worse than the brief panic he experienced looking into a wormhole, or standing on the edge of the roof of the Carceral Archipelago, an irrational vertigo he mastered with ease. *To others they're monstrous creatures, terrifying in their sheer impossibility,* he thought, looking down at the girl writhing in mindless fear on the deck. *Its psychic defences are driving Ruth mad, but to me it's just a giant. So much for Max the coward. Hark at me now.*

Ragaleis turned and walked eastwards, fading as the fog swirled around him. The ground trembled with each footstep. *He's escaping,* realised Max with relief, *he's not going to try and rescue Bassandis.* With luck the dreadnoughts headed south towards Metacarpi and Ragaleis could evade them. Max dragged Ruth into the cabin. Samson stared out of the bridge window at the Thumb, his face covered in sweat. Max remembered Olaf in the engine room of the *Bricolage,* fingers gripping the controls, eyes filled with the same fear. Max heard the muted thunder of Ragaleis's stride behind him. He released Ruth. She crawled into a corner, wrapped her arms round her knees and rocked back and forth, chanting the same lullaby he'd heard her sing in front of her dead father. He told Samson to spin up the dynamos and the ship sped away from the house.

As they raced towards Metacarpi Max realised what lay ahead. An impossible task faced him. He had to stop his father unleashing the one thing the old man thought capable of saving the city. The Lord of the Carceral Archipelago would think him a traitor, happy to abandon them all for the sake of a fantastic story about giants. When did Herman ever pay attention to his son? How could Max get through to him after years of impatience and contempt? Abductor Pollicis Brevis lay in ruins and the dreadnoughts responsible bore down on Metacarpi. The only chance it had to defend itself was a monstrous titan, which may or may not prove a match for the invaders. Then out of the Wasteland arrives Max the scavenger, the idiot son who couldn't even follow the simplest order to take Ruth home, and he's babbling about his childhood friend the giant, who just happens to be part of God's mind. *Forget the city Father, we've got to save my childhood playmate Bassandis, whatever the cost.*

Max fumed. Put like that, he knew which choice he'd make. He'd be lucky if Herman just laughed at him. He paused as a chilling thought caught him off guard. His father said he'd sent him away from Metacarpi to save his life. If he knew Ragaleis lurked inside his head, then he must have realised Max had led the giant to his brother. So did the Black Roses, that's why they'd tried to kill him on the chain. By secretly dispatching him north, had Herman hope to throw Ragaleis and the Black Roses off the scent? Did Herman know what Bassandis really was? Impossible, his father embodied stone loyalty and an unflinching dedication to duty so ingrained it turned him into a machine. He would never betray humanity's Great Task. *He must still think the giants are simple monsters, tethered by their thoughts to each other and to me.* Max shivered, his hands trembling. *Riddles within riddles, more madness, focus on the problem. What can you possibly do to make that sour-faced bastard believe your story?*

Odilon. He smacked his fist into his palm. Samson jumped and the ship veered off course for a second. The Lord of the Carceral Archipelago listened to the Watcher in the Tower. Last time they'd found the giant a day's flight from Odilon's spire. Max scanned the landscape. The ship didn't carry any charts of this region, but if he could spot a landmark he recognised he could guide them. Odilon wouldn't pour scorn on Max's story. The man might be as mad as they come, but he understood more about the universe than anyone else Max knew, and his father trusted him. If he could persuade the Watcher then he stood a chance of stopping Herman. He took a gamble. After the *Beatrice*, Odilon had probably accompanied Herman to Metacarpi to prepare the defences, but he hoped against hope the Watcher had returned to his tower. This ship outran the *Bricolage*. Less than a day to find the spire, four days to reach the city. He prayed they'd stop his father before the dreadnoughts turned up.

By sheer luck they passed a mountain of machines he recognised in the afternoon and within minutes he worked out their position relative to Odilon's tower. Ruth and Samson recovered, though the guard kept his hands clamped over the controls and wouldn't tear his gaze away from the Wasteland ahead. Ruth watched Max with fearful eyes. He guessed he'd impressed her by being alive and not crumpling into a hysterical puddle in the shadow of the giant. He told her about Bassandis, and their race to stop his father unleashing the monster on the battleships. She stared at him open-mouthed.

"You can speak to the mind of God," she whispered. He didn't particularly want to be reminded of his talent. The look of awe in those purple eyes bothered him. Once it would have made him happy with desire, now it conjured up images of himself as some kind of oracle. *No, not me, not Max the raggedy scavenger. Find someone else.* He couldn't ignore a horrible feeling he'd be seeing that expression on other people's faces in the future. Besides, Ruth still angered him. Getting Bryony to her father might have stopped the fleet in its tracks . . . but there

was no point harping on about her stupidity. Seeing Ragaleis had clearly brought home to her the enormity of
what they were trying to do. Max was relieved to see her
arrogance gone and didn't mind her stewing a while
longer in fear and guilt.

At last Max spotted Odilon's tower. Relief quickly
turned to worry. Night descended but no lights shone
and when he tried to hail the spire on the radio it stayed
silent. Samson set the ship down outside the hangar
doors. They remained shut. Despairing, Max realised
he'd wasted his time on a futile detour.

"There's someone up there," said Ruth. She pointed
at the upper stories. Max followed her gaze but saw
nothing but steel and glass rendered indigo by the fading light.

"Are you sure?" *She's probably seeing things, her
brain's scrambled by the sight of the giant.*

"There's someone there," she replied, her voice
tense. No-one else lived in the spire. Unless she jumped
at shadows it had to be Odilon. Perhaps he was hiding
because he thought they came from the dreadnoughts,
after all they arrived in an imperial ship. They couldn't
get into the tower at ground level, but higher up might
be easier, as long as the Watcher didn't decide to take
pot shots at them with an antique weapon he'd finally
got to work. Max told Samson to ascend. He searched
for the gun emplacement he'd found last time. The outside of the spire was a haphazard chaos of aerials, pillars, vanes, sculptures and buttresses. He found himself
wishing for the rough stone monotony of the Carceral
Archipelago. At the point he was about to give up in
frustration he spotted the outline of the plastic cannon.
Samson brought the ship next to the platform and Max
jumped down. Ruth followed him. He almost banished

her back to the flyer, but relented. If it wasn't Odilon inside, her combat skills might prove useful.

It took him a moment to break in. On his last visit, electric lights had illuminated the interior. This time darkness filled the metal passageways. Pale radiance from hidden sources outlined some of the oddly-shaped blocks in the walls. To Max the feeling of climbing his way through the guts of a dead clock grew even stronger. He called Odilon's name, but heard nothing but his own voice echoing down the corridors. Where would the Watcher hide? How many damn studies and laboratories did he have? Max had no idea where to look. He cursed under his breath. The dreadnoughts flew towards the city, remorseless and deadly. He didn't have time to play hide and seek in this stupid labyrinth with a man who clearly didn't want to be found.

He realised he stood at the entrance to the library where he and Abby shared a bottle of wine. It felt like aeons ago. Without thinking he stepped into the room. Something cannoned into him. His gun flew through the air and landed in a heap of books. He smashed into a set of shelves, dislodging a heavy volume that thumped him on the head. Before he could react he'd rebounded and ended up on the floor. A weight landed on him, driving the breath from his lungs, pinning his arms to his sides. *You stupid idiot, it's the one you didn't see that always gets you.* Where the hell was Ruth? He felt someone grab the collar of his uniform and yank his head painfully up. A mouth closed over his in a kiss so hard he felt his teeth cut into the back of his lips. His eyes re-focussed only to be filled with a web of red hair.

"I thought you were dead, you stupid bastard," yelled a voice. *Abby?* Hands grabbed his shoulders and shook him till his teeth rattled. His head fell back onto the floor with bang. Abby sat astride him. God but he'd never realised how beautiful she was, and how much he'd missed her. She looked up and her face hardened. Max craned his head back and saw Ruth in the doorway. She'd had the sense to stay back as soon as she saw Abby. His friend's thoughts were written over her face so Max decided to put an end to it once and for all. He reached up, pulled her down and kissed her back, pouring all his love for her into that embrace. He felt her tears on his cheek.

CHAPTER TWENTY

"WE CAME HERE first," said Abby as they flew over the Wasteland, "they made us take an imperial flyer and your father said the city fleet'd blow it out of the sky the second they spotted it. Odilon swapped it for one of his. I thought I'd lost you, I was in a state. He gave me something to make me sleep. When I woke up they'd gone."

Max heard the unease in her voice.

"Odilon drugged you?" He found it hard to believe. The Watcher doted on the Fabrice sisters. He could understand him wanting to keep Abby out of the way when they released Bassandis. Even so, her words shocked him.

"I tried to make them take me too," she admitted sheepishly. He'd seen Abby's persuasion techniques, and there'd been times when he'd have cheerfully knocked her unconscious himself. Even so, the idea that the Watcher had doped Abby still bothered him.

"He's protecting you," said Max, unconvinced. Not that Odilon's ruse had helped. Here they were, speeding south, trying to stop a titanic battle to decide the fate of humanity. When he thought of it in those terms he had to sit down until the dizziness passed. He told Abby what happened since she left the *Beatrice*. At the end she stared silently out of the window at the passing terrain, refusing to meet his eyes. That bothered him more than anything. Was Abby scared of him as well? He could talk to monsters, but that didn't make him one. *Has this changed everything? Just at the point I realised I truly love you?* To his relief she caressed his cheek and kissed him.

"Let's leave, you and I," she said, nodding towards Samson, who hadn't moved from the controls since they left the spire. "Dump these two and journey to the Thumb."

"What do you mean?" *You know what she means.* It was so tempting it hurt.

"The city's finished," she whispered. "We can't stand against the fleet. You won't stop your father unleashing the giant. Out there we'll discover whole new worlds; cities of philosophers filled with wonderful books, the mercury river, the Steel Queen, the court of Theuderic, Lord of the Machine Men. Come with me Max, together, just the two of us, like old times."

She looked into his eyes, making a desperate call, one he knew she didn't believe herself. Instead of answering he took her in his arms. She bunched his shirt in her fists as if she feared being torn away from him there and then. Max cursed the fact they were crammed in a tiny flyer with Samson and Ruth and no chance of being alone together. Their love would have to wait until after. After what? After they all got killed?

Abby didn't mention the Thumb again. Instead they talked about stopping his father. Max decided there was no point heading for Metacarpi. They'd be shot down as soon as they reached the outer defences. He knew the fleet hadn't fought against anyone for hundreds of years. Inexperienced and jumpy captains would panic if an enemy flyer turned up. They'd head straight for the fortress beyond the Forbidden Sea instead, hoping to get there before the dreadnoughts arrived at the city. Abby agreed with the idea of persuading Odilon first. Herman might listen to his old friend.

Samson hid inside himself. He rarely spoke a word, and when he did he only talked about the flyer, its engines and their course. Max understood it was his way of coping with the giant. For the guard nothing existed outside the machinery powering the vessel; its dials, switches and dynamos. Beyond the walls of the cabin lay an insane universe the poor bastard no longer knew, while on the panels in front of him needles and digital readouts spoke of precision and surety. Max didn't dare disturb him. Wrapped in his fear, the man posed no threat and he flew the ship well.

Max did worry about Ruth. She sat on the front deck of the airship, her arms round her knees, staring out at the Wasteland as it sped beneath them. Max realised that Samson's withdrawal left her completely alone. The only other people she knew flew in the two dreadnoughts towards a storm of destruction.

"I'm going to talk to her," he warned Abby, in case she got the wrong idea.

"Why?" she asked, too sharply for Max's liking.

"Her father died and we might need her help," he said. Abby shrugged. Max bit his tongue and joined Ruth on deck. She turned Alaric's ring on her thumb, watching the light glint on the carved hair.

"I'm Lord of the Long Lock now," she said. He tried to read her face, but it told him nothing.

"In the house I dreamed I was the giant Bassandis," he said. "Four of us walked out of God's head, two women, myself and Ragaleis. We stood at the opening of the Acoustic Meatus. To the north I saw God's hair, like a wave of black flecked with silver, pouring out of the universe onto the singularity."

"Those are cities clinging to the filaments. When I look up from my home they appear as clouds of light hanging in the darkness. Crystal ships bigger than the *Beatrice* float between them. One took me to the Anti-Helix on the day I pledged myself to the service of Crysanthe Uella."

Max remembered the ice-cold features of the woman in the speaking mirror. Ruth made it sound like a profound honour, Max wasn't so sure.

"If we can't stop my father unleashing Bassandis then we might have to return to the *Beatrice* and rescue Bryony," he said. "I'll need your help, and your promise that you won't fuck everything up like last time."

Ruth nodded. *That'll have to do*, thought Max, and went back inside.

On the morning of the fourth day they crossed the shores of the Forbidden Sea, flying so low their ship kicked up a wake behind them. Max made Samson reduce speed. The last time he and Abby came here the moving turrets on the outer wall nearly blasted them out of existence. He guessed they'd only survived because the artificial mind controlling the weapons had recognised his father's ship. This time they piloted an enemy vessel. Max hoped that ages of neglect left gaps in the defences. They could only find them by flying close enough to trigger the guns and praying they could move out of range in time. He told Ruth to scan the skies in case the iron box turned up. He knew their ship had precious little in the way of defences; half a dozen rockets and a couple of machine guns, anti-personnel weapons hopeless against plate armour. The gun on the *Zephyr* had barely dented their pursuer while its cannon chewed them to pieces.

Once he thought he saw Ragaleis in the distance, but the towering shape turned into a thunder cloud. He almost regretted telling the giant to flee. The clapped out old arsenal ahead wouldn't give him too much trouble, a few strides and he'd be over the iron walls. Max closed his eyes and tried to summon memories of the room and his mother. Faded images teased at the edge of his mind, without the startling clarity of the visions the giant had created. *He's not in my head*, he guessed, *he's too far away.*

Max watched glumly as they approached the line of blocks, broken wheels and rusted armour. The dreadnoughts were another matter. As frightening as the giants appeared to mere mortals, he'd no doubts the guns of the *Beatrice* could slay them. He stopped himself. Mere mortals? He sounded as arrogant as Ruth. *You're Max the raggedy scavenger, just because you can talk to bits of God's mind doesn't make you special.* Holiness might creep up on him unawares. He laughed out loud.

"Nothing's moving." Abby said, turning round at his voice. Damn, he hadn't been paying attention.

"How near are we?" he asked. Far beyond the prow of the vessel the metal boxes sat on their wheels, doors and hatches firmly closed.

"About two hundred yards closer than last time," said Abby. Max dared to hope. *Machines don't play waiting games, they've broken down or something's deactivated them.* He told Samson to keep moving forwards. Nothing moved, no lights flickered on the console. *Father and Odilon turned them off*, thought Max, *this is too easy.*

They left the defensive wall and entered the plain of spires. Max tried to see their summits but they lofted into space. Once above the glowing atmosphere their stone and metal walls faded swiftly into blackness. Samson steered the ship between the blades and through the tunnel piercing the inner wall of the fortress. Still nothing moved. No hidden weapons sprang from the ruined towers on the battlements, no other ship appeared in the sky. Max began to doubt. Perhaps his father hadn't come here at all. Perhaps the whole thing was a ridiculous fantasy and the cylinder held neither giant nor wonder weapon. To the north the remnants of the fleet flung themselves in suicidal attacks at the imperial battleships, his father yelling desperate commands from the roof of the Carceral Archipelago. He felt Abby's hand grasp his. She saw the anxiety in his face.

"Come on, you coward," she said gently. "We'll survive, we always do."

The cylinder rose before them, the doors still shut. Max couldn't see any other vessel. He told Samson to take them up to the hidden shelf. As they approached he saw the gouges left by their attacker's shells. The memory of the explosions came back to him. He knew now that a Black Rose had controlled the iron cube, intent on stopping him reuniting Ragaleis with his brother or freeing Bassandis. He'd no doubts it watched him even now. Perhaps it clung to one of the spires where it rose above the atmosphere, watching him from a perch in space, hidden by the airless darkness. He shuddered and wiped his palms on his shirt. *Keep calm, keep focussed.*

He saw the wreckage of the house and sadness superseded fear. Their attacker had destroyed the front, and shattered glass and wood littered the concrete. He noticed a passage cleared through the debris leading into the next room. *They're here, but where's their ship?* Samson set the flyer down on the flat space in front of the wreckage and Max and the two women disembarked. He asked the guard to stay with the ship in case they needed to leave in a hurry.

Instinct told Max to keep quiet as they crept up to the house. He only expected his father and Odilon, but caution kept him from striding into the cylinder yelling their names. The next room showed less damage, though a shattered table and chairs traced the path of half a dozen stray shells. Miraculously the guitar still sat against the wall, untouched. If they got out of here alive Abby could have it as a present.

The room where he'd played with Bassandis looked intact, but something had changed. Max no longer saw it as a place of childhood wonder and comfort lost. With Ragaleis gone, nothing picked out his emotional needs and gave them form in enticing visions of his mother and her kindness. For a second he hated the monster for playing with his memories, and he stared at the empty room in disgust. He heard noises from the corridor. He peered down it and saw a dot of light. *The door's open.*

They walked along the passageway. Max imagined Bassandis in his human form fearfully making his way to meet the woman and her child. He remembered how he'd felt when he stood with the other giants, looking down on the singularity with its thin coating of dirt and air. He'd been frightened, tentative yet filled with excitement at the possibilities spread out before them. How did he end up here? What did he think of the games he played with the child? He tried to put himself back into the mind of the creature but it proved impossible.

He stepped through the door. Abby and Ruth followed him, fanning out on either side. Ruth carried Samson's machine gun, Abby a revolver she'd picked up from Odilon's spire and Max still had the derringer he'd found on the *Beatrice*. Not the greatest massing of firepower, but his father was the only hostile creature he anticipated meeting and he wasn't about to shoot him, no matter how tempting. Yet old habits died hard and Abby certainly seemed to perk up at the thought of a firefight.

The passageway opened out into an immense vault. A mist hung in the air, tenuous above, growing thicker below. A walkway curved away on either side, hugging the walls. To his left Max made out a cluster of machines. Orange lights winked on panels, but the dim light and haze made it hard to see any detail. He looked for signs of life. Nothing. Where in God's name were his father and Odilon?

To his right a set of stairs led down from the walkway into the mist. Abby moved towards them but Max stopped her. He'd heard something.

"What's this fog?" she whispered. Max took a guess.

"I think the giants generate it to hide themselves from us so we can't see them in their true form."

He'd never seen Ragaleis full size in daylight, only a silhouette in a cloud, but judging by the terrified response of the people around him that was enough. He imagined he'd look like the man he met in the house, pale faced, white hair, dark suit. He remembered the grey skin and black fingernails of the hand gripping the ridge and wasn't so sure.

He looked more carefully at the fog. It drifted back and forth slowly, like waves on a shore. With it came that sound he'd heard before; the wind blowing rhythmically, rising and falling in time with the tendrils of mist curling over the inside of the colossal doors. *Only it's not the wind is it? That's the sound of Bassandis breathing.* He caught Abby's eye. She'd recognised it as well. She swallowed and jerked her head towards the steps.

Max glanced around and ran some calculations through his head. They'd come into the cylinder about two miles up, so if Bassandis stood his head would be more or less on their level. Max saw nothing. *He must be sitting down or even lying, though this place isn't wide enough for him to stretch out.* They'd find out by climbing down. Max descended the stairs.

He'd barely taken ten steps when Abby hissed at him. He turned to see real fear in her face. Her gaze flickered back and forth. Sweat stood out on her forehead. Behind her Ruth leaned against the rail. She too looked ill.

"What is it?" asked Max.

"I don't know," Abby said, gasping as she massaged her temples. *She's having a panic attack*, thought Max. The idea was ridiculous. *Not Abby Fabrice, for God's sake.*

"Something's happening inside my head," she whispered, "images, ideas, horrible things, bloody faces, screaming at me."

"It's the giant," said Ruth. "I felt like this when the other one appeared. It's inside my head too, showing me things. I didn't kill her, she tripped and fell." Ruth slapped her hands over her mouth and stared in horror at Max.

"I can't go down there," she said in a tiny voice. "Don't make me."

He took pity on her desperation.

"Go back to the flyer, he said. "Stand guard with Samson." She nodded, her purple eyes filled with desperate gratitude. She fled back up the stairs. Abby sat down on the steps and put her head between her knees, a string of her more colourful oaths spilled from her lips.

"How come you can't feel this?" she asked, irritation briefly breaking through terror.

I can talk to giants, thought Max, *they don't affect me.* He closed his eyes and listened to his mind. Something lurked in the background, a sense of anger, like an argument heard in another room, but nothing more. He put his hand on Abby's shoulder to reassure her. She froze, looking at him with astonishment. She placed her hand on his wrist, removed it and stepped back.

"Oh god." She stumbled, one hand pressed to her temple. She took Max's hand again. Abby gasped in wonder.

"It's gone," she said.

"What do you mean?" he asked.

"When I touch you, it stops." She took his hand and he saw the pain in her eyes fade away. He swore. He really didn't want this. He could cope with the ability to bear the giants and whatever psychic poison they sprayed around themselves, but apparently his mother turned him into a demigod with mystic healing powers over others. *No thanks*.

But Abby descended the stairs again, clinging to his hand, pulling him after her.

They came to a wide platform stretching into the mist. Abby held onto him as they walked across it. He looked up and saw shadows emerging amid the drifting strands of vapour. He stopped, pulling Abby towards him. He put his fingers over her mouth, he didn't want her to cry out, and nodded upwards.

The silhouette of a man sitting in a chair towered above them, his hands resting on his knees and his head bowed. Through the fog Max made out dark strands of hair hanging down from the giant's scalp, forming a veil that fringed his face.

"He's the size of a mountain," hissed Abby when he removed his hand. She instinctively pulled back, but Max put his arm around her shoulders. Although he couldn't see the creature's face he recognised the giant. *It's Bassandis*, he thought. *I became him in the vision*. He noticed the rage lingering in his mind. It bothered him. *Giants don't think like this, we're innocent, untainted, like ethereal children*. He pushed the unease to the back of his thoughts and led Abby onwards.

They stood on a level with the giant's lap. In the distance Max saw a spiral staircase wrapped around a pillar. It terminated at a platform in front of the creature's chin. *That's where they speak to him.* How did his father cope with the psychic distortion Bassandis emitted? *The old man's made of iron and stone, not flesh and blood, that's how.* He imagined the horrific images that overcame Ruth bouncing off Herman's impenetrable will like balloons. They walked towards the stairs. As they drew alongside the giant's hand Max stopped. *Something's not right.* He peered into the mist. At this distance everything merged into a mass of shadows but he could make out a band circling the figure's wrist. *What in God's name is that?* He started to walk towards the fingers. They towered above him. A sick feeling of horror and anger swelled up in Max's mind. *He's chained to the chair, the old bastard's put him in manacles.* That instant he hated his father more than he'd done at any time in his life. No doubt the stupid, ignorant old shit crowed to himself for taming such a mighty beast. Bugger persuasion, he'd be happy to put a bullet through his heart. The angry voices in his mind grew momentarily louder and he felt Abby's hand tighten around his. *We're sensing his feelings,* thought Max, *they're mixing with mine. That's why I'm so angry.* He mastered himself with difficulty.

"The idiots made him a prisoner," he said to Abby. "God knows how many years they've kept him like this." How long could you chain anyone to a chair, drip feeding them poison about fighting and war, before they went mad?

They climbed the spiral staircase. Abby insisted on holding Max's hand all the way to the top. It slowed their progress and nearly had them over the rail a few times. Eventually they stood in front of the head, It looked like a mountain hanging in the air. Max knew he must talk to Bassandis, but he dreaded what he'd find. He summoned up his courage and approached the titan.

It was worse, far worse than he'd expected. Ragaleis appeared almost ghost-like in his human form; pale-skinned, slender, with a languorous manner and soft voice. Max guessed this appearance was designed to put humans at their ease. When he'd played with Bassandis, Max had seen him as a doe-eyed nervous young man. The giants in his vision looked the same. The Machine Men deliberately turned them into dreaming poets; fey and otherworldly. The monster in the chair formed a grotesque, diseased travesty. As Max fought the nausea, he wondered how much of this horror came from his father's callous stupidity and neglect. Abby buried her face in his shirt, whimpering in fear. He forced himself to look at the giant's face.

He saw pale skin blemished with grey and blue stains, lank hair made of white and yellow strands, each as thick as his finger. The sound he'd heard on the gantry came from cracked lips, a whistling foulness that surged around him every time the creature exhaled. The gloom cast by the down-turned face made it hard to see the features, but Max thought the skin and flesh sagged, as though it could no longer bear its own weight and slowly pulled away from the skull. *It's too late*, he thought. Pity for the creature overwhelmed him. His nose prickled and he felt tears running down his cheeks. *Father, what have you done? He can't defend the city, he's dying. He'll never make it back to the Head, he'll never see his brothers and sisters again.* The face moved a little and Max's heart raced. Now came the time to speak, but the last thing he wanted to do was look into the giant's eyes.

CHAPTER TWENTY-ONE

"WHO'S THERE?" SAID the giant. His voice sounded like a mudslide. A wave of foul air billowed around Max.

"Bassandis, it's me, Max," he said.

The creature's head still hung down. He reminded Max of Alaric before he died, fighting the black clouds in his head as they leached his thoughts away.

"Is it time? I'm very tired," said the giant.

Time for what? thought Max, *time to go and fight the dreadnoughts?* So his father and the Watcher had filled his head with thoughts of battle. *God knows what they've told him.*

"Bassandis, I met your brother, Ragaleis," he said, as gently as he could. "He's looking for you. God is finished, it's time to return to the Head."

"People," said the giant and the stench of his breath washed over them. Abby turned and retched. "Always people, full of their stories and their explanations, their hatred and their lies."

The face moved. The creature looked up. Max didn't need any psychic attack to turn his mind to hysterical mush. He stood a hundred yards away from a rotting face as big as a hill. The giant looked half-made. Pores big enough for Max to fit his fist inside pitted the skin.

Matter and dirt fell from the features in a constant drizzle.

Bassandis stared at them. Gravity dragged his features down. His eyes bulged from their sockets. Max thought he looked like a child's painting left to smear in the rain. Abby curled up on the platform beside him. Her nails bit into his wrist.

"I remember you," said the giant. Amid the knee-buckling terror shrieking inside his skull Max saw his chance.

"I played with you when I was baby," he forced himself to say. "My mother and I taught you about humans."

Moments passed. Max looked into the creature's eyes, searching for some echo of the shy man who jumped in fear when a toddler laughed. Bassandis tried to smile. It was frightful. Splits opened in his lips and white fluid and gobbets of flesh oozed out. *He's decaying, he's falling apart.*

"Your mother loved you," said the giant. The words stunned Max. In his head she'd become the symbol of everything he'd lacked since her death; affection, happiness, the feeling of being wanted. To hear this vindicated from the mouth of a monster as big as the Carceral Archipelago threw him into utter confusion. He struggled to frame an answer.

"We taught you about humanity. Do you remember? Now you have to take that knowledge back to the Head and reunite with your brothers and sisters," he said. "God is finished."

Bassandis nodded.

"It's a long journey, I need to rest, I tire so easily these days," he said. A tear as big as Max trickled over the pitted flesh of his cheek.

"Ragaleis will help you," said Max.

The giant's head slumped down again.

"Are the battleships here?" he asked. Max's heart sank.

"Listen to me, you must not fight the dreadnoughts," he said, trying to ignore his rising panic. "My father lied to you. You're not a weapon, you're part of the mind of God, you mustn't go into battle. They'll destroy you."

"The city is under attack," mumbled the giant. "Two huge ships fly above it and rain death down upon its people. They're our enemies."

The giant stared down, its lips slack. A river of drool oozed past its broken teeth. *This is hopeless, thought Max, it's like talking to a mad man or a drunk. Well done father, you've done a great job. This is the weapon you think will save the city? You're as deranged as this sad monster.*

The tip of a tongue as big as a boat flickered briefly in the shadows.

"I'm sleepy," murmured the giant. "It's such a long way to the city. Do I have to go today?"

"No!" yelled Max. "Not today, not ever!"

"Ragaleis," said the giant.

"He wants to find you, to help you," said Max.

Bassandis moved his hands. Chains rattled. *They must be as big as the ones that anchor the Carceral Archipelago to the ground,* thought Max.

"He abandoned me, he left me here, a prisoner of these petty men," murmured the giant, his voice sour and truculent.

Max realised he'd wasted his time. The creature's memories of their games, of his brothers and sisters and the reason for his existence, were hopelessly mixed up with the poison his father had dripped in his ear under the stupid belief he prepared a weapon to defend Metacarpi. He must find the Lord of the Carceral Archipelago and try and keep his temper long enough to persuade him not to unleash the giant. He picked Abby up and led her to the stairs. He felt the eyes of the monster on his back. The rage that seethed on the periphery of his thoughts mingled with new uncertainty. He'd sowed doubts in the creature's mind, but was it enough?

Once they arrived back at the gantry ringing the interior of the cylinder Abby turned away from Max and threw up. When she'd finished she looked at him with horror in her eyes.

"What has your father done?"

"He's shut the door on mankind," said Max, "that's what he's done. My mother knew what that was." He pointed into the mist. "She knew it was part of God's mind, and he didn't listen to her, did he? The stupid bastard thinks he's going to save the city with a two-mile high zombie."

Footsteps rang on metal. Someone walked towards them through the murk with swift, confident steps. Clearly not Ruth or Samson. *Here we go*, thought Max, *time to talk to Father*. This would take all his patience and powers of argument. He braced himself.

Odilon the Watcher stepped out of the fog. Abby flung herself into his arms. He grinned happily, then his expression switched to one of concerned anger.

"Abby? Why in God's name are you here?" he asked. He looked at Max.

"Max, you're alive! You shouldn't have brought her," he said like a grandparent ticking off a wayward child. "This place is very, very dangerous."

So's Abby, thought Max. It surprised him how little the wise sage understood the Fabrice sisters.

"Where's my father?"

"I'm not sure, in the environment control room I think, why?" Odilon's eyes narrowed. Max had the uncanny feeling the Watcher read his thoughts. It wasn't the first time, and it always made him uncomfortable. This time he hoped whatever he found would add weight to his argument.

"What's going on, Max?" said Odilon.

"You mustn't release the giant, it's not a monster at all, it's part of the mind of God."

Odilon's expression was a treat. For the first time Max saw him genuinely shocked. Odilon stared at Abby.

"Is this true?" he whispered. She nodded.

"I spoke to the other giant in the Wasteland, the one we searched for in your mirrors," said Max. "God is ready. All the giants must return to the Head to form his mind." He explained as quickly as he could about the eight spirits, the vision in the house, Alaric's mission and Hathus's betrayal. When he'd finished Odilon placed his hand on Abby's shoulder and took several deep breaths, looking for all the world like a fish dumped on land.

"Good God, Good God!" he said. "Your poor mother was right."

Max stared at him. Odilon knew?

"We found it on the shores of the Forbidden Sea," he said, wringing his hands. "It was lost, like a child. It had no memory, or none that made sense. We brought it here to study. Your mother was a great philosopher you know." Max didn't care, all he knew was that she'd told Odilon, and he'd done nothing.

"Your father believed it was a monster from a wormhole," continued the Watcher. "When it didn't die he thought he could use it as a weapon in case the city ever came under attack. Your mother studied it, and I think she realised what it was. She started to bring you here."

"We were teaching it about humanity," said Max. He could happily have hit Odilon. A few words from the mystic fool and so much of this could have been avoided.

"She was about to tell us," said Odilon, "I'm sure, but then she passed away."

"And you did nothing," said Max. *You're all the same, stupid old men who don't pay attention.*

"I'm sorry Max, I wish I'd listened to her," said the Watcher. His eyes filled with tears. He wiped them away with the hem of his robe.

"I genuinely thought they were monsters," he continued, "they possess psychic powers that drive men insane. That's why we sent you away, we knew the Wasteland giant was using you to try and find his companion. The enemy realised it too. We made you go north to get away from both of them, to save your life. Everything you see the giant sees."

The more I tell you, the more your life is in danger, his father had told him on the last day in the Carceral Archipelago. *Every scrap of information in your head, no matter how trivial, marks you as a target.* Max almost forgave his father for his bone-headed refusal to explain. He'd put it down to contempt for a stupid son, now he realised the old man tried to protect him. Even so, the sheer monstrosity of his crimes against Bassandis couldn't be so easily absolved.

"Odilon, if the giants die, God dies," he said. Max saw the Watcher's composure falter. He looked scared.

"We must speak to your father before he opens the doors." He ran back along the gantry. For a reclusive dreamer the old man moved fast and Max struggled to keep up. As they passed the corridor leading to the room of his childhood a hand yanked him back. It was Ruth. He shook himself free.

"We've found Odilon," he snapped, angry at the interruption.

"The iron box is back," she said her voice tense with fear.

Damn, that's all I need. He prayed the defence mechanism had merely reactivated another machine to blunder through the skies, but in his heart he sensed the presence of a Black Rose. He remembered the boiling column of petals on the chain outside his father's study and shuddered. He gripped the derringer, this time he'd be ready.

"Watch my back, it's after me." Her combat skills might prove useful. The universe conspired against him. Not only must he persuade his father to abandon the city to its fate, but he'd have the discussion while waiting for a blade to slip out of the fog and finish him off. Odilon and Abby were nowhere to be seen. He ran after them, Ruth at his heels. He glanced fearfully around, looking for shadows floating through the cloying vapour. It grew thicker, and he couldn't see the control panels he'd spotted when they first entered the vault. He wondered how long it would take to release Bassandis and open the doors.

He found himself among the machines. From a distance he'd only seen a few, but now he stood in a maze of boxes. Some hummed with power, but most lay inert. The mist thinned, but he still felt vulnerable. Every alcove and corner might conceal an enemy, and a Black Rose could just as easily fall on him from above.

He turned a corner and saw his father standing at a control panel, his back towards him. He froze. The last time he'd seen Herman they'd watched Theodore fall to his death from the balcony of the dreadnought. Max had disobeyed him by bringing Ruth to the heart of her enemy. He tried to remember the expression on the old man's face as the guards took Max away. Anger? Fear for his safety? Whatever passed for regret and fatherly love in his flinty heart? He realised he hesitated, a victim of the old fear of the Lord of the Carceral Archipelago. *Come on you coward.*

"Father?" he said. Herman turned and gasped.

"You escaped from the dreadnought," he said. Max saw relief break across his stony features for a second, then the familiar mask came down. Where were Abby and Odilon when he needed them?

"Father, listen to me," he said, "the giant is not a weapon, he's part of God's mind. You mustn't release him."

"He's right, Lord Ocel," added Ruth. *Lord Ocel*? Max was impressed. She tried hard, all her arrogance gone. She practically begged.

"He's one of the eight spirits that form the consciousness of the Deity," Ruth continued. "The Emperor sent my father the Condottiere Alaric to find him and tell him to return to the Head. Captain Hathus betrayed them. Hathus is in league with the Black Roses. They don't want God to wake because they fear mankind. They want all the giants dead. If you send this creature to fight the dreadnoughts he'll perish, and the enemies of humanity will win."

Max spotted a movement in the shadows beyond his father. He panicked, thinking it was the Black Rose. Instead Odilon and Abby emerged between two machines. Odilon motioned for Abby to stay where she was, and approached the Lord of the Carceral Archipelago.

"Listen to her, my old friend," he said.

Max waited for the scorn and anger, but none came. His father said nothing. That threw him even more than the contemptuous tirade he'd expected.

"Mother knew," he continued, "that's why she brought me here, to teach the giant what humans are like. That's why they walk among men, so that God will understand us. She meant to tell you before she died."

Herman looked at Odilon, who nodded.

"This is madness," said the Lord of the Carceral Archipelago. "Why are you telling me this now? The city will fall unless we unleash the creature."

"The whole of humanity will fall if you do," said Max desperately. *Please Odilon*, he thought, *he'll listen to you. For God's sake stop him.* Herman leaned against the panel. He seemed to have difficulty standing. With an unexpected wrench of pity Max no longer saw the stern tyrant who threw a shadow over his son's entire life. Here was a sad old man, clinging at straws, trying to make sense of a world crumbling around him.

"Father, for Yvette's sake," he said, trying one last gamble. His mother's name felt strange on his tongue.

"He's right," said Odilon, placing one hand on his father's shoulder, "the giant is part of the mind of God. If he dies, God dies."

Max started forward but the Watcher held up his hand. He stopped. Could Odilon actually get through to his father? He didn't think it would be so easy. He realised the Watcher was probably the only friend left for the Lord of the Carceral Archipelago. Everyone else he'd lost or shut out from his solitary life. Perhaps Herman always had doubts, but stubborn pride kept them at bay.

"Have you started the process to release the creature?" asked Odilon.

"Yes," said Herman, "what have I done?" Max heard the sorrow and desperation in his voice. *Thank God*, he thought, *he realises what's happened. We may save Bassandis yet.*

Odilon nodded and gave his father a smile full of understanding and forgiveness.

"You did what you thought was best, you weren't to know," he said.

The Watcher pulled out a long knife from beneath his blue robes and stabbed Max's father through the heart. Herman's legs buckled and he fell in a crumpled heap at the foot of the machine. In one movement Odilon reversed the weapon and used the handle of the blade to smash the controls.

Max stared at his father's body, unable to comprehend what he saw. It felt like watching a play, or reading a story book full of outrageous tales bearing no relation to reality. Abby stood on the other side of Odilon, her mouth a horrified O. Time froze around them. *What do I do?* asked a detached voice in Max's head. *Do I run and gather my father in my arms? Try to staunch his blood? Do I charge Odilon and kill him? What do I do?* He had no-one to help him, Abby and Ruth remained as paralysed as he.

In a second the universe came rushing back in a torrent of fury and grief. He stumbled forward, aiming his revolver at the Watcher's head.

Odilon broke apart in an black explosion. Something hit Max in the chest and he hurtled backwards to crash against a control box. Ruth flew past him, firing at the creature now standing over Herman's body. A tendril curled through the air and tossed her into the shadows between the machines. Her gun bounced across the floor. A revolver fired and sparks and fragments burst from the panels above Max's head. Abby shot at the alien from the other side, but her bullets passed through it as if through smoke.

"Abby for God's sake stop shooting," he yelled. "You're going to kill us all."

Mercifully she had the sense to hold fire. The creature withdrew its tentacles until nothing remained but a fountain of black petals. Max watched it, waiting for it spring on him. He recognised the knife now. He still bore its scar across his ribs. He got to his feet, frantically thinking how to defend himself. He knew the Black Rose studied him, but he couldn't see anything like eyes in the fluttering mass.

"Max," came Odilon's voice from the centre of the Black Rose, rendered strange by the echoes of an infinite space beneath the words. At first he'd thought the alien had consumed the Watcher, falling from above and slaughtering him in some unholy way. Now he realised the truth.

"Odilon. You're the Black Rose."

"Yes," answered the creature. *That why he's always been so weird. The odd mannerisms, the exaggerated expressions, the way he peered into our faces as if he couldn't quite understand how our minds worked. He was an alien pretending to be a man. I thought he was just eccentric.*

He'd known Odilon since childhood. He remembered the mysterious sage in blue robes who walked the night corridors of the Carceral Archipelago with his father, whispering advice into his ear. He'd always been kind to Max, he'd listened to him more than Herman ever did, but the boy found him sinister and resented the attention he got from his father. Now the idea an alien sat in the centre of his family, watching, plotting against humanity, made him sick with anger. A horrible realisation stole over him. It nearly drove him to his knees.

"You killed my mother," he whispered.

"Yes I did," said Odilon. "She realised who Bassandis really was. She wanted to tell your father and asked my advice as a friend. I couldn't let it happen, I needed to keep the giant here until I could find a way to destroy him."

"And you tried to kill me," Max said, "on the chain, and then with the iron flyer."

The alien terrified him but the questions crowded into his mind and his need to know stifled his fear.

"The giant Ragaleis is in your head," said Odilon, "looking out upon the realms of man. I didn't want him to find and free Bassandis. I persuaded your father to send you north and planned to kill you in the Wasteland. You came here instead."

"But you were with my father the night I was attacked on the chain," said Max.

"We move swifter than fliers. When he slept I roamed the skies at will. It took me less than an hour to return to Metacarpi," said the creature. The avuncular tones of Odilon lingered in its voice, gentle and persuasive. Max saw Ruth appear out of the shadows to his right. She stared at Odilon in fascinated horror. Max had no doubts the alien would finish her if she attacked again.

"Why? Why do you want God to die?" asked Max. "You helped us create him, you built the singularity and the worm holes, the Black Roses guided us through the Great Task from the very beginning. What's changed?"

"My brothers and sisters helped you," conceded Odilon, "but many of us realise you're not fit to enter the next universe. Look at what you've done in this one. You poison everything you touch with greed and cruelty. We won't allow you to do the same again."

A low grinding noise came from the mist behind Max, the sound of titanic manacles unclasping and falling away. The gantry rocked beneath his feet. *Bassandis is trying to stand,* he thought.

"Abigail," said the alien, "come with me. And Max, you too. I'm truly sorry for all the suffering I've caused you. It gave me such pain. You are my favourites in all the worlds of man. You represent the little good left in humanity, and I will take you both. We'll return to the god of the Black Roses, and your children and their children will see the light of the new universe."

"Fuck off," said Max.

"Abby?" asked the creature. Silence. She stood on the other side of Odilon, and Max couldn't see her past the writhing column of darkness. *She's not going to say yes, is she?* He couldn't stand the thought of losing her. He wanted to cry out, to stop her. Surely she wouldn't leave him to go with this monster into the void? God, it was precisely the kind of thing she would do, flying through the space to see the other Gods in all their grotesque splendour, ready to peer through the door of light at a new cosmos filled with stars and worlds. He saw her cradled in arms of tattered smoke, speeding through the gulf towards unbearable light, while he lived on without her, alone on this wretched, hopeless Wasteland next to God's corpse.

Odilon exploded in a cloud of petals as something came flying through him, shrieking in fury. Abby crashed into Max and they fell backwards onto the floor. Her skull cracked against his. She rolled off him, clutching her forehead and swearing. Lights danced in his vision. Beyond them he saw Odilon reform and hurtle up into the vault. For a second the creature hung in the air like a bird, then vanished into the mist.

Max rolled onto his hands and knees and crawled over to Abby. He prised her hands apart. An evil-looking bruise marked the centre of her forehead.

"That hurt," she said.

"You stayed," he answered.

"God's cock, of course I stayed," she grumbled. Max wrapped his arms around her, holding her tight as if he'd just plucked her from a flood.

"No time," she said, "the giant's escaping."

Max remembered his father. It took all his courage to approach the body. Mercifully Herman's eyes were closed in death. Max stared down at him, trying to understand his feelings. Crippling sorrow lurked there, deep inside. He knew it bided its time. At the moment only disappointment and anger at the Black Roses filled his heart. His father lay in a heap on the floor, a broken statue of an old man. The face bore the same expression he'd seen in life, a mask worn against the world and his own loneliness.

"Max," Ruth limped over to them. Blood trickled down the side of her face. "Stop the giant."

Max tore himself away and ran back through the mist. An immense shape rose into the vault. Bassandis reached down, grasped the edge of the platform in front of his seat and threw it aside. The crumpled metal slammed into the wall high above Max. Rubble cascaded around him. If the disc fell onto the walkway it'd crush him. Instead it rebounded, span over his head and disappeared into the gulf. The gantry sagged, but he kept going.

A vertical light appeared ahead. It widened. *The cylinder's opening.* Max called out the giant's name, but the sound of the hinges drowned out his voice. Bassandis swayed back and forth, and for a second Max thought he was going to fall. Instead he leaned forward and put his shoulder against the doors. Max saw how desperate he was to escape. How long had his father kept him clamped to that chair, telling him day in day out that he was nothing but a monster, a weapon built to destroy the enemies of the city? He despaired. Whatever lessons about humanity his mother had taught the giant lay buried under years of hatred.

"Bassandis," he yelled one more time. The giant paused and looked down in his direction. *He can't see me, I'm too small.*

"Don't go to the city," he shouted, "you'll die, go back to the Head."

If the giant heard him he gave no sign. He pushed again. The hinges screamed. One of the doors broke free and fell out into the arena beyond, crumpling under its own weight. With a bellow of triumph Bassandis groped his way into the light.

CHAPTER TWENTY-TWO

MAX RAN BACK to the corridor. The gantry tilted behind him as it broke away from the inner wall of the cylinder. Ruth and Abby joined him by the entrance.

"Odilon?" he asked. Abby shook her head. Max expected the alien to attack them any second and both women kept glancing fearfully up into the vault, but he had to stop the giant. He ran back down the passageway, Abby and Ruth at his heels. Beyond the wrecked rooms he saw their flyer and, to his astonishment, the iron box. It sat next to the imperial ship, its landing gear nothing more than four metal spheres stuck to the bottom of the cube. A side hatch lay open and on the ground below Samson sprawled in a pool of blood. Max realised in a second what had happened. Odilon had hailed their ship, claiming to be a friend. He'd murdered Samson as soon as he landed, to keep him out of the way while he hunted for the others.

Max, Ruth and Abby dropped into defensive positions among the ruins of the supply office. Max cursed in frustration. He could hear Bassandis walking away from the cylinder. With each titanic footfall dust fell from the ceiling and the debris around them shifted. He realised the giant was moving slowly because of his weakened condition, but knew that any doubt he'd seeded in the titan's mind would quickly fade. If Odilon waited inside his ship, the second they stepped out of hiding he'd destroy them - but this was their only way out. Abby's bullets had passed through the Black Rose without harming it, but enough concentrated fire might distract the alien long enough for them to get to their flyer. They'd have to charge the cube.

Abby walked past him. He tried to grab her but missed. *What in God's name is she doing?* One burst from the box's cannon and she'd be torn apart. She put her hands on her hips and stared at the black slit across the top of the vessel. Nothing happened.

"Aren't you going to kill me then, Odilon?" she called, her voice trembling with hatred. "Come on you alien shit, surely my life is as meaningless to you as all the rest? You only pretended to care for me and Becky, didn't you?"

She lifted her gun and fired into the hole. Nothing moved. Max refused to let her die alone. He ran up beside her, also shooting into the slit. He heard a bullet ricochet inside the machine, nothing more.

"Look," Ruth pointed up into the sky. Max peered upwards and his heart twisted. Far above them a rag of darkness tumbled through the sky towards the giant. He realised the alien had either fled or was shadowing Bassandis. Abby stared at the Black Rose. She started to shake and tears filled her eyes. *We've both lost parents of one kind or another*, he thought, and put his arms round her. She clung to him and burst into tears. *God, how often have I seen Abby Fabrice crying like a child? Never.*

"No time," snapped Ruth and vaulted onto the deck of the imperial flyer. Abby pushed herself away from Max, wiped her nose on her sleeve and followed. In a few seconds they rose from the ledge and aimed for the giant.

For the first time Max looked at a full size giant without its concealing mist. The sight defied all reason. He was a grotesque mountain. Through the rents in his clothes Max saw grey skin bulge and sag. Shreds of flesh hung down from his face and limbs. *He's rotting, he's falling apart*, thought Max, *we've come too late*. He could have wept with frustration. Bassandis staggered away from his prison like a drunk. One step took him over a collapsed section of the inner wall, and then he was climbing through the wrecked defences, crushing the rusted strong points under his feet and scattering fragments of machinery with every step. A wheel he'd kicked free rolled out across the Forbidden Sea like a child's hoop bowled over a playground. Max remembered navigating the *Zephyr* between its spokes when they first arrived at the fortress.

He told Ruth to fly them up to the giant's head, a stupid risk, but he wanted to reason with the titan one more time. He saw in the women's white faces and hollow eyes the incessant litany of rage from the creature's mind taking its toll. He put his hand on Ruth's shoulder and held Abby's hand. They both relaxed. Among his own thoughts he sensed a constant grinding undercurrent of anger, but in him it just manifested itself as a gut ache and a pain behind his eyes.

Ruth managed to position their ship in front of the giant's face. Max knew he didn't have much time. As soon as he took his hand away from Ruth she gave a cry and slumped across the controls. The ship rocked, but she cursed and brought it back on course.

"Hurry up," she hissed, blood trickling from her nose. Max grabbed Abby's hand and they ran to the rear deck. She could keep an eye out for the alien while he tried to speak to Bassandis. He hoped Odilon's affection for the girl would stop him attacking.

Above the ship the giant's face formed a grey cliff of misery. Max saw upturned eyes and a mouth fixed in a drooling grin of pain. He forced himself to remember the delicate youth peering at him from the shadows, his face filled with the happy anticipation of playing a game. Pity overwhelmed him.

"Bassandis," yelled Max as loud as he could. "Listen to me. You must return to the Head. Your brother and sisters are waiting. God is ready."

The thunderous footsteps and the whine of the ship's dynamos drowned out his voice. Behind him Ruth battled with the hatred flooding her mind and the flyer listed. Max thought he spotted a fluttering shadow high up on the giant's forehead, but mist gathered around the creature, making it hard to see. Sick at heart, he took Abby back into the cabin and put his hand on Ruth's arm. Her eyes filled with gratitude. They dropped away from the monster, speeding over the water towards Metacarpi.

Max fought against despair, frantically racking his brains to come up with an answer. If only he could get through to the giant, but the creature stayed locked in the agony of its death march. Even if he managed to communicate, how could he convince Bassandis to stop? The warped mind of the titan clearly believed its sole purpose to be the defence of the city. *How stupid can I be? I played games with it when I was two years old. It won't listen to me.* The Lord of the Carceral Archipelago had dripped rage and pain into its veins every year since. He remembered his mother's words and smiled bitterly. *"When I play with Max and sometimes chide him, it speaks of patience and loving kindness". I doubt there's much left of that after you've been chained to a chair for thirty years.* He looked at Abby. She sat in the corner of the cabin, knees under her chin, pale and shaking. He cursed himself for ignoring her. He realised she was still in shock about Odilon.

"He gave thousands of coins for the theatre," she said. "He brought wonderful gifts for Becky and me, he became another father. If he hates us why did he do that? Was it some kind of sick joke?"

If his own grim father had turned inside out to reveal a fountain of churning darkness he wouldn't have been too surprised, but the memory of the Watcher embracing Abby and the fond expression in his eyes made his betrayal doubly hard to bear. He tried to think of what he could have done, or what he should say now to ease the pain. He took Abby in his arms, but her body stayed rigid, locked in sorrow, and he realised he wasn't helping. He let go and she buried her face in her arms. He remembered his father lying on the floor at Odilon's feet, all power gone, leaving nothing but a broken stick of a man. The shadow puppets in Abby's theatre possessed more life. He couldn't believe he'd never hear Herman's voice again. In the back of his mind lingered the unsettling suspicion that the Lord of the Carceral Archipelago still waited for him at the top of the stone tower.

"Do you remember where you met Bryony?" asked Ruth. Max jumped. He'd forgotten about her. She looked haggard, her beauty eclipsed by exhaustion and fear. He described the rooms. She nodded.

"It's the only chance we have left," she said. "If we can get her back to Captain Andagis I might be able to persuade him to move against Hathus and stop him before he attacks the giant."

Max wasn't so sure. The *Beatrice* was only half the problem. Even if the dreadnoughts stood down it wouldn't stop Bassandis attacking and the ships retaliating out of self defence. He racked his brains for another way to get through to the monster.

"We've no choice, Max," she said. "I can't get near enough to Hathus to kill him, and Andagis will arrest us if we turn up empty handed."

"That creature's inside our heads," she continued. "It's generating a psychic field. I'm guessing it's weak now. A focussed attack might cripple the battleships, or at least distract the crews long enough for you and I to get in and out with Bryony."

You and I? He'd rather Abby came with him, but he didn't trust Ruth enough to put her in control of their only escape route. At least he could keep an eye on her while they hunted for the girl. Abby would have to pilot the ship, taking them in and plucking them out again, if she could stand the monster's cloud of hate for long enough.

"What other weapons does it have?" asked Ruth.

Max hadn't a clue. *Its fists?*

"It's not a warrior," he said. "All it's got is rage and madness."

Max walked onto the rear deck and looked back at the giant. The mist extended miles on either side, Bassandis a shadow moving in its depths. How long would it take the titan to reach the city? He reckoned half a day behind their ship. He wondered if Odilon watched them. Perhaps the Black Rose returned to the void, thinking his task over. Max imagined him tumbling up into the darkness of space to join the others. Max remembered his words. *Many of us realise you're not fit to enter the next universe.* That implied some of the aliens still wanted to help humanity. Perhaps Hathus knew. A day or two in the Steel Room would get it out of him. He caught himself in shock. *God, is it that easy to slip into the shoes of a dead tyrant?*

Night fell, mercifully hiding the giant. They took it in turns to fly the ship. Max managed to grab a few hours of sleep after midnight. He woke from hazy dreams of corridors, but they felt like the echoes of older visions and he'd walked through them alone, without Bassandis, Ragaleis or his mother. As dawn revealed Metacarpi ahead of them Max's heart sank. Beyond the cruel silhouette of the Carceral Archipelago he saw two jagged shapes floating over the northern edge of the city.

"They're here," muttered Ruth, her voice tight. Max looked back across the sea. He couldn't tell whether the distant haze marked the approach of the creature, or the light tricked him. Perhaps they still had time.

Abby handed him a pair of binoculars. Through it he saw the city's fleet gathered in a ragged formation over the centre. *They're insane.* It looked like a handful of flimsy toys. *Their only chance of survival is if the enemy gunners are too busy laughing to aim properly.* Even so, he told Ruth to take them in low, flying almost at roof height. They travelled in an imperial ship and it only needed one nervous captain to decide they presented an easier target.

He flicked the radio through the frequencies to see if he could overhear any traffic. To his surprise he found himself listening to a conversation between an officer on the *Beatrice* and Maria.

"Surrender her to us immediately, and reveal the whereabouts of your giant, by order of the Emperor Demetrius." The man's voice sounded tense, exasperated. *He's got Hathus breathing down his neck,* thought Max.

"Ruth whatever-her-name-is isn't here, and we don't have any giants either, or goblins, or pixies, or unicorns," came Maria's reply, majestic in its contempt. "So turn round and fuck off back to the Ear."

She's playing a dangerous game. As much as he admired her courage, he knew the only reason Hathus hadn't reduced the city to a flaming ruin by now was the imminent arrival of Bassandis. He wondered if Odilon had managed to tell him that the giant was approaching.

Max watched the *Beatrice* float across the northern walls, its spotlights drifting slowly back and forth. He momentarily had the impression that the sky blossomed with new suns after billions of years of emptiness. As their own flyer sped over the warehouse roofs and into the narrow streets he saw a few people on the streets stop and gaze up at the drifting battleships before scuttling into the safety of their tenements and cellars. The city looked empty and Max hoped these fleeting shadows were just stragglers too scared or too stupid to join the exodus. The fleet of city ships moved forwards but the dreadnought ignored them. The *Geryon* slid into position behind the flagship. *Good, close enough*, thought Max, *once we have Bryony this ship'll cross the gap in seconds.*

"You can keep repeating the same nonsense till you're blue in the face, young fellow-my-lad," Maria said, "but it won't make the slightest jot of difference. That woman you're after is a thousand leagues from here by now, and, as you might have noticed if you'd bothered to look out of the window, we haven't got a giant."

"Can you cut in?" asked Max. "I need to talk to Maria. Tell her you're Yvette Ocel."

He guessed Hathus wouldn't recognise the name. He was right. Abby broke into the conversation, pretending to be his mother. After a thunderous silence Maria cut contact with the *Beatrice* and turned on Abby.

"Whoever you are, you little whore," came the voice, "you'd better have a very good reason for pretending to be her." Abby's face turned white, and Max felt relieved that the two weren't in the same room.

"Maria, it's me, Max Ocel," he said, interrupting the tirade. "We have to talk, but the dreadnoughts mustn't know I'm here."

"Max? You wretch," he heard relief mixed with whatever passed for affection in Maria's head. "You're supposed to be on your way to the AntiHelix."

"We don't have much time," he said. "My father's unleashed a weapon to defeat these ships, but it's out of control. You must evacuate the Carceral Archipelago now, get everyone out, and the fleet away from the city."

"What kind of weapon?" asked Maria. He could hear the suspicion in her voice. Did she think he was playing a trick to get the tower to surrender? How could he persuade her?

"I asked you about my mother, remember? You said she took me on journeys when I was a baby," he said. "I found out where to. My father thought he'd discovered a weapon to defend Metacarpi and he kept it beyond the Forbidden Sea. My mother took me to see it. But it's not a weapon, and it won't save us."

"What is it?" asked Maria. *Here we go*, thought Max.

"It's a giant," he said. Silence. Max stared at the Carceral Archipelago, its walls mute, the four chains dropping down into the city.

"Where's your father?" asked Maria. She suddenly sounded very tired. The question took him back to his childhood. What did they used to say? *You're not making sense boy, where's your father? You shouldn't be here. Why aren't you in your rooms? Where's his father? He'll sort him out.* Abby shook her head. She clearly thought he wasted his time. *Father won't sort me out now*, he thought bitterly.

"He's dead," said Max.

This time the silence stretched forever.

"Maria, my father is dead and I am the Lord of the Carceral Archipelago, I command you to evacuate the tower and withdraw the fleet immediately."

Maria cut the connection.

"Look," said Ruth. A stream of black ships dropped from the underbelly of the *Beatrice* and headed towards the Carceral Archipelago. *Too late, it's starting*. The fleet scattered as the enemy formation lanced through.

Cannon flashed on two of the Metacarpi ships and Max saw smoke trickle from the rear of an Imperial scout. *The suicidal idiots*, he thought. Max didn't get a chance to see which of the enemy ships returned fire. The attackers simply erupted in a cloud of debris. Flaming wreckage spiralled down into the streets. All hell broke loose and he didn't want to hang around, so he told Ruth to aim for the *Beatrice*. With any luck they could slip past the others in the confusion.

He felt so sorry for Maria and the others hiding behind the stone walls. They didn't stand a chance. Decades of lording it over a mere city convinced the inhabitants of the Carceral Archipelago they were masters of the universe. Ten minutes disabused them of that fantasy. From their vessel he saw cannon fire pouring from the narrow windows of the tower's parapet. Imperial ships landed on the roof amid columns of smoke. Squads of troops leaped out of the craft. They carried machine guns and used them to cut a swathe across the landing area. Sporadic defensive fire came from the open hatches leading down to the upper levels. Max saw men and women, routed by the ferocity of the attack, race across the stone and leap into city flyers. They rose into the air to dip behind the fortress out of the line of sight of the dreadnoughts. One transport wasn't fast enough and a cannon shell blew it apart as it took off. Burning bodies and wreckage scattered across the landing field. He thought he saw a knot of guards at the shattered window of his father's study. Was that Maria wielding a heavy machine gun, screaming defiance while a harried clerk fed an ammunition belt into the breech? They flew through a link in the chain *Joy* and Max lost sight of the defenders.

Ruth dropped the ship down into the streets again, and they sped past empty windows and over rain-slicked cobbles. The underside of the *Beatrice* drifted above them, blotting out the sky.

"Max, the mist," said Abby, pointing back along the boulevard. The distant buildings dissolved into shadows wreathed in tendrils of fog. *Damn, Bassandis is here. It's too early, we don't have time.* Abby's screwed her eyes up and touched her temple, as if she'd been hit by a sudden migraine.

"It's ten times worse than before," she whimpered. Ruth shook her head and he heard her sob. He pulled Abby towards him and put his hand on Ruth's shoulder. He could feel it too, a growing rage within him. The shadows in the street grew longer, the universe darker. Images of death burst into his mind. He saw men and women ripped apart by cannon fire, shrieking in agony as they burst into flames, leaping from the windows of the Carceral Archipelago. He fought back. *Imagine he's a frightened stranger again, in the room with Mother.* In his thoughts he rolled a dice and plucked a wooden sheep from her hand. The rage subsided. Kind memories of Bassandis buffered the onslaught from the giant's wounded mind.

The flyer rose up under the body of the dread-nought, weaving between clusters of weapons pods and transparent turrets. Many of the guns slowly swivelled to point in the direction of the Forbidden Sea. Max realised that Hathus could see the mist, and knew what it was. A voice crackled over the radio, asking the ship to identify itself. Ruth shouted a garbled reply about a faulty dynamo and cut the connection. Max hoped they'd believe her. The communication light continued to wink as they drifted up the side of the vessel.

Max searched the hull of the dreadnought, trying to spot the window he'd escaped from. Beside them spread a wall of machinery. Wherever he looked he saw forests of guns, aerials, smoke projectors, fins, baffles, armoured vents, portholes and rifle slits. He searched desperately. They could enter the ship at any point, but then they'd have to fight their way to Bryony's prison, if she was still there. The ship loomed massive in the daylight, a city in itself. Max despaired. A flash of light on the upper hull distracted him. A hole appeared in the window and fragments of glass scattered over the controls. Ruth swore. *They've found us out*, thought Max, *they're shooting*. Ruth dropped the flyer out of sight behind a cluster of turrets.

"Max," cried Abby in panic. He looked over his shoulder. A titanic form coalesced in the mist far to the south. Bassandis. For a few seconds silence descended on the universe. The dreadnought next to them shifted and a pod of guns as big as a house swung towards the giant. They didn't fire. Perhaps they were still too far away and Hathus didn't want to leave anything to chance. If he merely wounded the titan it might escape. *He wants to get him into the city*, thought Max, *nice and close so there's no room for error when those cannon open up*. A sudden wave of rage hit him. Abby and Ruth cried out together and the flyer lurched, scraping against the armoured hull. Sparks sprayed over the front deck. Max helped right the ship, and saw a torn strip of bed sheet caught in a vent fifty yards ahead of them, its ragged end flapping in the wind. Max looked beyond and spotted the porthole. He almost laughed. The lazy bastards hadn't bothered to repair it.

Abby handed him her revolver. He took her face in his hands and kissed her.

"We're going into the ship, can you keep her here long enough?" he said.

She nodded. He could see in her eyes how hard she fought the torrent of loathing pouring from the giant's mind.

"Don't be long," she whispered.

"If we're not out in fifteen minutes get away from the city, go to the Thumb," he said.

"Bugger that, ten minutes and I'm coming after you," she replied.

CHAPTER TWENTY-THREE

RUTH AND MAX ran onto the deck holding hands. It felt bizarre and he couldn't shake the sensation of Abby glaring at the back of his head, but it was the only way he could help Ruth fight Bassandis's psychic attacks. Portholes popped open on the hull and Max saw guards aiming rifles and pistols at their ship. A handful of bullets ricocheted off the deck at their feet. Max never liked aiming one-handed, but he drew a bead on a soldier and fired. The man flipped back, dropped his rifle and tumbled out of the ship. A second clatter of bullets struck the underside of the flyer's prow. One round plucked at Ruth's hair, another hissed past his ear.

They floated a few yards from the broken window. No lights shone inside. The gunfire from the *Beatrice* increased. Ruth and Max fell to the floor as another cloud of bullets passed overhead. Max swore as the flyer dropped suddenly, its side banging into the dreadnought's hull. He glanced behind, fearing that Abby was wounded, but she still stood at the controls. She mouthed something that looked like *get on with it*.

"This is no good, Max. It's impossible," yelled Ruth. A round had laid open her shoulder and blood soaked her top. The gunfire increased. *We're pinned, they'll lock onto us in a second and that'll be it*. He banged his fist against the deck and let out a wordless yell of frustration.

Bassandis roared. Max heard it as a thin sound, barely audible, but it brought with it a sick pain behind his eyes. Horrific images danced through his mind. *Good God, and I'm protected.* Ruth clasped her hands to her ears and screamed. Blood poured from her nose. Cries of pain and horror rang out from their attackers and the gunfire ceased. The flyer shot upwards, the edge of the deck scraping along the metal skin of the dreadnought in a shower of sparks. Max grabbed Ruth and jumped.

They landed on the hull above the broken window and immediately began to slide down the armour plating. Max held onto Ruth's wrist. Her feet struck the lower sill of the porthole and she disappeared into the room. With both hands free Max snatched at the upper window frame and managed to swing after her. He saw the flyer fall away from the dreadnought, listing dangerously as it tumbled down towards the city. He watched helplessly as it dropped between a row of tenements, hoping against hope that Abby still lived. A second later it re-appeared at the end of the street, weaving between the buildings to throw off any pursuing fire. Max yelled in relief and admiration. Abby Fabrice was as tough as they came, and he loved her for it.

They ran along the servants corridors, threading their way through the maze of apartments. Ruth seemed to know where to go, carefully choosing her direction as they came to each new junction. Their boots padded over thick carpet designed to mask intrusive footsteps. She stopped and pushed a panel aside. They entered a room ringed with leather sofas. A guard stuffed a cello into a case while another held Bryony by her upper arm. A third guard lay curled on a chair, his hands clasping his crotch as he groaned in pain.

"I don't care if your father's the Emperor's own catamite. You will play a beautiful fugue for Captain Hathus on the bridge while he destroys this city, you fucking brat," snarled her captor, a bearded mountain of a man. "And if there's any more impudence I'll thrash your arse so hard you won't sit down for a year."

Ruth shot him in the chest. The force of her machine pistol kicked him backwards on top of his injured colleague. Max grabbed Bryony and pulled her towards him, firing at the remaining guard. Splinters erupted from the cello as the heavy rounds passed through it into his abdomen. He sat down suddenly and Max put a bullet into his forehead before he started screaming. Max turned to cover the door. He didn't want to know what Ruth was doing behind him, but the soldier with the injured balls suddenly stopped moaning.

The girl kicked him on the shin, wrenched herself away and hurled herself into Ruth's arms. *The ungrateful shit,* he thought. She clung to Alaric's daughter, covering her face in kisses and running her hands through her hair, babbling and weeping out her terror. He rubbed his leg ruefully.

A second wave of rage thundered through his mind. For a second he felt an overwhelming urge to shoot the two snivelling fools in the head and have done with it. They meant nothing to him any more, they were a pair of whining children. He gasped, appalled the giant could affect him so much. Abby and Ruth collapsed, howling in despair. The *Beatrice* lurched beneath his feet. *It's not going to be that easy, is it, Hathus? Bassandis has the power to send the lot of you insane and then all the guns in the universe won't save you.* He grabbed the women and hauled them to their feet.

"It's a psychic attack," he told Bryony, "don't let go of my hand ."

No other guards appeared. Max guessed Hathus thought he needed only three to drag the girl to the command centre. Even so they pushed a heavy sofa in front of the main door before wending their way back to the galley. They went like children, holding hands, with Ruth leading the way. Back at the porthole Max peered out and his heart sank. The flyer was nowhere to be seen and the *Beatrice* flew so close to the Carceral Archipelago the links of the chain *Sorrow* were mere yards from the hull. A constant barrage of small arms fire filled the space between the dreadnought and the tower, though most of it came from their side. Max saw with a sick feeling of defeat the shell holes pitting the wall of the fortress. Splashes of soot poured over its surface and most of the tiny windows smoked from inner fires. They'd only been ten minutes, where was Abby? He heard shouts behind them in the corridor. *They've sent more guards, we're trapped.*

Ruth turned to Bryony and hugged her. *You're not just friends, are you?* thought Max.

"Do you remember when we danced through the rigging of my father's crystal ship?" she asked. Bryony nodded. Ruth kissed her and before Max could intervene she jumped onto the edge of the porthole and launched herself into space. While he watched dumbfounded Bryony followed, dropping out of sight with her arms spread like a bird's wings. *They've just jumped to their deaths, now what do I do?* He looked out of the window. Below him Bryony landed on the inside of the nearest link, rolling forward before standing up in the arms of Ruth. *That's a good fifteen yards away.* He'd break a leg if he was lucky, or end up plummeting to the streets below. He tried to focus, searching for that kernel of courage amid the panic in his head. With a shock he realised it wasn't there. For the first time in his life he found nothing but fear. A bullet smacked into a shelf to his left, shattering a stack of plates. A voice behind him yelled. Max jumped out of the window.

It felt like Odilon carried him through the air again but without control. He tried to scrub off speed by pressing his hands against the hull but he fell away from the ship almost immediately. He smacked into the rust and grit on the inside of the link. His knee cracked painfully against the metal. He skidded and rolled, realising with horror that the surface beneath him sloped down and he was gathering speed. Hands grabbed him by the collar of his waistcoat. The lizard scales contracted around his chest, holding onto him, and Ruth and Bryony dragged him back from the edge.

He hauled himself up and looked west. Bryony shrieked and buried her face in Ruth's shoulder. Ruth swallowed, grey faced. Max prayed she wasn't going to be sick.

To his right the *Beatrice* drifted away from the chain. To his left Bassandis emerged from the mist. Appalled, Max saw how much the journey had taken its toll of the monster. His face sagged, caverns opening beneath his eyes, the corners of his mouth dragged down by tons of flesh. His hands swung listlessly at his sides. *He should be dead, the poor bastard, God's mind or not, someone should put an end to his suffering.*

Two multi-turreted flyers dropped from the underside of the *Beatrice* and angled towards the giant. He opened his mouth, the jaw sagging as a wave of drool poured over his tongue. Max watched in disgust as it splattered down the creature's front and onto the stones far below. The wind blew some of the spittle towards the tower. When it hit the wall Max saw the masonry turn black and start to smoke. *What in God's name's that?* To his relief the wind blew it away from their chain. He wondered if all the pain and misery Bassandis suffered manifested itself in such lethal fluids - cruel acids capable of eating into metal and concrete. *Hathus may have more of a fight on his hands than he thinks.*

He saw the pilot of one of the flyers panic at the sight of the giant and yank back on his controls. A wing tip clipped one of *Hate's* links. The ship slammed sideways into the Carceral Archipelago and exploded.

Bassandis spat. Max watched in fascinated horror as a lump of congealed air struck the nose of the remaining attack vessel. For a second, as the roiling cloud spread over the craft, the metal bulged and became porous like the skin of long-drowned corpse. The craft disintegrated, the explosion from its collapsing engines tearing through the miasma and raining fragments of steel and iron into the streets below.

The giant took a step forward and roared again, the skin of his cheeks ripping under the weight of his jaw. Even though Max held their hands Ruth and Bryony shrieked, and Max fought hard against the insane urge to gather them in his arms and leap into the gulf below. The dreadnought shuddered, cannon turrets swinging wildly back and forth as the force of Bassandis's psychic attack hit home. The giant leaned forward and grabbed at the leading edge of the *Beatrice*. His fingers ripped a section away, the metal cutting lumps of flesh from his hand. Max jumped as a cannon thundered. The shell caught the side of the titan's hip and exploded, tearing a house-sized crater in the top of his thigh. Bassandis went down on one knee. Rubble from shattered houses fountained into the air, rattling against the wall of the Carceral Archipelago and the chain beneath them. Their link rocked violently. Max struggled to keep his balance. He'd given up the idea of taking Bryony to the *Geryon*. He only thought about survival. How could he get them off the chain before they got caught in another attack? He saw no way of climbing up or down the links. The wall of the Carceral Archipelago was too far away to jump.

A few shots ricocheted off the metal above his head. *They're firing at us, we're sitting targets here.* He looked up at the parapet of the tower. Smoke pouring from the upper windows hid it from view. A flyer shot through the rolling clouds and angled down towards them. Ruth raised her machine pistol, ready to fire, but Max caught her arm. He recognised the ship. As it approached he saw Abby's face staring at him through the shattered window.

She guided it next to the link and Max and the two women scrambled aboard. Without a word Abby twisted the vessel away from the chain and dropped it beneath the dreadnought, aiming for the *Geryon* floating on the other side of the flagship.

"I thought you were dead," Max said. Abby gave a hollow laugh.

"I think I am," she said. The relentless psychic attacks of the giant had left their mark. She looked ten years older and her lips were caked with blood. He realised she'd been chewing them. He placed his hand on the back of her neck. The bones of her spine felt so sharp they dug into his fingers, but at his touch she relaxed and life returned to her eyes.

Ruth worked the radio. A babble filled the cabin. Max heard frantic shouts, screaming and hysterical crying as the crew of both ships fought the horrors in their minds. A few calm voices dispatched orders, but they sounded few and far between. Ruth gave up trying to pick out the *Geryon's* signal and called for anyone on the ship to respond. After what seemed an age a woman's voice demanded to know who hailed the dreadnought.

"This is Ruth an Vircana," Ruth yelled, "firstborn of the Condottiere Alaric, I demand to speak to Captain Andagis immediately. I have his daughter with me and we're bringing her to you."

Abby guided the ship out from under the shadow of the *Beatrice*. Max spotted a turret swivelling towards them. He realised they'd heard Ruth's message and planned to blow them out of the sky before they reached the sister ship. He yelled to Abby and she dropped the flyer. A cannon fired. The shell sped over them with an ear-splitting whistle. The vessel swayed in the wake of its passing. Far below an explosion blew apart the bottom floors of a tenement and it crumbled into the street.

"Andagis, we have your daughter and we're under attack," shouted Ruth. The cannon turned. The next round would catch them dead centre. Straight ahead a row of the *Geryon*'s own guns pivoted in their direction. *They're either defending us, or joining in the fun*, thought Max. A movement to his left caught his eye. Bassandis lurched to his feet and took another swipe at the front of the *Beatrice*. His fingers ploughed through plate armour, ripping turrets from the superstructure. They fell to the ground like glass marbles, trailing cables and tumbling bodies.

Rigid with horror Max stared into the face of the giant. The skin of the titan's right cheek lay in tatters and his jaw hung at a crazy angle. Yet even as the head turned towards him, he still saw echoes of a frightened man peering out from those ruined eyes.

Ruth pointed at an opening between two cannon on the hull of the *Geryon*. Abby twisted the ship towards it, barely avoiding another shell. This missile clipped the underside of the dreadnought ahead and ricocheted downwards, detonating harmlessly over the Brick River. Max's stomach dropped into his ankles as Abby yanked the vessel's nose up and they hurtled into the landing bay. The flyer hit the floor, span round and slammed into the far wall. One of its dynamos exploded, hurling lightning into the ceiling.

Before Max could stop her, Ruth kicked open the door and strode out into the hall. A dozen guards pointed their rifles at her. Max motioned for Bryony to stay inside and he and Abby joined Ruth, standing either side of her with their guns ready. Max saw fear, hatred and panic in the faces staring at him down the barrels. Ruth lifted her hand so the ring on her thumb caught the light.

"Behold. I am Ruth an Vircana, Lord of the Long Lock and Condottiere of the Emperor's fleet." It sounded like pompous nonsense to Max but to his surprise three of the guards knelt, then another two, laying their guns on the floor beside them and bowing their heads. *They believe this crap*, he thought, *we might yet live*. A young officer in flying overalls saluted and offered to take them to the bridge. Ruth called for Bryony and she came out of the craft. Max heard a murmur pass through the squad. *We're heroes now*, he thought. He nearly dropped his own gun as relief and exhaustion took hold.

But it wasn't over yet. The officer led them through a ship in disarray, half the crew disabled by fear while the others struggled to keep the leviathan aloft and battle-ready. Everywhere Max saw bodies lying on the floor, men and women clutching their heads and whimpering. The ones still standing gawped at Ruth as they passed by, many of them snapping to attention or dropping to their knees. Thirty years in the shadow of his father taught him a healthy contempt for self-regarding majesty but even so some of the awe he saw in others began to rub off on him. Max started to understand how powerful this woman was in the echelons of the empire.

They came to a passageway leading to the uppermost gun cupolas. From an observation window between two turrets Max looked out over the city as Bassandis roared again. Abby clasped her hands to her ears and screamed. Several of the crew collapsed to the floor in their own vomit as the sound rose and fell. Ruth went pale and stumbled back against the bulkhead. Max clenched his fists, fighting against the rage and hatred. *Destroy them all*, the thoughts filled his mind. *Wipe them from the universe, pluck handfuls of these filthy little insects from their ships, fling them into space and watch the blood burst from their eyes and mouth in sprays of red ice.*

As he fought to keep control he saw a tangle of distorted air speed from the mouth of the giant and slam into a section of the Beatrice's prow. He watched armour bulge and twist, holes opening in the metal as the plates peeled back like scabs. Somewhere in the depths of the battleship a circuit failed and an explosion engulfed a cluster of turrets. Debris pattered across the hull of the *Geryon*. Max staggered as the shockwave pushed their dreadnought sideways. Windows shattered along the corridor and a guard collapsed in a spray of blood.

They arrived at the bridge and stepped through the open hatch into chaos. Max saw one officer standing by the windows pulling at his hair and screaming. Another fired his revolver through a broken pane. The rest of the crew hammered at the controls or yelled orders into radios and speaking tubes. Before he could stop her Bryony gave a cry and flung herself into the arms of an officer standing in the centre of the room. He looked like one of Maria's clerks, a skinny man in a faded uniform who fussily adjusted a pair of wire-framed glasses before he wrapped his arms around the girl. He looked over her head at Ruth, his expression unreadable. Max thought he saw a tear on his cheek. Bryony pushed herself back and beat on the man's chest and face with her fists.

"You abandoned me," she shrieked, "you left me there, with that monster, I hate you, he forced himself upon me and you did nothing!" She crumpled at Captain Andagis's feet. Her father staggered, grabbing onto a console for support. Max tensed, dreading what the man would do next. He might have incredible inner fortitude to withstand the giant, but now he stood over his daughter, knowing she'd been raped by that filthy animal Hathus. *If he goes to pieces, we're all dead.*

"Captain Andagis," said Ruth, "you must stop the attack on the giant." The captain mechanically removed his glasses and polished them on his lapel. He stared through Ruth as if she wasn't there. She shouted his name and he jumped.

"Hathus is a traitor to the emperor and I will personally make sure you get a chance to exact your revenge upon him and his family," she continued, "but now you are under my command and you will disengage from the giant, and put this ship between the creature and the *Beatrice*. On no account must the giant be harmed any further."

"But it's still attacking us, how will we defend ourselves?" he asked, his voice quiet, reasoned and utterly terrifying. *He's another one of these cruel lords of the Ear. God help Hathus when Andagis gets his hands on him.*

"Do as you are told," screamed Ruth, holding up her father's ring. Andagis flinched, calmly spoke into his radio, and the ship creaked around them as it started to drift between the titan and the *Beatrice*.

It's too late, thought Max, looking through the window at the giant. Even if the dreadnoughts stopped, the maddened creature would continue. If only he could get through to Bassandis.

The monster staggered through the city. A shell from the *Beatrice*'s largest cannon struck his hand, punching a tunnel through the skin. Another round smacked into his shoulder. His face crumpled like a sad child's. He held his arms up to protect himself and his jaw, no longer supported, unhinged, hung for a few moments and then fell into the streets. Max wanted to close his eyes, but couldn't. He had to watch. *I was you once, in a dream. We were noble and good, like gods ourselves. Look what man has done to us. Odilon's right, we're not worth saving.* The bone crashed onto the houses, sending fountains of debris into the air. Bassandis slavered unintelligible sounds through the rent in his face and waved his hands at a storm of shells that sped through the air towards him. More and more slammed into his body, boring holes through the flesh and exiting the other side. He sank to his knees.

The firing stopped as the *Geryon* blocked its sister ship's line of sight. Max heard Hathus's voice on the radio.

"Captain Andagis," he said, his voice soft and reasonable, "my sincere compliments, but you're in our way. Would you oblige me by moving your ship so we can finish our task?"

It was Ruth that replied.

"To all the crew of the *Beatrice* and the *Geryon*. This is Ruth an Vircana, Condottiere to the Emperor Demetrius, Commander of the Dogs and Admiral of this fleet. Hathus is a vile traitor and I order you to hand him over to me immediately. The giant is not our enemy, the Emperor commanded us to lead the creature back to the Ear."

Nice try, thought Max, *but it won't work as long as the giant keeps attacking*. Hathus chuckled.

"Ruth an Vircana, all the Dogs are dead and the only traitor here is you. You are at a tactical disadvantage, caught between the monster and my ship. I really don't want to use force to get you out of my way."

Max realised what he had to do. He turned to Abby.

"Knock me out."

"What?" she looked at him as if he'd gone insane.

"Hit me, knock me out, do it, now!"

She saw something in his eyes that made her own go wide, then socked him as hard as she could. God it hurt, he always forgot how strong she was. As blackness washed over him he hoped she hadn't broken his jaw.

He stood in the room, but it had changed beyond all recognition. Now it was a cavern of misery and fear. His breath clouded before his face. The carpet beneath his feet squelched like mud and a cold flickering radiance replaced the lamplight. The stench of piss and blood filled the air. Shapes changed and shifted, shadows looming, then retreating. *It's unstable, the vision is fading.* He looked at his hands. They were his own. *At least I'm not a child.* Something foul and multi-legged scuttled over the ceiling above him. He didn't dare look up.

Incoherent sobbing came from the corridor leading into the cylinder. Max called out Bassandis's name and the noise became a desperate wail for help. He ran into the passageway. The pale man sat on the floor, propped against the shifting stone wall. The stench filled Max's nostrils, making him gag. He saw that Bassandis lay mortally injured. He hadn't looked at the giant for long as he lurched through Metacarpi, the sight was too terrifying, but here he saw the full enormity of the creature's wounds, the delicate flesh ripped, the ragged mess of his lower face. The giant looked at him with eyes filled with anguish. He stretched out his arms. Max, weeping with sorrow, took the delicate hands in his own, trying not to crush the broken fingers.

"Bassandis, you must stop fighting," he said between sobs. "You must leave here, run away from the city."

The giant shook his head. He struggled to sit up, but fell back with a cry of pain.

Can I carry him? What happens if I try to lift him? thought Max, desperately thinking of a way to save the creature. *He's a giant, how can I possibly take him to safety?*

He caught a movement at the end of the passageway. A shadow hurtled towards him. Sorrow gave way to mindless fear as a voice shrieked in his mind.

"Max," it howled, "you wicked wicked wicked child, what have you done?"

It was his mother, rendered monstrous. Eyes like bloody caverns glared down at him, her mouth, a void filled with a thousand teeth as sharp as knives. She blotted out the universe itself, claws reaching down to rend him apart.

I didn't do it, it wasn't me, it was Father.

He opened his eyes, shrieking in fear and struggling to get away as Abby pinned his shoulders to the floor. Beyond her he saw Ruth and Andagis looking down at him.

"Ragaleis," he managed to gasp, "he's here."

CHAPTER TWENTY-FOUR

"SIR?" SAID ONE of the crew, staring out of the window. Max got to his feet and looked north. An iron castle floated in the sky, drifting lazily towards them like a cloud. Max struggled to understand what he saw. He peered into the distance. Was that the silhouette of a man far beyond the houses, bending down and tugging at something in the ground?

Max saw the missile hit the *Beatrice* between two of its engines. The vessel lurched, its frame twisting like the spine of a dying fish. The immense clump of metal sank into the vessel, puncturing the armour and tearing through floors, leaving a hole as big as a field. *He's pulling up the outer defences and throwing them at us.* A second shape lifted into the air, shedding fragments of iron behind it like a comet's tail.

"Get us out of here," he yelled. He knew it wouldn't be long before those hill-sized lumps of wreckage headed their way.

Fighting Bassandis had driven half the crew from the two battleships mad, though he'd been weakened by his years of imprisonment. The psychic attacks he aimed at the fleet came from a sick creature, barely able to walk. They were bad enough. Even Max, buffered from the effect of the giants, struggled to control the random surges of psychopathic hatred sweeping through him on the *Beatrice* and the chain. Ragaleis was unharmed, and driven by a focused rage at the humans who dared to hurt his brother. Max knew he'd caught the tiniest fragment of the giant's mind in the dream corridor when the demonic vision of his mother came for him. It was more than enough. She'd haunt him for the rest of his life. Even he stood no chance against the power of Ragaleis's fury at point-blank range.

The second flying ruin headed straight for the *Beatrice*'s engines. Max hurled himself towards Abby.

"Get down!" he yelled, grabbing her round the waist and slamming her onto the floor. The windows of the bridge blew in with a roar of sound. The explosion on the other ship shoved the *Geryon* violently away. The floor tilted. A radio operator flew over Max's head and smashed into the bulkhead with a sickening thump. When he fell to the floor he left a man-sized patch of blood smeared across the steel. Max felt the ship sinking. He hauled himself up. To his amazement Andagis stood unmoving at his post, polishing his glasses to remove the dust. Bryony cowered at his feet. Ruth sat on the floor a few yards away, shaking her head as if trying to clear the noise from her ears. Bodies littered the deck around her. A choir of klaxons echoed through the ship and lights flickered on the control panels that had survived the blast. Most were red. Max grabbed the captain.

"We have to abandon the *Geryon*," he yelled, "you can't fight two giants."

Andagis shook him off.

"We must defend ourselves," he said. The idiot was in denial, he simply didn't see him. Max didn't have time to waste. He yanked Bryony to her feet. She screamed and tried to pull away. Blood ran through her hair from shrapnel cuts on her scalp. Max pushed the girl into Andagis's arms.

"Do you want to lose her again? Abandon the ship!" he shouted. A shadow passed across the shattered window, another colossal lump of iron ripped from the ruins of the defensive walls. He caught a glimpse of Ragaleis, arms above his head, about to hurl a fourth missile. *He's miles away, yet every one is bang on target.* Max prayed the giant still only aimed at the *Beatrice*.

He didn't wait to see if he'd got through to the captain. He grabbed Abby and ran from the bridge, trying to keep his footing as the dying vessel shuddered beneath him. Ruth joined them, her hair grey with dust and her uniform ripped.

"We need to get off this ship," he said. She nodded. He could see she'd lost hope of preserving the fleet or Bassandis, all she could do now was save herself.

They fought their way along shattered corridors. Max heard Andagis's voice echo through the ship, calling for the crew to abandon the *Geryon*. Thank God the man had seen sense, though his orders merely created fresh chaos. Max reckoned that Bassandis's attacks lingered in the crew's minds, so when the order came to flee their last shreds of morale collapsed and the evacuation turned into a hysterical rout. He'd sensed nothing in his own mind for a while now, and a horrible suspicion fell upon him that the titan lay dead in the streets. Even so, he knew that as soon as Ragaleis tired of hurling pieces of the landscape around he'd fall upon the city and anyone caught in the full force of his rage would perish shrieking in seconds.

Max had to shoot a couple of crew members to get at one of the intact scout ships in the narrow hangar. Fleeing vessels jostled at the exit hatch. A fighter tried to squeeze past a lumbering transport. The pilot misjudged the gap and smashed into the side of the tunnel. The ship exploded, sending a ball of fire rolling back into the bay. Max yanked Abby and Ruth out of the way just in time, dragging them into the flyer as the oily flames billowed past. Fighting panic he powered up the vessel. Ruth stood at the open door brandishing her machine pistol. Good, she could keep the bastards at bay until he managed to get the damn thing airborne.

He heard another distant explosion as the flyer kicked into the air. He couldn't tell whether it came from the *Beatrice* again, or the *Geryon*. The hangar tipped violently so the exit lay at the top of a steep slope. The remaining flyers not tied down or in the air slid down the incline, thudding into each other and the walls. Max heard screams from the injured and dying above the sound of tearing metal.

He almost panicked, but managed to push the terror away. He opened the flyer's throttle, dodged a tumbling gunship by inches, and in a second flew free of the dreadnought. An explosion in the hangar behind them wreathed their ship in fire. Max felt as if someone kicked him in the back as the shock wave sent them spinning into the air. He wrestled to bring the vessel under control, pointed the nose beyond the houses and aimed for the shore of the Forbidden Sea. After a moment Abby touched his arm, her green eyes filled with fear. She struggled to find the words. In the end all she said was "Ruth". Max didn't want to look round. He knew what he'd see. In the end he did anyway. Flash burns scarred the frame around the open door. Ruth had vanished.

He couldn't go back. They'd die. That's what he told himself. The dreadnoughts were finished. The onslaught from Ragaleis had triggered explosions in the *Beatrice*, ripping her open from stern to bow. Her sister ship lay so close that the force of the blast and the shrapnel had torn her to shreds. No-one in the vicinity would survive. He thought of Ruth and the spear-tip dance. She was made of steel and glass, a creature from the airless wastes of the AntiHelix, surely she couldn't die like that, in the bloody mess and chaos of the hangar bay? No matter how much he wanted to he didn't go back. Their only hope of survival lay in getting as far away as possible. No time for the luxury of guilt.

The air around them filled with escaping ships, fleeing the two crippled dreadnoughts. Max accelerated past the warehouses on the southern edge of the city, speeding along the edge of the sea. Six miles out he landed. He couldn't go any further. He had to know what happened to Bassandis, if he still lived or whether the hope of humanity perished with him. He knew Abby wanted to keep going, to put as much distance between them and the battle as possible, but something in his face made her bite her tongue.

He stepped onto the shelving concrete shore and looked back at Metacarpi. Abby took his hand, and he was grateful for the feel of her fingers between his. Trails of smoke drifted up from the distant city. The Carceral Archipelago rose into the sky like a hole cut out of the universe, its four chains binding it to the singularity. He gave a bitter laugh, he'd never be rid of that damn tower. The *Beatrice* had vanished. Instead a wall of black smoke filled the sky to the north east. That must be where it fell once its engines exploded. Further to the left he saw the *Geryon*. Remarkably it still hovered above the houses, but it listed badly. As he watched it sank behind a long row of tenements. Flashes of light outlined the blocks, followed by a low rumble a few moments later. Two of the buildings collapsed from the force of the shock wave. Max hear cries of dismay around him, and turned to see more flyers landing on the edge of the sea. Men and women in imperial and city uniforms stumbled out onto the shore, their faces streaked with soot and blood. All wore the same expression of dull pain mixed with a strange fascinated horror. He knew what they waited for. They all should have fled long ago. They were exposed, vulnerable, and yet they stood and watched the sky above Metacarpi.

Ragaleis stepped through the smoke like a man wading through a corn field. A loud gasp erupted from the crowd behind Max. At this distance he couldn't see the creature's expression. Was he triumphant? Angry? Filled with sorrow and a monstrous desire for revenge? He didn't want to search his own mind for any link with the titan, he was terrified of what he'd find. Instead he pushed all but his most immediate thoughts away and focused on the scene ahead.

The giant paused and looked around, as if searching for something. He seemed to see the Carceral Archipelago for the first time. A few steps took him next to it.

"God," murmured Abby. *Ragaleis was right*, thought Max in wonder, *they're the same height*. He watched, his body and mind numb, as Ragaleis took the chain *Joy* in one hand and gave it a tug. Gouts of stone erupted from the staple fastening the last link to the wall. The giant yanked again and the metal hoop broke free. Ragaleis tossed it away. The chain arched from the tower in a gout of dust and rock, clipping off chunks of stone as it scraped against the walls. The metal hit the sea and a few seconds later came an ear-splitting roar.

Max sank to his knees. *This can't be happening. My whole life lies in those stones. It's immovable, like my father.* He remembered Herman's crumpled body among the control panels in the citadel. *First the Tyrant, now the Tower*. The Carceral Archipelago lurched to one side. It canted towards the distant shadow of the Thumb. Ragaleis clutched *Hate* in two hands and pulled. Several of the house-sized rings of iron parted and the second chain plummeted into the streets. Finally the giant put his shoulder to the fortress and pushed, like a man forcing open a door.

The remaining chains tightened, links howling in protest as the rusted metal twisted and tore. In an eruption of debris and water, a pin half a mile long burst out of the Forbidden Sea, whipping sideways across the surface. It roared over the city trailing twisted links behind it. The Carceral Archipelago toppled over, its bulk breaking apart from the base as it collapsed. Lumps of masonry dug trenches in the sea. A cloud of soot and dust rolled over the water. The tide of noise swelled and subsided.

Ragaleis stood up amid the rubble and brushed the dust from his hands. He turned and looked across the water to where Max knelt on the shore of the Forbidden Sea. He felt as though the titan's eyes stared straight into his, and an odd thought crept into his mind. *You did that for me, didn't you? Was it to punish me, or to free me?*

The giant picked his way through the ruined city. He stopped and knelt down. When he stood up again Max saw he carried Bassandis in his arms. Behind him someone started sobbing. Max felt nothing. All that remained inside was an emptiness over which his consciousness drifted, fragile and alone. *Too late, he's dead, part of God's mind is lost forever.* Ragaleis turned his back on the sea and strode back through the wall of smoke. Max watched his silhouette recede, fading into nothingness as mist rose up to hide him and his burden.

After a while - he didn't know how long - Abby coaxed him to his feet. She cradled his cheek in her hand.

"We did all we could," she said.

Did we? He didn't know. He instinctively searched for the Carceral Archipelago but couldn't find it. *Of course, it's gone, like my mother and my father. Shadows, stone, steel, uniforms and faces; all vanished. My life is wiped clean. This landscape is utterly strange to me. It's going to hit me some time soon, the enormity of it all, but not now.* Max felt like a hollow doll, his mind filled with nothing more than light and possibility.

"Max?" said Abby behind him. He looked round. To his surprise Andagis stood at the head of a knot of men and women in imperial uniforms. Bryony sat on the shore beside him. Max saw her arm bound in a sling and a man dabbed at her forehead with a cloth. Beyond the crowd figures made their way towards them. While he'd stared at the ruin of his home more flyers had landed on the shore, bringing refugees from the dreadnoughts and the tower. For a second he thought he was alone among enemies, but then he saw that the will to fight had long been driven from the hearts of the survivors.

"You're Lord of the Carceral Archipelago now," said Abby. Her voice sounded full of regret.

She's right. By law I'm the ruler of the city. I've stepped into your shoes at last, Father, he thought wryly, *you got what you wanted.*

He approached the captain. Andagis took off his glasses and polished them. Max noticed one of the lenses was missing.

"Ruth an Vircana?" asked Andagis.

In his memory Max saw her standing in the door of their flyer, ready to repel attackers. He shook his head. Andagis winced. *If he's going to be the one to tell Crysanthe Uella I don't envy him.* Bryony started crying.

"What about Hathus?" Max asked.

"The giant destroyed the *Beatrice*. Its engines blew," answered the captain in his cold, dry voice. "Few escaped. Of these survivors, barely a handful come from the flagship. Captain Hathus must have perished in the explosion. So the universe punishes the treacherous."

Andagis looked Max up and down, contempt tussling with admiration in his long face.

"You're the man responsible for the death of a filthy monster who usurped my Lord's rightful authority and who stained the honour of my daughter, I am in your debt."

Max thought the pompous moralising out of place, especially when surrounded by the haggard faces of the wounded and the barely sane. Nevertheless he accepted it graciously and bowed.

"This doesn't look good," murmured Abby at his side. A group of ragged soldiers marched purposefully towards them from the city, armed and angry-looking. Behind Max a few guns swung in the direction of the newcomers. At their head strode a tall woman in a soot-stained uniform of steel and wool. Despite himself Max laughed out loud in amazement. Maria's hair spike had collapsed at some point during the fight, and her grey locks hung around her face, but there was no mistaking the hawk nose and glaring eyes. She stopped, drew herself up to full height and pointed at Andagis.

"Arrest that column of piss," she declared, "and free the Lord of the Carceral Archipelago from our enemies."

Max quickly stepped between the two groups before anyone started shooting. He could see Maria wanted to do nothing more than clasp him to her bony chest, but she wasn't going to allow a shred of affection through until she'd crushed her foes utterly.

"They're not enemies, Maria," said Max. She stared at him as if he'd lost his mind. She gestured behind her at the ruins of the Carceral Archipelago, and gave him a look that said *notice anything different you stupid boy*? He took her by the elbow and led her to the water's edge. He gestured for Andagis to join them.

Once out of earshot of the crowds, Max explained to Andagis and Maria about the eight giants and Alaric's mission to return them to the Head. When he described the betrayal of Odilon, Maria's hands flew to her throat and her eyes filled with tears. She insisted on immediately sending a flyer to retrieve his father's body from the cylinder.

"Now what?" she asked, after finally agreeing to make her peace with Andagis.

"Once my survivors are all accounted for we'll need to contact the AntiHelix and get them to send ships to take us home," said the captain. "It'll be months before they arrive, so we'll help you rebuild the city."

Maria sniffed. Max elbowed her in the ribs. She glared at him, then nodded at the captain.

"But not the Carceral Archipelago," said Max. Maria's mouth dropped open. She looked at him as if he'd just slapped her. He knew she thought he betrayed his father, but he couldn't bear the thought of that tower rearing once more into the sky. She pursed her lips and looked away. Max saw tears in her eyes.

"What about the mind of God?" asked Andagis. "Is all hope lost?"

Max didn't have an answer. He doubted Bassandis had survived the battle. In the decaying remnants of the dream room he'd looked mortally wounded. The giants possessed powers he hadn't dreamed off, they could rip men's minds apart, but whether they could bring back the dead he didn't dare to guess. In the wake of the battle they had no reason to look on humanity with anything other than hatred. It was a chilling thought. What could he do? Contact the giants once more, beg forgiveness from the titans? Who knew where the other six roamed. Perhaps they'd also fallen to man's ignorance and stupidity. What about the Machine Men deep in the mind of God? He remembered the glittering insects crawling over his hands when he sat at the table with four sisters and three brothers. *They're not bugs, they're our creators.* If the Machine Men had fashioned the mind once, could they do it again? Someone had to journey to their realm and explain what happened. How would they react? In the end Max couldn't think of any answers, and Andagis and Maria exchanged fearful glances.

They brought his father back at twilight in an imperial high speed scout. Maria organised a pyre on the edge of the sea, built with fragments of wood from the abandoned warehouses along the shore. Max laid Herman's body on top. The old man felt so light, as if all his weight came from the stone and iron tower. Now the Carceral Archipelago lay in pieces nothing remained but an empty shell. *I'm looking at myself,* Max peered into his father's face, *decades into the future and unstrung by death.* He found it hard to measure all the regrets, all the lost opportunities. He suspected his mind saved them for a later date. Now he merely felt sorry for a man who thought himself master of a city, but who had lost control years before his friend betrayed him for an alien power. Herman had known all along of course. When he spoke with Max in the Steel Room he'd talked of spies and treachery. He just didn't realise the enemy was Odilon, his closest confidant.

A crowd gathered, survivors from the city and the battleships. After they'd scattered oil over the wood he tossed a brand onto the pyre. As the flames roared into the sky Maria's steely resolve finally gave way and she collapsed in a heap, sobbing uncontrollably. No-one had the courage to go and comfort her, so Max put his arms around the grieving woman. She clung onto him as if she feared he was next.

Later, when everyone drifted away, he sat on the edge of the sea and looked at the Thumb. The fire warmed his back. Abby sat down beside him. Thousands of miles away lights flickered on the skin. Nighttime turned it into a black wall stretching up into space. Beyond it lay the Palm. What would it be like to stand so high above the atmosphere? Did anyone live there? Did the white-haired philosophers really drive their trains across the lightless skin like they said in the old story books? He remembered the vision of God, floating through space on the singularity, and it filled him with wonder. Abby rested her head on his shoulder, pressing against him for comfort. He said nothing, but a plan was forming in his head. At midnight he stood up, held Abby and kissed her properly for the first time. She whimpered with happiness when he whispered in her ear that he loved her.

"Come on," he said, and led her along the shore. She probably thought they searched for a secluded corner in an abandoned warehouse where they could make love. When he took her to one of the few surviving city flyers standing on the beach she looked at him curiously, clearly thinking they needed somewhere a bit more discrete. He lifted her up onto the deck, climbed aboard and started the engines.

"What are you doing?" she asked.

"We're going to the Thumb," he said. Her mouth dropped open, then she grinned,

"Really? We can't, can we?" she pointed outside. "What about them?"

"They'll be fine." Between them, Maria and Andagis could rebuild the city, they didn't need a new Lord of the Carceral Archipelago. He realised that as long as he stayed in Metacarpi he would carry with him the weight of the stone tower, casting its shadow of cruelty and oppression over everything. *Bugger that, I'm free at last, and the entire Body of God is waiting.*

Before Abby could protest any more he coaxed the flyer into the air. Someone shouted from the beach, but within seconds they raced along the water's edge, away from the guttering embers of his father's pyre and into the night.

CHAPTER TWENTY-FIVE

THE NEXT MORNING found them speeding towards the Thumb. Max didn't want to stop, he feared Maria would send flyers in pursuit, but by late afternoon they were both exhausted. It would be dangerous to continue, so he looked for a place to land the ship.

After half an hour he spotted the first of a cluster of tents in a valley. Soon he found himself flying over a refugee camp. Tents became warehouses and eventually he saw the wormhole building itself, a pyramid sheathed in copper long turned green by the passing of the centuries. The courtyard contained a camp that spilled down the streets between the storehouses. Men, women and children, the dislocated citizens of Metacarpi, stared up at the flyer. Max saw a few shake their fists, and a bottle bounced onto the deck, hopeless gestures of rage from the dispossessed. He didn't know how they'd react to seeing the son of the Carceral Archipelago land in their midst, but they couldn't continue. Besides, they brought news of the enemy's defeat and he hoped that would earn them a meal and a place to sleep at least.

When he and Abby stepped onto the deck the crowd fell silent. He wondered if they recognised the raggedy son of the tower, covered in blood and soot and stinking to high heaven.

"What's the news from the city?" a woman shouted.

"The battle's over, the dreadnoughts are destroyed, you can return," Max called out. The crowd stared at him in silence. *They don't believe me,* he thought. A woman in the front row started weeping and a few cheers broke out. As the news sunk in more and more people joined in until a shouting mob surged around the ship, hurling a barrage of questions up at them.

"Well done," said Abby sarcastically, "now what do we do?"

Half a dozen men in caps and leather coats elbowed through the crowd. They carried rifles. *Anarchists,* thought Max. He hadn't bargained on them, but now it made sense. They'd organised the first evacuation when his father refused to take the threat seriously. He guessed that turned them into heroes. They recognised Abby. A couple of them broke into wide grins, but when they looked in his direction their expressions turned cold and contemptuous. Max began to think he'd made a mistake. They should have continued to the Thumb. He'd been too naive to trust himself to the good will of the citizens. After all he was now the Tyrant of the Tower, even if nothing remained of the Carceral Archipelago but a line of smoking rubble in the sea.

The Anarchists managed to get them away from the crowd. They took Max and Abby into a labyrinth of warehouses, eventually stopping at a side door where more armed men and women sat on packing crates around a couple of braziers. The leader of their escort knocked. The door opened and he motioned for Abby to enter. Max tried to follow but the man pushed him back. Max almost hit him, but managed to control his temper.

"Not you," said the man. He nodded to an upended crate next to a fire. "Wait there."

Max toyed with the idea of imitating Ruth, loudly declaring himself to be the rightful ruler of all and demanding entrance, but he could guess the response he'd get. He sat down and brooded. At least Abby would be ok, these were her people. He'd always suspected she was closer to the underground than she admitted.

"How's the Tyrant in the Tower?" asked a woman sitting opposite. A couple of the men chuckled.

"Dead," said Max. He couldn't be bothered to rise to the bait. He was too tired.

"So you're the king of the stones now," she bowed, "your Lordship."

"The tower fell, a giant pushed it over," said Max. That shut her up. He closed his eyes and started to nod off. Something bumped his leg. He opened his eyes. A man knocked a bottle against his knee. He took it, the woman lifted up her mug.

"To the fall of tyrants," she said. Max couldn't help but laugh. *Here I am committing high treason, but God knows, I'll drink to that.* The wine tasted good, the tingling in his throat told him it came from a cellar on an ancient world.

The door opened and Max was astonished to see Abby re-emerge with her sister Rebecca. The owner of the Theatre of Angels gave him the once over.

"Well, well, Maximilian Ocel, the old dramas play out and the lord becomes the beggar," she said with a half smile. *Here we go,* he thought, bracing himself for a very public dissection.

"You're the leader of the Anarchists," he said. Laughter erupted around him. *Why do I ever open my big mouth in front of this bloody woman?*

"Maximilian, darling, what's the first principle of Anarchism?" asked Rebecca. *No leaders, right.* He shut up.

"Do you remember Peter Löwy?" she continued. He shook his head.

"I told you he founded the Theatre of Angels hundreds of years ago. He built a corridor in the cellar so a giant could come and watch the plays," she said.

My God, he knew Bassandis. Long before his father found the giant a crazy actor tried to teach him about humanity in a theatre. *Peter Löwy could speak to giants, like me.* Rebecca gave him a knowing look, she'd read his mind.

"I bet us theatricals made a better job of teaching that giant about what it is to be human than your father and that fucking alien," she said. As ever Max had no come back.

Rebecca turned to Abby and hugged her, burying her face in her sister's hair. After ages she stepped away, turned Abby round and gave her a little push.

"Go on, fuck off," she said gently. She spoke to the Anarchists around her, wiping her eyes with the heel of her hand. "Get them a decent flyer and supplies, and you . . ." she turned to Max. The sardonic mockery had vanished and she looked deadly serious. Despite himself Max felt his blood turn cold.

"Take care of my sister or so help me God I'll find you, rip your head off and stuff it up your arse."

She went back into the warehouse.

Max didn't want to hang around and get embroiled in the politics of the new order. The ancient energy in the wine woke him up. The Anarchists gave them a swift two-man scout which they loaded with supplies, including, to Max's delight, a tin of pomegranate seeds. They resumed their journey, aiming for the mottled wall of the Thumb four thousand miles to the east.

Abby didn't say anything for the first couple of hours. She sat cross-legged on the forward deck looking out at the red landscape as it sped past. Once in while she wiped her eyes. Max decided to leave her alone for the time being, he knew she'd return to him when ready.

The effect of the wine lasted a day. By nightfall Max found himself falling asleep at the controls. Abby sat on the floor of the cabin, her back against a corner, her head lolling forward. Fearful of crashing, Max set the flyer down in the shadow of an abandoned engine. He gathered Abby up and half-carried half-led her to a bunk at the back of the ship. He pushed her onto the bed, curled up on the floor beside it and fell asleep.

He felt as though he'd only closed his eyes for a few seconds and when he awoke it was still dark. Frustrated by his inability to sleep he got to his feet and looked for Abby. She'd disappeared. He went onto the bridge but that too was empty. He checked the chronometer and saw, with a lurch of panic, that a whole day had lapsed. Swearing at his own stupidity he ran through the ship, finally ending up at the prow, peering into the gathering gloom beyond. Abby stepped round the side of the engine and waved.

"Come and see," she called. He could have cheerfully throttled her. In the past her recklessness had driven him mad, but now it came with the added twist of anxiety that love brought. He hadn't realised how bad it would be.

Biting back his anger he clambered down the side of the ship and followed her. She led him to a square lake of glowing blue water encircled by a colonnade of black arches. Beyond the pillars Max saw a line of hills built from jumbled polyhedra. *We're far to the west, I've never seen a landscape like this before.* Around the city the Wasteland was filled with broken machinery; tools that once had purpose. The disturbing shapes scattered over this part of the singularity made no sense that he could see.

"At last. We both stink," said Abby. She stripped off her clothes and dived into the water before Max could stop her. After a few seconds she surfaced a few yards away, shaking the drops out of her hair and stroking it back from her face.

"Come on, you coward," she called.

He undressed, slipped into the pool and followed her. She swam over to him and started to wash the grime and sweat from his chest and shoulders. He wanted to see her properly, but the only illumination was the blue radiance of the water. It faintly under-lit her breasts, arms and face as she moved around him.

"You never looked after yourself," her voice came from behind as she rubbed at his back, "you're a mess." Her hands felt fierce and insistent.

"Hark at you," he said, feeling the muscles unknot, "you're the maniac, not me." She pressed herself against him, her arms sliding round his stomach. He could feel her small breasts against his back. It took his breath away. He turned and she put her arms round his neck, dragging him down into a long, warm kiss. She nuzzled at his neck. Subtle and delicate weren't the immediate words that sprang into his mind when he thought of Abby Fabrice. Most of their career found them in conflicts of one kind or another, scrambling up or down things, plunging into danger with her screaming ahead and him trying to keep up with his teeth clamped tight and one eye squeezed shut in terror. Relaxation consisted of drinking, falling asleep in chairs or standing up, or getting into marginally more friendly fights in bars. Yet now her touch was so delicate, her kisses the brief glance of an insect's wings across his neck and chest. Before he knew it she'd wrapped her legs round his waist.

"About time," she hissed as she ground against him with a steady urgency. She grinned, flicked her hips and he was inside her. Her muscles gripped him hard and all thoughts fled from his mind. The tendons in her back rippled under his fingers and he smelled the warm cotton scent of her hair.

A long time afterwards they sat naked and cross-legged on a heap of blankets on the floor of the flyer, a bottle of wine between them. In the lamplight Max looked at Abby, noting every detail; the torrent of freckles down her breasts, the corded muscles in her shoulders and stomach, the slight pulse in the hollow of her throat. She folded her arms and cocked her head on one side.

"Comparing scars?" she asked.

"We have enough." replied Max.

She looked down at herself and laughed.

"I don't think I was destined for the fragile ballrooms of the AntiHelix, do you? I look like a boxer with a pair of tits."

"You're beautiful Abby," said Max and he meant it with all his heart.

Abby crept up to him on her hands and knees. She kissed him on the side of the neck. He brushed the hair out of her eyes and smiled. She glanced around.

"What shall we call her? She's our ship now."

"How about the *Bricolage*?" said Max.

"Perfect," she said, pushing him onto his back.

Max woke many hours later. The cabin was filled with daylight and universe beyond the windows glowed paper white. For a few seconds Max felt disoriented. He looked down at Abby, still asleep with her head cushioned on her arm. Sex with her was as exhausting as it was inventive and he had the bite marks to prove it.

He stood up and looked out across the Wasteland. A hideous dread eclipsed every thought and he nearly fell. *No, not now, not this.* All strength drained from his limbs.

The whiteness came from a wall of mist, and just in front of it sat the giant's house. The crazy angled door stood open. *He's come to punish me, to kill me in some unimaginable way for betraying Bassandis. He'll take my mind and rip it apart.* Tears of sheer terror blurred his vision and he struggled against the urge to be sick. He glanced down at Abby. He couldn't wake her, not now, not to see this. She looked so peaceful and happy. In seconds it would all be destroyed. At least he had the power to grant her a few more moments of peace.

He looked back at house. A white haired man in a black suit stood in the doorway watching him. Max waited for the horror to fall. The monstrous vision of his mother he'd seen on the *Geryon* had almost driven him mad, and he'd been at the very edge of Ragaleis's attack. Now he stood right next to the titan. He hoped his mind would collapse quickly under the coming horrors. A few minutes passed. Nothing happened. In his head he found only his own thoughts. He calmed down a fraction. Ragaleis continued to watch him from the doorway. Eventually Max summoned the courage to pull on his clothes and step out onto the deck of the flyer. To his surprise the giant beckoned to him.

He knew he had no choice. He wasn't going to flee, Ragaleis would crush him instantly. He stepped down onto the ground and walked towards the house. He didn't believe his feet capable of carrying him towards that door, at each step he thought his legs would collapse. He almost wished for it so he could surrender himself to the fear and madness, but he forced himself to keep going. He wanted to plead for Abby, to beg the monster not to harm her. His heart hammered in his chest. At last he stood in front of the giant. He tried to read the creature's expression, but Ragaleis's face told him nothing.

"Max, come with me," he said and stepped back into the house. Max looked over his shoulder at the *Bricolage*. If only he'd had the chance to say goodbye to her. He prayed the giant would let her go. She'd mourn him, but the body of God and all its wonders still waited for her and he didn't know anyone as resilient as Abby Fabrice. He entered the building.

He stood in a white-walled room with no doors or windows. Silence filled the air, a stillness so powerful it felt like an unseen animal stood at his back, watching and measuring his every thought and movement. In the centre the body of Bassandis lay on a steel table. Ragaleis stood next to the head, looking down at his brother with an expression of deep sadness.

"I healed his body, but I came too late," said Ragaleis. Max looked at the dead titan, forcing himself to ignore the sensation of falling towards the corpse. He saw a young man with pale skin and white hair, made whole again, without any of the hideous wounds caused by the battleships and his long imprisonment. The large eyes were closed in death, though the lids looked almost translucent. Max remembered a game with wooden animals by a fire long ago and tears of sorrow ran down his cheeks.

"I'm sorry, I'm so sorry. I tried to stop them, my father and Odilon poisoned his mind." What could he say?

"So Bassandis is dead, and my heart overflows with hate," said Ragaleis. "Perhaps I should leave this realm, walk away from your God until I reach the edge of the singularity and cast myself into the void. If I find my brothers and sisters and we reunite, God's mind will be part-formed and tainted by my rage."

There's a sour irony to this, the Black Roses feared we'd destroy everything, and if we have a mad god on our hands their prophecy will come true. Now he realised Ragaleis wasn't going to punish him immediately, his mind started to work, hunting for anything that might give them hope.

"There must be something we can do," he said. "What if I journey to the realm of the Machine Men? Perhaps they can make another giant."

When he saw the pain in Ragaleis's eyes he immediately regretted his words. Another giant wouldn't be his brother. The creature shrugged.

"Perhaps," he turned to Max and held out his hand.

"You're going to let me go?" gasped Max.

"What purpose would it serve to hurt you?" asked Ragaleis. "If there's going to be any redemption we'll need people who can talk to giants. There are very few of you left."

I'm shaking hands with someone two miles high, thought Max as he took the titan's hand in his own. It felt ordinary, human.

"Goodbye Max," said Ragaleis.

He paused and looked at Max curiously, peering into his eyes. Max thought he saw the flicker of a smile. *Please, not again. Now what's he seen?*

"Yes, go and talk to the Machine Men, perhaps they can help after all," the giant said. A door opened behind Max.

As he left the house he spotted Abby standing naked on the deck of the flyer holding a machine gun in her hands and gazing towards him in an agony of fear. When he climbed on deck she flung herself into his arms and they almost pitched backwards over the rail.

"It's OK, we're safe," he said. She slapped him hard across the face, twice, then shrieked a string of curses at him. How could he have left her there and gone into that house alone, did he care nothing for her at all? He grabbed her fists until the insults turned into incoherent sobs and she buried her face in his chest. *It's going to take a while for me to live this one down. Love turns us all into cowards, time was when you'd be running towards that house with a gun in each hand,* Max thought, looking down at the woman crying in his arms.

He glanced up. The house vanished and the mist dissipated. He heard the sound of monstrous footsteps retreating. *He's heading north,* he realised, *he's not going to jump off the singularity after all. What did he see in my eyes that made him change his mind?* He felt no different, only the returning desire to flee west with Abby. They went inside and moments later the ship lifted into the sky.

At last they came to the Thumb. Max watched as the wall ahead slowly turned into the underside of a cylinder six thousand miles in diameter. The *Bricolage* flew beneath the curve of the Proximal Phalanx. It lowered over them a hundred miles above, plunging the ship into twilight. Max and Abby stood on the bridge, holding hands, wondering at the bizarre landscape drifting over their heads. The skin became a patchwork of walls, boards, planks, stone and metal, a collage of debris from all the factories, warehouses and ruins since the beginning of time. Here and there gaps in the surface exposed the girders and beams beneath. In several places giant chains, metal bars or ropes as thick as the Carceral Archipelago itself dangled down. Nailed, welded, sewn, tied, soldered, riveted, stapled, glued, folded, fused together - the body of God was testament to a million years of labour.

The *Bricolage* coasted south beside the Knuckle. To the west Max thought he could see a line of light between the landscape below and the skin above. He gasped in wonder. *I'm looking at daylight from the space between the Thumb and the side of the Palm.* The distances overwhelmed him. It was one thing to know how big God was, but the final experience wiped all reason and understanding from his mind.

Their flyer dipped and rose as it negotiated forests of chains and ropes, giant assembly mechanisms and scabbed outcrops of scaffolding. Abby steered back towards the light on the left and started to rise up the curve of the Knuckle. She brought the flyer closer to the skin, kicking up a backwash of dust, grit and wood fragments, weaving it left and right to avoid the larger outcroppings.

"Is it all like this?" she asked. Max heard fear and wonder in her voice, tinged with disappointment. *Where are the cities and realms I dreamed about, the lights that shone from the skin at night*? he thought. All his life he'd looked to the Thumb and imagined the worlds and civilisations within the body of God. In his mind he'd created empires and kingdoms with histories, fantastic sciences and wondrous creatures; Kings, Queens, Dukes, Lords, Mad Philosophers and women with gorgeous faces and dark appetites. This wilderness appeared no different to the Wasteland.

There's more than this, he told himself, *this is merely the Thumb*.

Abby let the flyer drift onto a shelf of wood jutting out from the skin in a wide arc. They disembarked and, hand in hand, walked to the edge. Max felt the same wrench of vertigo as when he looked over the balcony at the realm of the white cities. Far below, the Wasteland spread into the haze. The dull red landscape was littered with trenches, pits, gullies, broken cranes, empty buildings bigger than a city, lakes, canals, mountains of brick, wood and iron, foothills of detritus and fragments of abandoned machinery larger than the Carceral Archipelago itself. From where he stood it seemed to Max that the floor of the universe became a vast page scored with marks, measurements, symbols and words, as enigmatic as a leaf from one of Odilon's books. Abby pointed.

"Look."

He peered down. Was that a man, walking slowly north, stepping over hills and the shattered ruins of vast machines? He couldn't tell, they were so high up. Maybe it was a trick of the light.

"Where's Metacarpi?" murmured Abby, one hand on his shoulder.

Max looked to the east. In the distance the landscape merged into bands of colour; red ground, ivory haze, the blue and purple of the atmosphere and then, above all things, the featureless black of the empty cosmos. Even if he knew where to look, he doubted he'd see their old home.

"Come on," he said and led Abby away.

Where the ledge met the surface the skin was a lattice of white wood punctured by an iron door. Some planks had slipped. They peered in through the gaps at a row of square archways. Beyond these a plain stretched into the interior of the Thumb. The gloom made it difficult to see detail, but Max could have sworn he looked at a forest of black trees a few miles away, and beyond that a cluster of spires reaching up to an impossibly high ceiling. He put his arm round Abby's waist and pulled her to him. Their cheeks touched as they gazed, entranced, at this new world. This is how it always started, he knew that now. They'd never spoken of it to each other, but in those brief moments when they stood side by side at the beginning of an adventure, with danger before them, nothing else came close.

"This is why we're here." Her voice was soft in his ear. They opened the door and stepped into the Body of God.

John Guy Collick was born in Yorkshire, England. When he was 10 years old his grandfather gave him a copy of *A Princess of Mars* by Edgar Rice Burroughs, and from then on he was hooked on science fiction and fantasy. He worked for Scotland Yard before moving to Japan for ten years to lecture in literature and philosophy. As well as writing science fiction he is also the author of a book on Shakespeare, essays on literature and several screenplays.

John Guy Collick lives in Hampshire, England.

Website: johnguycollick.com
Twitter: @johnguycollick